Cuddy
ITEM RE
NOR H
FREE LIB
COLLECTION

ITEM RETIRED FROM
NORTH KINGSTOWN
FREE LIBRARY
COLLECTION

Lois A. Cuddy

North Kingstown Free Library
100 Boone Street
North Kingstown, RI 02852

Penelope's Song © 2015 Lois A. Cuddy. All rights reserved. Big Table Publishing Company retains the right to reprint. Permission to reprint must be obtained from the author, who owns the copyright.

ISBN: 978-0-9908413-3-3

Printed in the United States of America

This novel is a fiction based on the fiction that we know as Homer's *Odyssey*, its characters, myths, legends, and setting. Freely drawing from Homer's epic and its major characters, this volume is the author's invention.

Cover Design: Robbin Cuddy
Front Cover Photo: Grace Farrell and Carl Treichel

Also by Lois A. Cuddy:
T. S. Eliot and the Poetics of Evolution

Big Table Publishing Company
Boston, MA
bigtablepublishing.com

3 0073 00365 9225

"Life shrinks or expands in proportion to one's courage."
~ Anais Nin

I dedicate this volume to
Lorraine Morton, Albini Chabot, Gregory McNab
Sister, Father, Friend
and to my children and grandchildren

Translator's Note

In 1997, on a site outside of the ancient city of Tyre, archaeologists discovered a bronze box containing a large trunk filled with early writing. Dr. Aram Abramson and Dr. Sara Basrum, directors of the project in Lebanon, contacted me to decipher this early, unknown language. With the most advanced technology, we subsequently dated this material to about 1200 BCE, the estimated period of the Trojan War. With the assistance of renowned linguists and anthropologists, we worked for ten years to find the key to this unique language, which we named Early Tyrian. I spent the next five years translating the writing on the sheets of parchment and leather that survived over three thousand years.

The book that follows is the translation of the story that emerged. It is the narrative of Penelope, wife of the hero Odysseus from Homer's epic stories of the Trojan War and its aftermath. Written about her world and her own experiences in youth and later on Ithaka, Penelope's memoir is a version of history that Homer did not compose—and probably never imagined.

This translation of Penelope's narrative has necessarily been modernized to include punctuation and paragraphs that were not part of the early written language, which united Phoenician, Mycenaean, and Ægyptian scripts. I have also provided contemporary forms of dialogue, English idioms and sentence structure, chronology, and organization of the text. While I accept full responsibility for any errors, I have attempted to remain faithful to Penelope's voice and linguistic rhythm and have worked tirelessly to be true to the story as Penelope wrote it.

L.A.C.
Boston, MA 2014

Contents

Map of the Mediterranean World around 1200 BCE

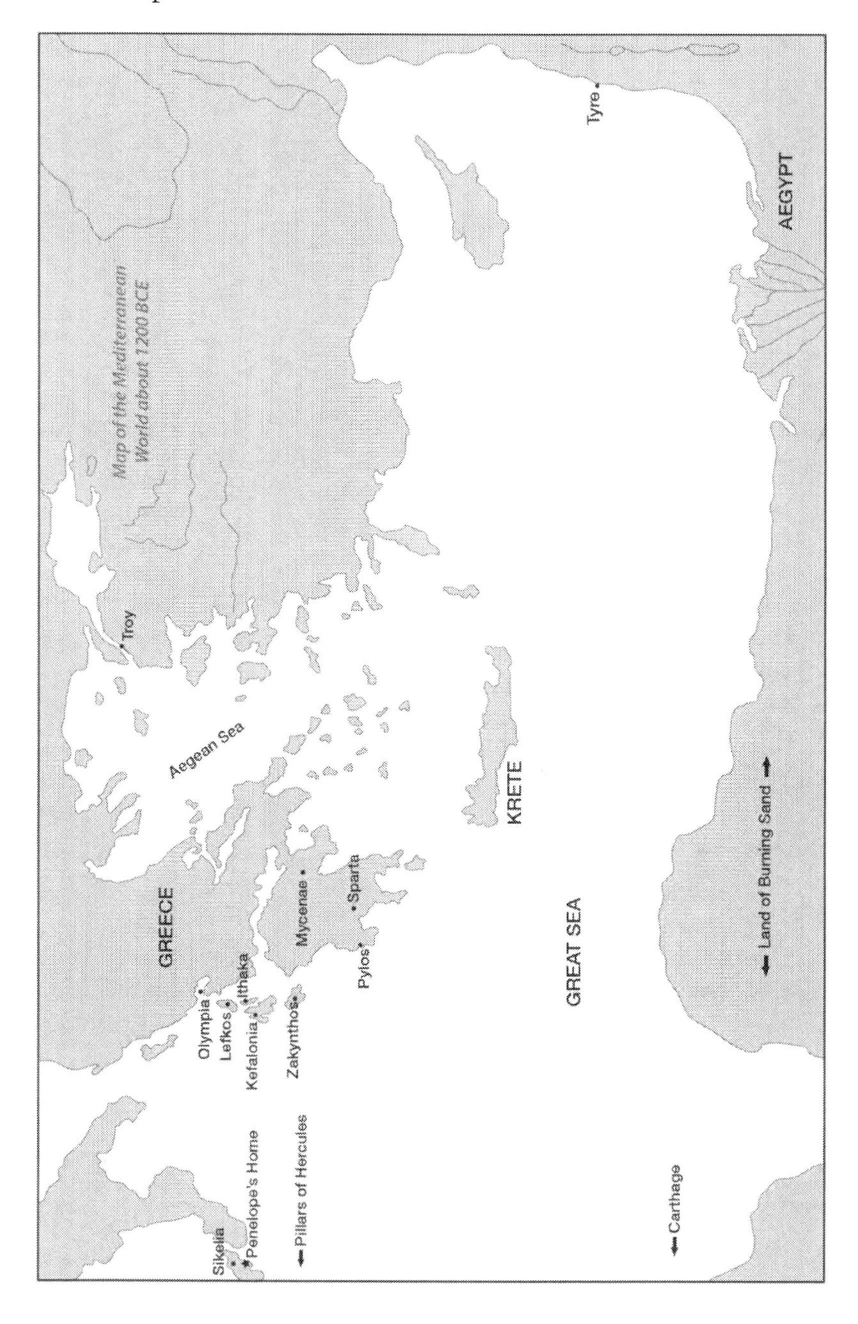

Prologue

I am no warrior and so may be forgotten.

I am Penelope, once Queen of Ithaka and always friend of Cadmus, the Phoenician merchant. That is how I wish to be remembered. But if I am mentioned at all in the long seasons to come, I will be known as the wife of Odysseus, hero of the Trojan War and favorite of gods and poets. I will have no shape apart from my Lord's, I am certain. Yet, I too have a story. My father was the godly King Ikarios from the island of Sikelia in the Great Sea west of Ithaka. I am descended from a noble line. However, on Ithaka, where the family of King Odysseus rules, I have struggled to create a name that would make my father proud. I earned fame, I am told, but I would have preferred a different fate.

While my lord Odysseus traveled over the world for experience and knowledge, as the Fates decreed, my journey had a different design. I have labored to understand the meaning and purpose of my life and marriage to a renowned but absent hero. Admittedly, at times my days were pleasant and challenging, even delightful, but too often they seemed baffling and filled with longing for what I could not have. Perhaps that is the nature of human life. Zeus says that we mortals bring on most of our suffering by our greed and folly. I wonder. I have been neither greedy nor foolish. Rather, choices were made for me that I would not have made for myself. I am a woman, after all.

As I now relive my experiences and reflections through my writings, I realize how fortunate I am to have known the love of remarkable men like Cadmus and my father and to have enjoyed the affection and pleasure of family and friends, weavers and artisans. I have shared in the history of a monumental time with heroes who will be forever revered, and I have been protected by gods and goddesses who made this long journey possible. For all this, I am grateful.

At this moment as I sit in my garden overlooking the glimmering sea, I re-read my story and await the arrival of the sons of Cadmus. They will take the chest full of my writing—my life, my memories—to their father who will at last know my heart. They also may take me with them—if I choose, and if it is not too late

PART ONE

1. Penelope Meets Her Future

My Master Odysseus has left me again. I don't know where he has gone or for how long. He does not tell me these things. He just leaves, and I am kept in the bedchamber at the top of the palace by his mother, who has taken even my loom, my daily comfort. Yet I feel liberated at this moment with my brush and ink as I dare to write in secret for the first time since coming to this rocky island. Perhaps if I write the story of the last days in my homeland, I may free my nights from the terrors of sleep. I may no longer relive those days, and I can bury them in the cave of nightmares for all time. So, in the silence of this night, with a tiny lamp, I relieve the darkness through the story of my sorry life.

It was the last glorious day of my childhood.

The Sun God was brilliant in a clear blue sky, the sea was calm, and a light breeze cooled the courtyard. Two galleys arrived in our port to herald the arrival of a king from an island called Ithaka. Always generous and welcoming, my father prepared a day of feasting and games to amuse the guest and his men. Word went out to the villages, and men arrived the following day to participate in the festivities. The men who attended the King called Odysseus also came into the field to enjoy the celebration. They ate and drank heartily at the midday meal and laughed at stories shared among them. Then the games began.

My father the King and my mother the Queen sat on high-backed chairs inlaid with gold and silver. King Odysseus sat next to them in an elegant chair reserved especially for honored guests. My brothers, sister, and I sat around them on the amphitheater benches with our friends and relatives. Men competed in quoits, balls, running, jumping, wrestling, javelin throwing, and bow and arrow. My childhood friend Tyndareus was proud to win the last two competitions, and he smiled at me and bowed to honor me.

He and I had been friends since we were babies crawling on hands and knees. I smile to think of it. As the son of our nearest village leader, he came to our palace often. As we grew, Tyndareus and I would run off to roam the woods and beaches. We would hide and play games until someone found us and returned us to my nurse who spent her days in fear for our safety. There was a touch of wildness in us for several years in our youth until the day arrived to teach us how to work. But before that day, we enjoyed the freedom that has no responsibility.

One day we found a cave that faced a beach, and Tyndareus decided that this would be our home when we grew up. He was almost eight years old.

"I will marry you when we are grown," he said, "and we will live in this cave."

I asked, "But how will we eat, and who will take care of us?" Even as a five-year-old child, I was more practical.

I remember his words as he said, very seriously, "Our servants will bring our food and clean clothes, and we will be free to live as we please."

We laughed, and that became our secret—that we would wed in the future. Gradually our families came to understand that Tyndareus and I were betrothed. They were glad and expected that when I was of age we would formalize the bond.

I looked at my handsome friend, now smiling on the field of victory, and felt my heart swell with pride that he would want me above all the pretty girls on Sikelia.

My father the King announced to the stranger called Odysseus that he could choose two games to compete for a special treasure that the winner could select. It was the law of hospitality in our kingdom to make such an offer. In the past the guest, knowing he would receive a worthy gift simply for being our visitor, waived that right and settled back to enjoy the banquet that would follow the games.

Odysseus, however, accepted the offer. He chose the javelin and bow and arrow, and he selected Tyndareus to be his competitor. No one on our homeland knew that Fame had carried the name of Odysseus throughout the world for winning in those games. A roar went up among our kinsmen, for Tyndareus was the best on the island of Sikelia. Odysseus marked off the distances, which were farther than we had ever seen, and designated the point to hit. He looked at the youthful Tyndareus and waited to be challenged. Tyndareus frowned, glanced at me, then stood tall and ready to begin.

Odysseus won both competitions, and Tyndareus bowed to the winner as heroes do in our kingdom. Without thinking about the consequences of his offer, my father the King told his famous guest to choose whatever prize he wished. My father pointed to a magnificent display set out on a table for all to see and admire. We assumed that Odysseus would select a beautiful golden bowl or one of the silver or bronze objects designed and inscribed by our gifted artisans.

Instead, the stranger said, "I will select my prize at the evening banquet." With a nod of his head, he and his men left the field in silence.

As Helios hid behind the mountain in the west and the lamps were lit around the Great Hall in the palace, Odysseus arrived with Mentor and two of his warriors. The rest of his men shared tables in the courtyard with the men of our kingdom. After paying tribute to our gods with a burnt offering and a libation, my father raised his golden cup to honor our guests. Then our family and invited guests sat down. We began to eat the delicious roasted fish and lamb, vegetables, breads, cheese, curds with honey, and fruits. The best of our wine was passed out generously. Laughter accompanied the conversation, Tyndareus and I smiled often at each other, and all seemed to enjoy the occasion.

Then King Odysseus stood and reminded all that he was yet to select his prize. In an expansive gesture my father again pointed to a table against the wall and asked our guest to make his choice. Without delay, Odysseus walked over to me and raised me from my seat.

"She will be my prize," he said in a clear, firm voice.

Everyone gasped. Some of the men laughed at his wit. He held my arm as I stood beside him. I thought that this was an amusing joke until I looked into his hard eyes.

I said very quietly, "No, my Lord."

"That is not possible, my Lord," my father said. "My daughter has been promised to Tyndareus. Besides, she is too young for marriage."

Tyndareus knocked over his stool when he stood up, the color drained from his face. Suddenly everyone realized the seriousness of the situation as warriors who served Odysseus entered the hall with their swords and stood against the walls and at the doors. No one could come in or go out.

In a voice that carried throughout the palace, Odysseus said, "I, King Odysseus of Ithaka and son of Laertes, was promised the prize of my choice. Princess Penelope is my choice."

Then turning to my father, he asked in a stern voice, "Do you make empty promises to all guests? Or do you keep false words only to dishonor Odysseus, son of the godly Laertes?"

As one of his warriors handed him a bow and quiver, Odysseus said, "I will have her. Woe to the man who stands in my way."

Tyndareus yelled, "No! You cannot have her!" Before anyone could stop him, he picked up a large carving knife from the table and ran toward this stranger.

Swiftly, Odysseus raised his bow. His arrow pierced the chest of my beloved friend.

I could not sleep that night for tears that wet my pillow, for sobs that shook my soul.

Sorrow overcomes me at the memory.

After the deaths of Tyndareus, his father, and my brother, the wedding ceremony was canceled. The stranger Odysseus planned to take me away the following day. Early the next morning I was summoned by my father and led to the Room of Justice. My father was seated in his high-backed chair and beside him sat Pandares, my oldest brother, and Menoitios, the eldest and wisest of our neighbors.

They will help me, I thought, as I knelt before the King, imploring him. "Father, please do not send me away. I beg you to give King Odysseus the treasures he desires. I will show you that I am worthy."

"Daughter," my Father began, but he could not continue. The tears filled the deep lines that I had never before noticed in his cheeks. He gestured to the old man to continue.

"My child," Menoitios said in a soft voice filled with grief. "Your father the King sent your godly brother and me as emissaries to plead your case to King Odysseus, son of Laertes. We offered the wealth of your father's kingdom in exchange for you. King Odysseus listened as we listed the treasures we are prepared to give to him.

"Then King Odysseus said in a harsh voice, 'That is what I expect for Penelope's dowry. Perhaps more than that after I examine the quality of those objects. Let me explain your situation and my position,' he said with the arrogance of a god.

"'I will have the Princess Penelope and you will choose the conditions.

"'First, if you challenge my decision, we will kill all your men, old women, and children and enslave the young women and boys to be sold along the shores of the Great Sea on my return home. Then I will burn your palace and gardens and all the surrounding lands of your kingdom. I have the men in my two galleys to accomplish what I tell you. I will then take the Princess Penelope as one of my slaves. I will decide later if she will be my wife or a whore to be sold at home in the wine houses of our marketplace.'

"Before I could speak he went on, 'Second, if you accept me as her wedded lord, without resistance, I will take her home as my Queen to be honored as the wife of Odysseus before all the world.' He stood up and said, 'Tell your King that Athene is with me and directs me in all things. It is your King who makes the choice for his daughter's future. Tell him that if the treasures are not carried down to my ships today when the Sun God crosses the highest point of the sky, I will take that as a sign of war and we will attack.' We were dismissed. I'm sorry, Princess. There is no compromise in this man."

My eyes were large and unbelieving as I listened. My father suddenly took me in his arms, and we wept together—so long, I thought that there would be no tears left for future sorrow.

Finally I pulled away from my father's arms. I looked at that beloved face and I said, "Father, I will accept him as my Lord and King. There is no choice for you or for my people. The gods have spoken. My fate is chained to this stranger."

Pandares, my golden brother, could not look at me.

My legs shaking, I stood up. I walked back to my room with my back straight, my head held high, to prepare for my leaving. I did not want anyone, even my nurse, to see my heart bleeding. It continues to bleed. I cannot write more on this.

My Lord and I left for Ithaka the following day. Since he had accepted the generous dowry that my father gave to him, he said that I would be married on his island.

Many villagers stood quietly on the shore as we sailed away. I tried to hide my fear as my brothers stood with heads bowed in shame. My dear father and sister wept, and my beloved nurse wailed like a funeral mourner.

My Lord told me to go below where I stayed for several days in isolation not to stir up his men. I lay in the stench of the hold and my own sickness until Mentor took pity and brought me up to the deck where the wind and the waves cleansed me.

In a storm they tied me to the bow of the galley and left me for days tied so I would not fall, or jump, overboard.

I learned something about war and cruelty when I was taken away from home. I will never forget those lessons.

I have tried to put the memories of that special terror and heartache out of my daily thoughts, but my dreams constantly remind me of the time when the Fates turned happiness to misery.

Hungry, exhausted, cold, and half-dead, I arrived from my homeland on the Great Island across the sea. I can remember only hazy images as they untied me in the bow of the galley and carried me up the mountain from the busy port on Ithaka to the palace where I will live forever. I remember the pain that attacked me as I lay on the hard litter, and I recall shivering with cold and burning with heat.

People seemed to be on each side of the road, their faces in shadows and blinding light.

"Who is she?"

"Is she the new queen of King Odysseus?"

"Is she dead?"

"Can you see her face?"

"Is she beautiful or ugly?"

Whispers flew around me as we passed the strangers, and they faded from my sight.

Men carried me up steep stairs, and someone removed my filthy clothes. I think that I had worn the same robe for all the weeks that we were on the sea. I was lowered into a deep container of hot water and scrubbed until the pain made me lose all memory of what happened and where I was.

Maybe it was all a terrifying dream—the storm when they tied me to the bow of the ship, the terrible thirst, the arrival on Ithaka—but I am now told that I have been in and out of this world for many days, too weak to walk or even eat. This was not the way I imagined my arrival on the island of Ithaka where I will be queen.

I was strong and full of vitality and joy in the palace of my father. Now I feel my bones and have difficulty walking up three steps to the small shrine where I can pray and make offerings to my goddesses. Here also I keep my story secret and hide my writing beneath the altar.

King Odysseus and his family are disappointed that he chose me for his wife. I have heard whispers.

One night when they thought I was sleeping, I heard my Master arguing with his mother. "I have promised to wed her," he said. "I have chosen the daughter of a king, a worthy choice despite her youth. It is true that she could not endure the trials on the sea for all those weeks," he went on, "but I challenged the power of a king to wed her and so must fulfill my promise."

"But she is not Greek," his mother hissed. "She may destroy us."

In a low voice filled with anger, Odysseus said, "She is not a barbarian. Her great-grandfather was Greek. In her homeland, she was beloved. Everyone admired her for her virtue, her beauty, and her gift of weaving. When I saw her, she was full of energy and pleasure. I believed that she would bear strong and handsome sons, and she would increase trade for our palace. I still believe it.

"Consider this. If she continues to be too sick to be a wife, I will send her home in disgrace for being unworthy of the King of Ithaka. For now you must try to make her well, or I will be the one to lose face."

I wanted to scream at his mother that I am Penelope, daughter of King Ikarios, but I had not the strength to shout. I remained silent. Odysseus' words finally quieted his mother who continues to watch me without a smile of comfort.

2. Life on Ithaka

Days, perhaps weeks, have passed since I awoke one morning and was no longer shaking with cold and fire. When I could walk with steady steps, we had the bonding ceremony that makes me belong to him.

After the sacrifice to Athene and Hera, there was a banquet where I met my Master's sister Ktimene. We smiled at each other and my heart beat with gratitude. I would like to know her, but immediately her mother separated us. I have not seen her since that day.

My Master Odysseus is again on a hunting trip, I am told, so I am alone in the night and can write my feelings and thoughts. Here, in the palace on the summit of Mt. Aetos, I always feel alone, even among the servants. I wish my nurse were here with me. But as I write at this moment, my father, sister, and Cadmus smile upon me, and I too can remember how to smile.

For endless days and nights I have wept privately for the loss of my family and friends. Ithaka is a dark and desolate place in the House of Odysseus. I have not been allowed to go beyond the courtyard. The dark walls of stone, the unpleasant smells of enclosed rooms, and the absence of laughter disturb me.

I long to see once again the palace of my father, where spacious windows brought light to our days. All the rooms had bright mosaic floors and walls and white lime ceilings. The Great Room of the palace had mosaic pictures of sacred scenes, of the glen where we offered sacrifices to the gods on the holy days each year, of olive and orange and lemon groves and grape vines that grew on steps that climbed the steep hills overlooking the sea, and of the mountain of the gods that protected and warned us. Our house was famous for its beauty.

From the palace we could see Goddess Etna in the distance, and we kept an altar fire in the courtyard where she could observe it always burning in homage to her power. The great mountain threw up fire and rocks to warn us of the consequences if peace and honor and piety should not rule our lives. If we were foolish enough to forget that she had absolute dominion over us, we were reminded when we heard the rumblings from her high peak.

Off the Great Room was the Room of Justice, where my father the King made rulings to settle disputes among our people. There he met village leaders and strangers who arrived to pay tribute for his benevolence and wisdom.

Home! My heart is dying! Will I never leave this island?

Last night at the banquet he grabbed my arm with such force that I thought it was broken. I cried out in pain as he lifted me from my seat and squeezed harder.

"You undo every man who sees you," my Master bellowed at me.

"Master," I whispered, "what…" My eyes were filled with tears and I thought that I would be sick with the pain.

"I have not yet caught you looking at him with those bewitching eyes," he said to me with clenched teeth.

"But I have seen you watching her throughout the banquet," Odysseus yelled at one of our guests across the table. "You have violated my friendship, and I could kill you for that."

"My Lord," the guest muttered, his face white beneath the tanning of the sun. "I…"

"Do not insult me with denial. You will never set foot in my house again. Now leave before I shoot an arrow through your heart." The guest arose with shaking legs and left the room in silence.

The pain of feeling nothing in my arm made me want to swoon. I knew that the man had been watching me throughout the meal. I had kept my eyes on my food and had stopped laughing when others were amused. I knew that something was wrong. I heard the change in my Master's voice and recognized his anger mounting, but I was not certain about the cause. I thought it was the wine. It was the guest looking at me.

"You cannot be trusted to share our banquets," my Master said to me. "You will remain in your room hereafter." Then he turned to Mentor and said in a menacing voice, "If you see her using those eyes to attract and destroy men, tell me." Back to me he snarled, "You will be hanged for your disloyalty. And hereafter, cover your eyes whenever you are out of our bedchamber. Eurykleia, take her to our room." He pushed me toward his nurse, and the pain in my arm would have made me fall if Eurykleia had not held me.

I began to walk, shame covering me. I fought back the sobs of injustice for his charges. I had done nothing. I had worn the veil that covered my whole face except my eyes so that I could see. Now I would wear veils that covered me from the top of my head to my feet forever. Even worse, at any time I could be charged with attracting any man who entered the palace and looked at me. The pain in my left arm had spread to my chest. I fell on the bed and lost all sight.

This morning he saw the black fingers of his hand on my arm when I rose from the bed. He turned and left the room.

I could not raise my arm to weave today. Pain makes me dizzy. Terror torments me.

There is nothing that I like about being a wife, even the wife of a king. Nights with my Master are unspeakable, but he becomes angry when I cry and warns me of my duty. I have learned to hold the sobs behind my teeth. I have lost the freedom to take long walks and to explore hillsides and beaches. Nor am I allowed at the evening banquets.

I was told that the weavers are my responsibility, and I am to teach them the art as I know it. Yet, my Master's mother often locks me in my sleeping room and away from the women. I do not know the reason for her decisions.

I spend my days in the bedchamber with the olive tree that connects earth with sky. My Master told me that he built the bed with a tree that lasts forever in order to remind his queen of the marriage that endures. I should be happy beneath the branches of such a tree. Instead, it stifles me. Why did he build the bed with a tree that forever reminds me of my prison? I am left wondering why King Odysseus wanted marriage without love or tenderness or friendship.

With longing I think of simple things like the waters that we all enjoyed on Sikelia. In my homeland, springs gave their water generously. In a public square a fountain and a large pool for bathing were open to all in sociable meetings and conversation. What pleasure we enjoyed from such daily interactions! Though I have heard of a spring called Arethousa that is located near the palace here on Ithaka, it is not a place for social gatherings, I am told. There are no public baths on Ithaka, and from what I now know there is little bathing by the people of this island. I am considered strange because I struggle to keep clean and sweet smelling, as in the past. The servants do not seem to understand why I want so much water brought up to our bedchamber. Every day they frown as they carry up pails of clear water for me.

Everyone seems to fear me. They leave me alone.

Despite my daily prayers and offerings morning and evening, this life torments me. Where are my gods?

My Master has gone on another hunting trip with his friends who feast and laugh with him each day and evening. When he is away, I thank the gods that there is calm during the sunlight hours and tranquility during the hours of darkness that allow me to write.

I rise after restless nights and visit my shrine where I stand praying to Hera, Athene, and my Lykaian Goddess to help me survive here. I bathe and my hair is brushed and tied. I dress in the same robes each day, eat the same grains and seeds with thick goat milk curd. Then I send word to the weavers to begin their daily tasks. I am pleased that I have regained my health and am permitted to weave with the women.

When I am not with the weavers, I look at the sea through the small window of my room. I am not allowed to leave the sight of my Master's mother even to find the herbs and roots that I love to collect and eat.

I sleep more and more when I am allowed and smile less and less.

I am amazed, especially after observing the men on Ithaka, that my father kept peace by making olive oil and wine that were desired by other kings and village leaders on the Great Island. One might think that those leaders would unite and overrun our kingdom in order to possess the groves and grapes for themselves. The Ithakans would have done that. On beautiful Sikelia, people from neighboring villages believed that my father knew secrets from the gods that made our oil and wine and weaving celebrated for their excellence. No one else could produce the same golden green oil from trees, they said, or wine that the gods would desire if they were mortal, or weaving inspired surely by secrets from the past. For these reasons the other tribes, who fought with each other in frustrated aggression and in drunken brawls over land and women, kept peace with my father. In turn, he was generous and fair in his trades. It must be said, though, that he kept the best oil—what he called with a smile "the virgin oil"—for our own people. The best wine and the best robes he kept for trading with the Phoenicians and for the royal family. But even our second best was superior to all others.

I try to imagine what life with a husband like my father might have meant to me, a man who was always at home to demonstrate justice without judgment and kindness without weakness. A man who never swaggered to prove uncertain manhood, never bragged about the women he ravished and the men he murdered or the women and children he stole from their homes.

How fortunate my mother was. Why did she not know or appreciate the gifts that the gods had given to her?

Memories have become my only friends on Ithaka, for my life was filled with such joy in the past—with kindness and love, banquets and the baths.

In the dark, stone palace on Ithaka men are always preparing for war, but I remember my homeland as a place of peace and prosperity. We had no army because none was needed. Our men were farmers and stone builders, carpenters and potters, herdsmen and athletes. Because there was no war, the people spent their time perfecting their arts. They produced the finest animals and sheep's wool, the loveliest woven robes, the sturdiest pots and building materials and leather, the most beautiful and intricate goblets and bowls. Men grew strong and handsome through hard work and through the competition of the games that filled their lives and made them proud and tall.

From childhood boys were groomed for the glory of peace, and girls dreamed of the man and children who would give them reason to age into wisdom that was respected by all. Everyone worked and the land was beautiful and bountiful and made the people proud of their participation in the wealth that nature's gods bestowed.

In our land, unlike on Ithaka, mothers were not afraid that their sons would be sacrificed to the Greek god of war, did not live in terror that armed warriors would enslave their daughters and murder their men for cups and blankets.

And then Odysseus arrived and taught us the ways of a dark world.

My father the King, like his father and his grandfather who journeyed from Sparta to Sikelia, kept harmony through unbroken treaties and trade. My father welcomed the merchants who stopped on occasion to give us gold and bronze and other articles that we did not grow or fish or produce for ourselves. Through one of these traders, the Phoenician merchant Cadmus, I learned to read, write, and appreciate words. I came to know plants and herbs and medicines that he brought from distant ports. I learned all things important in the world from this man who became my trusted friend.

Yet, as a wife, I am not allowed to use my knowledge and must keep hidden all that I have learned. If they knew what I hide, they would call me Witch and have me stoned for bringing fear of the unknown to their island.

Despite the danger, only my writing and my memories of a former life bring me comfort on this desolate rock called Ithaka.

Athene! Hera! Hear my prayers! Help me find a way to escape this rocky prison! Help me to find a way home! Let me see Father and Cadmus once again!

I look down from the battlement. There is Chaos below me as the soldiers in armor slash the people in the courtyard with swords and battle-axes. Women and girls, boys and babies scream as the blood flies and javelins and swords rip through soft flesh. Men, trying to protect the helpless, curse and moan as they too are hacked to pieces. Arms and heads fly everywhere, and the ground is covered with blood and gore. Several soldiers start to climb steps and ladders toward me, and I know that I am next to taste the blood of their rage. There is no place to go. It is too high to jump. Suddenly my Lord's mother approaches from below, she points up at me, and the wind increases to a gale. I hear her laugh with the fury of a huge vicious bird, and the sky is covered with black wings that shriek and shut out the sun. She calls again like a giant screaming hawk, and the fierce black birds are also screeching as they attack me in waves. I put my arms over my face and head, but the beaks and talons rip at my back, my arms, my stomach, my legs. My robe is in tatters, my flesh exposed, blood covering my feet. The birds fly away with chunks of skin in their beaks and make way for the next surge of wings. They too rip at my bleeding flesh while endless numbers of large black birds shriek uproariously, waiting to get to me. So many, the sky is too small to hold them, the flapping wings so loud that the gods cannot hear my cries. I cannot breathe, my ears are breaking with the roar, and the pain and terror go on forever as my flesh is torn from me.

I awake. My face is bathed in tears. I am sobbing. My gods! Why does Morpheus torment me?

This palace is so dark and ugly. Beauty has been lost to me. How do these people live buried in stone and shadows? And why do they treat me as less than a slave?

I want to shout, "I merit respect and deference for my family line."

I want to scream, "I am the daughter of King Ikarios from the Great Island of Sikelia. My grandfather was King Machaon. My great grandfather was Prince Amyklaios who left Sparta to find freedom and peace. The gods favored him in his honorable quest." Yet, despite my noble heritage, here I feel invisible and useless.

I do not deserve the harsh and cold treatment that surrounds me on Ithaka. I do not deserve the sorrow of being a wife in a palace so cruel.

Or do I deserve it? Have I, while growing up, been unkind or ruthless? Have I hurt people and then willed forgetfulness of my deeds? Often when the Sun God sleeps I search my memory for offenses that I may have committed.

Then I ask, "Was I too happy on my homeland? Did I ignore the pain of others in my selfish desire for pleasure? Can I blame a child for enjoying such an easy life of love and laughter? Is this my punishment for youth?"

Despite my search through memory and dreams, I can discover nothing that merits the sadness of this life. I am left with only darkness and misery that deprive me of sleep.

Are tears, like years, endless?

I hear the nightingale singing its song of woe. I think of the long seasons confronting me, and I want to run and scream. Instead, I remain as silent and submissive as I was when I arrived on this island. It is the only hope for better seasons to come.

Sometimes when the darkness of night crushes me, I want only to descend to the cold home of Persephone and Hades. Perhaps the shades are kinder in the Lower World.

I hear someone…

I have returned to my own weaving. For a full moon I have not been allowed to weave or spend my days with the weavers. I do not know the reason. I begged for my loom and finally it was brought to my Master's sleeping room for me. Now I can weave all day, and when I am not allowed to participate in the evening banquet, I can weave in our bedchamber. This comforts me and brings me peace.

My Master's mother was so pleased with the robe I made for her that she relented and allowed me to work with the weavers again. I keep another loom in the weaving shed, and we share our fancies and work on new ideas together. I showed them how I use my fingers between the threads to create designs. That makes them smile. Since I have been with them, I can see their improvement. I am brought to their enclosed weaving shed on the far side of the Great Room each morning and remain there all day, except for the mid-day meal. Then I eat alone.

There is so little air and light in the weaving shed. The windows are small and high to protect us, I am told, and we are surrounded by grey stone. It is dusty and noisy from the activities of the craftsmen and servants and storage facilities near us. Yet I can take the veil from my face when I am among the weavers. That allows me to breathe.

I feel free among these women, though they are slaves and can never have their freedom. Neither can I be free, so we are all one.

I think that I am sick. My food returns after every meal, and I have no energy.

My Master's mother only smiled when I told her of my illness. She orders the servants to bring me more varied foods, but the meats are too rich and heavy. I long for roasted fish, fresh vegetables, and tasty broths, but even those foods might make me ill. I am afraid to eat.

"Am I being poisoned?" I want to ask Eurykleia, but I am afraid.

Despite my attempts to bathe often for my own cleanliness, the stench of the palace increases my illness. And I am not allowed to go into the fields to search for rosemary and other herbs to calm my stomach. His mother does nothing to help me. Why does she hate me? I do not trust her.

Only when my Master is away hunting or plundering the settlements of strangers can I write my story and feel these moments of freedom. But I must be careful. His mother watches me and comes to my room in the middle of the night. When I hear her at the door and listen for her soft steps, I kneel in prayer with my robe over my writing. I told her that we stand to offer sacrifice on my homeland, and sometimes we also kneel when we pray alone. She accepted this explanation. So now, when she sees me kneeling before my altar with one tiny lamp to light the small room, she walks down the stairs and leaves me in the peace of night.

Once I was honest and would never have altered truth. But this house has made me fearful of everything. I hate her spying, but I dread his return. The papyrus sheets remain hidden under the altar shelf in a box covered by a ceremonial robe, and the ink must be carefully cleaned up and put away in a sack behind the box where they never look.

Cadmus, you would know how to help me. Where are you?

After writing, I always feel certain that my life will be happier in days to come. I can sleep.

I have been in this prison palace for too many swellings of the moon. My body is growing, and one day I mentioned this.

The weavers giggled, and one of them said, "You will have a gift when the cold season comes." They all laughed.

"What is the gift? Will I like it?" I asked in simplicity. They laughed and refused to say more.

I finally realize that I am with child. My weavers told me so. I believe them for as the weeks pass, my waist is beginning to enlarge. I have always been slim and energetic, but now I see a slight bulge where once I was flat. And the growing of my chest amazes me. The thread they use to measure me is getting a bit longer. They seem to be excited about it. I am not.

What kind of world can I offer to a new life? To a baby girl I give my own imprisonment and danger. To a boy I give the character of these Ithakan men.

Why are the men of Ithaka so unlike my dear father whom they disdain for his weakness? I do not see him as weak. I remember him as gentle and kind, willing to use reconciliation to end discord between men. Both men and women on our land admired and loved him. I cannot say that of the King my Master on this island. Here, since Laertes gave over his throne to his son, everyone fears the King and his anger. He rules with hardened eyes, booming words, and a quick sword. Power without justice rules this land.

I too fear my Master though he no longer forces my submission. He now goes on hunting trips each week since my illness began. When he is home to rule, I lower my eyes and remain silent.

I try to shut my mind to my homeland. In the darkness of the night Morpheus tortures me with images of my dear father and sister, proud Tyndareus and our palace, my brothers and friends, the fields and shore where I ran freely like wind. I pray that my dreams will be beautiful. Instead, I awake with tears washing my face and with images of my brother and Tyndareus bleeding in the Field of Asphodel. Then I lock all sound behind my teeth. My Lord gets angry when I weep.

The weavers have begun to smile at their own work. They see the difference in the quality of their fabrics. I am teaching them how to set up the looms to create more intricate patterns in the fabrics, and they seem excited about learning new things. I will have to go out to gather plants for dyes after my confinement. I have trouble with my own weaving now. Reaching across the loom with the shuttle is so tiring.

The weavers smile softly with me when my Master is away, and we have become friends. Except for the discomfort, work has become almost like the joy I knew on my homeland. Then my sister and I would work with the weavers who were both servants from our palace and free women from the nearby villages. They would tell stories and gossip, and we spent long parts of the day laughing.

How I loved those days. And how excited we all were when a new idea for a design or a color was suggested. We would work at those ideas until we made them into beautiful patterns that brought praise and trade of value to my father and the Sikelos mountain tribes.

Inspired, I would sometimes return to my room where my own loom sang long into the night. Even my mother's scolding the next day did not keep the smile from my tired eyes, for I knew the beauty of my work. Each time I brought a new cloak or blanket to the weavers, they looked with large eyes and open mouths at what I had finished in my room. In those moments, I knew what happiness was. They clapped their hands with joy and begged me to explain what I had done. I did, and we loved each other, these women and I.

I long to create the same kinds of friendships here, but it is not easy with slaves who fear my Master and even fear me. Perhaps they think that I might tell the Master that they enjoy their tasks. Then the work will be made longer and harder.

I am determined to make their lives easier, even if they cannot be happy. I must think of strategies to give satisfaction to these women, to give them glimpses of the joy that I have known, and to decrease the desolation in their eyes.

I have now seen a different aspect of my Master. Men on Ithaka, who own land and keep slaves to do their work, often spend their days in games or in drinking, talking, and idleness at the palace of Odysseus. Sometimes they accompany my Master in his hunting expeditions on Ithaka or to distant islands for more slaves. In the courtyard of the palace, the games they play for competition are boxing, running, jumping, javelin, bows and arrows, and swords. They also now play with quoits and heavy balls, which Odysseus brought from Sikelia when he stole me. Odysseus never competes with the bow and arrow or the javelin because he is famous throughout the world as the best in those games. I have also heard it said that the massive strength of his shoulders and arms makes him a wrestler to fear.

Several days ago Prince Zetheus from the kingdom of Sami on the western coast of Kefalonia stopped at the busy port of Ithaka to meet the famed Odysseus. As always, my Lord treated him with the respect and hospitality accorded all strangers who cross our threshold. To honor the guest, my Master ordered a banquet for the evening, and to fill the hours of the day organized a competition between the men who accompanied Prince Zetheus and the men on Ithaka. I was allowed to observe the games from a hidden corner of the courtyard.

Unfortunately, Prince Zetheus broke the bond of courtesy between host and guest. The day was hot, and his men were losing most of the games. As he drank more and more wine cut with too little water, he became increasingly boisterous and arrogant. He began to direct his taunts to his host, and his men encouraged his jibes and insults with laughter and applause.

My Master sat quietly as his face became dark and fierce.

Finally, the prince faced his men and said, "Surely the king of Ithaka has a reputation that far outweighs his abilities. Why else does he not show what he can do with bow and arrow? Like all kings who are cowards," Zetheus said with a sneer, "my host hides behind Rumor invented by an ally or a friendly god."

That was the final word. With careful deliberation, my Master picked up his bow and arrow that sat at his side. Like a warrior my Master stood up, and Zetheus added to his insults by laughing at his stature.

My Master said in a voice for all to hear, "You, Zetheus. You with the empty mouth can take an arrow through your chest right now. Or you can accept the challenge of competition with my bow and arrow. The loser kneels at the feet of the winner and offers a gift of great price to the victor."

Without hesitation, Zetheus accepted the challenge and directed his men to select a distant tree and to place on it a circle for the target. My Master announced that each would have three arrows, and the arrow closest to the middle of the circle on the small tree would be announced the winner.

Zetheus laughed with contempt at the ease of winning such a contest. He took a long drink of wine and sent out his three arrows. All hit the tree but only one hit the edge of the circle drawn on the bark.

My Master planted his legs firmly in position and with keen eyes swiftly shot his three arrows into the center of the circle. Zetheus was furious and did not acknowledge the victor.

After he conferred with his men, Zetheus again raised his voice with a proud and haughty manner as he challenged my Master to a boxing match. The young prince was tall and strongly built with long legs and arms. They are about the same age, but the prince assumed that he had a great advantage over Odysseus whose legs are shorter.

In courtesy to a guest, my Master warned the prince that he was an experienced boxer. But vain and intemperate as he was, the prince accepted the challenge with an angry sneer. Odysseus rose and threw off his mantel to expose his huge shoulders and the muscles of his great arms and back and chest. At the unexpected sight of his foe, the prince lost the rosy flush of wine and sun and took on the color of green fear. He seemed suddenly sobered but still felt required to make boasting and insulting remarks to his host. He attacked Odysseus at a run and started to punch in all directions.

It was clear that my Master was also in a rage, but he remained composed and thoughtful as he deflected the punches that grazed his cheeks and shoulders. The men of Zetheus cheered and laughed as they threw insults to Odysseus. Suddenly my Master moved quickly to the side to avoid a hard punch and hit Zetheus straight in the face. Blood splattered over both of them as Zetheus staggered back, his nose smashed into the well between his cheeks. His men yelled for him to fight back, and as he moved forward in a daze, my Master hit him again with a powerful smash to his chin. We could hear the bones of his face break. His head snapped back, and his body fell in a heap. Even from my place of hiding, I could tell that his neck was broken.

The breath of life escaped through his shattered teeth.

Silence enclosed us.

Then my Master, with frightening anger, ordered the guests to carry Zetheus to their ship as he announced, "No one from your kingdom will be welcomed on Ithaka in the future. Your people do not honor the laws of hospitality. Anyone from the realm of Zetheus will be sent to the cold home of Hades if he steps on the shores of Ithaka. Let my words be sent out across your kingdom and other nearby islands," he said. "And let it end here." Then he turned and entered his hall.

Throughout the boxing competition, I had been turned to stone and could not move. Autonoë, my handmaiden, took my arm and led me inside. I began to shake.

The useless violence made no sense to me. A man was alive and then was dead for no reason that I could see. Why do men do these things? Why did the young prince need to show his pride in this foolish way? After my maids bathed me and brought me some mint tea, I realized two things. I recognized that everyone in the palace was proud and grateful for the power of Odysseus to protect his subjects.

I was also aware that my Master had shown amazing restraint in dealing with his guest, far more self-control than his quick temper has ever revealed in my presence. Perhaps his reverence for the gods' laws and his position as King take precedence over his own weaknesses and over his consideration for mortals. He seems to fear only the gods, never men. I dread him more than ever.

I have made some changes in the weaving room. For the larger robes and blankets, I now have two weavers working together on one standing loom. With this method the weavers do not have to walk back and forth with the shuttle to keep the threads straight. I have also requested that the head carpenter should make some benches so that we may sit for part of the weaving of the robes. Perhaps that may help to relieve the pain in our backs and legs. It might—

Work cannot be joyful on Ithaka or it is not seen as work. Only free men can laugh and find joy in the work of hunting and war. All others—slaves and women who labor and farm and sweat and serve— must spend their days in frowns and stifle the laughter that is as much a part of our nature as the tears. Why have the Ithakans not learned this lesson about the laughter within us that waits to sing? Why do they believe that their gods approve of human pain and suffering but disapprove of happiness? I find myself seeing their way until I make these lovely marks that sweep away my fears. Then in the darkness of the night a small lamp and a brush shut out their way of thinking.

Instead of feeling despair and pain, I become part of my writing and remember my home and the wonder of pleasure. I become part of my gods—the Lykaian Goddess and Athene and Hera who rule all mortals. I remember that every day was new and exciting and full of love and friendship. And though my mother required submission and frowns when she occasionally visited the weaving shed, the days were filled with sunshine and the energy of ideas and creation. That is what I hope to bring to my slave weavers on Ithaka.

May the rest of my life not reflect the days of Sisyphos.

Have I defied the gods in such thoughts?

The benches have been made, and the weavers seem more comfortable and frown less. The pain is somewhat relieved, but weaving is still hard work. Perhaps over time I can make other changes in how we work. I hear…

As I walk across the Great Room with my veil hiding my face, I take the opportunity to look into the rooms that make up the lower level of the palace. I am always appalled at the meanness of the rooms. On the first floor the rooms are small and dark with only a tiny window for air and light. That is for protection in case of assault, I am told. There is only space for a bed and a place for a robe and sandals. There is no color, only grey stone. The rooms on the first floor of the western and northern sides are the rooms for my Lord's mother and his father, his guests, and their personal servants. Only the size and placement of the rooms distinguish royalty or other positions. But they live little better than the guards and workers and slaves whose rooms are on the southern side adjoining the work sheds.

On the second floor, the rooms are no larger, but at least the ones on the side of the gardens and fields have a small window. These are for the maidservants. The rooms on the side of the craftsmen's sheds and kitchens have no windows because of the noise and dirt. These rooms are for maids and weavers. The roof covers the whole second floor, but my Master's bedchamber is the only room completed on the western side of the second floor.

Though my Master's bedchamber is larger than other sleeping chambers, it is also dark and drab with its stone walls and floors and low ceiling. The people on Ithaka do not seem to know any other way. Beauty is absent from their lives except for golden goblets and other riches taken as my dowry, and the occasional treasures from my Lord's raiding expeditions.

I have been thinking about the difference between my Master's bedchamber and the other rooms that I see in the palace. This is the only room that overlooks the sea.

The Master's chamber is surprisingly large by Ithaka's standards. There is the bed with leather slung between three posts and the olive tree that makes up the fourth post. A heavy oak door in the corner of the Master's room opens to a narrow balcony and stairs that lead down to the Great Room. Our sleeping room has small shelves in two corners for personal items and weaving materials, and there is a narrow door to the three steps that lead up to the small shrine. There is just enough space for a large loom and a smaller loom and for robes hung in a third corner. There is a small window overlooking the sea in the distance. I love and hate that window. It is just wide enough to offer me a vision of the world that I loved but will never again experience. My Lord planned this room where his Queen would spend most of her life weaving, praying, sleeping, and making warriors for the future of Ithaka. I shudder when I think about it.

As my body swells, my back aches. I have difficulty standing or even sitting straight to do the weaving by the time the Sun God moves over us in the sky. I can't imagine how the pain will be when I become really big. I never realized the agony that weavers endure as they become older or with child. I remember the complaints among the weavers on my homeland when they began to grow large, but I was a child and did not understand. Now I begin to think about how to alleviate the sharp ache that feels like a knife through my back and sometimes down my legs. The benches help, but not enough.

3. Creating a New Life

Two days ago I knew happiness when Cadmus the Phoenician merchant arrived on Ithaka. He has found me. I am not forgotten.

My servant came to my room, bowed, and said, "Lady, a merchant has entered the palace and asked to trade for fabrics. What should I say to him?"

"I shall come down to greet him," I answered. I stood at the top of the stairs, ready to descend. But then I heard my Master speak.

He said, "My Queen, who is in charge of the weaving, is confined and cannot greet visitors. We shall talk."

Disappointment overcame me. I returned to my room choking back sobs.

Cadmus said nothing. He did not say that he knew my family or me. He did not say that he brought word from my father or sister. But I was happy just to see him—tall and dark and well muscled from the challenges of sailing the powerful seas. My friend. My forever friend.

The next day, after my Master indicated that a merchant had arrived from Phoenician Tyre, from Krete, Libya, and elsewhere over the seas, I sent down to Cadmus my finest cloak. I was listening at my door and smiled when I heard him thank my Master for his generosity. He praised the cloak and its exquisite work.

Inside the folds I had inserted a sheet of parchment telling him about my happiness in seeing him again. I did not describe my life. He could see it all around him. The squalor, the filth, the stench. Rather, I told him that secretly practicing the writing of his marks in the silence of my room was my greatest pleasure in life. I wrote that I hoped he would return after my confinement so I could greet and honor him.

I know he found my note because later he flattered my Master with a wondrous gift for his queen. It is a beautiful trunk of carved oak with bronze corners. It is lined with Lebanon cedar. There are designs of leaves and flowers on the top and sides. I opened it in my room and was touched by its contents. Hidden under skeins of silk yarn from the East were many sheets of papyrus and thinly pounded leather with ink dust and brushes for my writing. He also included powdered dyes from plants that I do not know. One dye is called Tyrian purple, which the Phoenicians make from seashells off the coast of Krete. I think I remember hearing about that famous purple dye. One of the most amazing gifts was another jar of purple dye from the shells of snails that live on an island beyond the Pillars of Hercules. His note told me this. He did not write it, but that dye must be the most valuable in the world. I was so excited by his gifts that I could hardly wait to try the dyes and compare the different purples.

But the most precious gift was the long letter that he wrote to me.

"Your father has grown smaller than when you left, my Lady Penelope. He no longer looks to the skies when he walks. Your mother's tongue reviles him for his weakness, and this makes no one happy. Your brothers work hard and prepare to rule the land when your father is no longer strong enough to do so. Your sister misses you. No one takes Penelope's place, so the laughter that once greeted each day and rang out beyond the walls of the palace has been lost."

I waited to continue reading until the tears subsided. He told me about his travels and taught me new words that I can now use. I will read this letter over and over until I can repeat it without the reading.

I wept quietly as I dragged the large trunk up to the small shrine and put it under the altar beside my other smaller box. It was fortunate that my Master's mother suffered from a headache and was in her room when the beautiful trunk arrived. Otherwise, she would have examined the contents and taken everything, perhaps even the trunk, from me.

I covered both the trunk and the box with the special robe that drapes the altar. I think his mother assumes that the robe is part of my devotion to the gods, as are the small statues and the silver wrought bowl for libations that decorate the top of my altar. I will hide my writing in this beautiful trunk forever.

That night from the top of the stairs where I hid overlooking the great banquet room, I heard my Master complain about his queen, "She has strange habits of making marks on the stone floor and walls." I do this occasionally as reminders of ideas for weaving new designs. Then with small stones I erase the marks that I have made.

My Lord continued, "Perhaps because she came from a foreign land, could she be a witch—like Medeia in the story sung by my bard? Merchant, have you ever seen such things in your wide travels?"

With deference but with a voice filled with the assurance of experience, Cadmus told my Master that I had been given special knowledge from the gods, "Few mortals have the gift of making these marks. Even the gods do not use them. These marks," he said, "show unusual creativity and skill that explain the beautiful weaving in her work. This is a skill of great value."

"This pleases me to know," my Master said. "But there are other things that trouble me. She bathes every day. Is that not strange? And she bewitches men with her eyes, those green eyes that drove me wild and still make me weak when she gazes at me. Other men cannot take their eyes away from her."

Cadmus was silent. Then he said, "Your queen sounds like a remarkable woman and one who is a treasure to a husband who appreciates her gifts. Her art of weaving offers great value to you. And I have known people in other lands who bathe daily, though that is not done in all settlements. As for her eyes, you say that they are green?

"It is rare to find green eyes in my travels. Only one woman have I found with eyes like the waters that wash up on the beaches of the Great Sea. What a treasure you have, my Lord. I think that Aphrodite would want to tell you to enjoy such beauty that is yours. I am sure that her virtue equals her loveliness, is that not so?"

"We have seen nothing that suggests that she is not a good woman," Odysseus answered.

"Then I can only advise you to appreciate all that she gives to you. You are a fortunate man."

My heart beats hard with gratitude at the memory of those words.

In the course of their conversation, Cadmus offered to trade bronze, silver, and gold bowls and cups, jewelry, and other precious items for my woven goods. "I would like you to consider holding your finest woven goods for me," he said. "If you agree and make our word our bond, I promise to stop at your island every two years in order to trade. I assure you that my generosity will be equal to my appreciation of your weavers' beautiful work."

"This agreement pleases me," Master said. "I assure you that my honor will equal yours. However, if we keep our work for that length of time and only for you, I will expect you to stop regularly for this trade. My word is my bond, and I expect the same from you." They shook hands in that special way that men do.

I feel weak with happiness.

My Master has not mentioned the trunk from Cadmus. It is useless to him, so he seems to have forgotten it. I will keep the trunk hidden under my altar where I visit the gods and write at night. I cannot stop thinking of Cadmus whose friendship gives me life.

I was born on the day Cadmus, the Phoenician trader, first came to the island of my father.

Of course I know that I came into the world long before amid the screams and sacrifice of my mother who told me many times that she cried when I was not another boy. But I do not speak now of the disappointment and despair brought on by my life, rather of the part of me that thinks, feels, loves, and dreams—the part of me that learned to read and to write. It is the part of me that remembers and was given life by Cadmus.

The Merchant was in my father's Great Hall when my young sister Iphthime and I returned from the shore. The day was hot and filled with sunshine. Iphthime and I had been running into the small waves that played with the pebbles on the beach. The waves had tickled our toes and had pulled the sand from beneath the soles of our feet, so we ran after the water to tickle it back. Eurynome, our nurse, had stood by helplessly as we jumped into the waves, our clothes and hair weighing us down. We had played for some time in the cold water, we had eaten bread and cheese and grapes. We drank fresh water touched with wine and lay down on a soft blanket to dry our clothes. We had told stories and giggled and fallen asleep. It was one of the free and glorious days that describe my youth and the love that enriched our days.

Then we started back to the palace. Our nurse was aghast when we insisted on going to the Great Room to say hello to our father and to show him the image of his two disgraceful daughters. We wanted to amuse him and hear his laughter when he saw us with seaweed in our hair.

"Father, Father, look at the seaweed! We brought the Great Sea to you," we called to him with merriment.

As we ran into the room with the sun coming through the western windows and the mosaics dressing the walls in color and golden light, we saw Father speaking to a stranger.

We stopped inside the large doorway. Suddenly I was ashamed of our appearance, for I was no young child like my sister of six years. I was not yet a woman, but I was almost ten years old and should have known better than to act like my ruffian brothers. I would have removed myself silently had we not been shouting with glee to get our father's attention, but Father and the stranger had already turned to see the source of this noisy interruption. My father frowned, the stranger looked surprised, and my face flamed with a fire that even the sun could not paint on my skin. I could not move.

I stood there for only a moment, but my discomfort seemed to last for days. I was aware only of the mosaic floors and walls reflecting the Sun God's brilliance. Finally, when I looked at my father's eyes, I saw his amusement beneath the frown. He smiled and—returning his smile—my sister and I ran to his safe arms. He enclosed us in the soft fabric of his robe, and I felt the kiss on the top of my head and heard my sister giggle.

Feeling embarrassed again, I moved away from him and stood as tall and as dignified as I could, considering the state of my clothes and the sand in my hair and on my cheeks. With my father's introduction I gave a formal bow to the stranger. Instantly I saw the kindness in his eyes and felt a glow of pleasure spread through my chest. He did not laugh at me, as my father had the freedom to do. He returned my bow, said something that I cannot remember in a deep and kind voice, and I felt in that moment that I could like and trust this stranger forever.

Cadmus, the Phoenician merchant, stood tall with pride, but without arrogance. Neither did he bow his head and shoulders with deference to the King like most other merchants. This regal

Phoenician, I learned later, was proud of his family name, his birthplace of Tyre on the eastern shore of the Great Sea, and his role as a trader in spreading learning and art throughout the many islands and ports of the world.

"This is a noble trade," he told me later. "We bring dyes, medicines, gold, jewelry, pottery, goods woven in new and remarkable patterns, seeds and new plants for growing and spreading in distant lands, and so many other objects that your parents need or have never before seen. I am proud of our mission in the world." I came to know and understand how he enriched all lands.

We had met many other traders on their way past our land, but never had anyone so changed my life as this man would do—this man with the curly black beard, tight black curls cut like a wreath around his head, and strange and beautiful clothing. At the evening banquets he wore long robes woven in striking colors and trimmed with precious stones. He was adorned with arm bracelets of gold and ivory and rings with stones of colors I had never seen. During the day when he worked, he wore a simple tunic from the waist to above the knees, and when he was in the palace he added a tunic without sleeves to cover his chest. Always he wore sandals of exquisite leather.

I came to realize that though he had the height and strength of a brave warrior, he also had the intelligence and wisdom of a seer and the tender and warm heart of a child. Despite his youth, his knowledge of trade and of the world commanded remarkable respect from my father who seldom deferred to any man. The Merchant's smile and those kind black eyes would forever haunt my dreams.

As I sit through the hours of night, I think so often of my Merchant with his gentle and knowing eyes. Cadmus the Phoenician became my friend.

Since I was a princess and he was a merchant, he treated me always with the respect accorded my position, though I was still a child and he was a man learned in the knowledge of the world. But a strange thing happened that brought us together for all time. He would teach me how to read and write in the months that followed.

On the first night of his visit to our island, he dined in the Great Hall with the King and Queen and with leaders of nearby villages while his men dined in the outer hall with the men of our palace. My three brothers and I were allowed to attend the banquet and to hear the stories that he brought from the outside world. I was now old enough to observe the festivities until the stories ended after dinner. I was thrilled. I loved stories and the songs of my father's bard.

Before that night, I had hidden with my sister at the top of the stairs when visitors came or when Demodikos, the King's singer, sang the songs that moved my heart. But that night I did not need to hide. I sat at the long table, prayed to Zeus and the Goddess of the Fields, and observed the sacrifice and libation performed by my father. I drank wine with water and shared in the meal of roasted lamb and sweet white fish, of vegetables and fresh greens, of fruit and bread, honey and curd. It was a glorious meal and one that I have never forgotten.

For dinner Cadmus wore a richly patterned robe with an elaborate collar of jewels, gold armlets on each arm, and gold rings with green and blue stones. He told stories of Greek warriors, of battles that made my father and me wonder why, and he sang songs in a voice that surpassed our own poet.

For the many days that followed, while he was my teacher, he dined with us every night and told us about the world. He told us about the islands he had seen, and how people lived, what they wore and ate, how they spoke, and which people were dangerous or friendly. He praised the rare tribes who were peaceful and enjoyed the glory of the gods, as we did in our land. He told us of rumors about monsters with one eye in their forehead, the beautiful Kalypso, and the dreaded Kirke who turns men into animals.

"I have not seen such immortals," he said, "but I have heard so many stories of them that they must be true. I have long wondered," and he smiled.

He told us stories of the gods and goddesses who loved rich kings like Agamemnon and his brother Menelaos, and he told us of a great kingdom called Troy, which shared the vast land where Cadmus was born on Tyre.

His stories made me glad as I compared with other heroes and other lands my father's strength and goodness and the gold and rich woven cloth that adorned my proud and commanding mother. There has never been a happier time in my life than those weeks of freedom and excitement in sharing his knowledge of the great world beyond our kingdom.

In return, we shared with him glorious Etna that breathes fire and sometimes wakes us with her rumblings. Her sparks reminded us of how small we are and how powerful is the mountain of the gods who watch us.

One evening after the banquet satisfied our bodies, Cadmus began telling a story that filled my head with Arête, the wise Phaiakian Queen from Scheria.

"These glorious people live in a palace that is more magnificent than even the great palace of Minos on the island of Krete." We had heard of the wonders of Krete but never of Scheria. "There, Arête helps her husband to rule the peaceful land. She travels throughout the hills and valleys to reach the villages to settle disputes. Her people admire her for her beauty and the love of her husband, for her judgments in settling disputes, and for her kindness to everyone.

"In their palace are high marble stairs embossed with gold and ivory, the rooms are many and large, and the town is busy and colorful with flowers and plants everywhere. The kingdom is surrounded by fields and orchards that produce in all seasons. The streets are so wide that two carts can pass each other at the same time, and the riches are beyond imagination. Only your peaceful kingdom," he said, "can equal Scheria." We were grateful for his kind words, but we all knew that Arête's land was more magnificent than ours and that this queen surpassed all other royalty, even my own mother.

I could not stop thinking of this queen.

Several days later I began to weave a robe with a design and colors that I had never before used. The fabric was very fine, and I hoped that it would be worthy to send to Queen Arête. I stayed up weaving long into the nights and when I finished the robe, I asked Cadmus if he should be embarrassed to give this gift to Queen Arête from me. He examined it carefully and finally looked in my eyes and said he would be pleased to bring it to her. My chest pounded with joy.

"I know she will be proud to wear it," he said. I have never forgotten that robe and will never make another exactly like it.

Then we began our daily lesson of writing.

However thrilling it was to hear stories of the world, my greatest joy was in meeting Cadmus. The second day on our island, Cadmus was sitting with my father as they discussed what would be traded between our island and the contents of his two long galleys. I could not hear them, but I watched as this stranger made marks with a long brush and black water on a flat stone. I was fascinated and wanted to know what the marks were and why he was doing that. My father also watched him but was more interested in what he was saying.

I moved slowly closer to them to see the marks. I had not realized that I was soon standing behind the Phoenician and watching every mark that he made. Sometimes the marks were different each time he wrote, but sometimes he repeated the same shapes. As I watched and listened, I realized that some of the words they spoke were followed by his making a mark or marks on the sheet. I was so absorbed in what he was doing that I broke into their conversation.

Without realizing my rudeness, I asked, "What is the meaning of the little groups of marks that you make? Why do you repeat some of the marks? How do you know what marks to make with certain words? Do these pictures have meaning or are they just marks for your amusement?" I was so excited that I did not give him time to answer my questions.

My father was angry that his daughter would dare to interrupt men's work. But the Phoenician seemed amused.

"My Lord," he assured my father, "I do not consider her questions as impertinence but rather as curiosity that reveals a remarkable intelligence that I have never seen in all of my travels." That is what he said—"a remarkable intelligence." That made my father proud, though still angry that a girl would intrude on men's business.

With quiet humility, the Phoenician asked my father for permission to show me what the marks meant after their business was ended.

My father looked at my face and saw how I was silently pleading. He also saw that I too was ashamed of my behavior, but that I longed to know about the marks.

My father said in a gruff voice, "Go away, Daughter, until we have completed our transactions. Then perhaps the merchant will sit with you in the Great Hall where everyone can see you."

Thereafter, for the next two months, Cadmus and I sat together for hours every day. He taught me the pictures that, he said, combined Phoenician, Mycenaean, and Ægyptian forms into a new written language. He taught me how to put the characters together to make the words that speak to us. And I repeated the lines and their signs over and over long into the night until I could make the shapes that he knew and recognized.

While I was weaving, I practiced the shapes in my mind. I even wove some of those shapes into the hems of the robes that I made during those weeks. We began to write whole pages with meaning to each other, and I learned about his childhood and his thoughts.

He wrote to me that his men were grumbling about staying on Sikelia for long weeks instead of setting out to make more trade and more riches. After two weeks of their idleness, Cadmus allowed his second in command to do some trading at our main port and to take the galleys to the nearby islands where he could transact business. That kept his men busy. He wrote that he later promised to give them out of his own share what they had lost in the two full moons that he was not leading them in the best of trades. He laughed when we discussed this situation, but at that time I did not understand the enormous generosity of his gift to me.

While we were practicing writing, he taught me many new words. I was amazed—that was one of the new words—at how I saw the world in a new way. Now I could explain how I felt and how the flowers and trees, the clouds and sea spoke to me. It was as though my world enlarged to embrace everything that ever was and ever could be. I never knew before how important words were, and I wanted to learn every word that he knew.

After he left our island, I read over and over all that he had written until the words he spoke became part of me. They will always be the best part of me.

It was at this time that I was born in a new way that has made my life both bearable and unbearable. And so I speak through these marks during many nights when everyone is asleep, and I hide the papyrus and leather sheets so no one will find and destroy them. Maybe someday, these words will tell him the story of my life and will whisper the silent songs of my memories and my heart.

This morning my Master asked me what changes can be made so that I can produce more woven goods. He has not asked my opinion before this day.

I know that what I say to him on this matter will change my life forever. I must make a choice between living always in these rooms at the top of the palace with the weavers or walking through the palace and being looked at by other men. It is a choice between living safely in a prison or taking a chance on being accused of something I never did and being killed for it. I have been considering this situation, and the choice is not an easy one.

"I have been thinking about using the long unfinished space attached to our sleeping room that makes up the top floor on this side of the palace," I said very quietly. "The space is now as long as the western side of the palace and would offer much room for many weavers and many looms."

I had been told that this great space had been planned for our sons' rooms as they grew. Now the unfinished space could be used for my own purpose in the present. I do not want to think about the large family in the future.

In a subdued voice, I suggested, "We would need one very large weaving room, a large storage room, and a smaller servants' room. These workrooms would adjoin our bedchamber so that the weaving will no longer be done across the Great Room. The outside wall will have large windows looking out toward the sea and surrounding islands so that Zephyr would keep the rooms airy and light and the weavers would work harder." I did not say that the weavers would have clean air, improved light, and the feeling of open space for the first time in their lives. "They could produce many robes in such a space."

My Master said nothing when I made my suggestions. He just stared at me and frowned.

My Master was so impressed by my Merchant's conversation and the possibilities for gain that he began to talk about building the rooms adjoining our bedchamber.

"The weavers could then be closer to me," I reminded him, "and I would not have to be seen by other men in the palace."

As we talked, he made a chilling observation, "These rooms together will make up your new home. Here you will live and work to produce the woven goods that will make Ithaka famous. I have made an agreement with the Phoenician merchant to keep your best products only for this trader who promises to stop at our island every time he passes this way. I have given my word, and you must fulfill that bond." I nodded my head. I did not tell my Master that his contract with the merchant is my only happy dream.

"If I am to keep the robes and fabrics in storage for so long, I must start collecting cedar and plants like lavender and bay to protect the material from insects," I said. "I must be allowed to gather the plants and to teach my weavers how to find them." He said that he would think on it.

My Master seems to speak to me with softer words since my Merchant told him of my value to the palace. I am even invited sometimes to the evening banquets where my Master speaks to me as though I have worth. Although his mother continues to frown at me, I enjoy those evenings and especially the songs of the gods and heroes of the past. I am getting accustomed to having veils covering every part of my body and head, except for my fingers.

My Master and I met with Alessos, the Chief Builder on the island, to discuss plans for the new weaving rooms. I was included in the discussion because I am the only one who knows the needs of the weavers. I was grateful for the opportunity and spoke softly and with appropriate deference.

"I realize that it will be a huge undertaking to build the additional rooms attached to our bedchamber," I said. "We need space for more than thirty weavers and their looms and for spinners. We must also construct a large room with shelves for storage of yarns and completed garments and a small room where my maidservants will sleep.

"In addition, we must plan for a small room with six seats for our physical needs. I want that space on the outside wall so that we can have a window over the seats." I kept my eyes lowered with embarrassment.

"With doors between these rooms, I will have access to all the rooms on this part of the second level without being seen on the balcony overlooking the Great Room. Doors leading from this balcony will have to be strong oak reinforced with bronze and be locked from the inside with an oak bar. This design is for safety, my Master says. This second level should be enlarged by building the rooms outward onto the flat surface of the cliff that protects the western side of the palace from attack. Is this possible, Alessos?"

Surprised, he said, "The weaving rooms will be three times as deep as the first floor sleeping chambers. Is that what you need?"

"Yes," I said. "The King is planning to enlarge our weaving trade beyond the shores of Ithaka, so we will need more weavers and much more space. Is that not so, my Lord?"

Frowning, my Master said to the builder, "That is my plan. I know you will succeed in this."

I then shocked my Master again, "Alessos, could you also build a large outside garden attached to the walls of our bedchamber and the weaving room? The floor of the garden could perhaps be built to the edge of the cliff and so would offer substantial space."

I added quickly, "It is necessary for plants and herbs to grow and flourish for our health. And even for dyes." I did not say that I needed a garden of flowers and greens that I can see and smell and work each day. I did not admit that the garden was a gift for me.

When I saw the frown on my Master's face, I reminded him, "I have been making teas for your mother's headaches and stomach pains. I had brought herbs like mint, rosemary, parsley, and oregano with me from my homeland, and the Phoenician merchant had also traded some herbs for fabrics when he visited the island.

"The medicinal herbs have been necessary to ease your mother's pain, my Lord, but they will be gone soon. I have not been able to walk through the hills and fields to gather the leaves and bark and roots necessary for dyes and medicines. I must renew our store of these plants, or she will spend her days in suffering. And I will run out of dyes to make the fabrics valuable for trade. With such a garden we will have the herbs and other plants that we need throughout the year."

"Enough," Odysseus said. "I have heard enough."

I did not mention the reasons why I have not replaced the herbs—his mother's refusal to allow me out of the palace. And I did not remind him that when I have all this space for weaving, we shall have to make new plans for a nursery. I have some ideas about that, but this was not the time to discuss that subject.

Kind Alessos, without looking at my Master, said to me, "This will be possible if you could tell me exactly what you need and want."

"We must collect rainwater in vessels in the garden. I also need a wide opening with two doors that will lead from our bedchamber to the garden balcony."

"This will be a huge challenge—to cut doors in the stone wall without bringing down the roof of the bedchamber," Alessos muttered.

"Alessos is clever and will manage to do whatever you need," my Master said. "Now I have other work to do." Alessos turned red with pleasure as my Master stood up to leave.

My Lord left us with Eurykleia, his nursemaid of long years past, to discuss my plans for a balcony garden. Only Eurykleia could be trusted to oversee me in the presence of another man in our bedchamber. Alessos and I talked for long into the day and made the designs on the floor of my bedchamber with a soft stone. Eurykleia sat with eyes wide during this long conversation.

I felt the excitement I knew in childhood when something wonderful was about to happen. Then I remembered that I was on Ithaka, and I should not expect happiness. Perhaps my Master would suddenly refuse me, or his mother would learn of the plans and become angry, as she always is with me. If she thought I was happy, she would end the dream. Or the gods would be jealous of my joy and punish me.

I have not mentioned the garden again to anyone.

Alessos says that he can bring hundreds of men and mountains of stone from all over Ithaka and surrounding islands. Soon they will be hard at work getting the stones up the mountain and making walls and floors, and roof, he said. They will also make wooden shutters for the windows when cold winds visit the Great Sea or storms remind us of Zeus's powers. I struggle with the waiting. I must learn patience.

Men who will start the building have arrived. I look down the mountain and cannot believe the huge mounds of stones that have already been brought to us. The pulleys that will carry up the stones are being constructed. I am amazed at the numbers of men and the hard labor required to make these great houses. I have never seen this done before. It looks like the work of Chaos, but I am certain that Alessos has everything organized. My Father's palace, which was much larger and grander than this one on Ithaka, was completed long before I was born. I accepted it without question. Now I realize how much of men's lives are used up in creating houses and other buildings. I am in awe.

We do not know how long it will take to complete all this work. Alessos says it may be at least twelve cycles of the moon. We also do not know if we may continue to sleep in the bedchamber during all this construction with the dirt and dust over everything. Ktimene, my Lord's sister, suggested at banquet the other evening that I might sleep in the room next to hers. I like her but have not had an opportunity to know her. We have been kept apart by my duties and by her mother. I wanted to say that I would like to be near her, but I know that if I express enthusiasm for anything it will not happen. So I kept my eyes lowered and did not respond. I hope she did not think me rude.

Since I came to Ithaka, my Master has begun to increase the number of sheep that give us wool. This island's weaving, never before known beyond these shores, was used only for the Ithakan people. Now that my Merchant has asked to trade our garments and robes, we need more wool as well as goat hair and flax that I sometimes mix with the wool to make a different texture of yarn. My Lord has arranged for fields and hills near the palace to be used for the flocks of sheep that he says can number over two hundred within a year and many more in the future. I told him that the best wool comes from neutered males, but their meat is tough. He said that he would see to it.

As the weather gets warmer, the sheep will shed their wool. What does not molt naturally must be combed from their hides. Women and shepherds, and often children, must retrieve the molted wool from the grass in the fields, comb it loose from the kemp, wash and dry it thoroughly, separate the lanolin, and take the dried wool to the dyeing shed. The Chief Shepherd for the palace is in charge of this process, which will require more workers and more careful supervision in the future. Though much of the fleece is left a natural color, especially for the workers' and slaves' garments, I need the dyers to create the dyes and then mix and produce the colors that I want. After the workers dye the wool, it must be dried and combed in preparation for spinning. This whole process requires expertise, so more men and women must be trained quickly. Finally my spinners and weavers can spin the wool into skeins of yarn for weaving. It is a long and difficult procedure.

All of this takes months of hard labor and many workers involved in the making of yarn before fabric is woven and made into garments. Though I consult with the dyers, spinning and weaving are my first responsibility in the palace.

As I get larger my backaches become worse, especially when I weave. My breasts also seem to be too heavy for my back to support as I lean over the loom. I have been thinking about a way to help my condition and enable me to weave more effectively.

Finally I decided to weave a long narrow piece of fabric that is tied around my chest, is crossed to lift my breasts, and ties around my neck.

I made one, and I feel so much better. All of the weavers should have one of these, but I think that they would be embarrassed if I suggest it. Maybe when they know me better and we have been working together longer, they may accept my help. Now, despite the use of benches, they still suffer with back pain from the long hours of weaving each day.

I spoke to Alessos today. He said, "The work is going faster than expected, Lady, but it will take several cycles of the moon to finish the weaving room and the tiny room for physical needs. The inner wall and balcony overlooking the Great Room are also being built now, and that is difficult. The storage and servants' rooms that complete the top floor of the palace will then be started. The outer balcony for the garden will be done last." I assured him that I am very grateful, and his face glowed with pleasure.

Alessos is a very gifted man. The plans and organization for such an undertaking are truly awesome. From the first sight of Dawn's fingers to the darkness, so many men are working that even Ithaka's marketplace cannot be so busy.

Soon they will be working on my garden, which will not be completed until long after my baby breathes air.

I have been spending my days in the weaving shed and sleeping in a tiny room next to Ktimene, my Master's sister. When my Master is away on expeditions, we are both pleased to be near each other, to know each other, and to speak of our childhoods and our families. She has been lonely too. We must be quiet when we speak and giggle or her mother will separate us. She sits in wonder as I whisper to her descriptions of my homeland and the people I knew there. Stories of my family also intrigue her.

"Tell me about how your family settled on that glorious island of Sikelia," Ktimene said one evening when I had been describing our palace.

"I'll tell you the story that my father told us one evening after a banquet. I may not remember the exact words, but this is close to my father's words." Then I began to recite my father's story.

"My great grandfather Amyklaios was an honorable man who worked to bring peace to the world. For that reason, he hated the warlike Greeks and their way of life and decided to take his family away from Sparta to another land. Others in Lakedaimon felt as he did and decided to follow him in his mysterious travels.

"They joined men with fishing boats, and they all sailed over the waves of the wine blue sea to the inlet at the base of a cliff on Sikelia. It was here that he decided to build his kingdom. With work that could have killed weaker men and women, they built steps up the side of the steep elevation that became olive and lemon groves.

"Even as they were building shelters for comfort, they were planting olive and fruit trees and grape arbors. Then they planted their farms and built homes. They made their kingdom on land that others had not wanted. My great grandparents' first years in this new land, however beautiful, were hard and precarious. Courageous and determined, they traded metal tools and other objects that they had brought with them for sheep and goats. They hungered while those few animals became flocks for meat, milk, cheese, and yarn. The sun and warm breezes helped crops to grow while they ate fish and uncultivated plants and wild animals until the earth gave its harvest. And it took many long years for the trees to mature and for my father's people to have something worthwhile to trade."

Ktimene's eyes were large with fascination. She said, "How brave they were. Would you have had the courage to do such a thing?"

"I don't think that most people have that kind of bravery—or the ability to work that hard, do you?"

She shook her head and said, "Go on. Tell me more."

"My father took a drink of wine cut with water then he continued. For some years other villagers on the island mistrusted our people, and peace was always uncertain. Eventually some of the Greek children grew to marry the natives on Sikelia. Over time the Sikelos people came to trust my grandfather and his followers, and with my father's reign friendship with all the families and tribes secured peace and prosperity for our kingdom.

"This was a story that I had never heard, and I remember how I looked at my glorious father with even greater love and respect. I realized why I had never heard of war and why we had so little fighting and violence in our kingdom. How I enjoyed that peace."

Ktimene, always kind and gentle with me, reached over and held my hand. Then she told me a funny story, and we covered our mouths as we laughed.

There is much that I do not tell her, of course, but I tell her about my sister and brothers and the weavers, my father's gentle strength, the games and guests we enjoyed, and the beauty of the land. I do not try to compare our palaces or our lives to make her feel sad about what she has never had.

I have come to realize how similar our mothers are, though I have begun to appreciate some of the more admirable qualities of my own mother since I have known hers. My mother's intelligence, laughter, and occasional warmth, for example, make me long to be back home when we speak of it. I hide from memory her last words to me and feel both blessed and tormented by reliving the happy childhood that I knew.

Tonight I walked quietly up to my shrine to write. Since I have been sleeping downstairs, I miss the freedom to write when my Master is away. The workers have enlarged our bedchamber and have created a wide double door from the Master's sleeping room to the spacious stone garden that has yet to be built. I can think of nothing else. Even the birth of my baby does not excite me more than my garden. The walls of the garden will be as high as my waist and have three levels for plants, like the terraces on the sides of the hills on Sikelia. The scent of rosemary, thyme, basil, parsley, oregano, bay, mint, coriander, cumin, fennel, lavender, and so many other plants will transform my world. Even Ktimene, my new and trusted companion, seems excited about the garden.

Today was a day of great pleasure. My Lord went hunting, and I took Ktimene, three of my weavers, and my serving girls to collect plants and herbs on the hillsides away from the men working on the palace. Mentor gave me his permission when I explained our needs. This is the second time I have dared to do this because our adventure went unnoticed the first time. Two trusted guards accompanied us for protection. It is strange that we never needed protection on my home island. The guards remained a distance away from us to watch but not be bothered by our chatter and laughter. We were actually free to laugh in the sunshine.

We walked slowly because of my condition, but we talked pleasantly. I pointed out the best plants of wild parsley, rosemary, fennel, and thyme. I found wild asparagus near a little spring and mushrooms growing in the forest. I warned about the poisonous ones, and gradually they will distinguish the different types of mushrooms by themselves. They looked proud.

No one ever taught these women anything about their world. Except for Ktimene and the three young weavers included in my group, these girls and women have just carried and scrubbed things all their lives. But even Ktimene, who is my age, has never learned anything about her world. Though I am younger than most of these women, I wonder how heads could be so empty of thoughts and questions.

During the day, as we walked and I talked, my girls began to ask questions. At first they asked shyly and even with some trepidation that I would be angry at their boldness in speaking. But gradually as I answered their questions, they spoke with pride and with some confidence that what they had to say was worthy of an answer. Whenever I complimented them for their clever questions, they smiled with pleasure. Ktimene seemed to look at me with new eyes, and I was happy that she took such delight in sharing this day with me. Perhaps she will begin to weave with us. I pray to the gods that today is the beginning of many days of such freedom and joy.

My Master's mother was enraged when she learned that my girls and I had been gathering plants and bark without her permission. She does not want me to leave my room or the weaving shed unless my Master is here to watch me. What does she think I will do? Robes and veils cover me from my hair to my sandals, and my girls surround me so no one can see my size and condition. Yet, she screamed so violently at me that I could not tell her about Mentor or Ktimene or the guards. She would not let me explain the need for herbs for her teas or the bark, flowers, insects, and lichen required for the dyes. I cannot bear to think that my world will forever be limited by these walls. Without the air of the fields and woods to fill my chest, I will not breathe.

Can anyone live this way every day for a lifetime?

When my Master returned with the wild boar, he was filled with the pride of success. I am told that his mother immediately confronted him with the evil of my actions in daring to walk freely outside the walls of the palace, especially in my advanced condition. He sent for me, his eyes black with his mother's anger. She accused me of doing or desiring to do dreadful things.

"Such behavior would violate my gods' laws and the beliefs of my father and mother," I said in alarm. If he believed her, he could have me hanged or stoned immediately.

Terrified, I said, "I swear on the altar of my goddess and on the thunder of Father Zeus that I never would do or desire to do such things to disgrace you or the house of Laertes and Odysseus. Please, may the guards be brought to speak for me?"

The favored guards appeared before my Master and his mother.

My Master glared at the guards and asked, "What did the Lady Penelope do today and who was with her when she walked outside the walls of the palace?"

In confusion, the guards looked at each other. They did not know what to answer.

"Speak up," said my Master fiercely.

The older guard stuttered, "Princess Ktimene and Lady Penelope's serving girls were with your Lady, my Lord. They gathered bags of plants and bark that we helped them to carry home. They ate a lunch, I think, of cheese, bread, and berries, like us. The Lady and her girls laughed and talked, but it seemed that they only talked about the plants that they were gathering. We were too far away to hear, but she was pointing to plants as she spoke and picked them."

"What is the color of Lady Penelope's eyes?" my Master asked suddenly.

"What, my Lord?"

The younger guard said, "We did not get close enough to see her, my Lord."

"Master," said the older guard as he went down on one knee, "Lady Penelope never took the veil from her face except to eat and drink. Then she kept her face away from us. Master, I swear that she was never out of our sight. At all times she behaved with the virtue expected of a queen."

"What is the color of her eyes?" my Master repeated coldly.

"All of the women on Ithaka have eyes the color of ox leather, I think, my Lord. Are there other colors of eyes?" Tears had filled his eyes with fear.

The guards were terrified that by being with us they might have violated some law of the island. They assured my Master that they thought I had permission to go on such an adventure.

"Mentor picked us to guard the Lady and her servants, my Lord. We would always protect her for you, my Lord."

After the guards were dismissed, my Master asked me how many times I had gone gathering with his sister and my servants. "We have been out once before when you went hunting, Master. I went out so that I could teach my girls what to pick. Master, I needed those wild plants for dyes and for the medicines that keep us healthy, especially the herbs needed for your mother's pains. I never meant harm."

He looked at his mother who could not be calmed. With a cold and sullen voice, he said, "Go back to your room. I will deal with you later."

I am not to go outside the palace again until my confinement is completed—and then only with the Master's permission.

I live in a constant dilemma. I cannot go beyond the door of the high wall that surrounds the courtyard and the palace, yet I need the plants that offer their dyes for our fabrics. Today I sent three of the weavers and two servants to gather the plants and bark. I sent them for Kermes oak for red and black dye, spartium flowers for yellow dye and spartium stems for weaving fibers, mallow for fibers, coriaria for dyeing, sumach for yellow dye, cotinus for orange dye, cochineal beetles and punica and dyer's root for red dye. I knew that they could not recognize or even find all of them, and I didn't expect them to see lichen, which is scarce on Ithaka.

Before they left the courtyard, I said to them, "Whatever you can find in season will be helpful."

They found nothing. After being gone all day, they returned with baskets of branches, but nothing that I can use. I was certain that they knew at least some of the flowers and berries to pick. Drawing shapes of leaves and bushes on the dirt floor of the weaving room with a small sliver of wood, I have been teaching them how to identify the differences in the shapes and colors of leaves. I thought they had learned something of that art. However, they came back with baskets of branches that were useless to me. If they had accidentally returned with medicinal materials that I could use, I would have felt content. Instead, they brought me branches that are lovely, but have no use for dyes or medicines.

When I saw the leaves, my first feeling was of anger. If I cannot go with them and they cannot identify the correct plants and bushes without me, how can I function in weaving or in creating remedies for pain and illness? I wanted to shake them. Then I looked at their faces. They knew by my expression that they had failed. They realized that I could use nothing of what they brought back to me. Tears filled their eyes with shame. I realized that I was hurting them, and I knew sorrow.

I smiled and said quietly, "You have not done wrong. You simply need more lessons. We shall all go out together soon, and then you will begin to learn the differences. It takes time and long experience to do what I asked of you, and I should not have given you such an impossible task."

I will never forget the look of gratitude on their faces when I said, "Come. You must be so tired gathering all of these branches. Let me make some mint tea for you, and we will relax together before resuming our weaving."

I sent a servant for hot water, and we went up to my bedchamber and had our tea. Amid the loud noise of the building we watched Helios begin his descent over the sea. I did not let the other weavers know that this day had been a failure. I simply made arrangements quietly to have the baskets removed from the shed. I must find a way to get out myself, and I will take these women and two other weavers with me.

4. Courage

I think often about a recent day in my life here on Ithaka. I try to put that day in the dark place beyond memory. Yet, despite my efforts, it keeps reappearing to remind me of the sadness of the children who are taken from their homes and enslaved by Odysseus and his men. Perhaps if I write that day, Morpheus will shut it in a cave behind my nightmares.

It was a lovely day of sunshine, soft clouds, and the whispers of Zephyr. Then I saw the brutality of a child who has become part of my life and tears.

My Master had taken his men on a journey of almost a moon's growth to bring back slaves as rowers for his ships. They also brought young girls, boys, and women to collect and process the wool and to keep the palace and gardens, the winery and olive groves in order. Some would be traded at the marketplace on Ithaka. I had never seen new slaves brought to the island. I had never seen people tied together with ropes so they would not escape, nor had I seen the bruises where they had been beaten.

Covered with veils and robes to hide my face and my condition, I walked from the wool shed, across the courtyard, toward the weaving shed. I looked up to see a great hulk of a guard push a small child of about seven or eight years. She had bruises on her face and arms, and she kept her head down with tears running down her cheeks. He leaned down and said in a menacing voice, "Go to the slave quarters with the others." He pushed her as he said, "I will come back to get you in the dark." She fell to the ground in a swoon, and a smaller boy leaned down to help her.

I ran to her, my face still covered. He pushed me down and away from her, and my veil fell from my face. My Master roared at the guard to leave his Queen alone, and the guard fell to his knees in apology and fear. My Master then asked why I was there and why I dared to interfere with their work.

The child had awakened and looked into my eyes with such terror and pleading that I forgot to be afraid of my Master. Then I looked at the little boy next to her, and our eyes touched before his filled with silent tears.

I looked up at my Master and said, "I am on my way to the weaving shed." I looked at the bruising around the little girl's mouth and the blood on her legs. I knew I must take care of her—and protect the boy who would also be used by these beasts that call themselves men.

"I need these two children for my weaving room," I said softly. "She is the right age to learn weaving, and the boy will be my errand boy and do work that I will no longer have time to do."

My Master responded in a harsh voice, "But she belongs to my guard. He has earned the right to this property."

For the first time I challenged his authority, though with a soft and deferential voice. I reminded him of his responsibility to protect his Queen.

I asked, "Does the noble Odysseus allow his servants to violate his family?

"He threw me to the ground and stripped off my veils," I said in a tone that showed my outrage. "I was working with the weavers and went to order more hair for the spinners. I simply stooped to pick up the child who had fallen. Do you give him the right to attack your Queen?"

The guard looked at me with contempt that I would dare to take his slave. I returned his gaze with equal revulsion.

"By attacking your Queen," I added, "this guard has violated the gods' decrees. He must be punished. Either I take his life or his slaves."

My Master studied my audacity for some time.

Then he smiled slightly and said, "You may choose. What is your wish?"

The guard looked at the Master with shock, then he looked at me, the color draining from his face. For long moments I considered him, then I looked down at the ground as though weighing my options.

Finally I raised my eyes and said, "I choose the children who will be my personal servants for the rest of their lives. She may never be touched again without my permission. The same for my errand boy who is too young to be trained for war or for serving on the battlefield."

My Lord agreed. The guard, with relief in his eyes, kissed the hem of my robe to show gratitude. I would have been amused by this new respect had the situation been different.

I asked Mentor to take the boy until I should send for him. Because I could not look at the other people who had been taken as slaves, I replaced my veil and lowered my eyes as I left the courtyard.

I took the girl into the weaving shed and sat her on a soft robe in a corner. She moaned with pain. She could not understand my language, but I tried to reassure her that she was now safe.

"No one will hurt you again," I said in a soft voice. "You will stay with me and with the weavers who will help care for you." Her eyes remained large with fear.

Moving slowly and speaking quietly, I gave her water and bread and curds, which she ate carefully because of the soreness of her mouth. I hid the rage that I felt for the men, all of the men, who allowed this to happen to her. I bathed her gently and saw the swelling and bruises and blood between her legs. I sent a maid to my room to get some herbs for a healing potion. I made a poultice to ease her pain and wrapped her in a clean, soft robe. Keeping my voice low and soothing, I told her to rest.

The child never uttered a sound, but tears filled her eyes and she started to shake. I held her in my arms and sang a song softly. Soon kind Hypnos came to relieve her fear. When she was asleep, I sent for the boy.

My weavers kept their eyes lowered, but tears and occasional sobs revealed the misery that we all shared.

How can their parents endure the thought of their children suffering in slavery? How can we do this?

My two young charges will not leave me. Their terror of being taken from the security of my eyes chains them to me. Until they realize that they are now safe, I keep them with me while I weave and even when I sleep. They sleep on pallets on the floor of the bedchamber I am using until the building is completed on the top floor.

I cannot go out for plants. I am too large and awkward to walk long distances and carry heavy baskets. It is getting close to my time, and exhaustion is like a blanket covering me.

My weavers will need coverings for their feet with the cold winds coming from the sea. I have no idea when we can move to the new weaving rooms on the upper floor of the palace, but soon the hard-packed dirt floor, cool in the summer and freezing in the winter, will cause pain to their bare feet. I asked them what they do in the cold season. They looked at me in confusion and said nothing.

"How do you wrap your feet to keep them warm in the cold season?" I asked them. They looked at each other and remained silent.

"Do you wear sandals? Do you have wraps for your feet and legs?"

Sida said quietly, her eyes not meeting my eyes, "We suffer, Lady."

Doria said, "We try to wrap old rags around our feet, but the cold from the floor comes through the material. The fabric gets dirty from the floor."

"Do you not have leather sandals?" I asked.

"No, Lady. We have never had sandals. We only have one robe that we are wearing," added Sida, feeling braver.

"How are they washed if you have nothing else to wear?" I asked. I had never noticed their robes and never considered their personal conditions.

"They are not washed often because we need to wear something to cover us. We have only two extra robes, so each week we send two robes to be washed, and the following week two other robes. Many weeks pass before my robe is washed again, Lady." That explained the aroma in the shed.

"Thank you," I said. I left the weaving shed and walked through the hall to the leather shop. As I passed the other craftsmen's shops, I realized that the rooms were warmer. They used braziers and other fires for their work. And I noticed that all the men making iron implements, clay pots, and other materials necessary to the palace wore heavy leather sandals. Even the maids had sandals. Only my weavers had bare feet all through the year.

When I asked the head tanner to make a pair of sandals for each of my weavers, he frowned. "I have never done that before, my Lady. Who orders these?"

"I am ordering them," I said. "I am in charge of the weavers, and they need sandals for the cold months. Please come and measure their feet, so that they get them very soon." Then I left his shop.

Soon after I returned to the weaving shed, Mentor and Father Laertes came to see me.

"Why did you order sandals for twenty weavers?" asked Laertes. "We have never given them sandals. They sit all day. They do not need leather for their feet."

"Their feet will be cold, and they will suffer in the freezing weather with their feet on the hard-packed earth. Their feet and legs ache from the cold."

"We have never had an order like this while the mother of Lord Odysseus was in charge of the weavers before you came to our island," said Mentor frowning. "Why do they need this valuable leather now after all the seasons that they have been here in all weather?"

"Perhaps my Lord's mother did not notice their suffering," I said with submission. Then I dared to add, "Or perhaps she did not care if their backs and legs ached until they moaned with pain. I do care." They did not seem moved by this argument.

Then I realized that I needed a better reason for my request and added, "They will work harder and weave more garments if they are not in pain. I also need a small brazier in each corner of the room. We will not use the fires unless it is necessary, but we must be warm, our fingers must be warm, in order to work efficiently. We must produce more fabric and robes for trade. My Lord told me so."

They looked at each other, and Laertes said, "We will think on it." They left.

After the Sun moved across the highest point of the sky, the head tanner came to measure my weavers and spinners for sandals. He bowed submissively to me and promised to get the sandals made before the cold winds arrive. After he left the shed, the weavers smiled at each other, and we discussed the pattern we would use for woolen feet and leg coverings. It was amazing how cheerful my weavers were for the rest of the day.

Now I must think of a strategy to get them more robes, and heavier robes, so that their garments can be washed each week and they can be warmer through the season that is coming.

My nurse ran for the birthing woman when the pain began to tear my body. I was terrified and longed to have the birthing woman from my homeland to assist me. Instead, Nerunome had been brought to the palace from the base of the mountain several days before the pain ripped me. She is known to be a gifted birthing woman and one on whom Eileithyia, the goddess of childbirth, looks fondly. The Sun God visited two times before my son screamed to life. I thought I had entered a realm where suffering is endless. I hope never to visit that place again.

After a day and night of agony and loud prayers to Eileithyia and to Paiëon, the god of medicine, Father Laertes sent for the Medicine Man who is known throughout Ithaka. He came with his strange looking robes and bird feathers in his long, wild hair. It is said that he lives in a cave where spirits teach him the art of healing.

His small black eyes stared at me from beneath heavy, fierce eyebrows. I was frightened when he sent away Eurykleia and Nerunome.

He wailed strange songs to Paiëon and moved throughout the room with frightening steps and a large knife in his hand. Then he started to cut my arms and made small cuts on my body. I screamed for him to stop. I had seen babies born on Sikelia when I assisted my mother in the birthing for other women on our island. No woman was ever cut. The blood drained from my wounds, and I went into the land of tormented sleep. After unknown time and bleeding, the women returned and he left me to heal on my own. I begged the women to cover the cuts with a salve that I make to aid healing and to bind the wounds with soft cloths. The tearing would not stop.

Secretly I prayed to my Lykaian goddess and to the goddess of childbirth on Sikelia. I promised myself that if I survived, the Medicine Man of Ithaka would never enter my room again. Finally, my goddesses listened to me, and my baby boy swallowed air. I heard him cry before I lost the world again.

When I see my baby, this tiny warm body, I know that he is mine and all that I endured was preparation for joy. When I hold him against my breast, the pain flows away like a soft breeze. I must sleep.

My Lord will see his new son when he returns from hunting on the distant land. He will want his son to be a hero like Father Laertes and himself. I dream of a son who twines the threads of my father and my teacher into a yarn of gentleness, peace, intelligence, and learning. Can this happen on an island like Ithaka?

My Lord's mother took my baby boy.

Frowning fiercely, she said, "I will raise him with the help of the nurse Eurykleia. She helped me to form the great hero who is my son, and we will create another hero in my grandson." I weep to think there will be another.

My breasts are filled with milk for him, but I cannot feed him. I cried and begged her.

"Your milk is too weak for the heroes of Ithaka," she said harshly. Then she walked out of the room with my beloved baby.

I long to hold him again, to kiss and hug him, to whisper loving words and sing softly the songs from my own land. I want my father to smile on him and bless him. Anger and sadness replace laughter that has been stolen from my heart.

My breasts are on fire. I hear a baby crying.

I hear him in the darkness and in the light. I know that if I hold my boy again, he will sleep. In my homeland mothers feed their infants. Only my mother the Queen desired a nurse to feed her daughters.

Memories float through the night air and twist the strands of longing. Where is my Merchant who would listen to my story and relieve the harshness of this life with his understanding?

My Lord returned to find his new son awaiting him. Odysseus was overjoyed and shared in celebrations for many days. Men from all over Ithaka and nearby islands came to honor the King and his new Prince.

When he finally came to see me, I begged him to give me my son, to allow me to hold him and feed him. There is no sympathy in my Lord. He said that this is the way royal sons are raised on Ithaka.

"My son will be a warrior," he said. "He does not need the softness of a weak and weeping mother."

There is no help for me on this cruel rock.

My whole body aches. The cuts have stopped bleeding, but there is swelling around each purple cut. My breasts burn with useless milk, and I continue to bleed from the birth. I have no strength, and I pray for sleep to stop the suffering.

When my Lord returned from his last journey, he had many treasures and new slaves. Two young girls who cry in the night have joined my weavers. I must teach them the way to silence and how to smooth the fabric of their days. How can I do this when I feel their pain and struggle to keep my own screams behind my teeth? Where is the beauty that I hoped was Ithaka when I was taken from my magnificent homeland? Where are the gods who smiled upon me in my youth? Why do they turn away when I pray to them each day?

Odysseus beat me because I no longer smile.

"I want my baby," I wept.

"You are not fit to raise a hero. Weakness has replaced the life I once saw in you."

I covered my face to hide the tears. I cannot eat and do not attend the evening banquets.

As the days pass, I feel weaker instead of stronger. Even the friendship of Ktimene cannot replace the warmth of my son, my beautiful son.

Ktimene and Eurykleia talked to my Lord, I am told. Today he ordered the nurse to bring the baby to me for a few minutes each day. My son shows me how to smile for my Lord so he will not beat me or keep me from the only joy in my life.

With the passing of two new moons, Telemachos grows strong and smiles with joy when we talk to him. His arms and legs move wildly, and he is never quiet. He makes sounds and squeals with delight when Argos, my Lord's dog, licks his face and nuzzles his neck and belly. They are already friends. Eurykleia lets me keep my boy with me a little longer when she can.

I am smiling again, and my Lord seems pleased with me. I am eating again and my strength is returning, as it once was. I hear…

4. Troy's Shadow

A messenger arrived from Mycenae to speak with my Lord. King Agamemnon of Mycenae and King Menelaos of Sparta urge my Lord to join their forces to attack Ilium. Helen, the wife of King Menelaos, had left her husband and gone to Troy with Paris, a Prince of that land across the Aegean Sea. She is my distant cousin, I was told in my childhood, and I wonder what drove her to defy the laws of matrimony. Was her longing to leave her marriage bed stronger than my wish to return home? Does our family line carry such defiance of propriety or does her great beauty excuse immoderate behavior?

My Lord was furious as he yelled, "I will not fight a war to get back a woman, even if she is the most beautiful woman in the world."

"But she was promised as a prize from Aphrodite to Paris, was she not?" I asked quietly. We heard this story from a merchant who stopped on our island.

Frowning furiously, he yelled, "I will not leave my land so others can take it over while I am fighting for a woman. No woman is worth the price."

Palamedes, who was acting as messenger for Agamemnon, had been standing silently while my Lord ranted.

Palamedes stood tall and when my Lord stopped for a moment, the envoy said bravely, "All the Kings of the Achaians, Danaans, and Argives on the mainland and on the great island of Krete and smaller islands of the Aegean Sea have committed their loyalty to Agamemnon. He only awaits the promise of the famed King Odysseus."

"My answer is No and that is final," and he walked out of the Great Hall.

The messenger, who had failed in his mission, walked back to his ship with his head bowed.

The days pass in smiles and laughter when Eurykleia carries Telemachos to the weaving shed. My weavers enjoy him too. He is held and kissed and squeezed, and he giggles with the pleasure of such attentions. She even brings him to my room sometimes, when my Lord's mother is busy elsewhere, so Ktimene and I can play and talk with him.

Telemachos is fascinated by the little animals that Alessos cut and smoothed from wood. Alessos is so kind and generous. He also brought shapes of wood that my son will learn to pile high as he gets older. Babies played with such things on Sikelia.

For now my son seems to love the songs that I sing and often falls asleep in my arms. Those are the moments that I cherish most.

We have received word that the celebrated hero Diomedes is on his way to speak to my Lord about joining forces to attack Troy. My Lord sent word to King Agamemnon that he is newly married with a baby son and has much to do on his island. The other leaders do not seem to be satisfied with his answer. My Lord is enraged that his courage should be challenged by anyone, but especially by the youthful Diomedes. My Lord sits silently with dark frowns awaiting the arrival of the hero. Meanwhile, the building and banging continue throughout the palace.

This morning Diomedes arrived as Agamemnon's emissary. I walked out of the weaving shed in time to see him walk audaciously through the doors of the Great Room from the main gate of our palace. Carrying a sword, javelin, and bow and arrow, he was prepared to fight.

In a loud voice, he asked, "Where is Odysseus, the king whose bravery seems to be exaggerated?"

The servants started running in all directions to find my Lord. Father Laertes walked across the courtyard and announced to the handsome and brazen young warrior that everyone was looking for my Lord and would find him. He asked for the warrior's patience.

After bowing to Father Laertes politely, Diomedes asked where the chambers of Odysseus were located. After Father Laertes responded, Diomedes brushed past him and ran up to our room at the top of the palace. When he came down the stairs, one of his warriors whispered to him. Eurykleia was holding Telemachos in her comforting arms as we stood together. Diomedes grabbed the baby before I realized what was happening, and he stated that he would find this coward who calls himself the King of Ithaka. Then Diomedes ran outside the walls of the courtyard, the baby wailing in his coarse arms.

Screaming for my baby, I followed him to the field where my Lord was covered in dirt and dressed in rags. He was strapped to a plow behind two oxen and was digging up the land that had been planted by the farmer only days before. I cried that his mind had been taken by Chaos.

Diomedes went into the field and lay my baby boy in the path of a furrow that my Lord was plowing. I screamed and tried to run into the field, but his men held me. Eurykleia was sobbing beside me. As the oxen approached the baby, I thought that my Lord would trample his son.

Suddenly, my Lord diverted the oxen and stopped the animals. He picked up his son, who was crying from lying in the dirt, brushed him off, and held him closely. My Lord walked to me and put our son in my arms.

"Wipe your tears," he said to me coldly. "You are the Queen of Ithaka."

Then he walked over to Diomedes and congratulated him for recognizing his trick. In a voice of amused self-confidence, my Lord invited Diomedes into the palace and ordered some refreshments for his guest while he bathed and changed his clothes. He then ordered a banquet for Diomedes and his men for the evening and told me to return to my work. I had been holding my son and soothing him. I gave my baby over to Eurykleia and my Lord's mother who came to hear the reason for all the noise. As I lowered my head and left the Great Room, I could not decide whom I hated more, my Lord or Diomedes.

I am told that Diomedes and my Lord spent several hours in private conversation before the banquet that I was not allowed to attend. This was a time for Father Laertes and Mentor to share a feast with my Lord and his guest. Later in the evening I was not surprised when my Lord came to the sleeping room, which we sometimes shared.

"I will be leaving with my men to fight against Troy and to restore the power and honor of Menelaos and the House of Atreus," my Lord announced. "We will leave soon to join the army of Agamemnon. My valor will not be questioned." I began to speak, but he interrupted me.

"The discussion on the matter is ended," he said as he turned his back to me.

My days are weaving and the brief time I am allowed with Telemachos. My nights I won't describe. The pain remains, and I cannot understand the meaning of husband love. I always thought that love was a gentle and beautiful gift, but instead it is dread.

My Lord is to leave for Troy when the Moon Goddess is round. I watch Selene's fullness growing and feel the same happening to me. I will not tell him that he leaves another life when he sails to Troy. I am ill again each morning, but I have said nothing about my condition. Though I am afraid to be left sick and alone on Ithaka, I want him to go.

The child who was violated does not leave my side except when I go to bed and then she sleeps on the floor of the weaving room outside of the bronze door to our bedchamber. When my

Lord goes hunting overnight, she sleeps at the door inside my room. My Lord was annoyed by her attentions to me but since he is soon to leave for war, he says nothing more.

I do not know her name because she never speaks a word. She works hard, does everything I ask, is learning how to make medicines and how to weave, but she never talks. Whatever happened to her before she arrived on Ithaka keeps all words locked in her throat. She always looks at me with gratitude, no longer fear. Once she kissed my hand, and I saw her smile. I call her Agape and told her that it means love, the love I have for her. That became her name.

My dreams about sad and hurt children torment me. They are walking slowly in long lines, their legs like tiny sticks, their faces gaunt, their eyes filled with the waters of sorrow. They are moaning and calling for their mothers. Sometimes they walk into the sea and sometimes they walk up mountains in order to jump. Always they are hungry and full of longing for home. I watch from a cage and cannot get out to help them.

I beg Morpheus to take pity on me and hide these nightmares. I beg Athene and Hera to take away my anger for the way children are treated here.

My Lord and his father Laertes returned from a journey to the island west of Ithaka. I can see the Ionian Sea toward my homeland between the mountains and lowlands of the island. They brought with them Prince Euphemos to wed Ktimene. My Lord tells her that she must have a husband before he leaves for Troy. The Prince is about the same age as Ktimene and I, so my Lord will not take him as a warrior. He is young and must produce a family to continue his family line and to honor Father Laertes who is lord of the islands around Ithaka.

I am heartsick. She has been my only friend since I arrived here. She plays with Telemachos every day, and he adores her, as I do. Although she is not one of my weavers, I have taught her how to weave so that she will have some value in her future life. And together we enjoy doing so many things, like gathering herbs and other plants. She even helps me to transplant wild herbs to the garden that the farmer cultivated for me outside of the palace walls. This is the garden that I will transplant to my balcony when it is completed. When I take my weavers down to the inlet to bathe, she always accompanies us and has a wonderful time with the women. She is the only member of her family who enjoys laughter and the pleasure of friendship. Without her, the palace will seem as desolate as it was in the first weeks after my arrival on Ithaka.

She told my Lord that she does not want to leave her home, but she told me that she does not care about her home but only cares for the baby and me. With tears, she says that she never had a friend before I came to Ithaka. I feel sad for both of us.

I remind myself that my Lord leaves for war in less than a half moon's growth. The building goes on.

I cannot describe the wedding feast of Ktimene and Prince Euphemos. It was a wedding filled with sadness. I feel only misery as I remember our tears when she left. I hope her life is better than mine and her prince is kind to her. I beg the gods to give her happiness. I lose my only friend on this island of rocks and goats, of cruelty and emptiness.

Only my beautiful son brings me joy for the short time I am with him each day.

Only days remain before my Lord leaves for Troy, and I am filled with relief.

Happiness blankets me for another reason. Cadmus arrived to trade with the island of Ithaka. He told my Lord that he would come every two years, but it is little more than a year since he came the first time. Perhaps he worries about me.

When Cadmus came the first time to Ithaka, some months after my marriage, I was confined to my room. Now, I can join in the festivities of the banquet. Of course Cadmus paid tribute first to the King, my Lord. I pretended that we had not known each other in the past, and he kept his eyes down also. He dined with us, and in the ways of all lands, the dinner in honor of the visitor was meant to be sumptuous. On Ithaka that means roasted goat and swine, yogurt and honey, and bread with wine, bad wine. I feel shame.

While his men ate in the courtyard with my Lord's guards and a few men from the nearest village, our family and guests enjoyed the celebration in the Great Room with songs by Phemios, our bard. Cadmus also told stories of his journey and the people he saw, and my Lord told of his feats. My Merchant glanced at me and lowered his eyes, but I know that his eyes held me. My eyes hold him. I remember the long hours that he worked to teach me to read and to write the Phoenician, Ægyptian, and Mycenaean figures that he said he combined to make the words that speak my thoughts. My dear friend… I hear quiet below. I hurry to hide this song.

This morning after Helios rode into the heavens, the Merchant began to trade with my Lord. I was sitting in the barren garden next to the counting room, according to my Lord's orders. I heard my Merchant ask about the woven goods that might be available for trade. Cadmus said that the people in this palace had patterns and colors such as he has never seen, and he was ready to take some for trade, as they had agreed on his last visit.

My heart was pounding with pleasure as Cadmus said, "The fabrics are admired by royalty in other lands, so I will buy more in the future, especially if more dyes are used. I have rare purple dye and other colors, bronze cups, jewels, cooking utensils, and other implements to satisfy the needs of your palace. I have also heard that the young queen might desire my special herbs for her medicines and potions, and I have roots and seeds for her garden. Her unique gifts are well known on your island and beyond."

Cadmus knows that I want all that he has for trade, though my Lord laughed at my foolishness.

Always wily in trades and stratagems, my Lord did not reveal that he was impressed by the offer made by the Merchant. Instead, my Lord called for me to join them. As I walked through the door from the empty garden, I joined them with my head lowered. I spoke softly as we discussed what I had ready to trade and what I could use beyond what my Lord wanted in sparkling stones and gold and bronze from other lands. I said that I had many robes and other fabrics that might interest the Merchant. I did not say that I had enclosed in the folds of a special robe designed for my Merchant a letter from my heart.

Instead, I said that in addition to the herbs and materials for dyes I also wanted trees for the garden. Cadmus asked what kinds of plants and trees I would want.

"I want a lemon tree for my balcony garden, and I want to plant fruit trees in the barren garden where I have just been sitting."

Before my Lord could stop me, I asked about fig, pear, pomegranate, apricot, date, almond, or any fruit or nut trees he might offer. Without hesitation, he said I would want two of each. He asked to see the garden to consider the size of the space and the size of the trees that would grow.

The three of us stepped into the garden, and Cadmus continued discussing the possibilities for planting and growing in that space. He said that he could give me some on this trip, and they could be planted immediately. He will bring others for trade on his next visit. I will watch them grow, and I will feel life around me.

As I listened to him speak I thought, "I will secretly call this space my Merchant's Garden of Trees, and I will feel pleasure in their beauty." I felt myself smiling behind my veil.

After the Sun God moved across the highest point in the sky, the Merchant was allowed to come to the weaving room to see my goods.

"My Lady," he said, "this weaving is the most beautiful that I have ever seen." He looked through my veil and into my eyes and continued, "Even queens admire your work and have asked me to bring more garments to them on my next visit. You will continue to keep your own special robes for me, won't you?"

"I am honored," I whispered. He takes my mind and my heart away with him.

I asked him in whispers about my father and sister and mother and about my brothers who still live. I am not certain how much Cadmus knows about my brother's death at the hands of Odysseus.

My eyes fill with tears at the memory.

Cadmus said softly, "Your mother is as she was when you last saw her. Your father, who always stood tall and looked to the skies when he walked, has lost his powers. He carries a burden of grief that crushes his spirit. Your sister tries to help him, but she is not Penelope."

"Please tell my father and sister that I am well and that my son is handsome and strong with the light of the gods upon him."

Our talk stopped as my Lord entered the weaving room. He seemed surprised at how many looms were at work, at how many weavers never stopped, at how much fabric we produced since I arrived on his island. He has never visited this room. It is a room for women and women are beneath him. He is pleased that the value of my woven goods gives him so much wealth in return. Perhaps my weavers would grow in his eyes if he were not leaving for Troy. I do not expect grand changes immediately. But the gradual changes that I see give me hope.

When Helios awakened and Dawn touched the world, my friend sent to the weaving room many boxes of sheep's hair and flax ready to spin into yarn. He also sent roots and flowers from other lands to use for dyes and medicines. We gave him the completed robes and the hair of many goats in trade. The goats on Ithaka are the pride of the island. We will be busy spinning and dyeing for many weeks while the best weavers continue to change yarns into my designs.

My best artists are beginning to weave lovely borders of various colors and designs and are even weaving images of leaves and flowers into the fabric. In the evenings when my Master is below drinking and laughing with the men, I do my own weaving with designs that no one else can do. I kept my best cloak, designed with the purple dye that comes from beyond the Pillars of Hercules, as a gift to my Merchant, my friend. That gift is a secret that even the gods cannot know, or Nemesis and Eris will punish me beyond the present torment.

My Merchant left Ithaka when our midday meal was served. I watched through the window of our sleeping room as the galleys moved out of the small western port of our island. I could not eat.

The Chief Farmer of the palace consulted with me about the design of my Merchant's Garden of Trees. I had made a chart of the design that Cadmus and I had discussed, and the farmer agreed that the placement of the trees would be correct in terms of sun and occasional rain. I wanted paths and places to sit as the trees grew higher than the walls. The garden will be lovely when the trees grow and flower, then again when the fruits are on the branches. It will be a beautifully scented, peaceful enclosure that will offer both pleasure and foods that I love.

I longed to dig and plant with Polykas and his assistants, but the Queen would lose face by kneeling in the soil and getting her hands and robes dirty. I wanted to take part in the new life that the men were creating as they planted the six tiny trees. Instead, I could only watch and think how I will plant my own balcony garden away from the eyes of men.

I have kept two small lemon trees in containers for the balcony outside the door of our bedchamber. My gratitude to Cadmus overwhelms me.

Today when the Sun God touched the eastern sky, my Lord and his men left for Troy. Mentor stood on the wall and watched the ships until they disappeared beyond the southern turn of the island. I know that he is desolate that he will miss the excitement of battle and the opportunity to be a renowned hero. I heard my Lord and Mentor in deep discussion several weeks ago when Mentor begged to be allowed to go to Troy.

"My good friend," my Lord said, "I need you to stay here and protect my home and my son, the next king. How can I leave if no one is here to assist my father who is getting older and cannot rule alone without your help? He looks to you now for support. I expect the war to be over soon with a thousand ships to defeat the proud Trojans, but what will happen if you and I leave together for long weeks or even months? You know the men of Ithaka. Any man on this island, with a few followers disloyal to me, could assault the palace and kill my family in order to take over my lands. How can I leave without my home's safety guaranteed by your wisdom and loyalty and friendship? I trust you, Mentor. My father and mother trust you and look to your strength. My wife trusts you. They will not be safe without you."

Silence followed this statement about our safety, and Mentor left the Great Room with his head down in disappointment. I am sorry for his sadness but feel grateful that he is with us.

My Lord has left for Ilium. I whisper my story of woe and bury my words in the leather and wood chest that protects them now and in time to come. No one must see them. The gods would be angry if they knew my feelings because they love King Odysseus as one of their own. I hope they care for his son as well. I want the gods to think that I am happy to be my Lord's queen, happy to wait for their favorite hero forever. Only Athene, I think, suspects my secret and asks Morpheus to punish me with the terror of nightmares.

In the dim light of early morning, I hear the cicadas call. I choke with loneliness and the memories of home. Since my Lord left for Troy my dreams fly away before I awake, and I cannot remember why I am tormented. I only know that emptiness fills me.

Long weeks have passed since I could speak my heart in the signs that give me my only comfort. So much has happened.

I was feeling sick every morning before my Lord left for Troy. I did not want to tell anyone. I drank bitter bark and pennyroyal teas and prayed several times a day to my goddesses. I begged them to make me well without enlarging my belly. Then suddenly I began to bleed. I was happy until the morning came and the bleeding did not stop.

My servants called Eurykleia. She sent the servants away and asked me if I were with child. I wanted to lie and say no, but she is wise. I knew she would not believe me in the future if I lied to her.

"I believe the gods had visited me and left a future hero before my Lord left for Troy," I said with eyes lowered. Then I murmured, "I think that the gods have taken it from me and left me with pain and sadness."

She was very kind. She bathed me and asked what herbs she should use to stop the bleeding. She made me tea and a poultice for my belly. The pains kept coming, and the bleeding continued for several days.

Only my Lord's mother did not seem alarmed and held my boy in her arms as she looked down at me and said with contempt, "It is bad luck for a bleeding woman to touch a baby." She would not let me stroke him, even when he held his arms out to me and wailed. He must think that I do not want him. To take such pleasure in our pain, she has to be filled with the evil brought by malevolent deities.

I no longer have the strength to care about the balcony garden. I often sleep in the small room next to Eurykleia, but sometimes when I need to write I climb the stairs to the shrine. I have been feeling weak with pain for weeks. The goddess Nemesis has punished me, and I am beset by furious deities who torment me day and night. I ask the gods for forgiveness. I tell these things in writing because I am certain that the Merchant will never see this. I pretend that I write to him, but I know he will never read what I write. Any day someone will find the contents of the chest and will destroy it. No one on Ithaka can read what I write, but they will destroy it all. I tell the gods that what I write is pretense, so they will allow me to continue to reveal these things without further punishment.

I fear that I have taken on the deceit of Ithaka and the hardness of its stone.

PART TWO

1. The Weavers' World

My strength is returning, and I thank the gods for restoring my health and forgiving me.

We have moved the weavers from the shed to the room at the top of the palace next to my Lord's bedchamber. The servants and I have worked for several days to prepare and set up the new room, and we are all exhausted. I decided that we would no longer use ground looms that take too much space and that are too hard on the weavers' backs. I am going to use only standing looms, many with two weavers working together, so that we can accomplish more than before. I ordered more standing looms to be made some time ago. We will see how effective this method is. I am too tired to write more.

It was an enormous task to get the weavers moved from the shed near the laborers and artisans to the new weaving room next to my Lord's sleeping chamber. We worked for two days from dawn to darkness in order to move and organize looms and materials in the new rooms. Each weaver established her place for work and storage. We were all so exhausted that we could not weave until the third day, but we are all happier now, despite the noise of the building that continues.

I watch my women look out through the windows at the sea and islands in the distance. It was as though they could not believe the beauty of the world that had been denied to them. I saw them breathe the clean air, and I knew how much they appreciated the light that they have never enjoyed before this time. The builders are working hard to finish the servants' room, which is almost completed. It is still very noisy, but the weavers can see what we will have when it is all finished.

There will be better days to come.

Just surviving on Ithaka is a great challenge. My weavers have been sick and starving, but I did not know it until they moved the looms to the weaving room at the top of the palace. On that first day after the moving, maids brought their noon and evening meals of bread and water to our room. I had never eaten with my weavers in the shed because my meals were brought to my room where I ate alone. I was surprised that they were getting the same thing to eat for their evening meal while I was brought my usual roast meat, yogurt, bread, and water with wine. I also had goat's milk because I had asked for it in preparation for the birth of Telemachos. I asked the maids why they did not carry up all the food together.

They looked confused and said, "This is all of it, my Lady."

I was angry and said, "Take my food down to Mentor and tell him that henceforth I shall eat what my weavers eat."

The maids seemed frightened to do this, but I sent them away.

My weavers looked at each other with lowered eyes, and I told them to eat. I sat with them and only drank water. I was so hungry that I could not imagine that this was their daily fare, but they said that it was. Each woman has a small loaf of flat bread and water three times a day. I wondered how they could survive on it. I realized why they get so tired and slow the pace of the weaving when the Sun God approaches the highest point of the sky.

Then I looked at my weavers. I really looked at each of them for the first time. They all seemed old and tired. I asked how many years they had been on Ithaka and how old they were when they arrived on the island. Most of them did not know, but two of the women had been making marks on sticks. One weaver made a mark each time the first cold storm arrived from the sea. The other weaver had made a mark at each blood time. I estimated that the first weaver was about twenty-five years old. She looked much older than my Lord's mother. The second weaver was about eighteen years old and already was stooped and dry. I was shocked. The weavers on my homeland were much older yet were robust and healthy.

I was enraged when Mentor and Eurykleia came to our rooms, but I held the angry words behind my teeth, as women must. We went into my bedchamber, and I closed the door to the weaving room.

"We cannot survive on bread and water," I told them.

"All the slaves eat this," responded Mentor, "and the weavers are slaves."

"But they get sick and fall into the cold home of Hades too young," I said.

Mentor said with indifference, "Then we replace them. We do not waste precious food on them. When slaves can no longer carry and clean, it is time for them to give up their breath. That is the way of it," he said.

I was shocked that these wonderful women had so little value.

Controlling my temper, I said quietly, "We can't easily replace weavers whose art takes long rolling years to develop. Just when they have the most value they are too sick to produce. I have lost two mature weavers since I arrived on this island, and several of the others are weak and struggle to work to my standards. You must realize that every time I lose a productive weaver, it takes many long swellings of the moon to teach and train another girl. It actually takes years to weave with the proficiency and talent that some of them now possess. These few weavers have the special skills that will bring wealth to our land, but I cannot produce enough of the highest quality for the trades if we do not take care of them."

I saw a new look in the eyes of Eurykleia as she stared at me. Mentor clearly had not thought such ideas before that moment. Slaves were nothing and therefore disposable to everyone in the palace.

Eurycleia said, "My Lord's mother would not allow more to be given to them."

"But these are artisans with a gift that cannot be easily replaced," I responded. "We must care for them as we care for ourselves because what they do brings honor and wealth to our land. I am so hungry after just one day eating what they eat that I could not survive. I will starve, and the world will learn how Ithaka treats my Lord's Queen." Mentor was silent as he pondered how to solve this dilemma. Then he asked me what I wanted for their meals. I said I wanted the same things for my weavers and maids that I had. He looked down without words while he considered the boldness of my request. Then he said that he would speak to Laertes, to the housekeeper of the palace, and to the cook.

Mentor continued, "I will not bother my Lord's mother with this matter. She is sick." Then he added brusquely, "I cannot promise to satisfy your request, Lady."

The next morning the maids brought bread, water, yogurt with honey, and small cups of goats' milk. The bread was fresh, even warm and savory, and there was more than just one small loaf for each woman. My weavers and maidservants were awed. I suggested that we keep the extra bread for the middle of the morning with the milk. I have never seen anyone enjoy a meal more than they did. For the noon meal, we had fresh bread, cheese, grapes, and water with a little wine. For the evening meal, we had roast swine, fresh greens with olive oil and tart wine, root vegetables, bread, cheese, and water with wine. The problem is that it had been so long since they had eaten anything harder than bread that they had trouble chewing the meat. I suggested that they dip the meat in the water and try to bite small pieces.

It will take some time for their stomachs to hold that amount of food, but they are still pleased with such bounty. We are no longer hungry, but I notice that several of the weavers hide their evening bread and cheese within their robes. Perhaps they fear that tomorrow will not bring these generous meals.

Now I watch to see how their energy will improve and if they produce more robes. That is essential for their value on Ithaka. But for me, their pleasure and good health are even more important.

The builders have finished the balcony, and I am now planting the garden. Workers are carrying up pails of soil and manure. Polykas is assisting me in transplanting all that Ktimene and I had planted in a plot outside of the palace wall. The Chief Farmer digs up the plants, and servants carry them up to my garden. Each plant that I touch reminds me of her and of the wonderful days when we found these herbs and flowers. It is a bittersweet task.

Alessos has done remarkable things with the space he created. The balcony is enclosed by a wall that is as high as my waist. Within the wall are three steps along the southern, western, and most of the eastern sides for plants on the three levels, like the olive trees growing on the sides of the hills at home. Down the middle of the balcony will be plantings in stone containers. Alessos made two large containers out of stones for my lemon trees that will eventually take up the northern side. Much soil was required to fill them so the roots will have enough room to grow and spread. I told him how impressed I am by his cleverness.

"Thank you," I said. "The gods have given you the art of creation." His face became red with pleasure.

I cannot see the trees now from the door of my room, but as the branches spread, I will see them on the right side of the garden as I look out to sea. The flowers and yellow fruit will be so beautiful.

I looked forward to the day when the weavers and I would have peace and light without constant banging, and that day has arrived. I am happy to be back in the soft bed that my Lord built to connect earth and sky, and the silent nights with open doors to the balcony are the answer to my prayers. No longer will I have to close the door of a sleeping room without air. I can breathe again.

I did not realize what standing all day for years of rolling seasons would do to women's legs until I saw the blue lines in the legs of Sida, one of the older weavers. I know that she has been in terrible pain, but I had no idea that it could be so bad. Her legs are covered with tiny purple lines and larger swellings like worms under the inflamed skin.

"Just standing is suffering," she said with water in her eyes.

When I saw her tears, I called for the Chief Carpenter of the palace. I directed him, respectfully, to make more benches of different heights so that the older women could work with partners first by standing at the loom, then by sitting on benches, then by sitting on a lower stool to finish the large robes. At least for the few women suffering the most, we will try this strategy as soon as the benches and stools are completed. Until then I have old Doria and Sida sitting on the floor to weave and to set up the looms by tying the warp threads on the bottom of the loom. Though it is difficult on the back, this position relieves their legs. I see the gratitude in their eyes.

Telemachos took his first steps today. He has been crawling on his hands and knees and standing for some time when he comes to my room. I think that he could have been walking several moons past, but my Lord's mother stops him when she sees him standing and trying to walk. I think it is healthy for his legs and arms to move and good for him to test himself. He laughs when he crawls away from us like Argos and we pretend to chase him. He thinks he is very big and strong. My heart melts for love of him. His legs are now strong enough to stand and take three steps without help. Then he sits down and laughs. I pull him up, and he takes three steps again before sitting down. That is our new game. Now he will not stop. Soon he will be running.

I long to go with him through fields and woods and along the beach. I long to share with him the freedom of the wind.

Telemachos has been making sounds like words for some time. I can even understand some of them. It is exciting to hear him and see his smile of pleasure as he thinks he speaks to us. I pretend that I am awed by his great accomplishment, and he tries to please me. He could never know that everything he does pleases me.

Today was a day of rare laughter. Eurykleia brought my beautiful son to the weaving rooms, as she usually does. Argos, my Lord's dog, follows Telemachos everywhere and waits outside the room for him. For some reason today Argos ran into the weaving room before anyone could stop him. He began to run among the looms. Telemachos screeched with delight and followed him on hands and knees. They ran in and out of the looms pulling the yarns while the weavers and spinners tried to stop them. Everything was moved by Chaos. We all laughed until our stomachs hurt and tears washed our cheeks. We tried to catch them, but the boy and his dog were too fast and slippery for us to catch without upsetting a loom. At first it was just fun and hilarity, then we realized that some of the hanging yarns were getting broken, and the yarn was unrolling and skeins were getting tangled.

I raised my voice with the demand to stop them just as my Lord's mother came through the door. From the Great Room she had heard the barking and voices and squeals and hurried up to see what was happening. She was furious. When she screamed, Telemachos started to howl with fear, and Argos ran to the boy to lick his face and soothe him. I picked up my crying boy and held Argos by the tail.

"You will be punished for your irresponsibility and recklessness," my Lord's mother shrieked at Eurykleia and me.

She hit Eurykleia and Argos with her walking stick then grabbed my son, who wailed even louder. When she left the room, Eurykleia was carrying my sobbing son, and Argos followed with his tail between his legs. I was left with tightness in my throat and chest, and I heard my son crying long after they left us.

Looking around at the disorder left for us, my workers and I began the long task of mending the yarns. As the sun moved down to the lowest point of the sky and order had returned to our rooms, they began to recount the hilarity of the morning—the cleverness of the boy on his hands and knees, the speed of Argos and his loyalty to the child. They even mentioned the startled and amusing looks on each other's faces. Gradually I heard giggling behind hands, and I too smiled. I felt the pleasure of the moment's freedom to be a child finding new adventures and to be a mother reveling in that freedom. This should be the design of every day.

I wondered if my little Telemachos were still crying and if the mother of my Lord had punished him for simply being a child. How does she reprimand him? Is she cruel to him, as she is to me? My beautiful, innocent boy deserves only love and kindness.

I think of Ktimene and wonder if she has a son—or daughter—who gives her such sadness and delight. I think how wonderful it would be to have her living nearby, so we could enjoy each other's pleasures and lessen each other's pains. I feel such emptiness without her and without my sister.

Today I had a thought like thunder. When I walked from my bedchamber into the weaving room, I thought, why could not my weaving women dance? I have not seen dancing in the palace, so I think that women must be forbidden to dance here on this island of mountains and stone. I dare not ask.

I see evidence of our narrow lives in the lined faces of women younger than I am. I see it in their stooped shoulders as they carry all the burdens of life here. I see it in my weavers who are chained all day to the looms and spindles while they fly beyond the seas and stars in the grand ideas they put into the cloth. Together we have created new fabrics, combining flax and wool and threads brought by the Phoenician traders, and new colors of dyes and new designs for our fabrics known and desired by kings and queens in far lands. I have been told how the merchants value our robes as we value their goods. Yet my women stand or sit all day with backs aching, legs turning to fire, and eyes longing to close. Even the bands I made for their backs and breasts cannot change the long hours of standing, leaning forward, and working.

And so I did the unthinkable—I told them to stand up, to stretch, and to tell us if they had ever danced. They all looked confused. I asked them who had seen men dance? Only two or three had in their childhood before they had been brought to Ithaka. No one remembered how to dance the steps. I too have not seen men dancing since my brief, halted wedding celebration on Sikelia, for dancing was a great and honored art in my homeland. How could I free their hearts to let them feel the movement of their bodies in freedom and joy?

I decided to make up the music and the steps. I warned them that we must move quietly with bare feet and keep our movements a secret from all others in our Lord's house and elsewhere on the island. This warning seemed to frighten them. Then I began to hum softly and move in my own dance. They began to giggle but would not join me. I took the arm of Autonoë, the youngest maid and the one with the smile still sometimes in her eyes. She began to follow me as I moved. She laughed quietly, and this gave courage to some of the others. She grabbed the arm of Agape who grabbed another then another until ten of us were dancing. The others were moving their bare feet and their arms ever so slightly. They were shy. When they returned to their weaving, they seemed to have new energy.

I have decided that until they stop us, we shall dance every morning and every afternoon.

Now when the weavers come to my rooms at the waking of Dawn, they take a few dance steps before I join them. When I enter the room, we pray to Athene and Hera, then we all dance together. They smile more frequently since that first day. They create new steps and new ways of moving the body, and as we move gracefully together, it is like a soft breeze coming through the room.

It is also good to move together, our bodies touching. Some of us are never touched, and the others are touched in ways that do not please.

When a girl not yet a woman is chosen to be a weaver, she knows that she will never have a husband or home of her own. She is a slave and was selected for a particular task in the Great House on Ithaka. She also learns that she may be used by men in the palace, or men who visit the palace, and she has no choice.

For the brief moments of dancing we touch with pleasure, knowing we are safe, if only here and now among friends.

And so my weavers smile and feel the wonder of music and movement.

I am feeling stronger.

I have used up most of my herbs and the roots for medicine. Last night I gave my Lord's mother the last of the herbs for her headache tea. I asked her if I could go today with my attendants and some guards to collect the plants for potions and dyes. It is a good season to gather some of the plants and roots that we need.

She became angry and refused my request.

Without considering the consequences of her refusal, she sneered, "Go back to your room where a proper wife should be. I will hear nothing more about this from you."

I sent for Eurykleia and told her that I need the herbs and dyes. I asked her to speak on my behalf to my Lord's mother. Eurykleia, wise woman that she is, told Father Laertes the problem. He and Mentor spoke to my Lord's mother. They reminded her that there would be no more teas for her headaches and the pain after she eats. She relented. Perhaps she realized that the cost to herself of punishing me was too high.

Eurykleia and two guards must attend us. Only she is again trusted to watch me. I have made preparations to go out tomorrow.

For the first time in many new moons I left the palace. My attendants carried baskets and our lunch. I carried Telemachos who was excited about every flower and stone and tree. No one has ever taken him outside the palace walls or talked to him about the beauties of the world. I felt sad to think of it.

But the sadness flew away quickly in the joy of having him near me and of hearing the new words that he is learning. He laughs and laughs at words like "bubbling brook" and so many other words that name the flowers and leaves and sky. He especially liked the poppies and the yellowcups.

We walked a long way to get the herbs. My attendants and I began to take turns carrying my boy, who is getting heavy, and following him as he ran to see everything. After each short rest he struggled to get out of our arms. I let him run for a time with one girl following him. I never heard him laugh so often. We all laughed. We sat on robes to have lunch. Our guards stayed a short distance away and ate together. We had a short nap because I was getting tired. Since my illness I have not had the endurance and energy that I brought to this island. We almost filled the many baskets that we brought, and I asked the guards to help us carry the baskets home. My attendants will be busy boiling and drying plants and roots for many days.

Over and over I think of our happy day in the sun. When we returned home, Telemachos put his little arms around my neck and hugged me and kissed my cheek. I have never seen him so happy. Since that day he keeps saying something that sounds like "out." We all laugh, and he runs to the door. Eurykleia promises that we will go again soon, and that seems to calm him. We do need to collect much more while the growing season is upon us.

Everything is so difficult and complicated on Ithaka. When I was home in my Father's palace, my maidservant brought me anything I wanted. If I wanted a cup of mint or rosemary tea, I just asked and the cooks knew how to fix it. Here on Ithaka, no one knows how to do anything that I want to eat or drink. I have to arrange for everything myself. Then after I moved the weavers, I soon realized the problems I would always have in being enclosed in the weaving rooms at the top of the palace. In the weaving shed I had to carry my herbs with me and would simply ask for some hot water so I could make my own teas or medicines for my weavers or myself. Nearby were the fires for cooking and baking bread, so getting hot water was an easy task.

But now being at the top of the palace makes even getting hot water more difficult. Hot water has to be hauled up from the kitchen every time I want a cup of tea. And how can I make teas for myself and not make them for my weavers who have headaches and pain each month and sometimes just need to relax with me at the end of the day?

I decided that I must have a place for fire and two large pots to keep water hot, not only for teas but also for making large amounts of the comforting potions and medicines that we require. I also began to think about making broths for my weavers, attendants, and myself.

I called for Mentor and explained my needs to him. He was reluctant to have fire near the door of my balcony, so we called Alessos the Chief Builder and told him what I wanted. At first he seemed confused by my request, but after making my garden balcony and seeing the richness of the growing plants he seems to accept my strange ideas and listened carefully to my directions. After thinking and measuring, he assured Mentor and me that he could make a place for fire that would be safe. It will be just outside one of the double doors that lead to the balcony but far enough away from the lemon tree on the northern wall. I am to have a small wood fire in stones that can be kept heated all the time. One of my maids or Medon, my errand boy who came with Agape, will keep the small fire stoked and bring the wood each day. On top of the stones and iron bars, I will have two large iron pots to heat water and make soup. Another large iron pot will be kept for medicines. I will also have large and small pots made of clay to hold large amounts of tea or small amounts for two or three cups. I am satisfied with this arrangement. I called the Chief Potter, and he will make the pots and the ladles that I want.

My herbs are growing in my garden, and I long to make my teas whenever I want them. Now that I live in these rooms, I must create a space that allows me my few daily pleasures. Patience is no longer a stranger to me.

Because my weavers are household slaves, they are at the mercy of all the men who live or visit in the palace. As the young ones grow into women, both guests and palace guards desire them. The men dare not touch me. The gods would torture them for violating the hospitality of our family. But I am sad to see one of my girls begin to grow with child because I know that she has been hurt. Sometimes I know when the young ones have been forced, for I see how they grieve. They suddenly realize that they will never be safe again, and they do not want to leave the weaving rooms at the end of each day. I know that I cannot protect them when they leave. I have tried.

There were times when I saw a child blossoming into a woman, and I would keep her hidden in my rooms. I did this for several girls and managed to hide each one for some time. When a guest or guard learned of a young virgin staying in my rooms, she became the object of their plotting. The weavers are my friends. Some are like my children, and I could not protect them. The guards' patience eventually weakened and they took the virgin from my rooms against my will.

When she returned to the weaving room, she too was quiet. It took some time before she would dance with us. It is not an easy life, but the dancing eases some of the pain and lets us pretend that we can protect each other when we are weaving together. I spend many nights weeping and plotting how I can change this situation.

My son will grow into a man, though yet only a child, and I do not want him to learn that men have the right and power to injure women, especially my girls. My Lord's mother does not object to men ravishing the girls so long as the men are kept happy. She wants only to please the men.

My weavers are the best in the world, I am told. Merchants stop at our island for my fabrics. They are unique, the merchants say. The colors, the designs, and the perfection of the weave—our fabrics are gifts from the gods to whom I pay homage every morning and night. The Nereids never wove fabrics more beautiful. I do not challenge the gods when I say this. I speak only because the merchants all praise the inspiration and talent that have created such beauty. My weavers take pride in their work, yet they are also humbled and delighted by the results of it. I also encourage them to offer ideas about designs and about mixing dyes to get different colors for the yarn.

Some of my women have extraordinary talent. I keep their robes, like my own, for my Merchant. The rest are for the other traders. These gifted women could have been managing their own weavers or their own shops and become rich and famous had they not been slaves taken by my Lord and his father from their homelands. It is sad to think this.

The only good fortune these days is that my Lord's mother seldom walks the halls of this palace to spy on us and to hear of our praise, for she would punish me. Since the seasons have taken her hero son away from her, she is often too ill to leave her room.

My Lord has been away to war for many years of rolling seasons, and I have made the weaving rooms also the sleeping rooms for my workers. I managed it this way.

Over time as I gathered confidence in my value to the palace and to our people, I gradually began to complain that my weavers could not concentrate on their work. One day I told both Father Laertes and Mentor that we were losing valuable time because my weavers were exhausted from lack of sleep and could not work. I said that they did not complain, but I knew that the men who live in and around the palace were responsible for this situation.

"Occasionally," I said, "a weaver is beaten and can not work, or a girl stops eating and becomes too weak to produce, or one becomes large with child and is too ill to work. It is apparent to me," I remarked, "that they only feel safe when they are in the weaving rooms. Please consider what can be done about these conditions."

Time passed and there was no change. Over some weeks of discussion, I convinced Mentor, who was left in charge of the palace by my Lord and Father Laertes, to allow the women to sleep and eat in my rooms. I reminded him that we could get much more work done efficiently if we all lived and slept together. We already eat our meals together and go down to the shore to bathe together. Except for the sleeping hours, everything else would be the same. I reminded Mentor, humbly of course, that our weaving brought much treasure to the home of Odysseus, and he would be pleased when he returned.

Mentor pondered upon this, consulted with Father Laertes and Eurykleia, and finally agreed to move the women up to the weaving rooms. He assigned trusted guards to stand at the doors of our rooms day and night.

Before they moved in, I insisted that they and their sleeping robes be cleaned. I took them down to the small inlet with a stream of fresh water flowing into the salt water. This is the place where the maids do the washing of clothes for the palace and where we sometimes go together to bathe. I brought lye soap from my Merchant, and we scrubbed our hair, our bodies, and each other's backs. Then we rubbed olive oil on ourselves until our bodies felt clean and soft. We will do this two times in the growing of each moon.

We organized the places for each woman to work and sleep. We also set up a small altar on a shelf in a corner of the weaving room so that our daily rituals will be pleasing to the gods. The weavers were delighted when I placed a silver bowl for libations and four small statues of goddesses to remind the deities of our devotion and gratitude. I did not know that the women never had a shrine for their use before they came to me.

My women seem relaxed and even content for the first time since I arrived on the dreaded Ithaka. Though we have to be very quiet so as not to attract attention to our rooms and though the men are angry that they cannot have these women, the weavers and I feel we have accomplished something wonderful.

Two of the girls want to get out to be with their men, so I allow them to live as they please as long as they get their work done, keep clean, and remain silent about what is done and said in our rooms. They know that if they violate that trust I will release them from weaving, and they will become servants doing heavy work without the comfort of good food and friends. They promise to protect our secrets.

My weavers are finally living without fear and pain. They are more excited about our work because they do not have to dread the coming of darkness. We have put aside our veils, and it is cooler and more comfortable for our work. Now they tell stories each evening before sleep, and I hope that over time the cries in nightmares will stop. One evening as we were all enjoying tea together, one weaver expressed for all of them the feelings of safety and peace that they now enjoy. Shyly, Karumna knelt to kiss the hem of my robe and they all lined up to kiss me. Tears washed my eyes and theirs also. I now wonder how such a simple thing as protecting women from cruelty and pain could not be part of life everywhere.

I smile remembering the day that I introduced my chest wrap to my weavers. It looks like two slings and even I am amused at the thought of its appearance. They all giggled and thought it was very funny when I explained how it works and why I feel better when I wear it. One woman said that since the wrap makes me feel better when I wear it, she would try it. She is always in pain, she said. Slowly, most of the others agreed. We chose the softest yarn that will not scratch or chafe, and as the weavers finished the robes on their looms, each made a long narrow wrap that is woven very quickly. We have also made wraps for the legs of the suffering women. They all say that they have been feeling better since they have been wearing them. That pleases me.

After many swellings of the moon when all of the weavers had been wearing the chest wraps that look like slings, I asked if they continued to feel better. They all agreed that it helps them. Even Eurykleia has been wearing one. It had been my impression that the weavers had been working harder and accomplishing more since starting to wear them, but there could have been other reasons for the improvement. I told myself that it might be my imagination or their new safety or the better food that they now consume. I am gratified that the numbers of finished robes for the people in the palace have increased greatly, and we have many more of superior quality to trade when Cadmus comes.

An interesting thing has happened. Agape and another weaver called Phedressa have become friends. For about two years after Agape joined the weavers, she did not look at anyone but me. She responded when a weaver called her to get something, and they shared their food or a piece of pretty colored thread with her for her hair, but she never spoke. The weavers all knew her story so everyone was kind and sympathetic. One weaver was especially gentle and attentive to her.

Phedressa was about ten or twelve years when she came to Ithaka, so the two girls were close in age. Agape helped Phedressa get through the first long nights and days of weeping, and gradually Phedressa watched over Agape. Now they are always together. I don't know when it started, but they are now inseparable. They eat and sleep together, and even began to talk together. I even see them smile.

This morning before the rest of the house stirred, one of the girls who wanted to sleep with her man came to me with sobs. She begged me to let her sleep in the weaving room. She said that she would never leave the room again. I saw red and blue marks on her face and arms, and her eye was closed with swelling and blood. Her ribs were broken, I think, and her mouth was cut and bleeding.

After I bathed and wrapped her wounds and gave her some tea for the pain, she became calm. She relaxed when she realized that I would not judge her. Then she told me her story.

"My man was angry that I spoke to another guard in answer to his question. I was only being courteous," she sobbed. "The guard misunderstood and grabbed my breast and kissed my neck. My lover saw this and went into a rage and called me names that cannot be spoken to you, Lady. Then he said he no longer would touch me. I am beneath him, he said."

After a time she resumed, "He offered me to anyone who wanted me. Five men accepted the offer and dragged me into an alley behind the pottery shed. I fought them with all my strength. I fought them and screamed, but no one came to help me. They beat me until I stopped struggling. Then they all did their deed on me. They laughed as they kicked me and walked away. I lay in the corner of the dark alley through the night. I feel such shame and pain that I dragged myself up to the weaving room before dawn so the servants would not see me."

She wept while she told her story and finally fell asleep in a corner of my bedchamber. When she awoke, I took her into my garden and put more salve on her wounds. I gave her rosemary tea and told her that she need not feel shame.

"The men are the animals," I said. "If Kirke were in our palace, these men would be turned into hogs."

I explained the story of Kirke, and she might have smiled if her lips were not swollen and broken.

In just two circles of the moon there has been disruption among us. In all the years that I have been on Ithaka, my weavers have been helpful and cooperative with each other. They supported each other whenever one of them was torn by pain, and they were warm and kind in dealing with each other. Bad temper was infrequent among them. Yet now they are not speaking to each other, they do not want to share stories each night before Hypnos spreads his blanket over our rooms, and they seem jealous and competitive over the weaving.

I think the cause is Lutto, a slave who was given to me after Mentor bought her from a trader. But I am not sure how she is doing this evil. I know that each time she gets friendly with one woman, that woman becomes filled with hatred toward others around her. Also, my best weavers, the ones with the greatest gift in their art, are now making errors in the weaving. I cannot allow this to happen, but I must determine the cause before I can decide what to do.

Agape and Phedressa have become attached in a different kind of friendship. One night I started down from the shrine where I had been writing, and I heard someone whispering. It was a soft whisper. I saw in the corner of my room near the bronze door the two girls wrapped in one robe. I think they were kissing, and I think I heard Agape speak softly. I heard them breathing harder, and I moved silently back up to the shrine.

When I went down to bed later, they were breathing the peaceful breath of love and sleep. I suddenly felt envious of what these girls have found together. Except in rare dreams, I have never felt the way they sounded, and I long for it.

With enormous sadness I knew that this love would never be part of my life. The only man who could make me know such pleasure, warmth, and desire was out on the seas in a Phoenician merchant ship. I also knew that no matter how much love I felt, we could never touch, never know the softness of each other's lips, the comfort of each other's arms. Desolation went to bed with me that evening.

I am left with empty dreams and shame that fills this vessel I call myself. Sometimes I want to scream until my throat bleeds.

I called Mentor and Eurykleia yesterday and told them about the trouble that Lutto has brought to the weaving room, "We are not completing the robes in numbers and quality since Lutto arrived. I have been observing her closely day and night when she does not realize that I am watching, and I know now how she manages to create the conflicts.

"Take her away from the weavers," I begged. "The sad thing is that she is a gifted weaver, but she cannot remain among my weavers. I believe that she was sent to Ithaka by some malevolent divinity. If we do not do something quickly, she will do terrible damage to my women as well as to Ithaka's reputation for weaving across the Great Sea.

"Take Lutto away from my rooms and put her in a small room to weave by herself. Then we can use her ability without the damage that she does to people."

They listened with trouble in their eyes but did not question my advice. They moved her and her loom immediately. I hope that the Litae will bring their blessings back to our rooms and will be able to repair the damage done to my weavers.

My weavers have been hostile since Lutto left us, and anger filled the room again today. I worried about what I could do to calm them and restore peace to our hearts. Though Lutto has been gone for three suns, the coldness remains in the weaving room.

This evening after we ate in silence and Helios began his wondrous descent over the far sea, I called the weavers and our servants together, told them all to bring robes for seating, and led them out to my garden. Only Agape and Phedressa have remained outside of the hostility. They had not allowed Lutto to damage their relationship and had simply ignored her. Thus, they walked into the garden holding hands and seemed to be amazed that so many good friends were angry at each other. The women were tense but were willing to sit closely together for the first time since Lutto had invaded our rooms.

The colors of bronze and apricot brushed the blue sky, and the scent of herbs and hyacinth surrounded us. I saw several women breathe deeply and almost relax.

Then I began to speak quietly, "How extraordinary our lives are, and how we live and create our beautiful art together would make most women jealous. However, lately the quality of our work has declined."

Gently I said, "We cannot be proud of work that is no better than what is produced on any other island. The weavers of Ithaka are known as the best in the wide world. Can we allow our feelings to destroy this fame? Together we have created a home that is safe, a place of kindness and caring, but Anger has invaded our lives."

I continued, "I have witnessed the hurt between women who have been friends for many years. Why have you let a stranger do these things to you and to each other?"

They looked shyly at each other.

Then Naela said, "I am angry because Marpessa has said hurtful things about me. I would never say such mean things about her."

Marpessa said with flashing eyes, "I have never said a bad thing about Naela. What did I say? I want to hear it."

I asked Naela what Marpessa was supposed to have said. Naela murmured that she could not say it openly.

"It shames me," she said with tears on her cheeks.

As we talked, it became clear that Lutto had selected close friends and told one woman that the other had insulted her by saying that she smelled bad or talked with stupid thoughts or was ugly or was a bad weaver. Slowly it became clear to everyone that none of this had happened. No one had insulted anyone else in the weaving room. Lutto had lied and out of jealousy had made up these stories.

She also had managed to pull threads out of the fabrics on the looms. I told them that she had done this in the night when everyone was asleep, except me.

"More than once I saw Lutto moving around in the light of the growing moon. I began to suspect how faults in the fabrics had been made by weavers who had never made an error before Lutto arrived."

As I spoke, my weavers began to relax, and I saw hands reach out to hands. Shy smiles replaced the cold eyes in faces that were again lovely. As they began to speak to each other, I made chamomile tea for everyone and felt gratitude to my Merchant who first brought this tea to me.

Surrounded by the sounds of katydids and nighthawks, we sipped our tea and were pleased to be together again. It will take some time for all the weavers to trust each other completely, but I am certain that the Litae have the power to bring contentment and peace back to my rooms. Being together in friendship and harmony is all we have.

The laughter of one of my young weavers set off a string of sister memories today. I think of Iphthime, my beloved sister. We are on the beach at home. She laughs and runs into the green-blue water and splashes me. The day is alive with sparkling lights shimmering over the sea and water rippling over the stones on the beach. The gods of day and sky shine down on us and on our servants. We fall on the blanket shrieking and breathing hard. My sister laughs her deep conspiratorial laugh, as she does when she peeks over her blanket too late at night for little girls to be awake to share secrets.

Now she is an infant in my memory. My sister is creeping so fast on the floors of the palace that it is my job to follow and help our nurse keep her from harm. She is delighted by her control over me as she changes direction and makes me do so also. What a beautiful baby she was and she owned me. I find myself smiling with such pictures of the past. My sister. My beautiful sister of love and of joy. I would have lived a happy life to be close enough to see her and hear her laugh each day.

We parted with tears and shrieks of sorrow. On that fateful day, Father the King pulled her from me, and Odysseus my new Master led me to the ship waiting to take me away from my home.

I sometimes hear the weaving girls speaking softly about me. Today I heard them laugh about the growing things that fill large clay pots on the stone floor and that cover the three steps of soil on the walls of the balcony outside my room. They think I am a farmer. On Sikelia my nurse and an old woman in the nearby village taught Iphthime and me about the great gifts planted in the ground by our gods, and we spent days in every season searching for the leaves and flowers and trees that would cure our bodies and feed us. Sometimes I felt that we worked more days leaning close to the ground and searching in fields and woods than learning how to weave, which was our main job. I liked the days spent in fields and among the trees and became very good at cultivating some of these wild plants. Near the back of our palace I had a little piece of dirt that my father gave to me for planting. These plants were like friends as they grew and shared their leaves and flowers and roots with me.

One day, not long after I arrived on Ithaka and I began to gain strength, my Lord proudly told me about our sleeping chamber high up on the floor above all others. He built this room, he said, with a plan to bring a wife to his home. One corner of the bed is an olive tree that connects earth and sky and is said to live forever, "like the bond that the Fates have forged for us," he said.

Because I was to spend most of my time in the weaving shed or in the bedchamber with my own loom, I asked softly if he would make a place for my plants. At first he ignored my request. Later, when the weaving rooms were being planned by Alessos the Chief Builder, my Lord agreed to attach an outside room to our bedchamber. I'm sure that he envisioned a tiny space for a few small plants, not the huge balcony that we now call my garden. It is open to the Sun God and the sea breezes in the long afternoon and evening, for my room faces the sea that welcomes the night.

My Lord has not seen the balcony completed so has never seen the garden in full bloom. He never saw how the servants brought endless baskets of soil to fill the three steps that hug the walls of the balcony. He has never seen me grow plants that I add to my food, seeds and twigs that I chew for sweet smelling teeth that do not give me pain, and leaves that my servant and I boil to keep my weavers, my Lord's mother, all of us healthy and strong. The plants bring me good fortune, and I have taught some of my attendants and weavers how to find the medicine and food plants on the slopes and in the flat fields and woodlands of Ithaka. Yet, the weavers still enjoy laughing at me. There is so little to give them pleasure.

I think fondly of the day that Eurykleia revealed her friendship for me. After my Lord left for Troy and his mother softened with sorrow for the loss of her son, Eurykleia brought Telemachos each day when Helios began to climb the hill of the sky and again when the golden god rode down the hill toward the sea. At each visit she allowed me more time with my beautiful son. The mother of my Lord was so grieved at her son's departure that she often did not leave her room for the whole day. She did not know that I had more time with my son or she would have ended this happiness.

Eurykleia was no longer filled with hatred for me as when I first arrived. I do not know why she resented me. Perhaps she was afraid that she would lose her favored position in the House of Odysseus. Now that I am kept prisoner in my rooms at the top of the palace, she seems to feel sad for me and shares the kindness that she keeps especially for children.

On this day I asked her if she was born on Ithaka.

In a rare confidence she said to me, "Laertes bought me from the traders who took me from my homeland when I was a girl not quite old enough to be a woman. He paid a high price for me, I am told. I was made the nurse of Odysseus and never allowed to bear my own child. Laertes would not allow anyone to touch me, though he could not fulfill his desires with me either." With her face flushed she continued shyly, "His wife, my Lord's mother, would not allow it. For that reason I remain bonded to the Virgin Goddess." So Eurykleia gives her love to my child and now some small part to me. I am grateful.

Perhaps she understands what I feel but I dare not tell her. Can she be trusted? I don't know. I only know that I enjoy each moment that is not filled with desolation.

For long rolling seasons I had been thinking about better ways of weighting the yarns near the floor. Stones are not effective enough for the special work that the weavers are doing. Mentor brought the ironsmith with the great muscles to our room so he could see our looms and understand our needs. Several days later he brought several different types of weights and we tried them on my loom. Something was wrong with each one until I asked him if an iron bar could be tied to the bottom of the loom. The next day he came up to our rooms and ran a bar through holes that he made near the bottom of the two posts of my loom. The yarn can then be tied to this bar until the garment is completed and the yarn is cut. This design works perfectly, so as each weaver completes her garment, the ironsmith puts a bar on her empty loom.

Why had we never thought to do this simple thing long years ago? Why had we simply used the old ways without considering a better, easier way? Sometimes I believe that we are locked into past teachings without thinking for ourselves. I must reevaluate everything that we do to improve our lives and methods.

All I know for now is that the weavers are pleased. We all want to sing, but we hum quietly.

My weavers and servants are so much more energetic since we started eating better foods, dancing each day, and walking down the mountain to the sheltered cove where we bathe and wash our clothes. We go two times between the new moon and the round moon. I would like to go almost every day, but we cannot spare the time from our main task of weaving. We start out just as the light is coming to our side of the mountain, and we return before the Sun God is over our heads. When we come back to our rooms, we rest briefly then begin our weaving for the rest of the day. It is a tiring day but one of pleasure.

Today I asked Eurykleia to bring Pheidopos, the Chief Potter, to meet with me at the top of the stairs. I closed the door to the weaving room so my weavers would not hear our conversation.

"I will be grateful if you will make thirty-eight small bowls for eating and drinking tea. Each one is to have a different color or a design with different marks painted on it. I have pictures of the marks," I said, and handed him small squares of pounded leather with the different marks on each.

I did not tell Pheidopos that each set of marks was for a weaver's name, for Eurykleia, and for our three maids. He looked baffled at these instructions. I also asked for thirty-eight small spoons and a large ladle for serving my weavers. I did not explain that I want to make rabbit stew and other soups in a large iron kettle on the fire of my balcony garden.

"All of this is to be a secret," I said, with a smile as I thanked him.

He was surprised but interested in his new assignment.

We went out again today and found a place where the crocuses grow in abundance. We will have enough yellow dye and flavors for our broths for some time. We have been collecting the early leaves and flowers that the mild season brings. We will do this several times before the hot sun covers the land. I feel almost free and happy on such days.

Telemachos has grown so that for long seasons past he has not come with us on these expeditions. It saddens me. I remember when he was little, and he pulled out grass and leaves and threw them into the baskets to help us. He looked so proud when he did this, and I wanted to hug him each time. He loved those days, and I remember thinking that he was the son of my heart. Now he goes with the men on their hunting days, but I hope that he still loves the fresh air and fields and woods as I do.

Today was a sweet and bitter day. I heard my beautiful son call Eurykleia "Maia." I am his mother, but he does not think about this.

Eurykleia looked both pleased by the name he calls her and shamed that I heard and must be hurt. I admit that when tears came to my eyes, I turned away and said nothing. She is good to me. I do not want to wound her. She never had a child of her own so she may dream that he is hers. Should I spoil her pleasure in being called mother? We have shared him since he was born. Why can we not continue to share him as he is growing up to leave us?

Today's bright sun heralded a surprise gift day for my weavers, for Eurykleia, and for the three maids who serve us and live with us. Pheidopos and his assistants brought up the bowls and spoons that I asked him to make. He also made a lovely blue bowl for me, a little larger than the others, with a golden sun and white slivers of moons.

I was very touched and said, "I shall not forget that you designed this lovely gift for me. The bowls and spoons are beautiful. We shall always be in your debt."

His face was red with pleasure, and he knelt to kiss the hem of my robe. I then carried the gifts into the weaving room and called the name of each weaver to give her the bowl and spoon. The bowls were of different colors, and each had unique and different colored marks so that each weaver would learn to recognize her own.

My weavers and maidservants were more thrilled than I have ever seen them. In all their years on Ithaka, they have never had anything that belonged only to them. Everything belongs to their Master and the palace. I told them that these bowls were theirs alone, and no one else can use them. They all cried. Then we had to decide where to keep them so that they are not broken.

Doria said, "They must be seen at all times while we are weaving." All the weavers and maids laughed quietly in agreement.

After several ideas, Naela suggested that we use a long shelf that has been used for storage in the weaving room. We removed some spindles and other objects from the shelf on the long wall and moved our small shrine to the middle of the shelf. Then they placed the bowls along each side of the shrine. With the colored bowls stretching out on each side, the small shrine assumes greater presence in the room. The weavers all stood and prayed to our goddesses. Some of the women had tears in their eyes as Naela led them in their prayers of appreciation. I have never seen such joy on so many faces. For some time, I kept hearing their words of gratitude and awe.

"Thank you, Lady. Oh, thank you, my Lady."

They are having difficulty keeping their eyes on their weaving. They keep looking at their bowls. I made tea for them this evening so they could use their new gifts. Immediately they recognized the shapes and colors of their own bowls, and they did so with such pride. I will make a rabbit stew tomorrow.

2. From Darkness to Dawn

I am happy to spend this night writing. For so many turnings of the moon, I have been weaving both day and night. Alone in the shadows of my room, I have been creating images of home on Sikelia to cover the walls of my room here on Ithaka. I am trying to transform this room with memories of warmth and comfort. I will ask Father Laertes to have the panels hung as each one is completed. Eventually I will open my eyes to the sunrise each morning over the Great Sea, to the high cliff of olive and lemon trees at home, to the image of my father's grand palace, and to Mt. Etna in the background of the palace gardens. The panels can never be as beautiful as my home, but the images will take away the darkness and desolation of the grey stone walls in my room. It will take many more rolling seasons, even years of seasons, to finish this dream, but the first panel can be hung tomorrow. My weavers will be surprised and—I hope—delighted to see the picture that I have woven while they slept. Each day I will awaken to see the sunrise that I have not enjoyed since I came to Ithaka and to this room, which faces only the descent of the Sun's glory.

I struggle to understand the ways of the gods. A curtain covers the answers to my questions and I suffer anew.

Since I had the panel of my homeland hung on my wall, I have been tormented. I had expected to be filled with joy in waking each morning to Dawn and the vision of Cadmus's galley sailing toward me. But each night Morpheus punishes me for that image. I am again dreaming of Tyndareus, the love of my childhood. For some time after I left Sikelia, I dreamed of him every night, then gradually he left me in peace. I think that the birth of Telemachos altered my dreams, but now my handsome Tyndareus tortures me each night as he reminds me of my disloyalty to the friendship we shared. My terrifying dreams berate me for turning my back on him and embracing the longing for Cadmus.

Last night's was the worst nightmare. I am in an olive grove. The trees are laden with their green fruit. I see their rotting flesh that covers the ground. I am running to reach a figure in the distance, and I must get to him. I am calling him and crushing the olives covering the earth as I run. He does not stop or turn around. I must see his face. My life depends on seeing the face, but he continues to walk slowly in the distance. No matter how hard or how fast I run, I cannot get closer to him. Then gradually I realize that someone is hiding behind the trees around me. It is Tyndareus, bleeding and weeping. I am terrified. He is behind every tree, left and right, ahead of me and behind. It is Tyndareus, but I cannot reach out to him. I cannot tell him that I will help him. I must reach the figure in the distance, but I begin to cry for Tyndareus. I want to stop his bleeding. I want to stop his tears.

Suddenly I am running through oil dripping from the olive trees. Every olive and every leaf is weeping oil that begins to cover my feet, my legs and knees. I am trying to run but the thick oil is up to my waist, my chest, my neck, and I cannot move. The figure in the distance turns and I almost see his face. I cry out to him to stop. He takes a step and disappears in flames.

Each twisted tree is Tyndareus, but I cannot speak to him. As the oil covers my mouth and nose, I hear Tyndareus sob, "It is time. It is time." I reach out to him as he dissolves into the bark of the trees. I awake.

"It is time, Lady," my maid says. "It is time to rise."

I cannot move. I am still in the olive grove, and I am covered with the sweat of oily terror. Then I breathe.

I wanted to be alone, to think of Tyndareus and the figure far away. I longed to read the dream and learn what the spirits tell me, but my weavers awaited me and I rose to meet the day.

The nightmare follows me. I struggle to understand the nature of my fate and look to my dreams for answers. They tell me nothing.

The nightmares continue. Tyndareus pursues me. I am afraid to sleep.

Last night I could not save Cadmus even as I was powerless to protect the young Tyndareus from the spirits of the Underworld. In my nightmare malevolent gods of Ithaka lay in wait for my Merchant, and I could not warn him. The trees, so beautiful in the daytime, were raging and shrieking and sending out arrows of branches. I do not remember other details of the nightmare, but I know that my Merchant was in danger and I must do something to fight the evil deities.

I have been thinking about the Lykaian Goddess of Sikelia. Once, on the night I arrived on Ithaka, I saw a vision of her. She was in the grotto on the side of the road as the men carried me up to the palace. The lamp in the grotto outlined her, and she held out her hand to me. Then she was gone, and she has not returned to me. For many circles of the seasons I have thought that the spirit was a dream, but my maids assure me that there is a grotto at that place on the side of the mountain. Now I am certain that my Goddess was there, at that moment, revealing herself to me. For what purpose I do not know. But perhaps if I can reach her she will safeguard my Merchant and keep him from harm. I cannot lose him or the light that he brings to my life. Is it my fate to safeguard him from harm?

If I appeal to her goodness and ask the Goddess for her protection and power, will she return to the grotto where she stood on my arrival on Ithaka? Will she speak to me?

"Lykaian Goddess, I beg you to hear me. Return to me for my Merchant's sake!"

I have been in my rooms, imprisoned in my rooms for many long dawns. Now perhaps I can write the unspeakable.

I thought that, as the Queen of Odysseus, I was safe. I had been roaming over the hillsides gathering my herbs and plants with guards overseeing our journeys. I believed that no harm would ever come to the Queen of a great hero. I was wrong.

I awoke from a lovely dream in which my beautiful Lykaian Goddess was inviting me to join her. She was in the grotto on the side of Mt. Aetos, and she was smiling in welcome. I put on a fresh robe and a veil covering my hair and face, I slipped past the sleeping guards at my door and at the gate of the palace, and I began the arduous walk down the mountain in the moonlight. The face of the Goddess was before me, and I longed to see her again.

Shame keeps me from writing what happened. I can only recount that it was in the sacred grotto that I was hurt and left bleeding. So much blood, almost like when I lost the weight that my Lord left within me when he sailed for Troy. After the assault, I lost all knowledge of the world. I do not know how long Hypnos shut my eyes. When I awoke, my body felt like fire. My breathing was labored as the pain in my ribs cut through me. Finally I left the grotto and pulled myself up with the help of a fallen branch. I walked slowly with terrible pain until I arrived at the palace gate. The guards were still asleep, and I crept silently to my room where I was safe.

I tried to clean myself and hide my garments, but Eurykleia came to my room early and saw my face and the dirt and blue marks on my body. The skin on my knees was ripped and bleeding as I had half crawled part of the way on the road up the mountain. Blood was still dripping down between my legs, and I had difficulty sitting up. She realized what had happened even before I could tell her.

She took my clothes with the blood and buried them. She told my Lord's mother that the gods brought bad luck to any household that did not bury in sacred ground the bloodied clothes of a woman whose womb was attacked by the Furies. She said that my body protected the rest of the household from the rage of the Furies, and everyone should be kind to me and grateful for my powers. My dear Eurykleia saved me from the stoning that my violation would have brought to me.

I must remain in my room though the swelling and blue marks on my face and the scratches on my hands and legs are almost gone. I cannot weave until my ribs heal. My dishonor torments me, and the pain in my ribs and elsewhere is a constant reminder. My weavers wonder at my absence as I hide in my room alone. Only Eurykleia comes into my room and then delivers my instructions to the weavers.

The memory will not leave me. I am terrified to think how all on Ithaka would blame me for walking alone to the grotto on the side of the mountain below the palace. How could I explain the prophetic dreams in which Cadmus was in danger from Ithaka and from the jealous spirits that wanted to punish him for our friendship? Who would believe me if I could say that I saw my Goddess in the grotto when I first arrived on Ithaka and knew I had to find her again? Who would understand, and how could I defend myself? I can only relive that night over and over.

I had waited and suffered through endless nightmares until my Goddess beckoned to me in a soft dream. I awoke on a calm and windless night that I thought the gods had blessed. Acting on an impulse, I decided to go alone and unobserved to the mysterious shrine. Allowing my maidservants the sleep they needed for the day to come, I made no sound as I wrapped my head and hid my face though no one seemed to be awake. I slipped silently past the sleeping guards outside my door and at the main gate. My heart pounded with adventure and anticipation. I walked carefully by the light of the moon and was grateful to see the small lamp flickering inside the grotto. All was silent, so I went through the door. I knelt down and touched my forehead to the ground and began to chant my prayer quietly.

Suddenly there was a sound from the door. As I turned to rise, an enormous weight came down on me. I tried to get free, but my robes entangled me. As I scratched at him, he began to hit me. I begged him to stop but he only hit me harder. I turned my head and saw the face in the light of the lamp. I could not breathe as he punched me and ripped at my clothes and legs. I felt the pain of him inside me but dared not try to scream. Too long I suffered the fiery tearing within me, then the man who smelled like a goat pulled away from me. He smiled as he ripped the veil from my face. Then his eyes opened wide, and he groaned with terror when he recognized me. He stood up and ran out of the shrine. I could not move. Then I lost all light.

When I awoke, I was terrified that a servant would come to the grotto for morning prayers or to replace the oil lamp and find me. I held the screams behind my teeth while I crept up the steep road in the dark. I began to sob only after I reached my room. When Eurykleia entered my room, I was frightened that she would call the palace to witness my shame, but instead she protected me. She bathed me, changed my clothes, and took away the robe that was ripped and dirty and held the signs of my dishonor. I knew then that she was my friend and ally. Yet, I cannot feel safe on this island.

Months have passed. I have been very ill, and Morpheus still torments me with terrifying nightmares. But now Tyndareus has left me once again, and the dark figure remains in the distance. I drink my strong teas, and I cannot speak or look at anyone. I cannot see Telemachos for the humiliation that I feel.

Finally, one day I could speak to Eurykleia about that night of guilt and disgrace. I needed to speak to cleanse myself of the filth. I thought that I would be punished, that I would be hanged or stoned. I prayed and welcomed whatever the gods felt I deserved. When I finished my story, Eurykleia had a look of darkness over her face. I thought she would speak sharply about my disgrace and how I deserved such treatment. But I was wrong. She praised me for my piety and desire to go to the grotto.

Then she asked, "Can you identify the man?"

"He smelled of goats. And I saw his face," I said in shame.

"Never speak about this matter again to anyone else." With a frown she left my room.

Several days later she came to my room and told me to hide at the top of the long staircase that led to the hall below. I was to pick out the one who defied Hera by touching me. As I looked down, a guard led several goatherds into the hall. Eurykleia held my hand so I would have the courage to look at the line of men.

I saw the wicked one and identified him. Eurykleia walked slowly and with dignity down the long staircase and stood before the guilty one. She pointed at him, then she turned and whispered to Mentor. She then looked up the stairs at me. I returned to my room until I was calm.

Later Eurykleia came to my room. We went up to my private shrine.

She said in a quiet voice, "The one who hurt you has been hurled into the Lower World. I told Mentor that the goatherd had pulled the veil from your face when you went into the courtyard to wait for the maidservants. They were out gathering saffron on a day when you felt too ill to join them, I told him. He was very angry that any man would dare to violate the Lord's Queen. The goatherd was made to kneel in the dust and lost his head from Lord Mentor's sword." Then she was silent.

With tears streaming down my cheeks, I hugged her knees and swore to be her servant forever. Then she did a remarkable thing. She held my face gently between her hands and with tears in her eyes she kissed my cheeks and hugged me. We stood together and prayed to Hera for forgiveness, to Lykaia Lakedaimoneia for my comfort, and to Athene for the protection of the House of Laertes and Odysseus. We were one in those moments, and for the first time since my Lord's sister left Ithaka, I did not feel alone.

I am afraid to sleep. Malevolent deities attack me when I shut my eyes. Sometimes I stay in my shrine most of the night and often fall asleep on the stone floor when I can no longer fight against my eyelids. Some nights I sleep on the stone floor of my garden. Other times I weave the panels of my homeland until I fall asleep on the floor and awake when light is creeping across the floor of my room. I quickly hide my work and walk to the weaving room to meet the day and my weavers. I pray that the gods will force the evil spirits to leave me alone, to stop torturing me with that terrible night and the pain that keeps me bleeding.

Telemachos is growing tall and handsome. He lives with the men and has become a great hunter, I am told. I miss the beautiful child that he once was when he laughed in my eyes and I held him close. I pray that some of that gentleness will soften the manhood that I now see in him.

The song of the sad nightingale awakened me, and I knew that someone was in my room. I lay quietly for an unknown time. Then I sat up and saw my beloved father standing at the foot of the bed that connects earth with sky. He wore the last robe that I wove for him, and his head was the color of cloud. I could not speak for the ache of longing.

He said in a whisper, "Penelope, my child, do not fear. I am here to see you this last time on my way from Sikelia's homeland to my new home in the fields ruled by Hades."

I heard my throat breathe the air of pain. Pleading, I said, "Father, stay with me. I will care for you. It is not your time. Do not leave me here." He smiled the last heartbreaking smile that I saw on his face before we parted long years ago.

"I know your life has been one of woe, my child. I have heard the nightingale sing of it to me. I will await you with the love that I save for only you, my daughter. This insubstantial world will soon pass, and we shall know each other again as we walk through the Elysian Field. Do not spend your short time here in regret. Know that you are loved and fill your heart with that knowledge."

My face was wet as I heard the voice of Eurykleia, "What is it, Lady? Are you ill? Has a nightmare enclosed you in fear?"

I looked at her and quickly turned to my father to say goodbye. At the end of my bed, the spirit faded and I lost him forever. I wanted to hug him, to hold him, but he was gone. I began to sob and lay back with my hands covering my face. I could not tell her about my father. I know that I did not dream him. He was here with me.

It will take some time before I understand the meaning of his visit. I am certain, however, that Fortune shed her light on me tonight, for I saw my beloved father one more time in this hard life of uncertainty and confusion.

A white mourning dove has been visiting me. It comes each morning and sits on the wall across from my balcony door until I go out into the garden. I have heard that mourning doves are grey and that they fly in pairs and mate forever. Perhaps that is true, but I am certain that this beautiful white bird tells of grief. It sits watching me. Then it flies in a circle above the garden and sometimes sits on the roof of the palace as it looks down on me. At first it was just a curiosity, but now it has come to me many days. It means to tell me something. Each time I see it, I think of my dear father, and I believe his spirit is with the bird. It is the bird.

This morning I spoke to this spirit, "I know you are my father and I love you. Beautiful bird, you have a home in my garden and in the garden of my heart forever."

In answer, he cooed his soft song then flew upward and circled three times above my head. A sad serenity overwhelms me.

Today the dove did not come to me. I went out frequently to watch for him, but he did not appear. It has been so comforting to see him and hear his soft cooing voice. Perhaps tomorrow…

The mourning dove no longer comes to me. My father's spirit has heard me, and I hope that at last he is in the Elysian Field where he is honored as he deserves. Somehow I know that I will walk with my father again in a time of peace and contentment.

It was the happiest day of my life on Ithaka. It began when I saw my Merchant's galleys come into the small western port below the palace, and I waited with excitement for Cadmus to visit my weaving rooms. It has been more than two circles of the seasons since he has come to Ithaka. It has been forever. At the brightest time of the day, when the Sun God touched the highest point of the sky, a servant asked if I could see the merchant Cadmus. Since I was not allowed to go down to the Great Room, he was brought to the weaving rooms. Eurykleia accompanied him. We exchanged words about our health and his travels and talked about the woven garments ready for him to trade.

Suddenly we heard a commotion below and Eurykleia left us. I asked him if he would like to have a cup of mint tea, his favorite drink. He bowed politely, and we walked quickly through my sleeping room to the garden where I clip the leaves and brew my tea.

While I prepared tea, I saw him looking at the panel hanging on the wall of my room. "It is magnificent," he said softly. Then he moved around the balcony touching and smelling the herbs and flowers. I turned and he was looking at me with shining eyes.

"How beautiful your garden is," he said, smiling. "No one else could grow so much in this space."

As he sat down, he said, "Despite my love for the sea and the sky, the color green forever draws me." He looked into my eyes then away.

"Surrounding myself with growing things gives me a vision of what time could bring in a better world," I said, revealing thoughts that I had never expressed, except in my writing.

"Telemachos seldom visits the weaving rooms because they are woman's place. He is now a boy growing into the warrior man that he will be. It is Ithaka's way."

Sadness enveloped us at that thought. We sat on benches softened by folded robes, and I served him tea and the bread and cheese that were to be my midday meal. Then I asked him about my father, although I knew what he would say.

"Your father has been taken without warning to Elysium," Cadmus said in sorrow. "His people still mourn him, and his eldest son Pandares sits on the throne of Sikelia. Your brother is a good king." He added, "Your sister was married before your father left the island, and your mother grieves in her own way.

"If she did not continue to bring misery to all who know her," he said, "her people might attempt to comfort her. Her enjoyment of pleasure somewhat eased the sting of her tongue in the past. But now there is no contentment for her, so your mother's frown is more frightening than ever." I could not breathe with the pain of hearing this.

Then the scent of herbs brought me back to the garden. I told Cadmus about my father's visit. I assured him that it was no dream. And I told him about the white dove.

"Have I lost my wits in believing that my father's spirit came to me?"

He looked into my eyes and said very quietly, "I have heard of such visits after the spirit escapes the lips of someone dear. I heard from a wise seer," he said, "that the spirit still tormented with guilt or desiring to soothe the heart and mind of one deeply loved has been known to return to the upper world for a short time. The visit may be in the form of a bird or in the form of his insubstantial shade. You are fortunate," he said. "Your father has come in the shapes that should comfort you. Now he can rest, and now you know that you are loved," he murmured, as he looked into my eyes.

My Merchant, my friend, always brings me peace as his special gift.

A soft breeze brought Courage, and Audacity wrapped itself around me. I continued my talk softly.

"When the men took my son's days from Eurykleia and me, I lost the only love on Ithaka. All softness flew with the man that he will be, the warrior who scorns gentleness and kindness to women as he grows into manhood. Only your visits remind me that a man can hold love in his heart, as my father and you taught me. Why cannot each day be filled with the peace and safety that I feel at this moment? Why was I chained to my Lord's fate, instead of a fate that I would choose for myself?"

Before I could feel shame at my boldness, he spoke in his deep and tender voice, "Since I have watched you grow to a woman, I have also considered such questions. I have asked why I must live a lifetime longing for what I can never have, living a life on the sea that fits what my people have made of me while I would gladly sit in this garden forever. I feel as though the shape of my character will forever be at odds with my desires, and sadness will always follow me." Emotion silenced us.

After long moments he continued softly, "I have a wife. She was given to me by the elders of my village, as is our custom. I had no choice. She is a good woman, not gentle or particularly kind or wise. We have little to say to each other since she has always lived in a small village of fishermen and gossiping women, and she is not curious about my adventures on the sea. Not like you. But despite her harsh voice, she is a good mother to my three sons. After the birth of our last son, she can have no other children. I had hoped to have a daughter, perhaps with green eyes. Exactly the color of yours."

He smiled and his eyes crinkled with amusement briefly before he continued, "I want you to know that my life has been measured out by my visits to this rocky island that claims you." My eyes became moist, and I was overcome once again.

As we sipped our tea, a thought came drifting to me from over the sea.

"Can it be possible," I asked, "that the gods have given us a treasure that has been given to no one before us? Is it possible that the friendship that we have, that must satisfy longing, is a richer gift than man and woman have ever been given? Perhaps the gods took pity on us for denying us the fullness that our lives could have been and gave us this special friendship instead.

"No other merchant would have taught me to read and write. No other man would have filled my dreams with such joy and anguish. No other merchant could share with me the words and knowledge that you carry across the Great Sea."

I stifled a sob, "And no one else could have filled this day with such beauty. Every day I shall thank Athene and my Great Goddess for giving me more than any woman has ever had." I touched the necklace of rich green stones that Queen Arête had sent to me long ago and that I wear every day.

Our eyes did not move from each other as I whispered these words.

He was about to speak when Eurykleia came to the garden with fear on her face. My Lord's mother followed, calling for the merchant. She was horrified that I had invited him into my sleeping room. She yelled that I had violated her son's bed and that this merchant would never come to Ithaka again. Guilt and fear kept me speechless.

Then Cadmus rose above us all and spoke with his soft but authoritative voice, "I would never violate the honor of the great hero Odysseus. I came to see the garden that the Lady Penelope has created. She was kind to offer me tea and bread and cheese. I had not eaten since last night, and I am grateful for her hospitality. The gods will repay you for such generosity and compassion. King Odysseus is known throughout the world for his hospitality as well as his bravery and cleverness. He would understand, I am certain, and would not accuse the Lady or myself of wickedness."

Before she could scream again, he continued, "The wife of the great warrior Odysseus is known throughout the world for her virtue and devotion to family and home. Other queens like Helen and Klytemnestra have violated their marriage vows, but the Lady Penelope remains alone in her room weaving in order to bring further glory to her Lord's home. He will be pleased with her and with Ithaka's reputation for the most beautiful woven goods in the world. She does honor to her Lord's name and to his house. You are fortunate that he chose her for his wife."

While she stopped screaming, she was not yet mollified. She repeated her threat that he shall never trade on Ithaka in the future.

He looked at her with a frown and said sternly but with appeasement in his rich voice, "Your son, the Great Warrior Odysseus, will not be happy with your decision or your judgment. Before he left for the bloody fields of Troy, he and I made an agreement. He asked that every time I pass near the island of Ithaka on my travels, I should stop to trade for his Lady's magnificent woven goods. I promised that I would give him more than a fair trade in articles that your household needs. No merchant would be more just than I am in this bargain. That was our agreement, and I honor my word." He continued to stare at her as he said, "My livelihood and my sons' future depend on my word and my reputation. The name of King Odysseus is also known across the seas for discharging his bargains. Would you defile his reputation while he is fighting afar and cannot defend his own name?"

I wondered if my own face were as white as the face of my Lord's mother. She said nothing while long moments passed. Then she said that he was to leave my rooms and never set foot in her son's sleeping room again. Cadmus bowed to her, apologized for offending her but reminded her that the bronze doors between the garden and the weaving room were always kept open. Then he turned to me, bowed, and thanked me for my hospitality and for my food.

He dared to add, "In my travels I will always remember the calm and contentment of your magnificent garden, my Lady." He left the garden, his head held high and his back straight with pride and dignity.

My Lord's mother glared at me in fury, then turned toward the door. She was so weak from her outburst that Eurykleia and a guard had to help her, almost carry her, down the staircase to her room.

With tears on my cheeks I went up to my shrine to relive the afternoon, to remember every word. I have lived that day over and over. Now I write it to hold it in my heart until I go to the Land of the Dead where Cadmus and I may see each other for all time. I pray that our talk is not considered evil by the gods. I remind myself that we did not touch, that we only talked. But those words fill the emptiness that has tormented me. I know that whatever happens to me in the future, his words and his looks will sustain me because I am more than nothing. I know love, and that is everything.

My Lord's mother punishes me by denying me even the rare visits with my son. Though she often remains in her room with illness, she still has the power to control and hurt. How long will the punishment last this time? Every day seems forever to me though Telemachos no longer seems to care about visiting my room. We have less and less to talk about.

He touched me again last night. It started like the other nights. I awake and he is standing beside my bed, and he whispers, "My Love, my Love, I am here for you." His voice is like honey, the scent of his lips like his favorite tea. Then he is in my bed, the blankets enclosing and hiding us, his lips soft on mine, his arms holding me, his hands bringing fire to my cheek, my throat, my breasts, the center of me. But unlike past times, this night does not end at that moment. Instead, we are suddenly alone on his galley, sailing across the Great Sea, the boat empty except for the two of us lying on the deck that is soft as cloud. There is no fear, for he and the wind hold me tightly and I am safe.

We are free! And I am on fire with a yearning that I have never known. The sea sings to us as we begin to ride the waves, first the small waves, then waves that grow bigger and bigger, our moaning mixed with the groaning of the sea and the wind. And we ride the waves higher and higher, up toward the sky, higher, higher—then the sky breaks open and the stars shatter and I melt into him.

I cannot move or speak or breathe.

His gentle arms of iron lay me down in the middle of an endless field filled with wildflowers. We lie together, our faces toward the sun and the clouds, and I begin to breathe again, sigh again, feel again. The chains around my heart are gone. I am released and open to the sky and the air—and to him. I hold his beautiful hand as tears cleanse me, not with pain or fear, but with the most exquisite joy. So this is the fire that owns my body and soul, this love that I give freely, openly to my only beloved.

Suddenly the song of the nightingale woke me, and I sobbed with the loss of a shining dawn that even Sikelia has never known.

For days I have wondered if Hypnos will allow my Merchant to visit me again when night protects our secrets. Will I ever know such bliss again? Desire overcomes me.

The seasons pass.

3. Etna's Warning

Mother Etna.

Whenever I hear the Thunder God's warning, I remember the fire and rocks shooting up like giant arrows covering the black sky. I hear the God's roar and terrifying screams all around me. I have been unable to wash away that fear. When the light flashes through the sky and thunder covers all other sound, I wait for the earth inside the mountains of Ithaka to come down from the sky and to cover everything with white dust. Is such power buried inside every mountain waiting for Father Zeus to send his lesson to the world? Or is Mother Etna alone in her warning?

Despite my fear, I would give the rest of my life to be back on Sikelia in the shadow of the Mother Mountain, waiting for my Merchant's visit.

We hear rumors that the war at Troy ended seasons ago. Traders bring us the news that the great kingdom of Troy was burned to the ground and all inhabitants were killed or captured. We wait to see who will be brought to our island when the men return. We hear that some Greek leaders and warriors of good fortune have returned to their homelands, and the rest of the heroes who escaped the grasp of Hades will soon be home. Rumor says that even Helen has resumed her life with Lord Menelaos.

Where is my Lord? Where are the men of Ithaka?

We have been waiting many circles of the moon, but we hear nothing of my Lord. He is alive, according to Rumor, but no one knows where he and his men are. On his return home, Agamemnon was murdered by his wife and her lover, and King Menelaos and Helen now live in harmony, so they say. But I remain waiting and alone, and my Lord's mother shrivels in her illness brought on by missing her beloved son. There is softness in her, after all, though she never shows it to me.

Telemachos becomes angrier as he grows taller and longs to know his father. Perhaps he feels abandoned, as I do. He is also angry that as time passes men on Ithaka and from other islands have asked when I will be made available for marriage. When will we agree that King Odysseus will never return? Despite our anguish and uncertainty, we are not ready to make that decision.

Woven reflections of my homeland live with me day and night. The nightmares of Tyndareus have flown away, so I now enjoy the sunrise that I see each morning on my first panel. My plans have changed over time, but the panels are essentially as I had first envisioned them. One is the image from my childhood bedchamber of the Sun God coming up over the water and my trader's ship sailing toward me in the distance. The next is the memory of my father's palace at the top of the great mountain with its steps of grape vines and olive trees going down to the beach. Those two panels and the panel of my father's Great Hall where I first saw my Phoenician friend are complete and now hang on the wall. The fourth one may be of distant Etna and the gardens where my sister and I played and drank from the stream flowing into the Great Sea, if I ever find the time to do it.

These panels are woven in the rich yarns called silk that my Merchant gave to me after my Lord took me to this dark place called Ithaka. Cadmus told me that the yarns were spun and dyed in the far lands of the East, beyond Troy and the world that we know. He has brought me more of that yarn with its vivid colors during the years that I have been here. I have three panels completed and I pretend that I am at home when I see them hanging on the wall facing the bed.

After these long years, my son is grown enough to lead the men in hunting. He is almost lost to me. Without the panels on the wall, I would have no joy. I awake every morning to the pictures on the wall and see the Golden God shining over the blue water, I see my father the King in the Great Hall with Cadmus, and I hear the laughter of Iphthime, my beloved sister. I smile. I look at the grey walls of stone around the bedchamber, and I feel grateful for the beauty of the panels.

Between the weaving of each long panel I wove smaller pictures of Ithakan landscapes. I put them on the walls of the weaving room, and one I gave to my Lord's mother when she became too sick to rule my world. For some time she refused to look at it. Gradually she became attached to the scene, and I now see her staring at it when I visit her room to bring her my herb broth that soothes her stomach.

She will not long have breath for this upper world. She has waited for her son to return from Troy, but she cannot wait much longer. I try to help her, but little can be done. It is strange, but I no longer feel the hatred for her that I once felt. It is a relief.

Cadmus has arrived and I asked him about Queen Dido. Until today I had not heard another word about the Queen of Carthage since Cadmus told me her story. On one of his visits, he left me the story on a sheet of parchment hidden under the skeins of silk. The beautiful and brilliant Queen of Carthage is related to the Phoenicians because Dido came from Tyre, the Phoenician birthplace of Cadmus. After Dido's brother murdered her husband Sychaeus, Dido fled across the Great Sea with a band of loyal followers to the shore of the endless kingdom that she calls Carthage. Out of loyalty to the peoples of his homeland Cadmus, like his father before him, had always stopped to trade at the Phoenician ports on the Land of Burning Sand. Cadmus continued the tradition, so he came to know Dido and the magnificent kingdom that she and her followers built.

Today Cadmus continued her story as he described "her passion for Aeneas, the Trojan hero who escaped with his father, his son, and a band of followers from the burning walls of Troy. On his way to found a new kingdom that would lead the world, according to the will of the gods, Aeneas was blown by the winds to the shores of Carthage. He and Dido fell deeply, wildly in love and assumed that this was the kingdom of the future that the gods foretold. Aeneas happily took control of the kingdom, its building and expansion, its governing and organization, while Dido spent her time adoring her hero and his beautiful son Ascanius."

I expressed my joy and wonder in their love. Cadmus looked at me with sadness.

"No, Lady," he said quietly. "Her love is not a reason for celebration. She lost herself in him. He retained the strength and leadership that are his character and his fate, but she lost all that was the treasure of Dido. When passion overwhelms all consideration for your people and your obligations, you have given up the best of who you are. That is what happened to Dido, and her people suffer for the weakness that Aphrodite inflicted upon her."

I was confused. He went on to say, "The gods forced Aeneas to leave Carthage to continue his quest for the empire that must be established by him, the half-mortal son of the goddess Aphrodite."

Cadmus said sadly, "I was in Carthage on the fated day and was witness to what happened. When she saw the ships of Aeneas leaving the port of Carthage, her sorrow so overwhelmed her that she fell on her sword then on the pyre that she had built of the bed and other tokens that she and Aeneas had shared in better times. The shining Queen was consumed by fire, even as her passion had consumed her."

He continued, "Her people lost all that she might have been and could have given to them in the future."

I sat in horror and could not speak. My friend rose and said softly that he would return later in the day to trade my goods.

So much I have to think about in the tale of Dido and Aeneas. So deep are the mysteries of fate and the human heart.

My Lord's mother is in terrible pain. Long ago a healer helped my father's mother when she was ill on Sikelia. In our homeland, we were kind to old and sick people and did whatever was possible to ease their suffering. I remembered that there were powders that we traded with merchants to keep my grandmother in the land of sleep rather than the world of waking agony. I asked Cadmus for such powders, and he gave them to me. I have also gathered the bright red flowers called poppies that grow over the meadows on Ithaka. My Lord's mother was grateful as the powder mixed with poppy relieved the searing pain.

For many long seasons, I had not known the condition in which she was living, and she did not want me to see it. I had been sending her medicine through Eurykleia. Finally, Eurykleia asked me to see my Lord's dying mother. The Medicine Man had been useless in relieving her suffering, though Eurykleia never admitted that.

I was shocked to see her. She had no flesh, only bone covered with dry skin that was grey. The room was very small and had only space for a small pallet. The air was fetid, and no one kept the door open for air until I demanded that air be allowed into her room, that she be cleaned of the lice that infested her, that she be bathed each day, and that the robes on her new pallet should be changed each day. I brought salve for the sores that had to feel like knives in her back. I had been sending her a small amount of my special tea twice a day, and I gradually increased the amount as the pain became intolerable.

She looked at me with gratitude each time I entered her room. One day she actually thanked me. She whispered, "Why are you kind to me? I hated you and punished you with that hate."

I was shocked by her candor. I considered for a moment then I told her, "We all need assistance going into the Lower World. I learned kindness in my homeland and have always tried to practice it to please the gods." Before I finished, she was in the twilight of relief and perhaps did not hear my answer.

Now she sleeps most of each day and night.

My Lord's mother joined Persephone and Hades last night. She was cold when I went to visit her this morning. Her spirit is no longer chained to pain, and I am relieved for her. As she spent so much of her life distanced from those who might have cared for her, she died alone. I have come to realize how empty her days were after Odysseus sailed to Troy. Love for her son seemed to control her life, and she wanted only to greet him in the Underworld. Now she must be in peace. Perhaps the shades in the Lower Realm will help her to understand why hatred dominated so much of her life. So useless is hate.

Life is so much repetition on this bleak island. Weaving and eating, weaving and eating, sometimes bathing and gathering herbs, or brief moments of dancing, but mostly weaving and eating are my lot and the lives of my weavers. Is there nothing else in what we call living? Only writing breaks the monotony and even then I sometimes cannot bear the loneliness in the shrine. How many seasons will I count in my life before I too can know consolation? Is this my fate?

My son has now grown strong and tall. He is a hunter. I have been told that he will be a great hunter and warrior like his father. For many rolling seasons he and Medon have been hunting rabbits and birds for my special stew that I cook with herbs and garden vegetables. I cook on the balcony where the stones were built for a small fire to make teas and broths for the weavers during their working hours. One of the large iron kettles bought from a trader some years ago makes wonderful stews. I also have delicacies like fresh and dried figs and dates and apricots, oranges and lemons, pears and pomegranates because years ago I planted two trees of each fruit in the private garden attached to the counting room. I remember the day my Merchant brought some of those small saplings to me on one of his first visits. They have grown large and healthy and give much fruit to my weavers and myself—and to others in the palace if they have the taste for them. Most of the people in the palace eat only Ithaka's traditional fare. It is a monotonous table.

It is always such a problem to keep healthy and clean and to keep the lice out of the heads of Eurykleia and especially Telemachos because they live among the others in the palace. Long ago I told the weavers that if they did not want to live with all the other weavers in our rooms, they would become palace servants and no longer weavers. I found that after they slept with the men of the palace, they returned with lice in their hair and in other places. I would not live that way. Finally I made a decision. Women who chose to spend their nights in the palace were replaced with others who wanted to be weavers and live in the protected space of our rooms. I have made only three exceptions to weavers who have special talent and who promise to examine each other and keep each other free of vermin.

I know that I am considered strange. But I have come to realize that we are healthier by the way we live with our herb teas, goats' milk, and our vegetables and fruits from the gardens. I believe that we are also healthy because of our regimen to be clean, our dancing around the room every day, and our isolation to keep the insects from consuming us. Each day we gently scrub our teeth with salt water and green twigs.

Twice during the growth of the moon all my women with Eurykleia still walk down the mountain early in the morning to bathe in an isolated inlet of fresh water mixed with salt. Guards protect us but remain a distance from us while we wash our hair and our clothes with harsh soap and lay out our clothes on the rocks for the sun to dry them. Of course we take robes to wear while our veils and daily robes dry. We continue to love these outings where we play in the water, eat bread and cheese and brined olives, and drink fresh sweet water on the small beach. Then we rest in the sun. The Sun God's rays, my father taught me, are essential for our strength, so each day my weavers come in small groups to stand on my balcony garden in the sun for a few minutes after they have eaten their midday meal.

The rest of the palace seems not to care about being clean or about being healthy. I am told that this is part of my eccentricity, according to the stories that circulate about me. My weavers did not care either when I arrived on Ithaka. They believed that my habits of washing every day and bathing every week were touched with lunacy, and they watched me carefully to see if my behavior became wild like the women who follow the warriors and mariners and are left behind when they become sick and fierce and untamed.

But now few people seem to question my strange ways. Even my weavers, who were old or looked old when I arrived, are spry and in good health. We do not suffer from the illnesses that bring pain and suffering to so many of the people on Ithaka, and my weavers trust me to have what they call "wisdom from the gods" that protects us. This amuses me.

One evening when my Merchant was on the island, I opened the door of the weaving room to hear the bard with his lyre singing the songs of gods and war. Karua asked how Apollo made the sounds of the lyre.

The next day I asked the bard to bring a lyre to the weaving room to show my weavers how it is played. He sat at the door of the weaving room as he played. They were pleased, but Karua was in awe as she watched him play. I observed the girl moving her small fingers and humming with him. I knew that she longed to touch the instrument with the lovely sounds. I asked Cadmus when he came to trade if he could get a lyre for me.

He asked, "Why do you want a lyre, my Lady? Do you not have one in the palace with your bard?"

"Yes, we have some on the island. However, I want one for my young weaver who longs to touch it and learn to play." Most men would laugh and scorn me for such an answer, but my Merchant smiled with amusement.

He said, "My Lady, I have a lyre and other instruments on my galley and will bring it to you this afternoon."

I asked him shyly, "What is your price in trade?"

He laughed softly and said, "It will be a gift that should remain a secret." When he brought it up to our rooms, he was accompanied by one of his mariners who knew how to play several instruments. The mariner, who remained at the door, was kind and showed Karua how to hold the lyre and how to get song from it. She was too shy to play while the men were in the room, but she held the lyre as though it had been her friend since she was an infant. She could not take her eyes from the beauty of it.

She is still a child, so I told her, "I will keep the lyre in my bedchamber and you may play it anytime that you are not spinning or weaving." The smile on her young face was amazing to see.

That evening after supper, like every evening after that day, I let Karua make music. From the first time she held the lovely wooden instrument, her fingers became part of the strings. Thereafter, every evening when the weavers told stories of memories or dreams or life as it might have been, Karua's lyre accompanied the stories. Sometimes when I hear her play, I almost believe that Apollo has given us our own Muse as a gift for the beauty that my weavers create.

Occasionally I let her hide at the top of the stairs to hear the singer's lyre in the Great Room at the evening banquets. She has learned the sounds just by hearing them. This child has been given a treasure from Mt. Olympos.

If Karua can play such wondrous music, why are there no bards who are women? I wonder how many other women, and slaves, might have a gift that is never fulfilled. Is giving or denying Karua a lyre a violation of what her fate might have been, or is it a fulfillment of her fate? Perhaps when Clotho spins the thread of life and includes a gift like the one that was spun for Karua, is it Lachesis who needs to add the element of luck in order to make possible what we can become? Was it Karua's good fortune, given by the Fates, to be a slave and weaver on Ithaka in order to play a lyre, which seems to be part of her spirit? And is our spirit aligned to our own fate, or are they in conflict for some, or all, people? These are questions that follow me.

Long ago I found an amazing surprise in the box of papyrus, ink, and brushes that Cadmus brought to me in secret during one of his visits. On a ring of gold one large green stone sparkled to remind me of the waters that lapped the beach of my homeland. With it was a note saying, "This ring is the color of your eyes. Wear it with good Fortune, Lady." I put the ring on my finger and wept. I wanted to show everyone my gift, but suddenly I realized that if anyone saw it, my Lord's mother would take it away. She would shame me and call me vile names. I knew I had to hide it.

After long consideration I asked Eurykleia to bring me a lump of soft clay to make an offering for my altar. I pressed the ring into the clay but left the stone uncovered. I made designs around the stone as though it were a simple votive. No one could tell that it is a ring. If I must lie and say that I brought it to Ithaka long years ago, I would do so, but no one comes to my altar. Sometimes I think about such deceit and feel ashamed to see what I have become so that I can hold a tiny ray of joy in my life. Every day I touch my lips to this ring as part of my ritual to the gods. Now that my Lord's mother is a guest of Hades, perhaps I can release the ring from the rock of clay and can wear it. I tremble with fear to do it. If they take away the ring, they will take my heart with it.

PART THREE

1. Secret Art and the Suitors

Last night the handsome and haughty Antinoös came to our palace with his father Eupithes to speak for my hand in marriage.

Telemachos sent a maid to tell me to bathe and dress in my best gown and come to the Great Room to share a banquet with guests. I have been eating with my weavers for long years since Telemachos enjoys feasting with his hunting friends. Few strangers honor us with visits, perhaps because the Trojan War ended and Odysseus has failed to return. What can people say to us?

I dressed with excitement, hoping that we would hear word of my Lord. When I went down to the Great Room with my handmaiden and Eurykleia, I met Lord Antinoös and his father. They bowed politely and we ate without speech. There was no chatter or laughter or clever stories, just the frowns of serious thought. I was confused and troubled.

Finally, when Phemios was about to begin his song, I dared to ask, "Do you have news of King Odysseus, where he is, and how long it will take him to get home to us?"

There was again silence as they looked at my son to speak. Not knowing what to do or say, the young Telemachos was speechless, and Mentor said nothing to help him.

Antinoös rose from his bench and spoke, "Lady, the men on Ithaka admire your beauty and cleverness. We have waited patiently for the homecoming of King Odysseus, but Troy was destroyed more than six rolling years past. With the defeat of Troy all living warriors returned to their homes. Odysseus alone has not returned with his men to his hearth. All Ithakans believe that the godlike hero and his men now reside in the Underworld with the heroes who left their breath on the sands of Ilium. It is time for his Queen, with her beauty and gift of weaving, to sit at the hearth of another. My father and I offer our home in the hills on the far side of Ithaka and will provide for you there. You will find no man on Ithaka worthier of your friendship and request your answer soon."

With a slight smile of satisfaction he sat down.

I could not speak. I took a sip of wine to take away the dryness of my tongue. A sudden thought came to me that this was the gods' test of loyalty to my Lord.

After some moments I began, "Lord Antinoös, I am honored by your offer of sharing your home with me. I too am wearied of waiting for my Lord's return. Nevertheless, I have been told by a great seer that he is alive and his homecoming is assured. The gods have prolonged his journey for reasons that only they know. I cannot violate my marriage bed by taking another husband while my Lord lives." I lowered my eyes and rose to leave the table.

Antinoös said in a louder, more demanding voice, "Are six rolling years not enough if he wanted to come back to you? Rumor tells us that he has found another to share his bed in these long seasons and leaves you to age until it will be too late for your future with another husband. It is time for you to decide on a man whose name and property earn him the respect of this island. There are many worthy young girls who would be honored by an offer from me. I will accept a reduced bride price from your son, but I will not wait long for your decision."

I gasped at his audacity and his arrogance. Quietly and with assumed deference, I bowed slightly, thanked him, and left the room. As I ascended the stairs to my bedchamber, I was accompanied by the knowledge of how the people of Ithaka see me as a discarded and unworthy wife. I wept throughout the night.

A trader came to Ithaka yesterday. He was a stranger, but he had heard about our fabrics and wanted to trade. Mentor led him to the top of the stairs where I could speak to him, my face veiled, of course. I had some robes to spare and asked what he had to trade. Mentor stood with me and smiled. The trader named some things that we did not want.

I was about to turn away when he said eagerly, "Lady, if you please. I have a slave that I bought at the last port on our journey across the Great Sea. It is true that the slave's trade is useless, but he is strong and can be used for hard work."

When I asked about the trade, the merchant said, "The slave told me that he made pictures from small pieces of stone." Then the merchant laughed at the foolishness of such work. Immediately I wanted to meet the man whose name was Periphetes, but I pretended to be indifferent.

I feigned boredom and said, "If he is as strong as you say and if he is submissive, he might be useful to Mentor. Perhaps we can look briefly at him."

Periphetes was brought to me, and I asked him many questions about his health and strength. In a few casual questions, I learned that he created mosaics, had been trained in the East, and worked on decorating a palace in a land far to the east of Tyre. One night he was abducted and later sold to this trader. I liked the manner of this artist and wanted to keep him on Ithaka, but I dared not show my interest.

I said in a tired voice, "We could use his muscles, I suppose. I have work for him to do carrying weaving materials and working in my garden. Mentor, you can always use him elsewhere, so perhaps you might buy him if his price is low enough." Mentor was reluctant, but he knows that I never ask for anything unless it is important to me. He said that he would think on it.

The trader, eager to rid himself of this useless baggage that he had to feed, lowered his price. After he lowered his price once more, I offered him six robes and three goats. He accepted. I believe he thought he made a good bargain, but the robes were of lesser quality and we have an abundance of goats on Ithaka.

I could not look at Periphetes as he stood in shame while we bartered for him. I promised myself that I would make up to him for the humiliation that he had endured.

With Mentor's approval Periphetes is now working for me. He and I have talked long about his art and how he can transform our weaving room and my bedchamber into a bright and beautiful place. He is very excited about the project, but we keep this plan secret from the rest of the palace. He is making designs for the rock floor and walls. For now, he says, he will make the mosaic tiles at night, and during the day he will prepare the walls and ceiling with a plaster that he saw in abundance sold at the marketplace. Pheidopos, the Chief Potter, who has helped me in the past and has become a friend, has agreed to help Periphetes make the tiles and to keep our secret.

The room will be light and clean and lovely for my weavers. Though we sweep the floors each night in order to keep the fabrics new, the room never seems clean. I am excited. Periphetes has started to put lime on the ceiling, and the weavers cannot believe how bright and cheerful the room seems already. He will begin the floor as soon as the walls are prepared and his tiles are made.

One day I said to this proud and gentle man, "I want you to understand that you are not my slave, though Mentor bought you for me. Rather, you are my assistant in transforming this palace into a thing of beauty. I look to you for guidance and vision," I said, "and I am grateful that you are here with us."

Periphetes bowed and touched the hem of my robe as he said with tears in his eyes, "Thank you, Lady. I will always be grateful that the gods brought me to the island of Ithaka and to you."

When he stood up he was taller than before. He resumed his work with a dignity that brings gladness to my heart. I am now more certain than ever that no man, or woman, should be enslaved and owned by another.

I worked on my panels almost every night for all the rolling seasons until long after the Trojan War was won and my Lord's mother traveled to the cold home of Hades. Then my Lord's father Laertes gave me permission to hang the last panel on the wall if I promised to weave a shroud for his time to leave the sun and sky for the dark region.

With that promise, he and two servants crossed the threshold of my bedchamber and attached the panel to the walls. He had not seen the other panels hanging. When he saw them covering the grey wall of stone with light and color, he asked me how I came to have such visions. I told him that they were the pictures of my home that I held behind my eyes.

He looked with sadness into my eyes. Suddenly he knew for the first time that Ithaka had never been my home and never could be. He had not thought about how I lived enclosed in the rooms at the top of the palace, never realized the freedom lost and the family gone. He left my life in the cruel hands of his wife, my Lord's mother, and she took away my choices and liberty to walk in the sun and soft breezes, to visit with my son and with guests, and to learn about the world beyond these cold walls. And after she departed this upper world, no one thought to alter my condition. He looked around and saw the prison of my rooms, then tears spilled over the edges of his eyes and he turned to Eurykleia who led him down the stairs.

I thought of that day when I awoke this morning, and I cannot get the picture of his tears from my mind.

Father Laertes is now living in the hills with an old Sikelos woman who cares for his needs. When I asked Eurykleia about him and his decision to leave the palace, she said with sadness in her voice, "Once he was the strong and proud King of Ithaka and surrounding islands, but gradually he lost the taste for power and the spear. After he gave over his throne to his son, he no longer desired to make necessary decisions and has left all authority on the island to Mentor."

Eurykleia continued in confidence, "Father Laertes has always been torn between his need for dominance, as King, and his nature as a kind and tender man, between strength as a leader and his desire for a life of love and friendship. Some men might see him now and call him weak, but once he was a hero, acclaimed and honored in this part of the world."

I think of her words, and I miss that gentle man and wish he would return to the palace. In the meantime, I work grudgingly and slowly on the robe that will dress him for his interview with Hades.

I had a dream that the giant with one eye threw my Lord onto the shore of Ithaka, but his breath had escaped to Hades. All hope for my future was lost. I sobbed.

I have kept close to my heart the dream that my Lord would return and free me from this chamber. He would allow me to dress in the beautiful robes that I weave, would adorn me with jewels in my hair and gold bracelets on my arms, and he would be proud of his wife who waited for him. I am not Klytemnestra who violated her bed and murdered her king upon his return from Troy. My Lord will be grateful and will not show his anger when he looks at me. We will eat together each evening with guests and will hear our bard sing the songs of Troy that will never again cut my heart. Our son will no longer bear a frown but will join us and smile because his father will be home. He could never take the place of my Merchant, but he is my husband bonded to me before the gods. Perhaps he would even be kind and gentle to me.

In such a future I will finally know the tranquility of a home that I am willing to accept. My Lord and I will age together in harmony and watch grandchildren grow with laughter and love. This has been my dream for the long rolling years.

And then I awake.

No man is allowed to enter my weaving rooms at the top of the palace, except for Father Laertes, my growing son, Mentor, Periphetes, Medon, and Cadmus. My Merchant visits our room briefly during his stops at our island to trade my woven goods for the treasures he collected across the world. I have never been allowed to be alone with my friend since the one beautiful day when we had tea in my garden. On the trading visits, he comes to the weaving rooms where I store the special robes for him. Always sitting near the door, we talk quietly about my patterns and the different weaves that he says he sees nowhere else across the sea. With Eurykleia and all the weaver women attending us, we can speak little and always with my eyes lowered. No longer can we share the color of our eyes or the peppermint of his shapely lips when he stands close to me.

I am excited only because I slip sheets of my written songs under the best robes that he says he keeps for himself. Under the special yarns and the Tyrian purple dye that he brings only for me—for my panels and borders and the richest of royal garments—he puts sheets and rolls for me to cover with silent whispers of ink in the long and empty years until he comes once more. He also leaves sheets covered with marks that tell me of my family and of his thoughts. I know that he shares my longing. I know it, and somehow that sharing, even the pain of it, comforts me, for I am not alone.

Antinoös was the first of my suitors. He has not been the last. Sometime after his first visit when I rejected his offer of marriage, he returned to the palace with several friends who joined him in their suit. As many new moons rolled on, more men joined them. They all seemed to be in the palace every time I looked into the Great Room or courtyard, so I began to leave my rooms only when it was necessary to go bathing and gathering. Since they drink and feast and play dice long into the night, they sleep into the day until

Helios is high in the sky. My forays outside the palace begin when the Sun God touches the sky, so I do not have to see these men I despise. Telemachos tells me that they often stay overnight in the palace, eat his wealth away, and sleep with some of the servants. Apparently they enjoy their life as suitors. I think that they no longer want me. They prefer the company of each other and their life of indolence.

Moon follows moon and my life remains desolate. Nothing changes. The servants are harried and exhausted and often mistreated by the men who have taken over our house. Animal pens filling the palace would be better than the suitors who fill this house with their smells and shouts, their arrogance and destruction. I do not like the anger I feel, but there is no help from anyone. No word of my Lord comes to us. We wait.

I have been shaking all day. I almost lost the panels that keep the images of my homeland in my eyes every day upon waking. Hanging in my sleeping room, they brighten the bleak rock walls that are my world.

Cadmus, my dear friend, arrived to trade with our palace and with some of the Ithakans. After spending the first day and evening honoring our elders and my son the Prince, who is now grown into a man, he asked permission to see me and the robes we have been weaving for him this last year or more. I lose the sense of time.

Cadmus came to the weaving room, as he always does, and remained near the door where my servants bring the robes to him. On this day, the bronze door of my own sleeping room was open, and he saw the balcony of plants and flowers. The lemon trees on the balcony were laden with fruit, and he could see and smell them from the door of the weaving room. His eyes widened with pleasure, and he asked to stand at the bronze door to see the garden once again more closely—if that could be permitted. Eurykleia nodded. He stood at the door and looked into my room where he has shared so many of my dreams. He smiled and praised the garden for continuing to thrive in its variety and usefulness. Then he turned and saw the panels on my wall. He was staring at the pictures of my home and my memory treasures when my son, looking tall and godly, entered the room with anger that this merchant would invade his mother's sleeping room.

Telemachos had never bothered to look at the panels that I had woven over the years when the rest of the palace was sleeping. He asked what they were and said he had never seen these places on Ithaka.

I said with quiet submission, "They are the pictures of my homeland."

With the quick anger of his father, he raised his voice, "Ithaka is your home. You dishonor my father when you call that place of the past your home. Rip those things off the wall."

I heard my breath choke me as he began to walk to the wall.

Without hesitation, my Merchant said, "Lord, those are very valuable wall hangings. Surely you do not mean to destroy them."

To my humiliation, my son turned to the Merchant and asked, "How much are they worth? Since these unwanted suitors have come for my mother's hand but she will not pick one to leave us all in peace, they are eating up our livestock and drinking up our wine. We need to find a source of wealth to support us. My hunting will not long sustain us. What will you give for these panels that have such value?"

The Merchant looked straight at my son and said in a quiet but firm voice, "I would give my fortune to have those magnificent hanging visions if the gods allowed it, but it would bring disaster on your home if I or anyone else took them."

We were all startled, and my son with frightened eyes asked the meaning of such words.

The Merchant said, "The Muses and the Gods of Mt. Olympos admire and protect such splendor. They esteem and defend the home that has created such beauty. This wall is a tribute to Athene and all the gods and goddesses of nature and the arts, and this home pays homage to the powerful deities in hanging these pictures. If you dare to harm them you will bring destruction upon yourself and your island."

"How do you know what our gods think?" my son asked in a sneering tone.

The Merchant said quietly, "My travels have shown me the power of the gods. I have seen lands glorified for their devotion and honor to the gods. I have also seen the gods' retribution when the laws of the skies have been defiled. I have seen astonishing devastation and would not bring it upon this house by desecrating that wall."

My son, with life drained from his face, turned and left the room.

I looked at the Merchant with the gratitude of my heart in my tears. And the weavers, hearing my Merchant's words, breathed with awe and relief.

I realized that Telemachos was so angry about my wall hangings that he did not notice the white walls and ceiling of the weaving room.

Would he deny me the mosaics if he knew what I am planning?

It is a huge problem to keep weaving every day while Periphetes works around my weavers to create the mosaic floor. We move two looms at a time into my bedchamber to make room for him to do small sections of the floor. And these two weavers must sleep on the floor of my bedchamber or on the balcony, if the weather is mild, until their section of the floor is dry. Then we replace those looms and take two more into my room, which is so crowded that I cannot weave on my own loom. There is no room for more than two looms in my room with the large bed. In the meantime, all the other looms are placed closer than ever in the large weaving room. Periphetes says that he has never worked under such difficult circumstances.

Despite the enormous challenge, he seems happy and filled with the joy of creation. The weavers, knowing the pride they feel for their own exquisite work, understand his feelings and remain patient and willing to accommodate his needs. They are also excited about the beauty of their room, so they work in this trying situation without complaint. Our room is the only one in the palace that is not shadowed and dismal. The weavers are overcome by the beauty of each section and feel privileged and grateful. When they see the mosaic floor completed, they will feel that they are the most important women in the world. And they are.

Creating beauty is a daring and courageous thing to do on Ithaka. I worry that my son may learn about this project and stop it before it is finished. Fortunately, he is so focused on the suitors that he does not know what else is happening in the palace. I know that he will think that the mosaics are useless and wasteful of time and materials. I worry more that his fury will be turned on Periphetes who could be beaten or sold away from the palace. My joy is always tempered by fear for this good man and great artist.

Yet, I am once again grateful to Mentor and Eurykleia for helping to make this happen. Mentor has ordered the materials and has made clear to Pheidopos, who is in charge of all things made of clay, that the work is being done for me and he is to keep silent about it. Since he made the bowls and spoons for my weavers, Pheidopos has been willing to do anything for me. I am told that when Pheidopos has some little time during his busy days, he helps Periphetes to make mosaic tiles for our floor even though the potter has never seen such art. He even made a bowl for Periphetes to eat his midday meal with us, and I invited Pheidopos to share our stew one day. He seemed to enjoy it so much that I often send my share down to him in my own bowl.

The work would go so much faster if we could have one or two other men working on our room, but men are not allowed in the weaving rooms. I am fortunate that Periphetes is recognized as my own slave so that he can come to our rooms each day.

We lost one of our weavers, the oldest one I believe, to Hades last night. She has been too sick to work for some time, but I have hidden that fact from Mentor. I am grateful that Eurykleia also kept this information a secret from the rest of the palace. When a servant or slave is too sick to work, it is the custom here to take the person away. She is never seen or heard of again. I fear to ask what happens to her—or him. One day Doria slumped over her loom and could not get up by herself. My weavers carried her to my room where she has been sleeping. Each day we carried her out to the garden and made her comfortable in the sunlight and the soothing scent of flowers and herbs. It was there that Thanatos came for her.

The weavers, Eurykleia, my servants, and I quietly prayed to our goddesses to take her to a happier place. Perhaps all of the hard work of her life will make her worthy of such laurels. We shed our tears then sent for Mentor who took her away to do what must be done.

We shall keep her bowl on the shelf with all the others.

Memories of my home on Sikelia—where I was free to roam and gather herbs and play and laugh. I sometimes lose myself in these memories, yearning for another time and place.

Now, on Ithaka, I tell my weavers to put their hands over their mouths to stop the brief happy sound from escaping. No one must hear our pleasure at being together. Naela laughed too freely one day when a manservant passed beneath our closed door. He reported our pleasure to my son, and Naela was removed for punishment. Lord Telemachos said in anger that our laughter wasted time that was better spent on weaving that can be sold. My lovely Naela forgot what the penalty for a moment's pleasure would be: she would become a servant to the suitors and would not be allowed to weave and waste time in laughter.

Enraged but controlling my voice, I said, "I need her work. She produces more than you could imagine, and she is one of my most talented weavers. Too much will be lost if she is not working for me."

In a contemptuous voice my foolish son said coldly, "After she learns this lesson, she will produce more than ever."

Then he took her out of our rooms. He knows nothing and feels nothing, yet he places himself above all others. I cannot speak the words that I feel for this man who was once my son in the long past but who has become this arrogant, ignorant, and impotent leader.

After Naela was passed around each night for too many nights, she returned to us. She kept her eyes on the floor or the fabric on the loom. A dark and angry frown replaced her beautiful smile. Her teeth closed off all sound. I want to reach out to her, but silence wraps its shadow around her.

We watch for the swelling in Naela's belly to remind us of the punishment for our woman's contentment together. We feel safe only with each other and the looms. Sometimes, as Naela teaches us, we are not even safe in this room. How can I forgive my son?

Rage and gloom are woven together to create the design of my days. I cannot look at my son, and I have no words to speak to him. He does not understand what he does to all women by his attitude and behavior.

Naela is close to her time, and we all pray that the gods prevent a girl from growing within her. No one should have a woman's life. How different it was in my childhood home with a father whose kindness shone radiance over our land. I will never stop missing my home and the pleasure of each happy day.

The gods brought Naela permanent suffering today. She pushed out a girl and all the women began to wail and shriek with grief for this innocent baby. My son and the suitors for my hand gathered in the Great Room at the bottom of the stairs to learn the nature of the screams. When they heard a girl was born, they cursed the gods for their bad fortune. They thought that our shrieks told of our women's disappointment that it was not a boy. After all, a boy is valuable to all, is he not? They did not understand that it was not a boy we wanted—not another boy to grow into a man on Ithaka. We did not want to inflict on another girl the suffering that is women's life on this island.

I sound bitter. When did my lips turn from perpetual smile to a scowl? When did I see men as enemies rather than friends and protectors? When did sour wine replace the sweetness of honey in my soul?

It is time to sleep.

Periphetes comes to the weaving room each day and works until the lamps do not provide enough light for him. He is always respectful and keeps his eyes away from my weavers. Yet, I have heard that he suffers for my attention, or from being in my presence. The other men in the palace push him and take his food and insult him. They make vile remarks about me also, I hear.

Periphetes does not say what he is doing for me and accepts the humiliation. He is just happy to be doing his art. I asked Mentor if he could provide some protection for Periphetes, but he doesn't know what can be done. I would have him sleep on the landing outside our door near the guard who stands to protect us day and night, but that might make his situation worse.

Usually Medon protects us each night when the men become drunk and rowdy after their dinner and too much wine. He was the young boy I took for errands when I asked for Agape long years ago before my Lord sailed for Troy. For all these years Medon did his work for me and also was a protector and friend to Telemachos. When Telemachos was crawling around the floor then walking, Medon followed him so he would not get hurt. When Telemachos began to run freely in the fields and woods, Medon was with him to watch over him. They have grown up together, become friends and blood brothers, though Medon is more than five years older.

According to Rumor, Medon has become proficient in hunting and warrior skills in order to defend Telemachos and to protect me. I love that young man who is like a better son to me. And so when the suitors began to take over the palace, he volunteered to stand by our door to insure that no one could beat down the door to our rooms. He stays until the early hours when all the drunken men are asleep, and then he is replaced with another guard. I always feel safe when Medon is nearby.

The mosaic floor is almost finished. It is beautiful. My eyes water with tears of remembrance when I think of the floors in my home on Sikelia. My father is before me, and I bow to Periphetes with gratitude. His eyes shine with pleasure. The floor is white with green leaves and small blue and purple flowers that reflect the skies and the flowers in my garden. Though surrounded by white walls and ceiling, we look down at the floor and we are walking across a field and feel new freedom in this enclosed space that now seems to be open without walls.

I took the mosaics at our palace for granted in my childhood, but now I know the wonder of such splendor, having been so long with so little of it. What joy I feel.

I laugh to see the delight of my weavers since their room for working and living has brought the nymphs of nature into their lives. They said that they feel like royalty, but immediately were sorry they dared to say such things. They thought that I would be insulted. I just smiled and then they smiled. We are all very happy. Periphetes says that he will create some mosaics for the walls, but I want him to do my room first. My ceiling and walls will be made white. Then he will create a mosaic floor for my bedchamber and my shrine. I am impatient to see it. The anticipation makes me want to laugh through the day. I know how my weavers feel.

How fortunate we are. Periphetes has told me that few lands that have seen the sun know how to create mosaics, or even what they are. Most royal houses have inside walls covered with other materials like plasters. Then colored designs are made in the plaster while it is wet or scenes are woven to cover the plaster walls. My homeland knew mosaics, but that is unusual Periphetes says. I think often about how Fortune touched us with light when she brought Periphetes to the House of Odysseus.

The men who have taken over our palace disgrace themselves and their families by treating visitors with disrespect. It is the law of the gods that all guests be treated like family, even better. It is the law of hospitality that strangers be treated with deference and esteem. Today the foolish men, loud and drunk even at the height of the Sun God in the sky, pushed my Merchant and laughed at him when he arrived to trade.

Throwing bags of yarn, goblets and bowls, herbs, and other needed materials over the ground in the courtyard, they gathered around the Merchant and his men and yelled, "Hey, Merchant, what do you plan to give the Lady Penelope today when you go to her rooms?"And they all laughed their filthy laughs.

"Who curls your beard?" "Who makes your women's clothing?" "Grab their bags and let's see what he has to offer." "Grovel on the ground, Trader." "Traders are cheaters." "Traders should be taught to bow to us." "Bow down, Trader, and all your men too."

Drunk and disgusting and dirty, the suitors humiliated and degraded my Merchant. I wept when my servant told me what she had seen and heard. Always he has been treated like a noble man because of his learning and the many years he has come to our island for the woven goods and other objects. Today they dishonored our gods' laws.

For the first time I feel hatred for these men so deep that I would destroy them with a lightning bolt if I had the power of Zeus.

Telemachos saw what happened to Cadmus, and he bellowed, "Leave that man and his men alone. When you mistreat this merchant," he said, "you desecrate our gods' laws and the laws of our house. I will not have it! What you are eating and drinking depends on this man and what he brings to the island and what he takes from us."

He ordered the servants to gather the bags together and bring them to my rooms. Medon stood tall behind my son holding a javelin ready to protect the Prince of Ithaka. The men grumbled and left the courtyard to find women and feel like men again. My Lord would feel proud of our son today.

Yet, I feel anger and shame at what the palace has become. All day the indolent suitors lie around or play games or assault the maids, eat and drink wine with water, leave their filth everywhere, and water the stone walls that surround the courtyard. The stench is disgusting and makes me sick when I am required to leave my room. I am almost grateful that my life is limited to the weaving rooms. At least we have fresh air, cleanliness, and safety in our rooms. The remainder of the palace is fit only for pigs, despite the work of the maids every day. This is no longer a home, for disorder and cruelty rule.

My Merchant is staying only one day on this visit. There are so many more suitors than the last time he stopped on our island. He says that he cannot endure seeing how I must live and the animals that I must live with. When we were trading the goods in my weaving room, he reminded me of the story of a witch named Kirke. I told him that I know that story well.

I said, "It is believed that she lives on an island, that she is very beautiful, and that she turns men into the animals that are their character. On her island there are pigs and wolves and mangy dogs that were once men. On Ithaka there are men who were once pigs and wolves and mangy dogs."

He whispered to me, "If there were any way to get you away from these despicable, evil men I would do it. I would give my life to free you."

"Many times I have thought of strategies, but there is no way to accomplish this dream. If Odysseus returned and learned of my abduction, he would track you down and kill you. I am not Helen. I could not do to you what she did to the Trojans. The gods have given me my fate, and I must live it."

I saw sorrow in his eyes, and he turned away. His hair is turning white and the sad lines crease his face. Yet he is still beautiful.

The only pleasure Cadmus and I had from that visit was his delight in seeing the mosaic floor and the white walls that covered the ugly stone that had enclosed us for so many years. He expressed his admiration for the design and the work and told Periphetes who bowed with gratitude.

In his quiet and humble way Periphetes said, "Lady Penelope has saved my spirit by allowing me the opportunity to serve the gods with my art. Working for her each day has been the glory of my life."

His respect and regard for me pleased my Merchant friend who smiled despite the pain that Ithaka brings to him.

Only once, except in dreams, our hands touched for a moment, and I thought that everyone would see the shaking in me. That was the day my Merchant looked through the door into my sleeping room and for the first time his eyes touched the panels on my wall. He turned to me with eyes so sad that my pain was unbearable. He suddenly reached out to touch my hand for comfort. My breath stopped, my throat shut down over my heart, my eyes closed and filled with the waters of sadness. Then Telemachos came into the room with anger that cut the softness of my friend's hand. That moment visits me often in dreams that Morpheus turns into nightmares of guilt and loss.

I hear them laugh and throw things, perhaps cups and stools, each night. People call them my suitors. I shudder. Mentor says that the silver cups are dented, and wooden furniture must be constantly replaced. Some time ago he asked me to hide the golden goblets and bowls and the most precious silver in our rooms behind stacks of finished garments. The suitors laugh at Mentor who is intelligent and kind, but he and my son are not strong enough to fight them all even with the help of Medon and their hunting friends.

No longer pretending to wield power on Ithaka, Father Laertes went up into the hills to live after my Lord's mother died. According to Rumor the sad old man wears rags and lets his hair and beard grow long and disheveled. Father Laertes has separated himself from the world that he does not want to see, so my son has no one strong enough to protect him.

Telemachos waits for his father to return to rid the palace of this vermin. While he waits, my son is tormented with confusion. He knows that the marriage gifts I must bring to a new husband would deplete the house of its treasures, and the loss of my weaving would further leave the palace in wretched need. He says that he wants me to return to my homeland, even in disgrace, but when I say that I will do it, he gets enraged. Rumor says that my parents will take me back if I want to return to Sikelia, but that is absurd. My father is in the Lower World, and my mother surely would not want me now when she did not want me as a child. I do not know if she still breathes the upper air. At other times, my son says that he will lose face if I choose my homeland over Ithaka or a new husband.

To help my son I could choose one of the suitors to marry so they would all return to their homes, but only Amphinomos is deserving of my attention. I hate all the rest, especially Antinoös who would slay anyone else I select.

More than once I have reminded Telemachos, "If we accept that your father has gone into the cold realm of Hades and you give away your father's wife, what will my Lord say upon his return? What will the gods do if my son forces me to violate my marriage bed?" I shiver with disgust at the thought. Telemachos says nothing.

I feel so sad for Telemachos. He cannot decide what to do or desire. I believe that my Lord will return, and my son also dreams of that time. With the strength and cleverness given to my Lord by the gods, I cannot imagine that his fate would be to lose his home, land, and family by not returning. And I cannot accept that he would leave his son in such desperate conditions. I don't know what to think. I only know that I am miserable for my son and for myself.

Zeus says that mortals bring sorrows upon themselves with their greed and recklessness. I have been thinking how this applies to the suitors and how I would define the nature of their avarice. They certainly yearn for the large bride price that my son would give to the man who would be my husband. And the man I choose would gain wealth from my weaving. Perhaps that is all they want, but I think the nature of their greed goes beyond even those measures of wealth. I think that being chosen above all others by the wife of the great hero Odysseus would gain a man a name equal to a king's power and reputation on this small island, and even beyond. I think that they are greedy for such power as they swagger through our halls.

It is not I they want because they do not know me. They have never even seen my face, never looked into my eyes. It is what I represent that they crave. I wait for the day that their greed brings down the wrath of Zeus on them.

The terror of sleep woke me, and I must write. The spirit of my Lord's mother visits me often since she gave up her last breath.

In my dreams, she has not found serenity since she left the Upper World, and her rage stalks me. One night when I visited her room while she still breathed the air of life, she told me that the goddess Hope had flown away from Ithaka, never to return. I have come to recognize that she was right.

Part of me feels relief at her passing, for she will never own me again. Part of me mourns, for I fear that I too will end my days in fury against the suitors who control me. Is her life a lesson for my own?

Perhaps I may someday be allowed to gather leaves and berries and roots when the growing season arrives, when the suitors are punished and there is peace. For now, my trained servants and weavers gather the materials for dyes and medicines. I miss the freedom of fields and woods, but the mosaic designs of flowers, trees, birds, and animals that now cover my bedchamber floor bring me joy daily. We could not use yellow in the floor design, for yellow is a woman's color and would insult my Lord when he returns. This belief is part of Greek tradition, I am told. I think of yellow as the color of the sun that grows the flowers and trees, that gives us life, but I abide by the beliefs of those around me.

Periphetes designed my floor with the blue and white of sky, the green of fields and woodlands, and animals of such beauty that this floor plan must please both man and woman. Perhaps it is a man's floor, for Periphetes had my Lord in mind when he designed it, but it is one that I love because it represents the gods of nature. Periphetes has just finished my floor and will now create the shrine floor. He said that he would put touches of yellow in the pattern. He is also making a design for one of the walls in my chamber in time for the return of my Lord. Then he will finish the weaving room walls.

Because of Periphetes, we have a world apart from the animal pens that are now the Great Room and the courtyard. Maybe someday this remarkable man may be allowed to transform the other rooms of this dreary palace.

Athene visited me with a wonderful dream. I was laughing and free in the fields, and Telemachos was a small child again. He put his arms around my neck with happiness, and I kissed his soft cheek. We were gathering herbs, and Helios was shining down on us in our excitement. I was dancing and laughing so hard that I woke myself with the sound of that joy. How foolish of me. I cannot leave my rooms.

The suitors control the palace, and I cannot be seen. They also own the fields outside of the palace, for it is there among the sheep that they have set up tents and temporary sheds for sleeping. What would they do to me if they found me in the fields? If I leave my rooms they might think that I was offering myself. It was not only my Lord's mother who kept me confined. It is Ithaka, its customs and unofficial rules, its ways of thinking about women and men. It is Ithaka that takes the independence from women even as my weavers and I are confined for our safety.

Last night I realized that I am fortunate to be imprisoned in my rooms for my protection. We were sleeping and the animals were drunk and carousing with the maids when suddenly there was a loud banging on the weaving room door. Two of the suitors wanted to get in. They attacked Medon, who was guarding the door for our protection, and they were trying to get into our rooms. The women were crying and shaking with fear. Fortunately the doors are made of heavy oak reinforced with bronze and with a heavy oak bolt on the inside. My clever Lord had ordered such doors before he left for Troy, and it takes a strong weaver to lift the bolt each time the door is opened.

I told the weavers to go to the windows and scream to the gods and local people for help. Suddenly the screams flew across the island, and I imagined that villagers began to run to the palace from all directions. The two men became frightened by the noise, and Medon threw one down the stairs and was about to put his knife through the other when a group of suitors ran up the stairs to get the two men attempting to penetrate the Queen's rooms.

I am told that Rumor spread the story about the state of affairs in the palace and the fearful situation of the Queen. For the first time the island of Ithaka and even the islands surrounding us must realize the danger we are in. Foolishly I expected assistance, but the men of Ithaka have done nothing to alter the situation.

Father Laertes sent word to ask me when his shroud will be completed. He expects to die before my Lord returns. I keep the shroud on a separate loom to weave a line each night, and sometimes I unravel some of it. I will not finish it for two reasons. First, to silence the suitors I have promised that I will choose one of them for my new husband when the shroud is finished, so I must not complete it. The second reason is that I also fear that my Lord's kind father will give up his breath to the gods of dark and cold as soon as the shroud is ready for his descent. He struggles to remain in the sun's rays only until the shroud is completed, he says. I will not let him go.

I woke in the night, tortured by Aphrodite. My sobbing and my longing for Cadmus wake me from nightmares of such joy that guilt robs me of all happiness. He was here in my arms when the nightingale's song tore me away from love. My tears confirm the images that I want to deny. I beg Aphrodite to allow me the serenity of sleep, which never seems to comfort me.

I fear the night. Only writing and weaving soothe me. Perhaps if I weave a few lines of the shroud, Athene will forgive me and intercede with Aphrodite.

In my homeland the gods were not so cruel, or was I just too young to know?

The suitors have been tormenting me with threats. They shout that they will invade my rooms in the night and take us all by force. They say that they will call a meeting of all the men of Ithaka, and together they will force me to choose a husband. Two guards are now posted at our door at all times each night and day.

They do not believe that my Lord will return, despite stories that the traders tell. There are stories of islands that my Lord and his men have invaded, of animals and women they have captured, of goddesses who keep him captive. But no one has seen him. They are only stories, but I must believe them. I am terrified of the threats.

To calm the suitors today I stood at the top of the long staircase and told them through my veil, "I promise again that I will choose one of you to marry when I finish the shroud of Laertes. Lord Laertes is a hero, so the weaving must be perfect, each line of thread delicate and worthy to take him on his journey to Hades."

As the men grumbled, I continued, "The gods have told me that the robe must be the finest that I have ever woven. You all know of my reputation for weaving. After a long day of labor, I am too exhausted to work on it long into the night. It is not an easy task to create a robe that will take this great hero away from us. My tears slow my progress. I ask you for patience. The gods ask you for patience."

Despite their desecration of our home, they fear defying the gods of the Underworld by interfering with the completion of the shroud. Sometimes their revelry makes them forget why they are here and they leave me alone, but every new threat creates fear in my weavers and in me.

Time passes.

A stranger in rags came to my rooms with a story about my Lord and where he is. He talked of storms that took him off course and of immortals that hold him captive. He said he talked to a seer, who is beloved of the gods and has knowledge of all things. He said that my Lord will return if I can endure a little longer. My Lord longs to return, he said, and weeps with pining for his home.

I have heard these stories before this day, but I gave him a new cloak and new sandals, food and drink, and thanked him for his kindness. After all, he may be a god in disguise.

Now there are over one hundred suitors prowling the palace. The suitors have waited for over two years of rolling moons for the shroud to be completed, two years of our suffering and our fear. I continue to unravel the shroud so that it will not be completed. The suitors cannot understand why it takes so long. I have again sent word with my son that the shroud of Laertes must be fit for the gods. He is a hero and the father of the great hero of Troy, and so this old man deserves the perfect shroud. I say that my days and nights are filled with weaving for trading, and I have so little strength to weave anything more. The men do not believe me and are getting too impatient for my son to control.

I have seen my Merchant only briefly since he was humiliated. The last time he came to the island, he brought his oldest son Lethos to trade with me, and I served them tea near the door to the weaving room. Then they left, and I watched the galleys move out to sea before the end of the day. I miss him. I miss the dream that is further away than ever.

For three long years, the suitors have tormented not only me but also the comely girls and women slaves in the palace. There are so many suitors now. I do not know the number, but they are loud and rowdy and enjoy fighting each other. Antinoös continues to dominate them all, I am told. They have insisted on speaking with me several times, so I go to the top of the stairs robed and veiled in my most beautiful garments and speak to them. I am afraid to make them angry, so I speak pleasantly and tell them that the time is coming for my decision. I tell them that the gods speak to me and say that it is not yet time to replace another man in my Lord's bed.

"I am not Klytemnestra," I said to them today, "and I will not take another man to face the wrath of the gods. I await word of my Lord Odysseus' place in the Underworld or this world. Then I will make the difficult decision among so many worthy and handsome warriors."

They laugh and cheer at such compliments. What silly fools they are.

"I assure you that when I finish the shroud, I shall be closer to my decision," I said with a firm voice. These speeches may placate them for a few more rolling moons until they yell, filled with wine, for me to make a choice. I hate them for their filth and their boorish behavior.

2. Restoration of Order on Ithaka

I have learned that my hero son has left Ithaka in order to find his father. Eurykleia knew that he was leaving, but she did not tell me. I am angry and hurt that I did not have the opportunity to say goodbye to him. She says that he was afraid to tell me because I would wail and beg him to stay for his safety. There is no justice in that statement. When have I wailed and lost control to my son, or to anybody? I hold all suffering within my heart since my Lord stole me from my home. All screams are shut behind the bars of my teeth.

I do not know if I will ever see my glorious son again, but I am proud that he had the courage to set sail to learn of his father and to gain knowledge of the world, as his father has done—and as I wish to do. Too often there are questions about a boy's father, while his mother is a certainty. Each time my son does something that his hero father would do, I believe that the gods point to his father as the model and deprive evil mouths of their cruel words.

I wait each day for his return. I have placed my loom near the open door to my garden that overlooks the small harbor on the western side of the island where my Merchant's galleys dock on his visits to our palace. When he chooses to trade with the market at the large port of Ithaka, he sails around the island where I can no longer see him. I don't know where Telemachos will dock when he returns.

It is strange that in the past I often did not see my son for weeks, yet now I miss him with an ache that never subsides.

Dread and Despair drain me of all energy. When my weavers dance or tell stories, I cannot do so. I sit in front of my loom and sometimes the warp and the woof seem confusing to me. Some days I cannot weave at all. I go to bed and sleep. Then I dream horrible images. Last night the Cyclops caught Telemachos who was not so clever in evading the one-eyed giant as his father was on our journey to Ithaka. Just before the giant ripped my son apart for eating, I awoke with a scream strangling me. I could not go back to sleep and lay trembling until I saw Dawn's fingers touch my window.

For long weeks I have not been able to write. Something is wrong with me. The nightingale sings the song of my terror and my grief for what I cannot have. I don't know how long I can go on.

The Merchant's son Lethos had only the weavers' fabrics to trade when he last arrived at our palace. They do beautiful work, but he asked for my fabrics and robes. I had two to send for Cadmus, but there was little else for me to give. He said that he would give that message to his father.

"My Father will be grieved that you are so ill," Lethos said gently. "Through the years my Father has spoken often of the Lady Penelope with the startling green eyes and the sun-browned skin touched with honey and apricot. Forgive me for my temerity, Lady, but I must tell you how he admires you, your strength and forbearance, your intelligence and cleverness, your kindness and generosity. His stories of you and all that you have accomplished have provided a model of what greatness should be to my brothers and to myself. And now I sit here sadly noting your weakness and must carry this dark tale to my Father. I hope that you recover for the future all that you have been in the past."

I could not speak as he said kindly, "My prayers and those of my beloved Father are with you, Lady." And he stood up and left me with my shame.

I went to bed and cried for many days. When will this suffering end?

The Moon Goddess has enlarged almost twelve times, and I lose hope for my son's return. If he is running across the Field of Asphodel with heroes from the Trojan War, I too want to go down to the cold home of Persephone. There is no more reason to stay above ground, for the light brings me nothing but misery and a different kind of darkness. I try to weave but finish so much less than in the past, and none of my work is inspired. I know that my weavers worry and try to help, but there is nothing they can do. My maidservants cook the stew, but they too miss the rabbits that Telemachos and Medon brought to us. We no longer go down the mountain early in the morning for our baths and to wash the clothes. If I had the freedom, I would not have the energy to romp in the water or even to wash my own garments.

My maids do everything for me. I am grateful. Even the mosaics do not raise my spirits. I do not want to write.

I am ashamed of my weakness.

Word came to me that Telemachos arrived secretly on Ithaka and remains in hiding. The suitors lay in wait for his ship and conspire to kill him. I am in misery that I can do nothing to help my son. I can only pray that he will remain safe. How impotent we women are in the affairs of men.

Telemachos has returned.

My happiness has no walls. I ran down the stairs to embrace my son, tall and grand and godly.

Before I could touch him he said with troubling authority, "Control yourself, Lady. A stranger has word of my Lord and wishes to see you. Return to your room and wash yourself, put on your best robe, and behave like a queen."

I was embarrassed, but I did as he directed and bathed for the second time that day and dressed quickly.

I was surprised that my son brought a stranger to my rooms and insisted that we meet in my weaving room. In silence and confusion I watched my son lead this beggar to the windows where they could look out at the garden and the sea. Then I invited them to the balcony garden, and the three of us sat on benches and I served tea.

The stranger was old and dressed in rags. His hair and beard were streaked with dirt and silver strands, and he limped. I noticed him looking around the room and at the flowers and herbs in the garden and was surprised at his curiosity. But when he talked, looking more at the floor than at me, there was humility that contrasted with the suitors and other men in the palace.

He said, "Lady, the hero Odysseus is on his way home at this moment. Unfortunately he is alone because the gods have seen fit to deny his men the joy of homecoming. Only King Odysseus has been spared because of the gods' love for him."

When I questioned the truth of a story that I have already heard too many times, he responded, "I assure you that my account comes from a source that cannot be disputed."

We spoke briefly about the suitors. I explained my situation and said that I would never defile my marriage bond. I thought that he had a slight smile on his face. Perhaps it was only the creases lined with dirt in his cheeks.

I mentioned Klytemnestra and he asked me to relate the story of that sad queen. I wonder how he could know so much about my

Lord and know nothing about that famed queen and her king who now reside with Hades. Despite my doubt, I trusted him while he was speaking, but now I begin to wonder how much he told the truth to me.

Only Odysseus would try to trick us with such deceitful stratagems. Or was he sent by Odysseus to see me and hear what I would say? Was he a god in disguise? Could this be? We did not speak very long. I am so tired.

I have been thinking about Klytemnestra and the song that our bard sang long ago. How she must have hated her Lord Agamemnon for the murder of their beautiful daughter Iphigeneia. To lay his daughter on the altar of Artemis and offer her as sacrifice to the god of winds that would take his forces to Troy is unspeakable. How could he perform such a vile ritual, even for his own glory in leading an army against Troy? I could never accept the murder of my child, even for the gods. Perhaps I too would kill my Lord upon his return if he had done this thing to our son. Of course a son would never be sacrificed as a daughter was. I no longer judge Klytemnestra as I once judged her. I feel her suffering and the emptiness of her life. But would I have acted as the beautiful queen did? I don't know.

I have more energy since my son returned. It is strange how my thoughts direct my body and its workings. My dreams are not of my son being hurled into the Lower Realm, as they were when he was on his journey. Last night I dreamed of geese and an eagle and the stranger who smiled, and the Sun God gave light to every corner of my bedchamber. I arose this morning ready to work. My weavers smiled at me for the first time in many turnings of the moon. All day they smiled.

Long days have passed since the stranger visited me, and my Lord has not appeared. I believe that story was a trick of the gods.

Today I felt, for the first time, a desire to go before the suitors in order to arouse their admiration and make them long for me. I cannot understand why I wanted to do this. I think that a god may have impelled me to do so. I asked Eurynome, my nurse, to help me get bathed and oiled, and I chose my best jewels and my most elegant gown that I had never worn before this day. Every choice I made today seemed to come from outside myself. I sent Eurynome to find Hippodameia and Autonoë to accompany me, but suddenly sleep overcame me. Never before have I fallen asleep in the middle of the day unless I was ill.

When I awoke, I was confused but knew I must present myself to the suitors. I took my two maids, one on each side, as we stood on the stairs and the suitors looked up at me with awe that I would be standing before them so brazenly. I heard sighs and words like "radiant" and "beauty."

Before anyone could speak, I began with words that came from a spirit speaking through me, "My friends, so handsome and godlike, my lord King Odysseus gave me instructions before he left for Troy. He said in his golden voice that I was to remarry if he had not returned from Troy when our son has grown into a man. That time is near. But I will not marry any man who violates our laws, eats up our house and home, and does not court a Queen with the gifts befitting my place. The gods would frown on me for that." Then I walked up the stairs.

After my appearance, I received a treasure of gifts that would have gladdened the heart of my Lord. There were robes, earrings, necklaces, and other jewels. They were brought from all over Ithaka from the families of the suitors. I felt both joy at how easily manipulated these foolish men could be and, somehow, shame at what I had done. I want none of the suitors—or their gifts—yet I pretended that I was eager to be remarried. What god is directing and tormenting me?

Two days later, Telemachos came to my room and told me to bathe my body and dress as befits a queen. Whenever he says this to me I feel anger. Does he think that I never bathe and must be told to do so? Does he think that I was not clean and dressed elegantly when I went to confront the suitors? He then brought the beggar in rags to meet with me again. I asked to meet with him in the maids' tiny room so that the weavers could continue working. The beggar was compliant, and even pleased that I put the work before our comfort.

There is something in this beggar that opened my lips to tell him things that I would not say to any other stranger. I found myself telling him about my imprisonment these long years since my Lord left for Troy. I told him that I have spent over three years weaving a shroud for beloved Laertes, father of my Lord Odysseus.

"Recently the suitors learned that I have been unraveling it at night. No longer can I delay choosing a suitor since I have no other strategies to use. It is almost beyond the fourth year, and I have used up all my deceits to delay them. I must make a decision to wed one of them, but I continue to resist making a choice, despite my son's urging." We talked long as the Sun God moved into the west.

As we drank tea brought by my serving woman, he said, "I saw my Lord on the island of Krete long ago and have heard that he is nearby as we speak. I assure you, Lady, that your heart will soon be glad when he arrives shining like a god."

This beggar troubles me. Somehow I feel connected to this dirty, disheveled man, his way of moving his head and hands, the way he sits, his golden tongue that speaks almost in the musical tones of poetry. Could a god be deceiving me? Is this my Lord before me? I know this is a foolish question, but the idea moves through me like a cold wind. I shudder with fear and trepidation, with hope and possibility.

Suddenly a god wrapped Audacity around me, and I felt a courage that has escaped me for many moons. Without plan, I told the beggar about my suffering through these years of dreams and nightmares that have tortured me as I have awaited the return of my hero husband. I told the ragged stranger about my recent dream of twenty geese that were feeding outside the walls of the palace.

"Suddenly a huge eagle swooped over the geese and they were left broken and mangled, the geese strewn over the grasses that had fed them. In my dream I was weeping," I told him, "and a mortal man appeared. He said that he was my Lord Odysseus come to tell me that he would kill the suitors who had turned my life to misery. Then I awoke." I asked this wise stranger what the dream could signify.

"The Goddess Athene has said it in your dream. The geese are the suitors," he said, "and the eagle is King Odysseus who is returning home as we speak. With the help of the gods who fly through the air like eagles, King Odysseus will destroy all the suitors."

Reluctantly, I answered him, "Dreams are so uncertain in their meaning. There are two gates through which our insubstantial dreams come. One gate is made of ivory, so seductive in its beauty that we want to believe that the dreams issuing forth from it are true. But we are deceived by those dreams. The other gate is made of polished horn, and through this gate dreams will be accomplished if only mortals recognize and accept them. I do not believe that my dream came through the gate of horn, but rather through the gate of ivory, which will bring disaster on me.

"In spite of my fears, tomorrow I will announce a contest. I will tell the suitors that I will choose to marry the man who can string the bow of King Odysseus and shoot through the twelve axe handles that revealed his unique skills before he left for Troy. Only my Lord can string that bow and accomplish this feat, so they will know that they are unworthy to take his place."

"You still have his bow and the axes after so many years?"

"Yes, they are where he hid them." I was pleased when the beggar approved of this plan and Telemachos, who had been strangely silent throughout our conversation, agreed.

As the beggar was leaving my room, I offered him a thick wool mat for sleeping. He thanked me and then asked if he might sleep near the fireplace in the Great Room. I agreed, and Telemachos led him away. Something about this stranger disturbs me, but I am too tired to unravel the mystery tonight.

Now that I have written about the beggar, this man who troubles me, I can sleep.

I long to tell my story of terror and death.

The morning after the beggar insisted on sleeping on the floor of the Great Room, I arose from a troubled sleep. I bathed and dressed. I stood before the altar in the weaving room and offered drops of watered wine with barley sprinkled over it as the weavers and I shared our devotion to Athene and Hera. Then I began to weave as I do each day. I waited calmly for my maid to serve me my morning meal with the weavers. I pretended that this day was like all others.

When the sun's chariot passed the highest point in the sky, I took the bow and sheath of arrows from the recess in the wall of my shrine where they have been hidden since my Lord sailed for Troy. I alone have known of their hiding place. I then sent Eurykleia with trusted maids to get the heavy trunk with the axes that were prized by King Odysseus. They carried our treasures into the Great Room where Telemachos sat frowning and where the beggar, the swineherd, goatherds, the cowherd, and the suitors were congregated in eating and drinking away my Lord's riches.

There above the Great Room I stood on the stairs, my veil hiding my face as always, and challenged the suitors, "I make a pledge to you that I ask the gods to secure with my life. I promise to marry the man who can string the bow of the lost King and shoot an arrow through twelve axe handles, as only the great Odysseus could do twenty long years past."

My maids placed the bow and quiver on the table before the men. Telemachos set the axes in a perfect line. Then I watched the men swagger and boast that they could string the bow with ease. One by one, grunting and cursing, several of the suitors tried and failed. As the arrogant Antinoös moved toward the bow, the beggar rose from his corner and asked to join the contest. I heard Melanthios, our goatherd, laugh and insult the beggar who stared at him with a black frown. Antinoös also laughed. He picked up the bow and tried to string it. It bent a little, and then suddenly it snapped back. He was straining and sweating. Even the gods he cursed.

Swiftly but quietly Eumaios, the swineherd and loyal friend of my Lord, walked up the stairs to kiss the hem of my robe while he whispered that I must go to my room immediately.

"Let no one into your rooms," he said. "No matter what you hear, keep the doors bolted and let no one in or out of the rooms."

Before I could turn, all the suitors were laughing and jeering at the beggar who asked again to enter the contest. Ignoring the orders of Eumaios, I stopped on the stairs and dared to challenge the men.

I said in a haughty voice that they had never heard from me, "This stranger, having lived a long life of hardship and suffering over the seas, surely could not be stronger and more heroic than my young suitors. Could you all be afraid that he is superior to you?"

I looked directly at the glowering Antinoös, the leader of these cowardly men. As all the suitors turned and stared up at me, the beggar walked to the bow and quiver and picked them up. My two maids and I moved quickly up the stairs. We entered our weaving room and bolted the heavy door. With relief I leaned back against the door and felt faint. Suddenly I was terrified at the consequences of my actions and trembled to think that our fate hung in the balance with the strength of one old man. Through the door we could hear the raucous shouts of the men challenging the beggar. Then a great roar arose followed by screams as Chaos seized the Great Room.

As Dawn arose to quiet the screams that filled the night, Telemachos banged on our door to gain entrance. It was a horrifying sight to see my son covered with the blood and slime of the dead men. Telemachos came to the weaving room to take away the girls who had slept with the suitors and were enemies hiding among us.

After my son took the three screaming women away, Eurykleia told me in a whisper that the beggar was my Lord Odysseus. I did not believe her. I thought it was a god with designs to trick me into taking an immortal into my bed before my Lord returns. But I said nothing of this to my friend.

She also told the story of other ugly things. "Our men hacked off the nose, ears, hands, feet, and genitals of the goatherd Melanthios whose disloyalty almost cost us the battle," she said. "Then they hanged him up for all to see."

Eurykleia seemed gratified as she continued, "Of the fifty serving women in the palace, twelve gave themselves to the suitors and therefore were foes of my King. These few foolish women had been serving and pleasing the suitors, had mocked and sneered at Telemachos and those loyal to your son, and had jeered at and mistreated strangers who visited the palace, including the beggar who helped Telemachos in battle for the palace.

"Lord Odysseus and your son had no sympathy for these women. Telemachos hanged them all after making them scrub and clean the palace of the blood and gore from the fighting. After the walls and furniture were scrubbed with the strongest lye soap and the earthen floor was cleaned and raked, the twelve women—all weeping in terror and squealing like the bats they would meet in the kingdom of Hades—were taken to the place between the roundhouse and the courtyard stockade where they were hanged."

I could envision them hanging until their toes no longer moved like birds' wings in the air.

Eurykleia continued, "These arrogant servants, with the suitors who thought they owned and controlled the palace, were punished as the cold hand of Hades greeted them. They received what they deserved, my Lady."

I knew that my friend was right. It was Justice that sent these women into the Lower World for their disloyalty. Yet, there is still such sadness in me that their characters were chained to a fate that shortened their lives by violence. I pondered how many of the girls gave themselves willingly to the suitors and how many were forced against their will. Was Justice really served on this day for all the women?

Eurykleia returned to our rooms later and told us that there would be music and dancing as soon as the people of the palace who survived the battle could dress. She had orders to begin festivities as though I had picked a husband from the suitors and the palace was celebrating. Men on the island must not yet know that their sons and other kin were dead until my Lord was ready to defend the palace from the rage of their families. Confused, I went to the top of the stairs when I heard the music from Phemios's lyre and watched the maids struggling to move to the music. They had no idea what to do because there had been no dancing on Ithaka since I arrived here, except for the daily exercises by my weavers. My Lord's mother banned dancing long ago.

I sent my weavers down to the Great Room where they led the servants of the palace in dancing and smiling. I was proud of their lightness and the pleasure they gave to the servants. I walked slowly down the stairs, hardly believing that I was free to walk through the palace without a suitor ready to assault me. The two royal chairs that Mentor had stored long ago had now been replaced next to the huge fireplace. I sat on the throne chair embedded with gold and silver and worried about what happened to my son and the beggar.

Suddenly I saw the godly figures of my Lord Odysseus and our son walking toward me. They had been bathed and oiled, their hair curled and shining, and they were dressed in the finest robes that my weavers made. Their beauty took away my breath. Odysseus had not aged. Instead, the gods had restored his youth while they had taken my best years and left me feeling dry and old. I rose trembling from my chair, wondering how I could test this man, this god, who tries to trick me into giving myself to a fraud. I did not move or smile as they stood before me.

In an angry voice so like his father's my son asked me, "My mother made of stone, why do you not welcome your King after twenty years of trouble in his struggles to reach home? How can your heart be so cold?"

Showing no warmth or submission, I pretended to be fearless as I said, "If he is truly my own Lord Odysseus, there are secret signs that will tell me so. I see and hear no such signs yet. He may be a god ready to trick me."

The godly man smiled slightly with his dark eyes still cloudy and ordered, "Go, Telemachos, and send the servants to their rooms. I will talk privately to your mother. It is her hard heart and clever wit that preserved the virtue of this house and the reputation of our name. Remember that and be grateful to her. Now go. We will speak together."

We stood staring at each other as the Great Room emptied swiftly and silently.

As Eurykleia was about to leave the room I called to her, "Take two of the strongest servants to prepare to move the bed in my chamber. Have the bed brought down to this Great Hall so that our King may have a comfortable place to sleep."

"Lady," she said, as she started to speak.

Before she could say another word, I frowned and ordered, "Eurykleia, bring the bed down to the Great Room without another word. And bring it down immediately."

As she walked up the stairs to our bedchamber, confusion in her face, this man standing before me bellowed in rage, "What god has destroyed the bed with roots in the earth and a bedpost made of the olive tree that lives forever? How I worked to make that tree smooth and to insure that mortal hands could never move that bed. Who did you allow into our bedchamber to cut down that tree?

Damage to that sacred bed brings down on you the destruction of the marriage bond between us."

I don't remember anything else that he said in his anger. I only recall feeling pleasure that I had tricked him. Suddenly he realized that I had tested him cleverly. He stopped shouting and smiled. He reached out and took me in his arms, both of us weeping, and I felt safe for the first time in the twenty rolling years since I left my homeland. I know that we walked up the stairs as he held my hand, but I remember little else, so overwhelmed was I with gratitude that he had returned at last and saved me from the suitors.

As the darkness of the night enclosed us in the softness of our bed, he showed me a gentler love than I had known with him so long ago. Then he told me of his adventures, why it took him ten interminable years to get home when the remaining Greek warriors had found home so long ago. He told me about Kirke and Kalypso and his longing to return to Ithaka, about seeing the Cyclops again and how he tricked the giant, and about the people who eat human flesh. He spoke of the kind Phaiakians and Queen Arête and so many other adventures, but I have lost the memories. At the end of his story, he told me about descending to the cold Land of the Dead, of meeting his mother and the heroes who had given up their breath in battle and the warriors whose cowardice or deceit cut the thread of their lives.

Finally he whispered the fate told to him by Teiresias. My heart shattered when he said that soon he would be going on another journey, this time overland to a place where the people do not recognize an oar.

"It is my fate," he reminded me softly. "I must take our household gods so the strange people will know our deities, and only then can I begin my journey home to rest with you forever. With the help of Athene and Zeus and the Fates," he said, "I will return again soon."

I asked when he would be leaving. Before he could answer, Hypnos threw a soft blanket of sleep over him.

I sit here writing while he sleeps. Since he related to me his story and the fate that awaits us, I am left with so many questions. When will he go? How long will he be gone, another twenty years? Will he return to die at home or die on the sea trying to reach home? Am I to spend the rest of my days alone, without the touch of a husband's lips or the security of his arms? He has learned much on his travels that might make up for the years of separation and suffering. I could tell by the way he held me and by the way he spoke in soft whispers to ease my anxieties. Perhaps now I can learn how to be a wife who knows love and not fear when touched. Why can we not live this way forever?

Though we are now safe, I cannot bury the terrifying memories of how my weavers and I felt during the battle with the suitors. Below us in the Great Room there were men running and yelling beyond what we have heard in drunken brawls. The screams were horrifying. At one point our loyal Eumaios pounded on the weaving room door. He yelled to keep the doors barred and let no one in. Then he too left to join the battle below. The cries of the men went on through the night. It seemed like forever. We huddled together, shaking in terror.

I whispered to my weavers, "Our Lord Odysseus has returned. He metes out the sentence of death to all who have violated his home these many years."

I did not feel certain of this information at the time, but I wanted to bring comfort to my friends. My weavers whimpered that the suitors were killing our King and his son and all who fought with them. I thought of Medon and feared for him also.

Lethia said in a shaking voice, "The few followers of our King can not kill so many suitors, for they are young and strong warriors. They keep fit by fights and games in the courtyard."

Something in her voice made me cold. She wanted the suitors to win. Then I recalled that she had not been sleeping with the weavers. Instead, she had slept with her mother each night, she said.

Her mother dyes the wool and other yarns and wanted Lethia with her at night, the girl had told me. Suddenly I realized that she had lied to me. She had been with a lover, not her mother. I felt cold Terror wash over me. She knows how strong the suitors are because she spends the nights with them.

If it is truly my Lord Odysseus come home at last, I thought, a mortal cannot fight all of the suitors, despite the love the gods have for him. Was his fate to return home only to be slaughtered by these vile men? And my son, what of Telemachos? I wanted to pull out the hair of Lethia for her disloyalty to me and to the palace.

We sat on the floor in darkness relieved only by small lamps and waited for our death. Suddenly a man was screaming and banging on the door. Melantho and Lethia jumped up to go to the door.

I yelled, "No. Do not open that door!"

I threw myself at them just as they were about to lift the wide bolt that protects us. Several other weavers also ran forward and dragged them down and away from the door. Then there was the sound of swords and the screams of death outside our door. I heard Medon and Eumaios the swineherd who yelled again to keep the door bolted.

Melantho, Thora, and Lethia wailed in sorrow and ripped at their hair. They tried to get free from the weavers who held them while we bound them with yarns. They would have unbolted the door, and we would have been killed or used to force my Lord into submission. They do not know Odysseus. He would never surrender, especially to save women.

Hours passed in terrifying sound, and then all was quiet. Telemachos came to the door, and I almost fainted with relief that he was alive.

I opened the door. He was covered with blood and gore, and he had Medon and two others with him, also in garments coated in drying blood.

He asked, "Who are the women who loved the suitors and despised the King?" I pointed to the women tied up on the floor. The brave warriors took the two weavers and Melantho away. The cries of the women could be heard as they were dragged through the Great Room. I could not stop trembling.

Helios began his climb into the sky, and there was quiet. After the sharp smell of sulfur filled the palace, another sound chilled us. From the windows we heard the servants getting their just reward for their disloyalty. I was glad that it was over, but I too sobbed that the women were murdered along with the suitors. I was certain that some of the women had been ravished by the suitors and had no part in the desecration of the palace. And yet they too were considered enemies of King Odysseus. The beggar banged on the door, and I opened it fearing that it was a god tricking me. He too wore the blood and filth of the suitors.

He asked, "Are there any more false wretches among you?"

"No," I said in a voice that could hardly be heard.

He looked long into my eyes and asked again, "No women who spent nights with suitors instead of among all of you?" I shook my head again, and he turned and descended the stairs. I felt like weeping with relief.

We sat long through the darkness and the rising light. I realized that living together had saved the weavers and our servants. Suddenly someone was banging on the door again. Then I recognized the voice of Medon who asked me to open the door. I forced myself to get up and give him entrance. He came with a servant who carried bread and water for us. We could smell sulfur so much stronger with the door ajar, and I thought that the palace was on fire. My weavers were close to panic.

Medon calmed our mounting fear. He said that the servants, including the few who had violated the laws of the palace, had scrubbed the furniture, walls, and stone and earthen floors, and the remaining servants were lighting sulfur to cleanse our house of the spirits of blood and waste. He said that when Lord Odysseus was finished bringing justice to those who violated his home in his absence, he would consider how to deal with the men of Ithaka who would be angry at losing their sons. After all this, he would come to me. He told me to bolt the door again. He said that servants would bring us food as soon as goats are roasted and more bread is baked. We were fortunate that with the water that I collect in large amphorae on the balcony, I could make strong tea to quiet the groaning of our bellies while we waited.

I told Eurykleia and the weavers to stay where they were. Their legs were so weak with fright that they could not stand. I made and served tea, and we all sat together quietly, grateful for our safety and our loyalty.

After my Lord awoke from his long rest, he left our room to plan the battle to defend the palace from the dead suitors' families. Three days of rolling light have passed and my Lord has not returned to me. I am told that he has been barricading the palace and preparing to fight the raging fathers and sons, brothers and uncles who seek revenge for their dead. The families of those who followed my Lord to Troy and who never returned also desire retribution for the loss of their men who were young when they left this island. I am told that they blame my Lord for surviving alone, while he did not protect their men from the terror of Hades.

How long will war continue and how long before peace comes to this island? When will I sleep again?

3. The Pleasures of Reunion

After the battle with the raging men from Ithaka and surrounding islands whose kin were suitors, after killing the fathers and sons of the warriors who followed their King to Troy and never returned, my Lord ended the battle with the help of Athene and Zeus. Then my Lord came once more to our room. He sent my weavers away with an order for Eurykleia to find rooms for them. They are not to stay with me, except during the day when they are weaving.

At first I still feared that this was not Odysseus talking to me. I believed that he might be a god in the shining light of Odysseus. Then after I accepted his mortal presence, I dreaded that he would compare me to the deities who were his lovers and would reject me in his disappointment. But gradually I came to trust in him and revel in our moments together. When he embraced me, I could hardly breathe. For so long no one had touched me. I had forgotten, except in dreams, what my skin and lips could feel. Is this the kind of freedom that I have dreamed of having over the years?

I thank Kirke and Kalypso for teaching my Lord gentleness, patience, and the generosity of love. Perhaps in youth, lust rules each man so that a woman's longing is irrelevant. Now knowledge and experience calm him, and time is endless in the arms of love. Once long ago, I was eager to have him leave for Troy, for I could see only terror and pain when I looked at him. Now, I weep to think that he will leave me again, and my bed will once again be cold and empty.

After my Lord returned from the horrors of Troy and his long years of struggle to return home, and after he rid our palace of the hated suitors, harmony settled over our land. Father Laertes, once King of Ithaka, no longer lives with the old Sikelos woman in a cave among the olive groves. He no longer lets his beard grow long or wears filthy rags to show his sorrow at his son's death. His son is alive, so gentle Laertes has returned to live in the palace and enjoy the comforts of his age and position. He has always been kind to me, and I am grateful. With my Lord's mother residing in the Lower World where she awaits her beloved son, and with the return of Father Laertes, smiles have replaced tears and tearing of the hair in the palace.

Eurykleia has resumed her service to Father Laertes, who becomes weaker with each new moon. They are now free to reveal their affection for each other and seem to feel pleasure in each other's presence. I suggested that he might enjoy sitting on the balcony each day in the soft breeze from the distant sea that reminds him of heroic times. He was pleased and now spends his days with us, Eurykleia at his side. I bring him tea and broth to give him strength, and each day he thanks me with a voice that gets softer. Yesterday he called me "Daughter," and my eyes thanked him with tears.

My weavers are in distress and are being injured. Since my Lord returned, my weavers have been sent to sleep in another part of the palace. They are no longer allowed to sleep in the weaving room, but come to me each day after their morning meal. We are all in misery. The new guards of the palace will not leave them alone when they leave my rooms. They are of different ages and many are handsome.

I told Odysseus about the situation, but he is indifferent. He says that his men need diversion.

As I have repeated so many times, I said again with submission, "My weavers are not getting the rest needed to work all day. And they come to me in the morning hurt and even beaten. Sometimes they cannot work for the pain. They require protection or our weaving will lose the tribute of the world," I told him.

"The traders want the fabrics and robes from Ithaka to sell throughout the world. Our robes have brought added fame to the legends told about our great hero Odysseus."

I dared to say to my Lord, "The names of Odysseus and his homeland of Ithaka are renowned throughout the world. Not only bravery in battle but also the trick of the wooden horse that ended the Trojan War will be part of Greek lore forever. We have heard this from the traders and travelers who stop on the shores of our island." Then after a moment I added, with humility, "My Lord, you will learn that the distinction of our weaving is also known over the seas."

Before he could scold me for a pride that challenges the gods—for only Athene, Arachne, or Kalypso could weave with such perfection—I assured him that I only repeated what the traders told me. He said that I was a gullible fool and that he would hear this for himself. He left me feeling shamed.

I understand that my Lord has discussed the matter of the weaving with Father Laertes and Mentor. Father Laertes told him that the weavers produce more when they are not hurt and beaten and that the palace has gained much wealth from what we make. The wise old man said that he learned from Eurykleia, Mentor, and merchants that I have brought honor and important trade to our palace and our island.

My Lord has given instructions that the weavers are not to be touched, on the consequence of death.

Why is life so filled with misery? Why is a woman born to be a vessel that can be broken or discarded after she is used?

My weavers came to work with smiles today. They knelt to me and kissed my hand. They have heard that I interceded for them, and for two nights they have enjoyed tranquility. They do not know this, but when my Lord goes on his next long journey, I will have my women return to the safety of our rooms.

How many of my women are already with child and will give birth within the next few moons? Only Time will tell us this sad story.

I have been thinking long on this subject. What is it in the minds of men that cause them to fight and die for the pride of one man? A wandering bard sang the song of Menelaos, who waged the Trojan War to avenge the abduction of his wife Helen by Prince Paris of Troy. To ensure the glory of their name and their manly stature, and of course to maintain the kingship that came with his marriage to Helen, Menelaos enlisted his brother Agamemnon to lead an army to Troy to recover the beautiful Helen. Despite the excuse of love and honor, many thousands of men fought and died for the arrogance, power, and pride of the House of Atreus. Why would so many men give up the breath of life to sustain such pride? Why did my Lord give up so much of our lives for this foolish purpose? No one seems to answer these questions. No one even asks these questions.

I wonder if Queen Helen went willingly with Paris, Prince of Troy, when Menelaos slept. Or had Menelaos left on a journey away from his kingdom when Paris took Helen? The legends differ. When Paris was selected to pick the most beautiful goddess on Mt. Olympos, he chose Aphrodite because she promised to give him the most exquisite woman in the world. Helen, who is connected to my family name from long ago, is known as the most beautiful woman in the world and Paris is considered to be the most handsome man.

Perhaps when Aphrodite linked the shining pair in love, they lost the power to resist. How does a woman withstand the temptation of such lust for a man or how can any man defend himself against desire for such a woman? Can the attraction created by Aphrodite defy the laws of hospitality and honor? In our longing for love and the satisfaction of desire, Aphrodite smiles and tortures us. I wish I did not think of such ideas, for the gods punish me.

The memories of my early days on Ithaka follow me, but my nights with my Lord make me comprehend husband love in a new way. I have a different understanding of Helen's passion for Paris and his desire for her. I wonder how one can give up a life approved by family and friends for stolen moments of gentleness and affection that carry us up to the blinding light of the sun. I have come to believe that I could never forsake family for my own pleasures. Cadmus was correct about the demands of responsibility and loyalty, but I can imagine the joy that a lifetime of love could have given to me.

Despite this yearning I am tortured with guilt and shame when my Lord touches me and I think of my Merchant in those glorious moments. Will I never find contentment in desire? Will fulfillment always be tied to dishonor and guilt?

My Lord was pleased with the changes made to the palace in his absence. The art of Periphetes astonished him. In all his travels he had never seen mosaic pictures, he said. He has forgotten about the palace of my Father on Sikelia, and I will not remind him of those terrible days. Both the weaving room and our bedchamber are graced with the glory of mosaic walls and floors and white lime ceilings. After looking repeatedly at our rooms, he decided that other rooms in the palace should be done with mosaics. Periphetes asked to consult with me on the colors and designs, and my Lord was surprised to learn that I am responsible for the improvements in the palace. He was impressed with the garden of fruit trees that I had planted from the small twigs that Cadmus brought on his early visits to trade. The large vegetable garden that our Chief Cook has utilized also interested him. On his long journey he tasted many new fruits and vegetables, herbs and spices that were not on Ithaka when he left, so he was happy with Ithaka's variety of foods on his return. He has ordered the Chief Cook to use them for our evening banquets. I smile.

My Lord was also shocked at the balcony garden attached to our sleeping chamber. When he left for Troy, the balcony had not been built. It was only an idea that I had suggested. Now he could hardly believe the size that exceeds several ordinary sleeping rooms, the lush colors, and the large numbers of different plants and herbs. The colors of hyacinths and alyssum and asphodel are interspersed with the buds of herbs in purples and whites and golds. He now drinks mint tea and chamomile tea.

But he most appreciated the poultices and salves that helped heal the wounds of his men after the battle to free our palace. He watched me mix rue, mugwort, and other herbs with Pramneian wine to keep his men from developing sores and losing limbs from their wounds. He observed me minister to his men and seemed proud that the plants I grow and gather in the fields helped his men to survive. When his men grew strong again, he gave credit to the gods for growing the herbs and instructing me in my work, but he speaks to me in a gentler voice—and listens to me now.

We were content for the turning of two moons. At times we told stories and laughed and enjoyed being together.

Then my Lord, hero of all warriors, announced that he would take Telemachos to find a wife. I shuddered, remembering how he found me and took me here against my will. I begged him to take a wife from Ithaka where all women desire the handsome son of the King. I recognized the signs and the frowns.

My Lord had been brooding silently, and I had watched with foreboding that the brief pleasures of laughter and song at banquets each evening in our home would soon be lost again. Contentment in the House of Odysseus does not last.

On a day of clouds and cold wind, my Lord and my glorious son set sail for the island of the Phaiakians. These are the kind and noble people who brought my Lord home after almost twenty years of trials and roaming. It is the land of Arête, their Queen, about whom Cadmus raved so many years ago and to whom I sent one of my woven garments. She sent a beautiful necklace of green stones back to me, and I still wear it.

The stories my Lord told me of the Phaiakian island and their way of life remind me of my own homeland. On that island are lush groves and gardens, harmony and justice, a King and Queen who rule with kindness and peace. My Lord told me of the opulence of their way of life, of their games instead of war, of their rule with law instead of fear.

I did not speak my thoughts, but I am certain that no girl from that island will find happiness on Ithaka. Yet my Lord plans to bring Nausikaa, daughter of Queen Arête and King Alkinoös of the Phaiakians, back to Ithaka to wed our son. She will be honored, he says.

Father Laertes is failing. No one mentions it, but I see that he is becoming weaker with each new moon. Perhaps the battles to defeat the suitors and bring accord to the island were too much for his aged body. Perhaps he already mourns his son's departure on another journey and cannot endure such emptiness. I must now finish his shroud.

Each day is again work and weaving since my Lord and my son left. The only pleasure is the occasional freedom to search outside the walls of the palace for bark and roots and the beginning of green plants. Several guards must accompany us, but they do not intrude on our lessons and laughter.

For the weeks after my Lord killed the suitors and their family members, I could not walk outside the walls for fear of revenge. After my Lord and his son called meetings to bring reconciliation to the island, the men of Ithaka accepted the idea of harmony among the families and tribes.

Gradually, I dared to walk a little further as the moon grew large and the people we met bowed in respect. Now I look to the guards to insure my liberty. We need the dyes and medicines, so I am indebted to them.

Once again the moon grows large, and I wonder how long my husband and son will be gone. Will my Lord take this opportunity to show his son the world that he knows from his ten-year journey? Will they be lost to us for many long years? Could this be the second journey that my Lord was fated to take, according to Teiresias in the Underworld?

What joy when Telemachos brought Nausikaa home to be his Queen.

After four turnings of the moon, my Lord and my son returned with their ship of forty mariners, and Nausikaa was indeed in their party. When I went to greet them, she amazed me with her beauty, youth, and humility. She smiled shyly, took my hand to kiss it, and knelt for my blessing. I would have a daughter to love, I thought. My heart was filled to overflowing as tears filled my eyes, and I raised her up to embrace her.

Then the voice of proud Telemachos disrupted the happy moment. He spoke haughtily, "Nausikaa, you will soon be Queen of Ithaka, and you are to bow to no one, not even to my mother, though she is the present Queen."

I saw her hide her tears behind her veil, and I felt my heart squeeze with pain for her and for me. There is so little respect for women on this island, and she has seen it on her first day among us. On Ithaka there had been few models of gentle and kind men for my son—few men like Mentor and Periphetes, like Cadmus and my father. He had grown up to be too much like the other men of Ithaka. I felt shame too deep to explain. I looked at my Lord who did not reprimand his swaggering son.

Instead, my Lord announced to all within hearing, "I will be leaving soon to fulfill the requirements of the gods in a new journey overland. Before I sail away to those strange and unknown lands," he said, "Telemachos will be made King of Ithaka. I plan to leave soon after our son marries Nausikaa in another ceremony for Ithakans, and the marital rooms are completed. Leaving as soon as possible will bring me back faster to the home that is part of me. Then perhaps I may rest."

Father Laertes, hero of Ithaka and surrounding islands, had no warm breath on the morning when the moon was full. He was wrapped with the cold of the Lower World. It was not a difficult or painful leaving. Softly, like the tender man he was, he walked to the

Land of the Blessed and gained entrance to the Elysian Field where he will find glory as befits him. When my Lord heard the news of his father's journey, he left the palace and disappeared while the funeral mound was being built. Mentor gave instructions. My maids and I bathed and anointed the old man in perfumed oils, and I wrapped him in the funeral robe that had taken so many difficult years to complete.

For several days the funeral field was prepared, larger and more regal than anything yet seen on Ithaka, I am told. Men from surrounding islands sailed to our ports, and people from across Ithaka walked to pay tribute to their beloved king for the long years without war while he reigned. He was buried on the side of a hill overlooking the sea that he loved. The rocks piled high over his burial mound will honor him in the endless years to come.

My sadness overwhelms me, and my Lord will not speak. I want to caress him in this time of terrible emptiness, but he will not let me near him. We look at each other across a wide and desolate sea.

In the weeks that followed her arrival, Nausikaa crept to my room whenever my Lord and my son—happy to be together at last—went hunting wild boar or deer or little hares for fur trim on royal cloaks. Fortunately, they went out almost every day, so Nausikaa came quietly to spend hours with me. She was very proficient at weaving, but we taught her more delicate weaves and different designs. She learned quickly. She said that the weavers on her homeland were very good, but we were the best she had ever seen. The weavers loved her almost as quickly as I did. We found time together to exchange stories from childhood. We laughed and cried together. She grew up happy, as I did, but her mother was warm and loving—while mine was not.

One day Nausikaa said with great admiration, "My mother Queen Arête has great power in our wide kingdom, not just in our palace. She settles all disputes among our people who have enormous respect for her wisdom and kindness and beauty. I do not boast," she said, "but our ways are different from yours on Ithaka."

In our talks over tea we learned that our mothers were different in many ways. I said, "My mother also wielded power, but she cared more for herself as she spent most of her days eating and adorning herself. Several times a year when I was a child she ordered new robes and too often had new longer belts made to reach around her waist. By the time she willingly offered me to Odysseus, her size had grown great."

At this Nausikaa said, "My mother remains young and beautiful for she walks long distances to reach the assemblies in different parts of our kingdom. Two servants follow her with mules and a royal cart so she may ride home when she wearies after the long assemblies and heated disputes that her decisions quiet. Sometimes she sleeps in a village far from home when night is descending. Her responsibility is great, as is the respect accorded to her."

I envied Nausikaa for growing up with such a mother.

Today Nausikaa and I lingered over our midday meal, and she asked how I met my Lord Odysseus. I responded carefully in order to shield her from the whole truth.

"I am told that Rumor has spread stories of my Lord Odysseus and his choice of me for his wife. One story, according to the wind, is that Odysseus was competing with many suitors for the hand of Helen, and he was very angry when he was not chosen to be her husband. So, to show that he did not care when Helen chose Menelaos, to show his indifference, Odysseus asked for my hand in marriage in front of all of Helen's suitors. He pretended that I had been his choice when he arrived, but I was a poor third choice, I suppose, behind Helen and her beautiful sister Klytemnestra. That's one story."

Nausikaa and I laughed. With the shining eyes of curiosity that I have come to recognize in her she asked, "What is the other story?"

"The second story that delights Rumor," I said, "is that Odysseus went to the meeting of Helen's suitors with the intent of choosing me instead of the most beautiful woman in the world. His wisdom and Athene told him that our fates were joined. He sat back with amusement and watched all the kings and leaders of important kingdoms and villages bow and beg to be the lucky man. Helen, her sister Klytemnestra, and I were on the dais listening to each one and admiring each man's elegant gift. I did not want any of them," Rumor said. "Then I noticed one man, not the tallest but one well muscled, standing apart and leaning against a pillar at the back of the assembly. I was intrigued. When he came to the front and asked for me, I asked who he was and accepted his offer eagerly. That is the second story."

"Which one is true?" lovely Nausikaa asked.

"Actually neither story is accurate. I was not born and raised with my distant cousins Helen and Klytemnestra on the mainland of Greece. My great-grandfather had long ago left Sparta to found a new kingdom across the Great Sea. I was born on the Great Island of Sikelia and grew up there happily. Then one day King Odysseus arrived, selected me for his wife, and my mother gave me readily over to him. My father the King objected, as did my betrothed and my three brothers and I, but my Lord was more powerful with his armed men. And so he took me to Ithaka where I have lived for over twenty rolling years. That is the true story." Nausikaa was shocked and was quiet for some moments.

"Have you been unhappy?" she finally asked with sadness in her eyes.

"I have accepted my fate," I responded with a smile. "Now it is time to resume our weaving. We shall continue our stories at another time."

She hesitated to follow me, and when I turned to her she asked,

"Does Telemachos know this history?"

"No," I answered. "And no one else is to be told these secrets that I share with you. All on Ithaka would resent me and punish me for telling you."

Nausikaa nodded her head and followed me to the weaving room. With sudden regret and fear for my trust in this child, I walked to my loom where I lost myself and my memories in the work of the moment.

Talking with Nausikaa has made me relive, in dreams and in waking, those wonderful and terrible days of long ago. My father and the father of Nausikaa were kings and equal in stature and power until Odysseus visited our island kingdom many long lifetimes ago. Then my father was made small by the threats hurled by the handsome hero without conscience. I did not tell Nausikaa all this in our ramblings.

I said instead, "Odysseus saw me, questioned people about my abilities and my virtue, and then told my father that he would have me for his wife. My father objected because of my age and because a promise had been made to the son of a ruler near our kingdom. The boy and I had been close friends since I can remember the joy of walking. My father was not yet willing to let me go so far away over the wide sea that separated our kingdom on the Great Island of Sikelia from Ithaka. But Athene was with Odysseus, and so the gods had spoken." I withheld from Nausikaa the rest of the story and my feelings about that stranger who claimed me.

Yet the story haunts me. I remember how I was told that the brow of Odysseus darkened when my father challenged his demand for me. To demonstrate his will and authority, he held his powerful bow and shot an arrow across the wide courtyard and long garden into the heart of one of our most trusted servants. I ran from the house into the courtyard to learn what new purpose my mother found for her scream that cowed us all. My father's face was a color I had never seen. I thought he was dying, and I ran to hold him.

My mother pointed at me and shrieked, "Give her to him. She is no use to us."

My father enclosed me in his arms and whispered that the gods willed that my life be payment to save my people. Odysseus was unflinching as we cried. Only then did the stranger promise to honor me by making me his queen.

I could not tell Nausikaa the whole story of how Odysseus killed my betrothed and how my mother ordered a feast for the following day to celebrate our marriage. At the banquet she proudly announced my marriage to the famous hero Odysseus with the shining curls and the bow that no other man could defeat. Like my father, I sat erect and without words as everyone raised golden goblets to me and to this stranger with the dark frown. The lamps were lit. The food that had been cooking all day was elegant and covered the tables. The wine that made my father's house the pride of many lands flowed like a stream. My father and I ate nothing and only touched our lips to the golden goblets. My mother ate and drank and laughed as she flirted with the man who would be my husband. My sister remained in her room crying.

Toward the end of the feast the doors to the hall opened and the relatives of my betrothed entered in a rage. His father's face was flaming, and he announced that he had come to avenge his son's untimely death. My brothers, who were furious with Odysseus, also stood. Odysseus stood up slowly and told the men to leave. When they refused and challenged Odysseus to fight, Odysseus raised his bow then shot an arrow through the heart of the godly father of Tyndareus. The hall was shocked into silence. My brothers moved to attack Odysseus who aimed an arrow at my youngest brother, who was the closest.

As he moved to stand between my brothers and Odysseus, my brave father said in a loud and clear voice, "Stop! There will be no more bloodshed in our kingdom."

Though I don't remember his exact words, I do recall that my father praised me for my courage and willingness to bring harmony between our people and this hero who honored me. His words almost choked his throat, but he stood tall with dignity and dared not look at me. Everyone left the Great Hall while my father knelt to hold his kinsman bleeding his life away. Sometime later, preparations were made to take the bodies of my betrothed and his father back to their own home.

After the bodies were removed and the kinsmen of Tyndareus and his father left, most of the guests returned to the Great Hall but sat silently at the feast. My mother was proud of the king who would be my husband and was delighted with the wedding that would make me queen. The gods were with Odysseus and against me.

Over his goblet of wine, Odysseus stared at me all evening, and I tried to tell myself that if the gods favored him, then they must have chosen me for good fortune. That night when cold death was removed from the Great Hall and all the guests were gone, Odysseus accompanied me to my room. He pulled the veil from my head, which was a violation of our laws. I was speechless with fright. He told me that I would be his queen and he wanted no more trouble. Then he turned and left the room without touching me further.

The next day my father, who had heard of my insult, once more asked this stranger to our ways to find another woman for his wife.

Odysseus put his hand on his sword and said menacingly, "I will kill anyone who tries to stop me. I knew the moment that I saw her that the gods had selected Penelope to be the mother of my children. It is in the stars," he said.

Fortune had turned her back on me.

Later that day I heard my brothers arguing with my father. They knew that though my father also objected to the wedding, he feared the further bloodshed that would come with challenging this stranger who had sent to his ships for his men to back him in war. My mother never asked me what I wanted. She sent servants out to announce the marriage to the villages nearest our palace and prepared a feast for all who could come. Few accepted the invitation since the story of death had spread over the island. She dressed me in the traditional red robes with gold in my hair and around my neck like a heavy chain. Then we gathered for the evening banquet that was to celebrate my marriage. I never spoke, never smiled, though I knew that everyone watched me. I was stone under my veil.

Wine was passed out freely, as is our custom, until my youngest brother Euminoös, urged on by the Wine God, challenged Odysseus. He stood up with his sword and charged Odysseus who pulled his weapon and with one simple move put the sword through my beloved brother. With blood streaming from his young body, my beautiful brother fell swiftly into the cold home of Persephone. As my mother screamed and my other two brothers rose to attack, the soldiers of Odysseus moved from the walls of the Great Room with their spears and swords drawn.

Once again my father yelled, "Stop," but in a voice that I had never heard. My brothers froze.

Odysseus, in a voice of authority, told everyone to leave.

"There will be no public marriage banquet in this land since your family does not deserve it," Odysseus said to my father. "Prepare her dowry. We leave for Ithaka tomorrow."

Later that evening, my mother came to my room and told me I was responsible for my brother's death.

"You do not appreciate the honor bestowed on our family by this great hero," she said harshly. "You have stirred up your brothers' anger and killed my son. You will never be forgiven by our people who will remember you with hatred."

She ended with a look of venom that can never be erased from my mind and said, "I ask the gods only that your life be our revenge for my golden son's death."

She turned and left the room. I never saw my mother again, but she must be happy that she has been avenged by the dark design of my fate.

I recall that my father sent emissaries to Odysseus to barter for my life. Refusing to compromise, Odysseus threatened to bring his skilled and experienced warriors to kill all our men and boys and old women, take the young women and girls, and burn our kingdom to the ground. Our men had not been trained to be warriors and did not know the ways of war. They could not stand up against the violent men of Ithaka.

I was doomed.

These memories return to me so vividly as Nausikaa and I talk of our families. I do not share all the details of this story with her. The scars are too deep to erase by talking or sharing, and I do not want to frighten her. I tell her only about the happy times in my childhood, and occasionally I mention the honor of my marriage.

I have known pleasure since Nausikaa's arrival on Ithaka. She comes to me whenever Telemachos leaves the palace with my Lord to hunt or visit other villages to bring calm between the men on this island. We talk about her condition because she is feeling sick each morning and has difficulty holding food in her stomach. Sometimes she cries for her family, but I try my best to act in her mother's place with kindness and understanding. My Lord and I eat at the evening banquet with her and my son who seems to be gentler than he was when he was growing up with men. Nausikaa is good for him, and he is proud that she is with child.

At the banquet last night I brought up the subject of justice and community. My Lord was not pleased and sat frowning. I expected the quick anger of the past. Instead, he remained quiet and allowed Nausikaa to talk about her homeland and how her mother and father kept peace by meetings of all the village leaders and by her mother's judgments in disputes.

My Lord said, "I have witnessed these proceedings on Scheria, and Telemachos and I were impressed with the results. However, having a woman giving out justice on Ithaka would not be sensible because the men of the island would not listen to a woman."

Nausikaa frowned as she considered the position of women on this island. I knew that she and I would have many discussions on this subject in the future.

I suggested with unusual temerity, "Perhaps a man could be appointed judge and hold meetings regularly to settle disputes without the warlike behavior that rules Ithaka."

"What kinds of disputes do you have in mind?" Odysseus asked with a smile too close to a sneer.

Undeterred, I listed several, "I was thinking of arguments over the ownership of women and slaves, over land borders, over animals that strayed, over children without parents, to mention only four examples."

My Lord and son raised their eyebrows as I talked and were surprised that I knew of such things. I wanted to tell them that though I was imprisoned in my rooms for many years, my eyes and ears were not closed when I was allowed to walk the palace grounds to inspect the dyeing of yarns and storage facilities or to gather plants and roots in the fields. Then I heard guards and maids talking quietly about quarrels and the bloodshed that resulted from such arguments. On our gathering expeditions I saw the hovels in which people lived, and I heard the loud arguments as we tried to avoid the small settlements. But I said nothing of these things to my Lord.

He and Telemachos agreed to speak more on the subject and make some decisions before my Lord left for his next journey.

I thank Kalypso, Kirke, Queen Arête, and all the women who softened my Lord on his long journey. I look at him with new respect.

Today there was a meeting of many village leaders in our Great Hall. There must have been at least one hundred men and their sons sitting on mats on the floor while my Lord the King and Telemachos the Prince presided over the assembly. Nausikaa and I sat outside the door and listened. My Lord told about the governing body and the accord enjoyed by the Phaiakians on Scheria. He spoke of the meetings and how they were conducted and how the men learned to respect other men's ideas and rights.

My Lord said, "There were laws decided by the assembly, and all men promised to abide by those laws. These are the ways of the most advanced people in the world," he assured the men listening.

"The ways of Ithaka must be changed in the future if the island is to become admired across the sea. Otherwise, if all men do not work together for the benefit of all, warriors from abroad will overrun the island and Ithakan men will continue to be wounded, to lose limbs or eyes, or to be hurled into the Underworld by angry neighbors."

Someone yelled out, "King Odysseus brought violence when he returned home, but now he talks with big words about law and justice."

My Lord said without anger, "Because there were no civil laws of behavior and hospitality on our island, my home was overrun by those who violated the gods' decrees, insulted guests, and cruelly misused my family and servants. And men across the island allowed this to happen to my family and my home. My Queen and her weavers were required to stay locked in their rooms for their safety, and this went on for years. Who would want these vile things to happen to your families and to your homes? In order to bring order to my home and island, I was required to punish those men as examples for the future." The men began to mumble to each other.

My Lord went on, "My son Telemachos will soon assume my position as King on Ithaka. He has been seasoned and tested by his travels and by our battles to defend our home. You can be proud of his heroism and fearlessness. The gods have chosen him to be your leader in the future. His choice, like mine, is for peace not war. We desire that your sons be brought up in a world of laws, of mutual assistance, and of respect among all men. With your help today, we want to make the rules that all will follow in the future.

"We want you to agree to accept one wise and respected man who will settle all disputes with good judgment and honor. And we want you to agree to a meeting monthly when the moon is full so that all parts of the island will be represented to follow the decrees made by this body of noble men. I believe that my son is ready to become leader of Ithaka. However, until Telemachos is old enough to command your allegiance and seasoned enough to preside, Mentor the Wise will be judge. You will assist him and he will assist you in all problems in the future.

"But first, let us eat richly and drink lightly before we get to work. Later, I will explain how we can bring organization and riches to our island."

At that point, Nausikaa and I went up to our weavers with the gladness that comes from honoring our Lords.

My Lord planned to leave on his journey at the turning of the moon, but the death of Father Laertes has taken energy from this man of action. Then organizing the men of Ithaka has not been an easy task. He and Mentor and Telemachos work night and day with small groups of men who quarrel among themselves. My Lord and my son watch the men get drunk on our wine. My Lord said their understanding of the assembly must be accomplished before he leaves so that Telemachos and Mentor can keep us safe. Though he has not said this aloud, I think that he may also want to see his first grandson born.

I feel protected now that my Lord is here on Ithaka. My weavers and I gather herbs and roots, bark and kermes beetles without the need of guards. Nausikaa has been learning about these things and walking has been good for her condition. She is almost ready for her visit from the Goddess Eileithyia. We pray to her and to Paiëon, the god of medicine, for an easy way for my lovely Nausikaa.

I called for Hippotho, the birthing woman, because it is close to Nausikaa's time. My lovely daughter asked me to stay with her, and I assured her that I would assist Hippotho. I suggested to Telemachos that he might want to go hunting when she began to wail, as his father did when my time came. He refused. He said that he must be near her if he is needed. I am proud that he has grown to protect and love this dear girl who is his wife.

The palace is in celebration. A boy was born to Nausikaa, and Telemachos showed great self-importance. He and my Lord celebrated long into the night until they and all of their friends took pleasure in the difficulty of walking to bed. Nausikaa stayed in our bedchamber with me, and after the long hours of pain she slept deeply until the following day. A milk mother came to feed the baby boy until Nausikaa has her own milk. Nausikaa refused the mother and says that she will feed her babies at her own breast. She says that she will be in charge of caring for her own babies. That is not the practice of the leading families on Ithaka, so I shall be interested to see how she manages to do what she wants.

Having the baby here reminds me of Naela and her lovely baby girl who has grown up with us. I remember how the baby was to be taken from Naela also and how Naela pulled out her hair and screamed. Eurykleia was sent up to take the baby to be raised by the serving women. Naela knew what that would mean for this girl's future, and I could not let that happen. I asked to see Lord Mentor, whose wisdom often served me well. We talked outside the door at the top of the stairs.

I said, "Naela is one of my best weavers and her sadness will take all life out of her fingers. Just thinking of losing her child has drained all energy from her. She now sits in a corner holding the baby all day," I said, "and I lose her weaving skills that bring so much wealth to Ithaka."

He responded, "The baby would take time from her weaving anyway."

What he said made sense, but I explained, "Though she cannot weave while she is feeding the baby, she can spin yarn. We always need yarn from wool and stem fibers, so our weavers take turns spinning after they eat their meals and take a rest for a short period. We never stop working," I said, "and we will teach the child to be a spinner and then a weaver at a very young age if she is left with us. If Naela's grief at the loss of her child takes all vigor from her hands, she will be useless to me, as she is now."

I suggested that he look into the weaving room to see her in the corner.

It was a pathetic sight. Naela was holding the baby in her arms and singing a song softly with the tears rolling down her face and wetting her garment and the baby's head.

Lord Mentor asked, "Has her mind gone to the realm of Chaos? Will she recover and be useful in the future?"

"Her mind is not diseased," I said. "She is a mother and all mothers feel as she does. Taking her baby will break her heart and her spirit."

He looked at me carefully for some moments and seemed to be perplexed, but he had come to trust my words. He promised to do what he could and walked slowly down the stairs.

Eurykleia came to the weaving room after the sun had begun to descend and told me that Naela could keep her baby with us only if she gets better and we are not delayed in our work. When Naela heard of the decision by Telemachos, she knelt and kissed my hand then rose and kissed my cheek. All of the weavers smiled widely with Naela, and we set up a tiny bed next to her loom in the space where she unrolled her bed mat each night. I took a piece of fabric and folded it to make a sling for the baby to sleep on her back while she weaves. She now works harder than ever before.

Remembering Naela, I spoke to Mentor on behalf of Nausikaa. I reminded him of Naela's situation and how similar it was to Nausikaa and her baby. I did not remind him of my own situation. Wise Mentor carried my meaning to my Lord and Telemachos. Now Nausikaa weaves with joy as she feels the warmth from her baby envelop her all day. Her nurse keeps the baby clean, and I hold him to feel the softness and to smell his baby skin.

Why could I not have done all that for my boy? My Lord's mother took him from me for the future heroism of Ithaka, she said. But I know that she wanted him for herself. I knew even then that she needed to be in charge and rule the palace, including me, the useless wife of her son.

I try to put bitterness out of my heart and concentrate on the joy of Nausikaa's baby boy. It is difficult.

I am shamed by my weakness.

Baby Laertes comes each day with Nausikaa, and I watch to see what a mother is supposed to be. I believe that Eurykleia expected to care for this child, as she did for Odysseus and Telemachos. But she is older now and her sadness over the death of Father Laertes has taken over her life. She would be unable to summon the energy needed for an infant. But she is happy with the child's name, which Odysseus requested. She stays with us in the weaving room and helps to keep the baby clean and to entertain him, though he can't see very much yet. He will be smiling soon and we will all enjoy that.

I ignore my Lord's preparations for his coming journey. I don't want to see it. Nights are without the searing pain of the past, and the warmth of his strong body comforts me. I enjoy my days of freedom in the fields, and banquets bring great pleasure. I have met a few wives of village leaders and enjoy them but will not see them again after my Lord sails away. So much I will lose by his leaving.

Why does my life depend on my Lord's fate? Does Justice close her eyes to my condition?

PART FOUR

1. The House of Telemachos

My Lord left this morning for his journey, as the Gods decree, to a new land that does not know the sea. I am alone again. Nausikaa held me in her arms, and I was grateful, but I do not know how Telemachos will treat me. He is now King of Ithaka and Nausikaa is Queen. I am again only head of the weavers and the strange woman who collects plants. How long before I lose that small value? Will my son allow me to remain in my Lord's bedchamber with my garden? I pray every night to my Goddess and to Athene and Hera.

When Telemachos is not hunting or pillaging on the shores of nearby islands, he wants Nausikaa with him. She does not weave with us very often now. She has a loom in a corner of the Great Room and weaves while she keeps her husband calm. I miss her. We all miss her and the baby.

I have learned not to appear too happy when Nausikaa is with us in the weaving room or on our gathering days. I do not want to incur the divine anger of Nemesis who may be jealous of our pleasure and punish me. Nausikaa is bright and cheerful most of the time, but she must please Telemachos who is too much like his father with quick anger.

The first time she saw my panels she was so excited. She wanted to know all about the story that each panel told.

Telemachos never saw the panels until they were finished, and then he would have been glad to sell them. Otherwise, he is indifferent to what I do, and he rarely visits me. For so many reasons I am deeply grateful for Nausikaa and all that she brings to my days.

Today Nausikaa and I talked long about her plans to transform the palace into a place of beauty. Since she first saw my mosaics after her arrival, she has been delighted with the weaving room, my bedchamber, and the bedchamber that Periphetes was transforming for her and my son. We discussed possibilities for the Great Room. She has asked Telemachos to speak to Periphetes about making the Great Room light and lovely. Though she had never seen mosaics until she came to Ithaka, she grew up with the arts surrounding her. She especially remembers with fondness the wondrous woven tapestries that graced the walls of the palace on Scheria. I suspect that she looks at the walls of stone here on Ithaka with the same desolation that I felt for so many years.

When they spoke to Periphetes, they called me to their meeting to plan the designs and colors for the Great Room. Periphetes has summoned the divinities of art and beauty to please his young Queen, and Telemachos has given him four new workers whom he must train to prepare walls and floors and to create mosaics. Periphetes also has two workers in the potters' shed to make the mosaic pieces. Nausikaa is elated and watches him work, even as we all did in the weaving room. Now she walks with the lightness that she had when she arrived on Ithaka.

It is remarkable what beauty can do for the spirit within us.

Nausikaa is again growing large with child. I have feelings that twist my heart. I long for a baby to hold again, but I fear the future for another girl or boy on Ithaka. The palace has improved since the suitors ruled us, but I never feel completely liberated. I am always dependent on someone else's decisions or approval. I do what I have to do and try to enjoy the moments of love with

Nausikaa and baby Laertes. I make her my herbal teas and cook special stews for them when my son is on hunting trips. I also have fresh fish, cleaned and prepared for cooking, delivered to my room. They are delicious and healthy. Even the weavers and maids have come to like the savory fish stews, though my son insists that they should be served only to the peasants.

Nausikaa says that I am like a mother to her and have made her life rich on Ithaka. I often wonder why life cannot be this way for all women. Love is so much more wondrous than hate and the strife of Eris.

Today may be the last time that Nausikaa and Laertes can share our gathering days, for she will be confined until some time after the baby comes. She wears huge robes to hide her belly, but she says she feels large and awkward. She has not the breath to walk far, and she cannot carry the large baskets even when we put them down and collect them on our way back to the palace. Yet just to have her and Laertes with us is worth collecting fewer plants and berries, no matter how important the herbs and dyes are to me.

Sometimes we pass the homes of peasants, and we see how whole families live in one room. Usually the people live in a small clearing with about five or six huts close together so that the men can work together to herd the goats or sheep, and the women can farm their tiny gardens, share gossip, and commiserate when they are beaten and have babies. Sometimes one hut stands alone in the hills, and then the woman must feel terribly deserted and alone when the husband is out herding, or working in the fields for a village leader, or being free to walk the hills and mountains. Always the woman stays at home.

Today we happened upon a small one-room hut in a clearing in some heavy woods. We had been looking for mushrooms. There were several dirty, listless children wearing rags and sitting near the door. I asked the oldest girl if I could speak to her mother. I had a feeling in my chest that something was wrong.

The girl said in a halting and shy manner, "Mau sleep. Da gone." She was holding a naked infant, one of the eight children who all live in one room with the parents.

I said as gently as I could, "I would like to see your mother. If she is ailing, perhaps one of my herb teas could help her." I made signs to indicate that I wanted to enter the hut. In confusion the girl led me through the door into a depth of squalor that I have never imagined.

Pale and bone thin, the poor woman was inside the stone hut. She was lying on one of the stone shelves that line the three walls. Except for the side with the door, each wall had two shelves built into the wall and used as beds with rough ragged blankets to ease the hardness of the stone. In the center of the tiny room there was a small fire on stones that held a large pot cooking something that smelled vile. There were no windows. We had to be careful not to set our robes on fire because there was very little room to move around in that space. The children found movement easier since they wore so little clothing. Even the girls who were almost women wore little to cover themselves.

When I examined the woman named Zeila, I saw the lumps on her breast and throat and knew that her illness was beyond my skills. Her pain was intense, and I felt that I might ease her suffering.

Between her moans, I said softly, "I am Lady Penelope of the house of Odysseus. I will bring you some herbs for tea to ease your pain. I will show your daughter how to brew the tea and how to use it."

I could hardly hear her when she asked, "Food for my children?"

"I will give them some food," I promised.

She took my hand and with a sob she kissed it and then closed her eyes. She might have shed tears if she had the strength to do so. Then we left the fetid air of the hovel. There would be no more gathering today.

When I could speak again, I asked Nausikaa to return with Laertes to the palace. I was concerned that they might become ill from the dirt and stench in the clearing or from the illnesses carried by each child. All the children had runny eyes or noses, puss oozing from sores or eyes, or coughs that would challenge my herbs.

With Nausikaa, I sent Naela and one of my maids to get the mixture of poppies, lotus, and other herbs that I kept in a dark blue bag. Each herb mixture has a different color bag so they cannot be mixed up. I asked Naela to collect blankets from the weaving room, some bread, cheese, goat's milk, grains, and dried fruit from the kitchen, some soap that we use for bathing, and two vessels to carry water and heat the tea.

"Please return as soon as possible," I said to Naela.

Nausikaa said, "I will see to it." Tears filled her eyes.

After they left, I sent another maid with two of the children to get water from the nearest stream. I realized that the family had only one bowl for water. I could not imagine how they survived with so little water, even if they only used it for drinking and cooking. I also collected any rags that I could find, so they could rinse them in the stream.

It was some time before they all returned from their errands. I made the tea and gave clear instructions to the eldest daughter, who was probably about twelve years old—though small for her age—and very fearful of administering the tea. I showed her how and gave her mother some of the mixture in a cup that was very dirty. Her pain must have been excruciating, for she moaned or cried out constantly. The tea soothed the woman, and soon she was sleeping softly. As she slept, I stripped her of her filthy rags, washed her burning skin in cold water from the stream, and wrapped her in a fresh garment. I put another folded blanket under her for softness. She weighed so little that I could move her easily.

Naela and the servants attended to the children who were ravenous. They tore at the bread and cheese and drank the milk. Naela had to show them how to drink slowly so they would not become ill with the rich milk. The baby, who hardly moved, had to be fed carefully with drops of watered milk. I thought of bringing the baby back with me to the palace, but I have no right to take a child from his mother without her permission, no matter that she is too ill to speak or nurse the baby.

We cooked the grains with fruit and left enough food for two days, and I said to the children as we left, "I will return in two suns. Be kind to your mother." As they watched me go, I felt choked by guilt and despair for them.

As we walked away from Zeila's hovel, I realized that I too have lived in a room for many years. But I began to compare her one-room hut with my room, now so lovely with the mosaics and the garden and the weavers who bring joy instead of burdens to me. I tried to put the pictures of that family from my mind as I smelled the salt breeze and the flowers and leaves that I love so much. I remembered the days when we had our lunch next to a small brook that sang its bubbling songs to us, the day Telemachos walked into the water and was delighted to see a butterfly. He scooped up the fresh water and laughed as he sprinkled all of us. The spirits of my sister and my baby son are with me on such days, and I feel almost content. In my long years of imprisonment, at least I have had some few days of freedom, I thought. And I have known beauty and enjoyed memories of treasured moments.

Zeila, I am certain, never had such gifts in her shortened life. And she never had a room that compared to my lovely rooms and garden. I realize that Fortune has given me so much more than these poor, miserable, burdened woman and children could ever dream. For the first time since coming to Ithaka, I thank the gods for my fate that could have been so much worse.

It had been two days since we saw Zeila, and I took Naela and three maids to visit this sad woman and her family again. Though Nausikaa wanted to come with us, I did not want her near the children's illnesses. Instead of gathering, as I had originally planned for the day, we brought food and milk, large jars for water, and woven garments for the children. As we walked into the clearing, the children ran to us, surrounding us and asking for food. While Naela started to feed the children, I went directly to see how Zeila was feeling.

The tea had eased Zeila's terrible suffering, but she was too weak to speak or move. I recognized the signs of Thanatos hovering over her. We fed the children and sent them with the maids to the distant spring for water. I bathed Zeila again and dressed her in a clean robe that I had brought for her. With the aid of the poppy tea, she moved gently into the realm of cold where all pain ends. Naela watched all that I did that day, and when she saw this mother of eight frightened children breathe her last breath, my weaver sobbed with the whole family. I love Naela for her gentle heart and the generosity to feel for these children and their needs.

Naela asked, "Lady, will we leave these children alone in the woods without food or care? Look at them. They live in dirt, their eyes run with tears and puss, and their coughing needs your teas if they are to survive."

I said, "I know. We shall bring them home with us. With food and care they will grow strong and healthy. If the father objects, he may come to the palace for his family and account to the King for their starvation and illness." Our eyes smiled at each other.

We have never seen this father whose children are in dire need of his help and support. Nausikaa and I fear that he may have abandoned his family.

The children's circumstances were appalling. The filth was beyond anything I had ever thought possible. They were clearly starving. There was not a morsel of food in the house, except for what I had brought. I asked about their father, but they said that they had not seen him for many suns. They had been eating grasses and berries, and they were all very weak and fearful. I sent my maids to the palace for guards and wagons to carry the children back with us. It was not a far distance for us to walk, but they were not strong enough to walk to the palace. I also instructed the maids to get more garments to cover the children. What they had been wearing when we first met them was useless and should be burned.

Instead of several guards, it was my son who arrived with Medon and one of the maids. He was furious.

"Why are you bringing these curs to our palace?" he asked. "We do not have responsibility for them. That is their parents' problem."

I explained, "Today their mother moved to the home of Persephone, and their father has abandoned them."

"That matters not to me," he said in anger. "We cannot feed all weak and dying children on Ithaka. Am I to support all the poor on this island? Let them join their mother who will be pleased to share them with Persephone."

In a soft but unyielding voice I said, "We cannot leave them here like this. Think of your own sons and how you would want someone kind to care for them if you and Nausikaa were lost to the world. I cannot leave them."

Before he could respond with the rage that his face revealed I said, "You have given my time and energy to your guards when they were close to the door of Hades upon the return from your sacking. I could have been weaving and earning wealth for you, as I do every day of every season. Instead, I treated their illnesses, and my herbs cured their wounds. Now I ask that you allow me to put some time and energy into these children who can grow strong and become servants and weavers in the palace. I will feed them with my stews that cost you nothing to provide to my weavers and to me."

Without giving him time to respond, I went on, "I have given my life to you and to your palace without asking anything in return. Now I ask to take these children back with me. They can sleep on the floor of my bedchamber and in my garden until they are ready to be weavers and servants. Some of the women in the palace would appreciate the opportunity to have children of their own if the babies survive and become strong enough to walk and run.

They will help the servants and slaves who have been denied families of their own. When the boys grow up, they can be hunters and help you. The Gods gave them birth. Now give them life. I ask it of you, and the Gods expect it of a great man."

As he turned and walked away, he said in a booming voice, "Let weaving come first in your time and work. I will be watching." He mounted his cart and bellowed to his guards, "See to it. Whatever she asks." He rode away and left Medon to assist us.

I smiled at Naela who kept her head lowered until Telemachos was out of sight. Then I said to Medon, "Attend to whatever is worth taking in the hut. When we all leave together, set fire to the inside of the hovel to make a pyre for their mother who lies cold and without breath inside."

Kind Medon said, "Yes, Lady. I will see to it all." Then he sent one of the guards back to the palace to secure more assistance as well as two large wagons and oxen.

My servants, Naela, three guards, and I took the children to the stream, bathed them with my strong soap, scrubbed their heads, cut their long wild hair, applied salve to their sores, and put new robes around each child. The youngest children were too weak and tired to walk back to their hut, so we carried them.

Some time later, a contingent of guards and wagons came to help us return to the palace. I took the children into the hovel to say goodbye to their mother. Without tears, each one stared at her with bewilderment. When that part of the funeral ritual was completed, we all stood outside to make our prayers heard. I asked the Gods to make her way easy on the journey to the home of Persephone and Hades.

On our way back to the palace, without the strength to observe or question what they had never seen, they all fell asleep with the comfort of full bellies and soft robes.

When we were out of sight of the clearing, the guards set fire to the stone house, and Zeila joined the spirits that now reside in the Field of Asphodel. I must believe that it is a better place than she has known in the Upper World.

It was late in the day when the children arrived at the palace, amid stares of confusion by our servants and slaves. I worked with Naela and Eurykleia to set up the sleeping arrangements for the children. I arranged for a milk woman to feed the baby until he is ready to eat soft food. She sleeps with the weavers so that she is available throughout the night. I told the weavers that I do not want them to be kept awake all night by a crying baby, but they simply smiled. They are happy to have the children with us.

The first few days the children were so weak that they ate little and hardly moved from the mats and soft blankets that comforted them. Now they eat eagerly and move around the rooms and garden. We are teaching them how to use the facilities and how to keep clean. In the past they had just squatted wherever they were, like animals, but now they are required to use the seats and to control their habits. They are sweet and want to please us, so they will learn quickly. Nights are the most difficult times. When they dream and wet themselves, the maids have much washing to do. But my maids are kind and patient and do not complain. They do not want my son to hear of the extra work, or the children would be forced to leave.

I have heard several of the children crying in the night. I hold them in my arms and sing softly until they sleep again. They miss their mother and their home, I am sure, despite the poverty and hunger that had been their lot.

I spent the night with Nausikaa as she labored to bring forth a new life. The birthing woman was called, and we all worked through the dark and the morning light to lessen her pain. We could do nothing to take the child sooner, and I felt the terror of losing her. It is a boy. He is called Alkinoös, named after Nausikaa's father. He is beautiful, and I already feel love in my heart for him.

Nausikaa is sleeping in my bed. I will sleep on mats on the floor next to the bed to be available to her if she needs me. We moved the older children to the balcony among the flowers and plants. They appear to love my garden.

I am exhausted.

Telemachos agreed to let Nausikaa stay in my room for several days until she is feeling better. She is very weak, and she needs care. Though I sleep on a soft mat and blankets on the floor next to the bed, I am happy to have her with me.

The children are fearful that she will be taken to Hades, as their mother was, though I reassure them that she will be strong and healthy soon. They whisper and try to stay quiet so they will not disturb her. It is touching to see their kindness. They are now clean, their sores and other ailments have improved enormously, and they are already starting to gain strength and weight. They even giggle now and then. Nausikaa smiles with me to see the change in them.

It was terrible. Telemachos sent Eurykleia to take the baby to the feeding woman. When Eurykleia told him that Nausikaa would not give up the baby, Telemachos thundered into my bed chamber, anger painting his face red.

"On Ithaka the Queen does not feed her own sons," he said to Nausikaa and to me. "The men have told me so. I am shamed that my woman did not have a feeding woman for Laertes. Now I will do it the right way, and I will see to it," he bellowed.

Nausikaa began to wail. The tears wet her cheeks and her gown.

With controlled fury I confronted my son and said, "Your wife grew up with different ways. The Queen on her island fed her own babies because her milk was richer than that of serving women."

I do not believe this, but I pray that the gods will forgive my lies.

I continued my argument, "The babies of Telemachos deserve the best that the gods can offer. Beautiful Nausikaa, daughter of godlike Alkinoös and Arête, was given to you by the great hero Odysseus and must be beloved by the gods. Therefore, she alone must give sustenance to your babies. Look at Laertes. How strong and healthy are his body and mind. If you defy the gods and the lessons that her gods taught to her," I told him, "terrible grief will descend on our house."

I said all this with subservience but with firmness. We talked at the top of the stairs while Nausikaa still sobbed in my bed. Telemachos was angry, his face flaming, and he said that he would think on it. He turned and walked down the stairs with fury in his shoulders. He was put in a position to choose between the stories of his ignorant men and the feelings of his wife. On Ithaka men care little for the feelings of women. And my son seems to learn nothing from experience as he repeats over and over the same insensitivities.

The children were frightened by my son's anger and by Nausikaa's tears. They hid in the garden. When I went out to them, several were crying, and the older children were holding the little ones.

Young Zeila asked, "Will man beat woman?"

I reassured them that such things do not happen in our home. I hope I told them the truth.

Today Telemachos agreed to have Nausikaa keep their son Alkinoös at her breast. But she must go back to their room. That is his Queen's responsibility, he says. It is clear to me that he must show his dominance over his woman or he will lose face with his men. I hope he lets her heal.

One of the guards fell from the top of the wall and ripped his leg in two places. He was bleeding from his arms and elbows also. Telemachos came for me and told me that his favored guard was ready to breathe his last, but he asked if I could make his leaving easier. Nausikaa had suggested that I might do that. I went to see the man. It was Ormenos, the soldier who relinquished Agape and Medon to me long years ago. He looked at me with fear, perhaps thinking that I would harm him in revenge for his hurting the child. I smiled and assured him that I would do what I could to help him. I asked my son to cut off his clothes so that I could examine him. My son was horrified that I would see a naked man. I wanted to laugh at his foolishness, but instead I told him to cover the man's body so that I could go on with my work. While they removed his clothes, I made some tea to relieve his terrible pain.

I believe that the guard had several bones broken in his chest and a broken bone in his thigh. I called the ironsmith who has the strength to pull the leg bone apart in order to reconnect the two sections. Then I wrapped the leg to an iron bar to hold the broken bone straight. I went up to my room to get some cloths to tie around his chest tightly and a needle and rabbit gut to hold the skin together. My maids carried many bowls of warm water and some soap to bathe the man. After his whole body was clean, I bathed the wounds carefully and put salve on the wounds before sewing them up and stopping the bleeding. His screams were ghastly but gradually my tea soothed him, and he began to moan softly as he slept.

After all this was done and he was wrapped in a fresh blanket, my son and his men carried him carefully on a wooden slab to a room off the courtyard. There Nausikaa and I could visit and selected servants could also attend to him. He became very hot with fever in the nighttime, and we took turns bathing him with cold water. I fed him special herb tea with lemons for several days until he opened his eyes and spoke without raving. I knew then that he would recover. He is aged, but time will mend his bones together, and he will walk again. My son, who had believed that I was delaying his appointment with Hades and had wasted time with all our attentions to Ormenos, knelt and kissed the hem of my gown and thanked me for saving his warrior friend.

For the last several weeks every moment of each day has been filled with weaving, helping Nausikaa and Ormenos, and bathing and feeding and ministering to Zeila's children. We had to feed them gradually with broths and teas, soft bread and boiled grain before making stews that would help them grow strong. I also asked the head goatherd to bring to me any milk that could be kept from making the cheese and curds necessary for the household. The weavers and I have also been giving our milk to the children. The children's sores have healed, their eyes are brighter, and they show signs of feeling better, of getting energy, and of wanting to speak to us. I made marks on the stone wall of the balcony over the Great Room to show their heights and how they would grow. These marks were set beside the marks for Telemachos and Medon as they grew tall and strong. The children who were old enough to understand were pleased at the idea.

Since the first night, when their sleep was restless and full of fear, the younger children have slept with the weavers who made room for them on their pallets. The songs of the lyre, the warmth of woman arms, and the softness of their voices soothed the little ones to sleep. The three older girls sleep on pallets in my room, and the two older boys now sleep with Thon, my boy helper, on pallets on the balcony. If their giggling is any indication of their pleasure, they love being in the garden.

The children no longer cry in their sleep with the passing of only two full moons. I feared for the starving infant, who was too lethargic even to cry, but he has been growing and his arms and legs are now waving around and showing energy and strength. His voice is louder than we care to hear, and he is actually smiling at us.

The children knew very few words when they arrived at the palace, so we have been talking to them constantly so they would learn quickly. They are now speaking in a language that we can all comprehend. They are so proud. We also gave them names because some of them did not have names, or at least answered to sounds that we did not understand. To the eldest, we gave the name of Zeila, like her mother. She wept with gratitude. The next girl attached herself to Nausikaa, so we named her Nausikeia. They were all pleased to have their own names.

As the six older children became stronger, they all took on their responsibilities. The girls sit with the weavers who patiently explain to them the art of weaving. The girls are delighted to "help" with the weaving. They are now learning how to spin and enjoy sitting with the weavers all day since I will not allow the girls to go out of the weaving room. The young boys follow Thon as he carries materials and goes on his errands throughout the palace. The boys show great importance in their work of carrying a ball of yarn or something else that Thon is delivering. I understand that these boys have become favorites among the maids and workers, and also Mentor, who greet them and give them treats.

The children are really quite sweet in their willingness to learn and to please us. They have learned to bathe and keep their bodies and teeth clean. Except for the youngest, they all use the grownup facilities instead of soiling or wetting wherever they are standing. They have learned the names of colors, and each has shown a preference for a particular color. Each morning the girls are delighted when we tie a bright piece of yarn in their hair. It is like giving them a gift.

These children are wonderful and have brought immense joy to our rooms. They are so grateful for their new life and want only to learn everything. I asked Pheidopos, who has aged greatly but is still the Chief Potter for the palace, to make bowls and spoons for each of them, and they were thrilled to receive them. In fact, they wanted to sleep with the bowls and spoons and gave them up only when we showed them the shelf that keeps their new gifts safe. The next morning we all smiled when we found one of the smaller boys sleeping below the shelf in order to protect their treasure.

Thon and the older boys of about seven and eight—they do not know their birth years—watch the little ones and have been remarkably successful in keeping the youngest from breaking my plants in the garden. They all learned quickly, even the smallest ones, not to pick the herbs and flowers without permission. When I let them water the plants or pick a leaf that I need for tea, they laugh with joy. They love the taste of the chamomile tea with honey that I give them when they do their chores well, which is every day. They had had so little in their lives that everything gives them pleasure. The weavers are happy to have them about, and they share their bread and stews and fruit with the children who cannot get enough of everything delicious. In just three full moons, they are stronger and growing.

I will be sorry to place them in the care of other women, as I promised my son I would do. One little boy of about two years of age I will particularly miss. He has become attached to me and follows me everywhere. We named him Pheres. He is too young to follow Thon throughout the palace, so he stays in the weaving rooms. I tell him the names of everything, and he learns quickly. He is beautiful, like the son I might have had if he remained in my care. I remind myself over and over that this boy too will be taken so I must not love him too much. But for now, I admit that I feel delight when he sits on my lap and enjoys my arms holding him and my songs soothing him.

We all take pleasure in their hugs and kisses, their bright eyes, and their excitement in learning. While they require work and time, it is a satisfaction for all of us to hear their laughter. Perhaps I can keep the three girls with my weavers, for some of the women are aging and need help.

I have so little time to write. I must weave at night to make up for the time spent with the children. Yet they bring so much laughter to our lives. Their questions, their answers to our questions, their pronunciation of words—all remind us of how new the world is to a child. It makes me feel young to see through their eyes.

It is amusing to all of us, but especially to Nausikaa, to see my grandson line up with the other children who can hardly wait for their share of the stews of rabbit or fish and vegetables. With their bowls full, they all sit down in my garden to eat and wipe their bowls clean with their bread, as the grown people do. Then they all wash their bowls and spoons, which they carefully place on their shelf to keep them safe. They play together after their midday meal. When it is time to work, my grandson goes off to practice being a warrior and the other boys fetch and carry. It is sad to me that as my grandsons grow up, they will be separated from these sweet children who are too poor to associate with royalty throughout their lives. My grandsons would learn much from these children.

Another boy has been born to my son Telemachos. This third baby is Ikarios, named after my father. Nausikaa begged Telemachos to grant me this gift, and I am grateful. The men in the palace are still celebrating after this third baby boy cried into the world. I do not celebrate. Nausikaa is not well. Three babies born within three years have been difficult for her. She is very weak.

I worry, but Telemachos requires that his Queen return to his bed before she is strong enough to care for herself and her baby. He does not understand. He looks at the peasants in their hovels and sees that women have ten or twelve children all living in one room. He thinks that if these poor women without the help of servants can do this, then his god-like Queen can certainly be a stronger model for his people. He does not realize that those women suffer miserably and work until they are glad to enter the cold Realm of the Dead before their time, while their children grow up sick and weak. Or they die at a young age. We have such children among us, yet he does not remember their earlier misery. This is not what life should be.

Telemachos came to my room and told Nausikaa that he does not take another woman or a boy, so he expects his wife to serve him when he comes to her bed—too often drunk with wine, I must say. I try to think what I can do to help her, but anything I say would only make the situation worse for her and we would both be punished. I feel disgraced by my son, the King of Ithaka.

I had hoped that Telemachos would feel happy about his life when he earned the respect of his people and when he had sons to make him proud. I no longer hold that hope. He is clearly the head of Ithaka and surrounding islands and enjoys the deference of his people. Moreover, his young sons look to him as though he were a god. He enjoys Nausikaa's company and her dignity and beauty as his Queen. Yet nothing seems to make him satisfied.

Is it his fate to feel the loss of his absent father forever or to desire a home and love while longing for adventures that have defined his father's greatness? Will my son never find peace and contentment despite the gifts that the gods have given to him?

Nausikaa is with child again, and she can hardly raise herself out of bed. I asked Telemachos to allow me to bring my teas to her and to bring the stew that my maidservant now makes for my weavers. I have no time to cook. I promised him that while I visit her I would continue weaving in their room and would use Nausikaa's loom since she is too weak to use it herself. I assured him that my weavers would continue to work hard by themselves. I would get them started each day, and Naela would be in charge while they continue on their own.

"If there are problems," I assured him, "they could call for me."

I now divide my time between Nausikaa, the weavers, and the children. Nausikaa has signs of redness and swelling and needs attention and salves to cure her or the baby may not breathe the air of the upper world. Telemachos seems worried, so I have his permission to attend her. She kissed my hand, apparently relieved to know that I will be with her, at least for a good part of each day.

Nausikaa is getting better, and my weavers are happy and reassured to see her. Occasionally, Medon helps her to climb the stairs, and she sits in my garden with the Sun God's rays touching her gently while I weave nearby. The sun and sea and lemon tea with honey soothe her even as she grows larger with each new moon. She has always been skilled with the spindle, so she is not idle. Though she gets fatigued easily, she still works her spindle each day when she is with us. I point that out to my son.

My grandsons come to visit with her, so I see them each day that she is here with me. I explain what the plants do and why they are treasures to keep. Only little Ikarios is delighted to hear about herbs and flowers and the petrels that fly over the sea and the palace. Only he wants to learn what I care about, but at least one of the boys is interested. He too will grow to want only bows and arrows and javelins, I am sure. But for now, at the age of almost two years, he speaks the words that name the plants and follows me around the garden. The way Pheres did. It is a wonderful age, and I do enjoy him.

I could not write about the loss of Zeila's children until now. Some time ago, my son informed me that it was time to leave the weaving rooms to the weavers. The children would have to go. He gave me permission to keep the three girls, who are the oldest and will be weavers, but I had to give away the boys. Periphetes and his wife Phylo, my weaver, took the baby, so I see him every day. More than a few artisans and their wives wanted one of these smart, polite, and well-trained boys. I chose according to my regard for the fathers because the mothers would be kind, I am sure. One boy will learn pottery, one will learn winemaking, one will learn to make iron implements, and Pheres went to the Chief Farmer and his wife. They are good people, and he will take pleasure in working with plants and the land.

There is an empty space where Pheres followed in my wake. I often turn to see him, but he is no longer there waiting to smile up at me. I cannot write more about this. Water fills my eyes…

Cadmus resumed trading with Ithaka after Telemachos and Nausikaa were married and calm came to our palace and our island. I am so happy to see him, but I do not reveal my feelings. On his last visit I mentioned that only Ikarios, the third son, cares about learning anything beyond hunting and the games. The baby is young and barely talking, but he watches my face and the plants that I explain. He smiles and tries to say the words. Laertes, an assertive boy of four rolling years, and Alkinoös of three years like only the bow and arrow and the javelin. They like to be with the men of the palace in the courtyard and watch them at their games and their practice to be warriors. Telemachos encourages them in these pursuits because Laertes will be the next king and will have to defend the home and the island. The boys have their own small javelins, which they carry everywhere, and their father the King is proud. So I look to Ikarios to learn what I know.

With a smile I said to Cadmus, "The boy may be interested in sailing and learning about the world that Cadmus and his sons know."

Cadmus seemed amused at my remark and said softly, "Such an adventure might make it worth continuing to ply my trade for a few more years." We were both pleased at the idea of what my grandson might become.

I could tell that Telemachos was disappointed that Nausikaa pushed out a girl, though he already has three boys. It pleased me that he did not show his feelings to her. I reminded him that he already has three sons and may have more in the future. I reminded him that Nausikaa is not strong because of having births so close together. We would not want to lose her, I said. He was angry to be reminded of his part in her illness. She looks so sick. Her skin is touched with shadow, and the color from the sun has gone.

I was both happy and sad. I would be happy for a daughter, but I knew that she would need all the protection and love that Nausikaa and I could give her. I promised myself that I would never take her from her mother. No child should be taken from its mother.

Despite her weakness, Nausikaa seems almost content. She holds the baby and feeds her, and I feel the loss again of never feeding my son or bringing him up to be the man I would want him to be. My son still shows anger without control, and only Nausikaa can sometimes stop the rage. She holds his hand and sits with him until he is quiet and then they talk. She has wisdom far beyond her years, and holding her baby girl has brought tranquility to her that makes me weep with tenderness.

The weavers and I are happy when Nausikaa and baby Arête are with us. She is named after Nausikaa's mother because my Lord told his son to do so before leaving on his journey.

"Queen Arête saved my life," he said, "and made it possible for me to return to Ithaka. She must be honored if Telemachos has a daughter."

Telemachos agreed and has fulfilled his promise and so little Arête, the child of beauty and love, brings sunshine into our rooms. I am so happy with her name because I admired Queen Arête long before I met Nausikaa. I still wear the lovely necklace with the green stones that she sent to me.

Telemachos, I believe, is disappointed that his child is a girl, so he does not care how she is raised. He sometimes allows Nausikaa to spend her days with me so that she will continue to learn the fine weaving that brings Ithaka fame and fortune. I also believe that he plans to take the weavers away from me and to put Nausikaa in charge of the weaving. Then I will have no value at all. But this may be in the distant future, after his sons are grown and Nausikaa is no longer bearing children. I put this possibility in the dark cave of forgetting.

Zeila, Nausikeia, and their sister Pero help with the baby between their spinning and learning to weave. I also allow them to visit their brothers who are now being cared for by workers in the palace. They are all growing strong, and I continue to measure their growth on the wall, as I did for Telemachos and Medon and now do for my grandchildren. We have never heard from their father since he abandoned them to die. He probably fears the punishment he would get for denying his duty and leaving them to starve. Or perhaps he just forgot them. I cannot understand such a man.

The child Pheres, who followed me everywhere while he stayed in the weaving rooms, smiled into my face and kissed me with tears on his cheeks as he left me. I wanted to keep him but kind Polykas, the Chief Farmer, and his dear wife chose him to care for as their son. I know that Pheres will grow tall with straight legs and strong back in the home of this couple. He will be a farmer and will grow my wonderful vegetables and bring them to me. It pleases me that I will continue to see him.

When Nausikaa and Arête arrive in the weaving rooms on those special mornings, smiles replace frowns. Eurymedousa, the nurse who came with her from Scheria, accompanies Nausikaa and her shining baby. My youngest grandson Ikarios comes to my room as the Sun God ascends the skies, and we keep him busy as we can. He asks questions about everything, hides behind the water urns and trees in the garden with one of the artisan's children. We often get permission from the new parents for the children to play together, and they delight in drinking the teas that I make for all of us in the weaving rooms. When I mix honey and yogurt with tiny pieces of sweet fruit, like figs or dates or apricots, they squeal with delight. They also like oranges and are learning to enjoy lemons when I sweeten them with honey. They take a great deal of my time, but I am so pleased to have them with us that I make up the weaving time at night when others are sleeping. I have little time to write.

I am always so happy when the months of cold rain and snow have passed. During those times of the year, we close the wooden shutters, light the lamps and braziers, put on our heaviest robes and foot warmers, and try to ignore the discomfort of cold. Then suddenly soft breezes arrive and light shines through the windows and into our days. This season is lovely. Before the heat of uncomfortable days, we work the flax, which grows in fields and rocky hills. I love flax because my Phoenician Merchant taught me how to identify it and use it for weaving cloth called linen. It has a different texture from the yarn and robes made from animal hair. It takes many months and much work to transform stalks into yarn, so it must be collected a year before we will weave with it. Linen is cooler than wool in the summer, so we try to collect as much as possible before the Sun God scorches the earth, and the yellowcups, anemones, cornflowers, and daisies dry up.

We also collect lichen from the rocks. One type produces purple dye, but it takes many rollings of the moon to soak and boil the plant before it is ready to use as a dye. This dye is not so regal as the Tyrian purple that Cadmus brings to me, but I use it for hems on garments that I do not give to my Merchant.

I have been teaching Nausikaa about these things so she will know in the future when I am gone. She is no longer large with child, so she can again walk short distances, but she is still weak. Something is wrong. She is not healing well, but she longs to accompany us. Today she could not go far to gather, so I left her with a servant and Arête so she could lie on a robe under an oak tree and rest until we returned. I think she is in pain, but she denies it when I ask her. When she is strong enough to come into the fields and woods with us, we shall take turns carrying the baby, watching Ikarios, and sitting together while she feeds Arête. These will be wonderful times when we can visit together in casual conversation. Usually, her time is taken with Telemachos who wants her near him when she is not weaving or with the baby who takes time that he resents. When her little daughter grows tall and strong enough, she will walk and run with us, as Ikarios does. What pleasure it will be to teach her without the interference of warriors.

Tomorrow we will return to a particular part of the woods for the kermes oak that provides beetles for red and black dyes. Nausikaa, Naela, her daughter Penelopeia, and selected servants are learning about the trees and flowers and roots and beetles and shells that give red, orange, blue, black, purple, and yellow dyes. It takes long years to recognize all of these wonderful gifts from the nature gods, but Nausikaa remembers many things and will learn all that I know in the future. And Naela and Penelopeia, who have listened and followed me faithfully, know much about the plants and about making the teas and other medicines. When I am gone, they can serve Nausikaa and the needs of the palace and the villages in the nearby hills.

Today we were searching for ruta, which makes a medicine for healing cuts and scratches and other wounds. We found enough today to fill several baskets. We collect other medicinal herbs while we search for food and dyes. We find nettle to cure sore elbows and knees and hips, and we collect the garden figs that we eat but also use to cure boils and other skin infections. It is also important to find the trees that give the gum and twigs for chewing and preserving our teeth and keeping our breath sweet. I have been taking Penelopeia with us because she has an extraordinary memory for plants, the shapes of leaves, and their differences. She also remembers the purpose for some of them. I think that she may make medicines for the palace in the future so that she will never be traded.

I also teach Nausikaa all of these things so she too will always have value in the house of Telemachos, even when she gets old and useless and undesirable in other ways. Unfortunately, she does not have the energy to remember anything in her present condition.

Mentor was first chosen to be judge of the assembly until Telemachos grew into greater wisdom. Telemachos is now head of the assembly and chief judge with the aged Mentor as his advisor and with several leaders of groups designed to control people who break the laws. All the men on Ithaka must know the laws, and the village leaders must tell their men what the laws are and the consequences of breaking those laws. Women on Ithaka are not important enough to know such things. No one on this island knows how to read or to write, so all decrees are passed on by words from one leader to the next. Long years ago, I had suggested to my Lord that the leaders must be reminded several times each year at the assembly about the regulations and the penalties, or men will forget. My Lord said that he would see to it. I felt warm that he would listen to me and that our son continues that practice with the men of the island.

After all these years, I still miss the sunrise. Before I was taken to this rocky island, I saw Helios and Dawn peek over the great sea each morning. In fact, I awakened with the servants so that I could welcome the shine of the chariot and the excitement of its light. On dark days, I felt sad that rain and clouds shut out the warm greeting of the sun until one day my wise father explained our need for rain.

"Without rain," he said, "we would have no water to drink or to bathe. We are fortunate that we have an abundance of both rain and sun to quicken our crops and give us the water we need."

With the assurance bestowed to him from the gods, he then led me around our high palace to the edge of our island. There I saw the storage of water from rain and from springs that led over rocks to the gardens around our home.

My father the King, with his great knowledge, explained that we must never drink the water salted by Poseidon, for that water creates thirst that could drive us mad. "But fresh water is a gift from the clouds of Zeus," he said. "We must always give sacrifice to our powerful god for what he sends to us." From that moment, I have prayed my gratitude to Zeus but thank him twice over for the days when he lets the Sun God shine through the veil of clouds in the morning.

I just awoke in the middle of the night wet with drops from my hair to my feet. Lately I am often drenched suddenly from a heat that devours me, but last night it was the sweat of terror. I was back on my Lord's ship when he took me from home. After many years I saw once again the gigantic Cyclops running toward the shore and the ship on which I huddled. For long years I have struggled to hold back these memories, but Morpheus makes it all so real—as he does in the middle of the night when he reveals to me what I have longed for and lost. I believe that the gods give me messages about what my life and days are worth, but I do not know how to read the signs.

After my nightmare of the Cyclops, I cannot bury the journey from Sikelia to Ithaka. The storm that threw us in a direction away from Ithaka kept us on the seas for weeks too long to measure. Winds and rain knocked us about. Zeus roared as he threw down his terrifying bolts of light, and Poseidon took pleasure in showing his power. Odysseus looked lost and afraid, but he bellowed his orders to cover his fear. I believed that Zeus and Poseidon were punishing my new Lord for what he did on Sikelia. I could not understand why they also punished me. I knew terrible sickness, hunger, and thirst for the first time in my life. I begged my Goddess to take me home. She was elsewhere and did not hear me. I don't know what god inflicted retribution on me, for I was so sick that I could not stay below in the hold of the boat. I just lay at the front of the galley trying not to move. Lord Odysseus tied me to the bow so that waves would not pull me overboard. I was terrified. I could not breathe beneath the waves that covered me.

Athene also ignored my new Master's appeals until we stopped on the shore of a lovely land with hills and many sheep. From the sea we could see the sheep grazing and a small stream of fresh water flowing into the sea. The men smiled for the first time in many long days. Odysseus and his men buckled on their swords and took their bows and arrows. When they left the ships, I was alarmed that they would leave me alone in this new land. I heard Odysseus give his orders and the men separated into two groups. One group went to fill goatskins with water, and the others climbed the closest hill to round up the sheep.

I lifted my head above the top rail of the ship. One seaman, who was left to guard the boats, stood on the sand near the ship with his back to me. I felt relief, and I looked around me. The land looked peaceful. Suddenly I thought that the people of this land might help me to return home. I tried to think how I could swim to shore without the guard seeing me. If I could untie my bonds, I could escape from the horror that had become my life. Before I could act on my plan, though, I heard a roar that shook land and sea. Odysseus and his men screamed with fear as they ran down the hill to the galleys. They managed to get only a few sheep and some water on board before a giant with one eye in his forehead came over the top of the hill. He roared again. The men were so terrified that they could hardly hold the oars as the giant came down the high hill. The men managed to row out to sea far enough for the giant to stop.

He was a terrifying sight. He was taller than the tallest tree, his hair was tangled and fell below his waist, his mouth like an open cave with black teeth. He wore the simplest pieces of sheepskin hanging from rope at his waist. He was so enormous that with his huge club the size of a sapling he could have broken the ships easily, but he seemed to be afraid of the water. He came into the water only to his knees but with such force that he made waves that almost tipped the galleys.

The men screamed while Odysseus roared to them to keep rowing for their lives. The deep channel saved us as the monster stood shaking his club at us. Only after our ships were far enough away from land to insure our safety did Odysseus and his men laugh at the giant. He roared again, and Odysseus swore to Zeus that he and the monster would meet again.

In his boasting I smelled fear in the man who shamed my father. I vowed that I would use his weakness to free myself from his power. Unlike my Lord's boasting, my vow was empty and I knew it.

Since Nausikaa came to Ithaka as the wife of my son, Morpheus has tormented me with dreams of the past beyond what I had already suffered for endless years. The nightingale's song fills me with mourning, and it takes some time after I wake up before I stop shaking and weeping.

I sit here in the shrine with my brush and purple water, and I am calmed. When Athene does not speak to me or protect me from dreams and danger, I have my writing to soothe the agony of my life. I can sleep a sleep of calm now.

The other day we found some white mustard, which gives delicious seeds to eat. We were also happy to bring home baskets of roots and shoots to eat with the roasted meats at dinner. Long ago I told the cooks how to use them with olive oil, onions, garlic, and herbs. Some people still don't like green plants and want to eat only bread and meat and wine, but I love the greens and flowers and roots that make my body feel alive and full of energy. And Nausikaa also eats my foods for the midday meal. Even my weavers eat what I bring home and are eager to try different tastes. Of course without the oil and wine and herbs, some of the greens like mustard, dandelion, asphodel, and other plants would taste bitter and may not be pleasant for most people to eat. I like to eat all of the wild plants that are edible and the vegetables that grow in the garden planted with seeds from my trader friend. I want to believe that these foods may help to keep me vigorous. For what purpose I do not know, but for my age I am stronger and healthier than most people I see who are far younger.

I am not sure that Telemachos is happy about that. Unless someone mentions all that I do for the weaving, curing illness, or gathering food, he seems to think that I should stay in my room and keep out of the way. He seems to want Nausikaa to himself, so only when we have guests and a banquet with songs by our bard does he accept my presence at the table. Most of the time I eat in my rooms with the weavers, as I did for so many years. I can tell that Nausikaa feels sad about his attitude, but we say nothing about it.

At the beginning of light this morning I looked down at the bay and saw two galleys coming to the shore. I knew immediately that they were the ships owned by my Merchant. I have missed him with a pain that goes through my chest like fire. I prayed to my special gods to allow me to see Cadmus, not just his clever and kindly sons. I felt my chest pounding, and I waited most of the day and kept going to my garden to watch the ships. As the light began to fall in the west, Nausikaa sent her maid to my room and invited me to the banquet feast to welcome the Merchant and his sons. I bathed and dressed in my loveliest gown with beads around my neck and green beads holding my veil in place. Telemachos was serious and refused to smile, though he was courteous to the guests. Nausikaa was delighted to have guests and was a lovely hostess though she was weak and tired.

Cadmus was clearly pleased and spoke with enthusiasm about his travels and the different peoples he encountered. Finally he told the story of Queen Dido, with whom he traded many times. He told us about Dido's great kingdom of Carthage that is favored by the gods. He described the temples and the riches of her palace. He told us about how Aeneas, the Trojan hero, came to love the Queen and her kingdom, how he began to lead her people and longed to remain there, and how his son Ascanius was beloved by Dido. As his song led to the fates of the beautiful and gifted Dido and her lover, we learned how Aeneas wanted to stay with her but was driven by the gods to leave and build a new kingdom on the land north of Sikelia. We learned of his sadness and guilt over leaving Dido, and we wept when we heard how Dido, wearing a splendid robe that I had woven years before, flung herself on a sword on the pyre in sight of Aeneas's departing ship.

Of course I had heard the story many years before, but I am touched that Dido was wearing my robe when she entered the Underworld. Nausikaa had never heard the story, and she was deeply moved. To change the mood of sadness, which will always be in my heart for Dido and Aeneas, we heard a song from our bard, we ate, drank wine, and talked. Even I talked. At my age, I am no longer required to cover my face with a veil, so I feel free and can meet the eyes of guests and family. It was a wonderful evening. The sons of Cadmus are handsome and friendly and full of laughter. I can only imagine a lifetime of evenings like this one. I am too excited to sleep.

Today Cadmus and his sons came to the weaving room to trade. My son accompanied them so he could watch and hear us. The Merchant praised our goods and showed his sons the differences in the weaves and patterns. He also asked my son's permission to show my panels to his sons.

Cadmus said, "I would like them to see the quality of the weaving so they will learn what extraordinary weaving is. We will stay near the wall as we approach the panels, King Telemachos." And he smiled at my son who nodded approval.

As they entered my bedchamber, the sons said that they recognized the place depicted on the panels. They said that they have visited and traded on Sikelia, and I was pleased that they could recognize the palace of my father. I longed to ask about my family, but I did not want to anger my son.

We arranged the trade, and I had the robes ready in woven sacks. Cadmus and his sons, with the help of servants, carried out the robes and gowns. They were surprised that there was so much for them to trade. My son was astonished at all that he received in return in tools, kitchen equipment, gold jewelry, leather goods, iron, bronze, yarn, and so much more. This evening my son smiled and was full of good cheer as we enjoyed another wonderful banquet. I said good night knowing that I would not see my friends again for perhaps two years or more.

I am worried. Nausikaa did not attend the banquet this evening and ate in her room alone. Too often she has been doing this recently. Often she cannot even rise from her bed. I know that she is ill, but my son will not allow me to see her in private conversation.

2. Family in Crisis

Nemesis is punishing me for loving Nausikaa and Arête and for being grateful that they care for me. I suspect that Telemachos is hurting Nausikaa. I hear tales that crying comes from their room. She no longer comes to our weaving room because Telemachos has isolated her, even as I am isolated from her. I hear that he has been beating her and screams at her that he will make her love him. How can I help her?

I am tormented. I can hardly sleep or weave or write. What can I do?

This is the first time in many turnings of the moon that I can write to express my grief. I cannot free myself from my son's brutality to Nausikaa since Arête was born. I have tried to hide it behind my eyes, but I cannot hold it any more. My son's story and what he did to Nausikaa has dishonored us all. Now I must speak it.

One night after drinking too much wine, Telemachos awakened me—and the weavers—by banging on the heavy door to our rooms. I opened the door and he stumbled into my sleeping room.

He smelled of wine and slurred his drunken speech, "Nausikaa has gone to the Land of the Dead. I cannot wake her."

Tears ran the rivers of his cheeks as he said, "I did not mean to hurt her. She has been disrespectful for long months since Arête was born. I have tried, as a King should do, to teach her what a wife should be for her husband. Tonight when I forced her, as is my right, she did not move or scream, as she has done in the past.

"She will not move," he repeated.

My throat closed. I could not speak. I longed to believe that he was wrong. I wrapped another robe around my shoulders and ran down the long flight of stairs to their room.

Nausikaa was lying on the bed unmoving. I felt her skin that was dry as parchment. I felt her neck for the regular movement of life. There was a slight movement, but her skin was on fire. Her nightclothes were stained with blood. I ordered my son to get two guards to move her up to my room where she could get care. He was so relieved that she was still clinging to life that he offered to carry her up the stairs by himself, but he was not steady on his feet and I was afraid to hurt her even more. I called for her handmaidens to get fresh clothing, basins of fresh cold water, salt water, and wine. I told them to start the fire on my balcony and fill the large pot with water. I ordered them to wake up enough servants to do all this at once and to keep the cold water coming to my room all night and the next day until I give new orders.

I sent one servant with a guard to find the birthing woman in the village at the base of the mountain and to bring her here immediately. I thought I knew what was wrong with my beautiful Nausikaa, but I needed certainty and help. Then I changed Nausikaa's clothing, so that others would not see her condition. I was shocked to see her bones without weight and the colored bruises on her body. They were blue and black and brown and yellow. So he had been beating her over the months since Arête's birth? I was stunned.

Why had no one told me? And what could I have done? As I moved her to take the robe from under her, she moaned without waking. I felt her bones beneath her thin skin and was certain that at least two of her ribs were broken. I felt an overwhelming hatred for my son. I despised him more than even the suitors. My son was a monster, but I reminded myself that I must care for Nausikaa now. My own feelings could wait.

The guards came with the litter to carry Nausikaa up the stairs, but we could not tie her to keep her from sliding. I was afraid that the ropes would hurt her broken bones, but I could not say anything to those around me. By this time, the whole palace was awake and watching from a distance. Arête was screaming, and her nurse was holding her tightly in her arms. I wanted to comfort her but could only see to Nausikaa.

My son turned and roared at everyone, "Go back to sleep and leave us to our business." They turned slowly and could not look at him. Everyone knew.

Slowly we walked up the long flight of stairs and entered my room. The oil lamps were lit and others had been brought. Eurykleia was weeping quietly as I entered the room and told the guards to put Nausikaa gently on my bed. Then they left the room. The weavers were frightened because they did not know what was happening. I told them that they might be needed and should not go back to sleep for a while. Gentle old Eurykleia turned her head to the wall to wipe her face then stood next to me for instructions.

I told Telemachos to leave my room, so we could care for the Queen. Carefully we undressed her and immediately started to bathe her with cold water taken directly from the cistern. Three servants and three weavers worked continuously as I showed them how to bathe her, starting from the hands and feet and face and head and then moving towards her body until the chest and belly were covered with cold cloths. I didn't want them to see the bruises on Nausikaa, but I needed help and decided that only these trusted women would be allowed to see her naked. Weavers found thick woolen blankets and cut them into pieces to hold the cold water. They started the fire for the herb tea, and Eurykleia began to put drops of cold water with honey down the throat of the unconscious Nausikaa. All of the weavers wanted to help. They had missed her deeply, as I had, and were glad to see her again, though not in this condition. I told them she had an illness from her last birth and had not recovered. That was true, but it was only part of the truth, as we all learned over the next weeks.

The servants brought Pramneian wine and they kept bringing water, for Nausikaa's skin was so hot that it turned the cold wet cloths hot almost immediately. The cold water was constantly renewed, and the plants in my garden never had so much water to drink. The servants were soon getting exhausted from running up and down stairs, so I asked the servants to bring the water to the bottom of the stairs and my weavers brought the water up the stairs to my room. They were pleased to contribute, though they too became weary because they were not accustomed to climbing so many stairs, so some rested while others worked. Thus, we all worked through the first night.

As Helios touched the far sky to announce the light, the birthing woman arrived and I asked Eurynomeia, the housekeeper, to organize the servants for the water and for running errands. We fed Nausikaa drops of water and tea with honey and lemons throughout that night and many nights and days. Nausikaa was the first priority of the palace.

When Alcippe, the new birthing woman, arrived I sent everyone else out of the room so we could talk in private. As Alcippe examined Nausikaa, I heard my weavers and the servants praying to Paiëon, the god of medicine, to make my lovely Nausikaa well. I heard their weeping and paeans to the God in their attempts to ward off the Gods of the Underworld. Nausikaa did not move.

Alcippe and I agreed that the place of the poison in her body was the site of the last birth and perhaps another one that never happened. Inside, she was ripped and was bleeding and full of thick yellow liquid, like the drain from an abscess or an infected wound. How to get to the source of the infection was the problem, and Alcippe admitted that she had never seen any woman survive such a condition as we saw in Nausikaa. I had to get salt water and medicine tea to wash out the infection. But I could not think how to do it.

When my women returned to my bedchamber, we continued to get drops of wine and herb tea with lemon and honey down Nausikaa's throat, and she swallowed without waking. We never stopped trying to get the fever to fly away, but she continued to look as though each breath would be the last.

When another morning touched the highest sky, a god inspired me. I summoned the blacksmith to the top of the stairs. I said I needed a very small pipe with a small bellows, so that I could put water into the pipe and push the water out with some force. Could he make such a thing immediately? He said he would try. I think he assumed that I would use it to get water into Nausikaa's throat. I let him believe it. Later that day, he came to our door with the implement. It was just what I needed and even better than I had imagined. I thanked him and said that this tool may save the Queen's life, if we can save her at all. He knelt down and kissed the hem of my robe and thanked me for the honor.

I put the pipe into hot bubbling water to clean it then began to wash out Nausikaa's wound with warm salted water from the sea. At first I used only salt water then alternated every hour or less with medicinal tea made with herbs brought by my Merchant for drawing and curing wounds. I would not allow anyone else to do such a thing to the Queen, so I was awake for many days and nights with only short moments for sleep. And all night and all day for many days we washed Nausikaa with cold water. One night I fell into a deep sleep, and the servants let me sleep for some hours.

When I awoke, Nausikaa's skin was no longer fiery and she opened her eyes. She was still warm but not on fire. I held her and kissed her.

Then she looked up at my tearful eyes and asked weakly, "Why didn't you let me go to the cold home of Persephone and Hades?" She continued softly, "I want to go there where I can walk freely across the Field of Asphodel and await my beloved mother and father. Only you have been kind and loving to me on Ithaka, the island of daily torture."

We sobbed together.

"Your life will be better," I promised her. "Your children need you to stay here. Their love will make your life worthwhile. Give us another chance to give you the happiness that you deserve. We need you. Forgive us for your suffering."

I called the servants to bring the children to her. They were so happy to see their mother that they hugged her and would not leave her side. I even saw a tiny smile on her wan, sad face.

I had not realized that Telemachos was kneeling in my shrine when Nausikaa awakened, and he heard her words and her misery. After she fell asleep and the children left the room, he came out of the shrine, his eyes wet, and knelt next to her bed.

Holding her hand, he wept, "On my word to the gods I promise never to hurt you again, my Love. I swear that your life on Ithaka will be one that is worthy of a goddess."

Unfortunately, Nausikaa was enclosed in a sleep so deep that she did not hear his pledge or his petition for forgiveness.

Thereafter, Telemachos came each day to the door to ask about her condition. He was subdued, and all anger was gone from his eyes that pleaded for her life. He realized how sick she really was, how he had ignored her bleeding and her pain, and how brutally he had treated her. In his attempt to force her love and desire, he had tried to beat her into submission. Several times he asked to pray in my small shrine where he would be close to her while he promised the gods to alter his ways. He was no longer drinking wine until the wine god overcame his senses, and he spent every evening inside the door so he could be close to his Queen. After his promise, I believed that his life would change and hers would be one of happiness—if she survived and could find a way to forgive him.

I no longer feel the joy of earlier times when I see the galleys of Cadmus sail into the port below Mt. Aetos because I know that he will be leaving too soon. Today Cadmus and his two sons left the island. Each of his sons mans his own galley now that they are men. I watched the ships set sail and move to the south as they made their way around the islands to reach home. I cannot stop the water from flowing from my eyes. My throat closes on the sobs of sorrow. I cannot write more.

After five round moons announced the passing of time, Nausikaa recovers from her fearsome battle with Thanatos. Death was defeated by life and the love we all have for Nausikaa. She is sharing our food, weaving for short periods of time, and sitting in my balcony garden during the afternoons when she gets tired. She sometimes sleeps in my bed, and I am sleeping on a pile of soft blankets on the floor. Arête cries to be with her mother, and we let her sleep in the bed to be comforted. I like having them with me.

Today Telemachos visited her as usual and they talked long and quietly. I did not mean to overhear their talk, but I was in the garden and too close not to hear.

He asked her to return to his bed, "I will not bother you unless you agree to lovemaking. I have had too many endless nights without you. Now I know that having you with me is the most important thing in my life. I promise never to hurt you again, my Love."

Because I had explained her condition to him in one of our discussions, he knew that she might lose breath to the Underworld if she had another child. They agreed that he could take a village girl or a boy to quench his desire, and she would be satisfied to accept this new kind of love.

"I know that my mother brought you from the door of Hades, so you must spend time with her and with the weavers when I am away hunting. I also understand that learning about herbs and dyes is important for the whole palace." He paused then continued, "I have learned much about the things that are important since your illness."

After a moment he said, "And I have learned of shame."

The windows of his eyes were opened to let in new thoughts without anger or fear. My son was finally growing beyond a brutal warrior. He led his wife to their room, which the housekeeper had prepared. Nausikaa, I was told, cried when she saw that he had hung the panel that I had woven of her homeland. He held her in his arms and they cried together. In this union, perhaps, is a new beginning.

I have been wondering why a man's desires rule his life and the lives of all around him. Perhaps Kirke, known as a witch, is only showing mortals the true nature of men. Perhaps she teaches us about our spirits and is not evil after all. I wonder what animal Telemachos or his father would be if Kirke transformed them.

I miss Nausikaa being with me every day and night. It was like having Iphthime with me again. When Telemachos went on his raiding party, she was with me every day but now he has returned. Of course I know that she belongs with her husband, and I am thankful that he is gentle with her. She too is grateful and smiles upon him as in the beginning of their life together. I wonder what she thinks behind her eyes.

I have to believe that an evil god directed Telemachos in his treatment of his wife and that he was never the monster that he seemed to be. There has been a gentle side of him in these past months that I always longed to see. I am surprised that I also miss the conversations that Telemachos and I had while Nausikaa was recovering. We talked as we had never talked before in his growing years. He asked me questions about women and how we feel and what I think about many subjects. I enjoyed these confidences and felt close to my son in these moments.

One night after we had talked into the evening, he even asked me if I have been content on Ithaka. I did not want to hurt him or insult his father, but I must be honest.

"I would not have chosen this life of waiting for my hero husband who had been taken for the gods' purpose and not for mine," I told him. "I would have wanted a life like the one on my homeland where women are treated with dignity and respect and love."

This statement startled him and he said, "But men on Ithaka love women and desire them. I love and need Nausikaa. Is that not the same?"

He could not understand how women should be treated differently from the way Ithakans behave. I tried to explain, but I do not think that it all made sense to him. I feared that little change could be expected if he could not comprehend the difference between respect and possession. He asked about my father and mother and sister and brothers. I told him the happy things but never about how Odysseus took me from my beloved home. I would say nothing against his father, for I fear the gods' retribution for my disloyalty.

Quietly I said, "The freedom to be with my baby as he grew up, to be a wife with a loving husband, to gather herbs and plants when the time was right, to walk down to the sea and put my feet in the water again, to leave this room that has protected me but also imprisoned me—these things I longed to be and to do. But all this has been denied me for the endless years that I have spent on Ithaka."

He expressed shock and said, "But I thought that you desired to stay in this room and went out into the fields and down to the inlet only when it was necessary to gather plants and wash clothes. I thought that this was your strange desire and your choice because no Queen washes clothes or gathers weeds. I have only seen you locked in this room when my father was gone. I believed that it was self-imposed exile and never thought to ask about it."

"No," I assured him, "this was not my preference. Would it be yours?"

"But I am a man and so must have my freedom to hunt and wander. If this life was not your desire, why then have you always been shut up in these rooms?" he asked.

I told him about my Lord's mother, his grandmother, who shut me away as soon as I arrived on the island. "She also took my son from me as soon as you were born so she could own her grandson. Only Eurykleia and Father Laertes helped me to see my son, but I yearned to have you near me even as Nausikaa desired to be with her babies." He seemed stunned.

I told him, "As you grew up and the suitors took over the palace because you did not have anyone to fight them, I was safe and my virtue protected only in this room with the bar on the door." His frown of confusion gave me courage to continue.

I reminded him, "You too imprisoned me to keep me away from Nausikaa."

With tears in his eyes, he knelt at my feet and said, "I owe you my life for saving Nausikaa. Henceforth, you have the freedom of the palace and the island with guards at your calling. You will never be a prisoner again."

I kissed his hand. I almost believe that there will be a new life for all of us.

I took my weavers down the mountain to the sea today. We found our small private inlet so that we could bathe and play freely. It has been too long since we bathed our whole bodies in the stream. They were excited and had forgotten, as I had, the wonder of the sea on our feet and legs, in our hair and on our bodies.

Nausikaa and Arête were with us, and Arête was delighted. She splashed us, and we ran after her, and she laughed and laughed. When our maids finished washing and spreading out the clothes on rocks, we put olive oil freely on our hands and faces and backs to soften our skin. It was a glorious day with fresh bread and cheese, pears, apricots, and cold water with wine for lunch.

While our clothes were drying, we collected and washed stones to take back to our rooms, to be placed on the altar in the weaving room as a votive to thank the gods for this wonderful day. We felt tired but happy on our walk back up the mountain. We will work harder at the weaving tomorrow to make up for our free half-day today.

For the first time since arriving on Ithaka, I can roam the palace grounds, the fields, and the woodlands without asking permission. Word has gone out across the island through the monthly meetings of village leaders and the Court that the King's mother is collecting herbs for medicine and for dyes and is not to be touched by anyone. Of course I am not alone when I walk away from the palace. I understand that there is still a problem of safety for women. I have been taking Naela, Zeila, Penelopeia and my other weavers, three or four at a time, with me so they too are liberated from the weaving room and will learn the art of collecting. We wear our veils and robes, but when we are away from the palace and no one is around us we raise the veils and feel the breeze on our faces. They even dance briefly in a clearing in the woods when no one can see them. And we laugh.

The heat of the days brings hyacinths and poppies, lotus, and plants that we gather for food and dyes and medicines. My servants and four of my trusted weavers spend whole days at this time of year collecting plants like spartium. I use this bush with large yellow flowers for dye. We roam over the dry slopes and woods. This bush offers stems for basket weaving and a fiber used for fabrics. It is also cooked and used for stomach problems throughout the year. Today was a spartium day and a pleasant one. If only Nausikaa were well enough to accompany us on these long and tiring walks, I would be content. I remind myself that she is improving, and I look forward to a new time.

Nausikaa loved the panels from the first time she saw them. In the early years she visited my room just to stare at the scenes of my homeland. One day, Nausikaa asked me to weave panels for her sleeping room. I asked her to describe her own homeland in detail. For weeks we talked and I drew images on slabs of slate. I could not show her my writing ink and papyrus. However much I love her, I could not trust anyone on Ithaka to know about my writing. I began to weave images of her home in silk and linen for her walls. I worked every night for months.

She made me promise to keep the secret from Telemachos. She was certain that Telemachos would be happy to have the beautiful pictures of her home in his room. I tried to suggest that he might not be pleased, but when the first panel was completed, she had the guards hang it while he was away for several weeks on one of his raiding voyages. Nausikaa wanted to surprise her Lord, she said with a radiant smile.

He was furious. He accused her of wanting her childhood home instead of the marriage home that he gave her. He accused her of ingratitude and not paying tribute to him. He left the palace for several days. When he returned, he carefully took the panel from the wall and brought it up to me. He was afraid to anger the gods if he damaged the beauty of the panel. He walked into my room with black frown lines on his face.

He told me, "Never interfere in our lives again." He threw the panel at me.

Before leaving he said fiercely, "You will remain in your rooms from this day. The rest of the palace belongs to me and my Queen."

That all happened many years ago, but I realized at that moment that all family had been taken from my life. And I have never forgotten that lesson.

For the endless rolling seasons I have spent on Ithaka, I have pretended to have family in my son's presence in the palace. I pretended to have family in the hope of my Lord's return from Troy. Later I pretended to have family in Nausikaa's marriage to my son, the birth of his sons, and Arête running around and talking and asking questions constantly and bringing joy to every day. I pretended to have family in my friendship with Nausikaa and her beautiful children. How I love them. I created a family with my weavers and my servants and a temporary family with Zeila's children. It was all illusion. When Nausikaa sobbed at my son's cruelty, I could not cry. I knew that even the pretense was past and that poor Nausikaa would learn about the prison that Ithaka could be. And she has learned the lesson too well.

But all that happened before Nausikaa's illness. Now the panel that I wove for her is hanging on the wall of their bedchamber, and Telemachos asked me to weave more panels of Nausikaa's homeland. He apologized for his behavior in the past and says that he wants to please her. Perhaps he has changed, but I tremble to trust it. There is too much revenge in Hope.

I have been working every night on the panels for Nausikaa. I have been too exhausted to write. Perhaps I have nothing more to say.

Telemachos took a raiding party to a land many weeks away from Ithaka. Now that he no longer uses Nausikaa for his needs he has longings for battle. Someday he will not return, I fear.

Rumor has tried to change my story but not even a god can do that. The eldest son of my Phoenician Merchant has been kind like his father in offering his friendship. Like his aging father, Lethos takes my woven goods that are still desired across the islands of the sea, and he offers what Ithaka wants. He also carries news from the outside world, even as my good and noble friend has done. Cadmus stands quietly listening with amusement at his son's humor, warmth, and enthusiasm. Today Lethos told me, with a smile in his eyes, that rumors of my new marriage fly around the world. Smiling with his mouth, he said that people everywhere believe the stories because my Lord has not returned from his second long journey across the unknown world. As he told the story and color drained from my cheeks, Cadmus frowned and later apologized for disturbing me. I assured them that I was grateful to hear what Rumor had to say. Here is what is whispered.

"Rumor says that Odysseus has a son named Telegonos by the fearful Kirke. Rumor says that the boy was born after Odysseus escaped from Kirke's island. After the child grew up he found Odysseus on the shore of Ithaka and killed his famous father. People who believe Rumor say you married Telegonos, my Lady, and Telemachos married Kirke."

"Such nonsense," I retorted. "I am fifty years in age, I think, and Telegonos is about fifteen years younger than my own son. I am not Iocasta. I do not marry a son, and Telemachos would not marry Kirke the Witch." We all laughed.

Of course the story of our weddings was wrong. I never married after Odysseus. I did not say this aloud but I thought, why would I put myself into another prison with a different marriage?

"It is time to put truth in history," I said to Lethos. "My son married Nausikaa of the Phaiakians. The marriage was arranged in a traditional manner after my Lord returned from his Trojan adventures. My Lord took Telemachos and sailed to meet King Alkinoös to ask for Nausikaa as a queen for our son. I think that he did not demand her. He asked King Alkinoös, who made his first return possible. After several weeks, they returned with the child bride who would become my mistress when Odysseus left for his next extended journey. My Lord has not yet returned." But I'll write about that another night.

"As for the rest of the story spread by Rumor," I told Lethos, "I have been married to only one man in my life. And beyond the childhood friendship with Tyndareus, I have loved only one man with my spirit, after my father." I did not utter the name of this man but let Lethos assume that he was my Lord and husband.

I said, "He only knows my lonely life. To him only do I sing my song."

While I denied the false story with words that did not speak openly, Cadmus watched me and smiled with his eyes. He knows the truth of my story. His son will someday take these writings to him, and he will know the entire landscape of my heart.

Rumors about me fly across the world, I am told, and I feel humiliation for what people must think of me. Yet, it seems to me that the people who tantalize Rumor with falsehoods and devise lies are believed and raised to the level of the gods. The innocent victims of the lies are treated with contempt and made to feel shame. Is Dikē, the goddess of Justice, without sight and hearing that she does not know this?

I have noticed for some time that the peasants bow down when we go gathering. I smile and bow back to them. This seems to please them. Now they know that the Lady Penelope is with the group of servant women picking the plants. They also know now that these are the plants for medicine that has helped to cure many of them in their illnesses. Many of the villagers and hill people in their hovels have come to the gate of the palace to ask for my help. Long ago the peasants spread word that I could cure boils and infections and other problems, especially for women.

In the light of the moon, women began to come to the side gate near the vegetable garden and ask for me. They told me about their family problems and begged for my ointments or my teas.

They still come and sometimes bring a daughter or a neighbor. They kneel to me and begin by saying that they have too many mouths to feed, and then they ask if I could take away the swelling that frightens them for the future. Too often the women say that they will do terrible things to themselves if I do nothing for them. After talking with the woman, I take some leaves from a sack and tell her how to make a tea that may help. I am willing to assist them, but I cannot always do so, and I am left feeling powerless and sad.

There was also a problem with the Medicine Man on the island because many people preferred to take herbal teas or use salves than to be cut and bled, particularly the women who could not reveal their secret problems. The Medicine Man was angry with me for taking his position of respect from him. I asked to meet with him.

He came part of the way to the palace, and we met outside of the house of one of the settlement leaders. He was accustomed to living in a cave and speaking seldom to anyone, so I found it difficult to understand his words. However, he asked in the simplest of language about what I was doing when people asked for my help. I told him about my salves and offered to share them with him and to tell him about the herbs that I use from the fields of Ithaka and from my native homeland. I explained that the people could not always go across the island to him, so those in the settlements near the palace came to me

He refused to learn about the herbs or the ointments and told me to stay away from his people. He kept shaking his head and saying "No."

"My place come family by gods," he threatened, "take you. Father and fathers past touched by gods to cure. People go Dark World from red swell and pain, it is fate." His voice became louder as he spoke.

Without waiting for me to answer, he said angrily, "I call gods Dark World take you. Stop you do. This my word!"

I realized that he was terrified to lose his position, and yet he would not—or could not—learn new ways. I told him to send out word to the people that I was not to give them anything for their wounds or illnesses. My submission seemed to appease him, and I have not seen him since that day.

People still come at night and in secret to see me, and I cannot turn them away. I tell them simple things like bathing their wounds in the salt water so they will heal faster. They would not believe the efficacy of that simple measure, so I tell them that Poseidon has blessed the waters for that purpose. Then they try it and find it to be successful. They believe that I am in league with the gods. I give them ointments and herbs for headaches or pennyroyal for teas when appropriate. I do what I can to help them. But I swear them to secrecy, and so far the Medicine Man has left me alone.

Hera directed me in my thinking and for some time I believed, but I was correct in not trusting happiness. For one short period of our lives, my son was gentle and loving, but that period is over.

Telemachos will not hear what Nausikaa and I tell him and instead closes out our voices. He thinks like a warrior again.

"What I say is law," he said when he pulled Nausikaa into my room one day recently. I do not know how this all began, but he continued.

"Nausikaa is forbidden to come to your room when I am in the palace or away," he said. "She belongs to me, though you try to take her from me."

I stood shocked, staring at him in confusion. How did he learn to be so jealous, cold, uncaring, and cruel? If I had the opportunity to raise him in the glow of my father's palace, would he be the same man today? If I could have kept him with me and taught him gentleness, taught him to love women instead of to feel contempt for them, taught him kindness instead of the rapture of possession and power, what kind of man would he be today?

Instead, he grew to think that I was the problem that drew the suitors who ate and drank his wealth away while I waited for his father to return from Troy. I brought honor to him throughout the world for my virtue and loyalty to his father, yet my son the King can only see me as strange for my plants and potions. To him, I am peculiar for my isolation in these rooms. Despite our extended talks together during Nausikaa's illness, despite offering him new information that should alter his way of thinking, these ideas remain with him. He enjoys believing that he is right in all things.

I fear that Telemachos will shut me away from Nausikaa completely. I miss her with the ache I feel for my beloved sister. The only thing I have left is my beautiful Arête who comes to see me each day whether her father is at home or outside of the palace or away hunting. She alone brings joy to me daily. Telemachos does not know this because he does not seem to care what she does. She is a girl so he does not see her. She comes to see me, and we eat together, take tea together, and work the garden together. I teach her how to weave, and she is pleased. She brings me stories from Nausikaa and the rest of the palace, and we laugh. Ikarios no longer joins us. He is required to be with the men and learn to hunt. Arête and I miss him, and I fear that she will be taken away from me also.

When I was a young bride, I wondered why girls were taken from their homes to live with the families of their husbands. Why could not the husband live with the wife's family, I used to ask myself. Now I know that it is to have control and power over the girl for her lifetime. The gods have given woman the fate of her husband for reasons that I do not understand. She is taken from everyone she loves, everyone who cares for her, and brought to a place where she must serve the new family. She must be grateful for even the food that she eats and the robes that she wears. She must defer to her husband and his family in all things though she is a queen. Even the guards or peasants who live nearby have power to keep her imprisoned for her safety. She can tell no one of her sadness or her loneliness. She is thankful if she is not beaten because no one is there to help her. She is grateful for the smallest kindness and the most limited freedom.

Even now, when I sometimes have the liberty to gather plants and to bathe in the sea, I am still limited by no longer being in charge as I dreamed that I would be if my Lord were here. And I still see Nausikaa only when my son leaves on hunting and raiding parties. Then she must come to my room at night when no one is watching. If someone tells my son that his wife defies him, we would be punished in ways that I can only imagine.

The shape of my life, and hers, is limited by the positions we hold, and I am subservient to my son and his wife. My only good fortune is Nausikaa's compassion, love, and consideration for me. And even that is limited by my son's demands. What gods are responsible for creating such lives for women?

I have thought long about the differences between my circumstances and the conditions of my mother and my Lord's mother. They had power. They deferred to no one. Perhaps the answer is in my father the King and in Father Laertes. These men were kind and gentle. These men, unlike Odysseus and Telemachos, cared more for peace than for power. My father tried to please my mother to avoid the lashing of her tongue, the screeching of her voice, and her vindictiveness. I remember that on rare occasions he resisted her rule. Then she would have me brought to her. As he watched, she turned to me with rage and slapped my face with her hard hand and pulled my hair until I thought I would have none left. My beating was *his* punishment. My father would immediately relent and promise her whatever she wanted. Holding tears in my throat, I saw her turn away with a little smile of triumph. She always knew how to gain victory over my father, and she controlled the palace.

My Lord's mother also ruled with cruelty. Father Laertes deferred to her. He learned to stay away from her and to take his son on long hunting adventures. Odysseus learned from his mother, not his father, how to wield power. And Telemachos also learned the art of living from her and the unscrupulous men around him. I wonder if these women were always cruel, even as children, or if they learned the ways of power when they arrived as new brides on strange lands. They gained control with fierce demands and with beating those with no power at all. I know that there was some softness in my mother, especially for her sons, but I do not remember it for myself. And I never saw softness in my Lord's mother, except in the love for her son and in the last days of her breath in this upper world.

I have long wondered if I could have altered my life by being harsh and ruthless. I wonder if my Lord Odysseus could relinquish control to a mortal woman when he fears no man but only gods. I question if it would all be worth the price one pays for such authority. My mother was feared and disliked by all who knew her. My Lord's mother was feared and hated in the palace. Even in her illness she held terrible power to hurt, but she was alone. When her spirit descended to the Realm of the Dead, a dark heaviness lifted from the palace to be replaced by relief and even smiles.

Would I choose such pitiless domination if it freed me from the prison of my room? I could not make such a choice. Perhaps I am too weak. This knowledge shames and comforts me.

I think of Helen and Klytemnestra, of Medeia, and of other women who are vilified for behavior that is evil. Is it possible that the only way for a woman to be free is to run away, regardless of the terrible cost, or to murder her husband as Klytemnestra murdered Agamemnon on his return from Troy? What virtuous woman would want to get revenge on her disloyal and deceitful husband by killing her children? Even the idea is horrifying. Why do women like Medeia make such choices? I refuse to believe that the reason is that they are women. Yet, when I remember how liberty and independence were taken from me by force and I recall the first months of my marriage and the treatment of Nausikaa, how can I judge a woman's actions in defending herself or in planning retribution? Do the answers to all these questions lie in the nature of the particular woman and in the fate that is linked to her character? Or is any woman capable of such action? I tremble to think it.

I have had much time to consider how I became what I am. I am like my father rather than my mother. I need to please and not to dominate by fear. At what point does one find and follow the path of one's character in life? And would I be different if I had the chance to change? I was taken by Odysseus against my will and with no resistance in order to protect my beloved family. With that moment of choice, my fate was locked in stone. Isolation was the only way to control me, like the weavers who are slaves.

Most women are slaves, I think.

It has been long since I have written my silent songs. My days and nights are filled with weaving both robes for trading and panels of Nausikaa's homeland, and so many other activities. As the children are growing, the family gathers together to welcome guests and strangers. My son sometimes allows me to join the family and guests and then those evenings are filled with banquets and grandchildren, with songs and games. I have learned so much about the Trojan War and its aftermath from the singers who live on Ithaka and those who visit our palace from elsewhere in the world. I wonder if the songs are true or if they are created to amuse and mystify. It doesn't matter. Life is so much better when my son is in a mood of generosity, and I am pleased with him during those times. He loves his Nausikaa and his children, and I am content to know that. I am also tired each evening and must sleep.

3. Unexpected Changes

The years roll on, and the children are growing tall and strong. I remember how they ran through the palace, and I was always pleased to hear their footsteps on the stairs leading to the weaving room. I kept tea ready for them with honey and lemon and their favorite herbs like chamomile, mint, or mixtures that I create. They loved the smell of rabbit stew and oxen broths with carrots, onions, garlic, and leeks (to ward off lightning) and herbs like parsley, thyme, savory, basil, rosemary, bay, or dill, and they ran up to ask when their food would be ready.

One time I told the children that I would teach the cooks how to make the stews for the whole family, or the whole palace, but the children squealed "NO" and jumped up and down. They said that they only wanted my stews and soups cooked in my garden.

"Only you make them taste delicious," they yelled. I laughed and promised to continue cooking in the huge pot in my terrace garden so that the food would take on the lovely smells of the plants and flowers and lemon trees. They laughed and hugged me. I do love them and the memories that warm me.

Now Telemachos and his oldest sons, Laertes and Alkinoös, often go out hunting with Medon for the rabbits or wild goats or birds that my servant and I cook with vegetables for my weavers and my grandchildren. The Chief Farmer Polykas tills and cultivates the fertile fields, and his green hands also tend my vegetable garden near the side gate of the palace wall. The celery and carrots, onions and garlic, peas and beans and greens and other colorful roots are available throughout the year. And Polykas has taught Pheres, Zeila's boy and the child I wanted to keep, the secrets of farming. The boy remembers our time together and often carries the vegetables to me. And it warms me to see how Polykas and Pheres enjoy being together and working the land. I praise them, and the boy smiles shyly. I know it pleases him. How easily I could love him. Indeed, I do love him. I am certainly happy to see him growing stronger and handsomer each year.

Telemachos has long stopped being angry when we go through the fields and woods on our gathering days. He has come to realize how important the plants are in feeding us and keeping us healthy. His tall, godly sons show him this daily.

It is a time of contentment that has affected the whole family. My son has changed and seems to be softer, but I still do not trust him. He alters like the tides, and I do not know what to expect as the moon alters. Yet I take pleasure in Nausikaa and Arête when they are allowed to spend part of each day weaving with us. Arête is getting to be very creative and careful in her weaving, and Nausikaa and I are proud of her work.

Ikarios, the youngest son, is exceptionally bright. Like his grandfathers, he has been touched with curiosity and cleverness and asks questions about everything when he is permitted to visit with me. I would like to teach him to write, but I dare not reveal to anyone what I can do. I show Ikarios some shapes of letters, and he understands how I put them together for words. We pretend it is a game. He is learning quickly, but I do not call it writing.

When Cadmus and his sons last visited our island to trade, Ikarios noticed the marks that Cadmus and his eldest son Lethos were making on a slate. He recognized some of the shapes and was proud to read some words as part of the game that he plays with his grandmother. Cadmus was pleased and smiled at the boy and said he plays the game well.

I asked Arête if she would like to play the game and learn the shapes, but she cares more for weaving and learning about the medicines and herbs. I teach her those things because they will make her valued when she is taken away in marriage. I pray to the gods that her bridal time will be long in coming, but she is a beautiful child getting too close to being a woman.

Each child is so different. Laertes is bold and rather a bully because he knows that he will someday be a king who must lead his people. He enjoys warrior activities and bossing Alkinoös and the other boys who attach themselves to authority. On the other hand, Alkinoös adores his older brother and follows him everywhere. He too has warrior skills, but he never challenges Laertes. Ikarios, the youngest boy who almost died of fever, is more independent. Full of energy and determined to compete with his older brothers in physical agility, he accompanies them on their forays, but hunting is not his preferred game. He loves to run through the hills, alone and free. I would like that too. His other favorite activity is going with his father and brothers to the great marketplace near the busy port at the base of Mt. Aetos. On market days he learns about different parts of the Great Sea and returns with stories and gifts for his mother, his sister, and me. He is generous and proud to share what he brings.

On meeting days when the village leaders of Ithaka gather to discuss the laws and bring justice to the land, Telemachos takes his three sons to meet the men and to learn about ruling. He has built a small amphitheater, and they meet proudly on that site overlooking the sea. Since Mentor went smiling to the Field of Asphodel to meet his wife and parents, Telemachos is now the leader and his wisdom has made him judge on the island. Mentor is deeply missed, but leaders from all over the island defer to Telemachos on most issues. My son is pleased about his position and proud to have his two warrior sons observe the deference that other men pay to their father. Ikarios seems indifferent to such displays of authority. Instead, he is fascinated with the laws and the process of making decisions.

I feel desolate without Mentor, my wise friend who listened and was kind and generous in helping me to improve life among the weavers. Always I could call on him, and I knew that he would try to make the changes that I desired, that were essential in transforming the weaving rooms if not the palace. He was a great leader for the many years that my Lord has traveled the world, and he assisted my son in growing into a strong King. Every day I remember and miss him.

For many years, since my Lord returned from Troy and saw the tile floors in our bedchamber and the weaving room and was glad, Periphetes has been given the freedom to transform the palace with his wondrous art. The Great Room has been beautified with mosaic tile patterns on the floor and walls. The ceiling is limed with a soft color like the seashore. Periphetes is an artist sent to us by the gods. It is a joyful time to eat together with guests in the splendid banquet hall. The tables are now set with silver and gold goblets and bowls that came to Ithaka as dowries or were traded for our weaving, and the food has expanded beyond roast goat, bread, and curds. We now have figs and dates, pomegranates, and other fruits and nuts growing in my Merchant's Garden of Trees in the palace. Varied meats and cheeses, vegetables, grains, lentils, and savory dishes are offered regularly at banquets. Lord Odysseus would enjoy these meals, as we do.

Gradually, Periphetes and his assistants have created lovely mosaics and bright walls in many of the sleeping rooms, and he will be busy long into the waiting years after he begins to transform the courtyard. To honor him and his glorious work, Telemachos gave him a wife Phylo who is one of my weavers. She told me that she was pleased and honored to be chosen. They have two children of their own and took Zeila's youngest baby. They have a servant who cares for the children while they both work each day at their art, and the children visit with us in the weaving room and garden. The family looks happy. Periphetes works from dawn to dusk with the dozen men who now assist him, and the palace has become a source of pride across Ithaka, instead of the grey, dark, and dirty place that I knew when I first arrived.

Much has changed. The gods have been good to us in letting my son grow into a man to be honored. We show our gratitude in prayer and with our patience in waiting for my Lord Odysseus to return. We have heard nothing of his place in the world. We wait.

Rumor has flown into my room to tell me that what seems to be satisfaction for all of us to see is a festering sore beneath the surface.

In keeping his bargain soon after Arête was born, Telemachos has let Nausikaa heal and grow healthy again but has taken other women to satisfy his desires. It is said that he enjoys other lives away from us. I am told that long years ago he took a peasant girl and made her his woman. Her family lives on a distant hill on Ithaka, and since she became the woman of the King, her large family now has food, their one-room hovel is now five rooms, the father has land for a garden to feed his children and grandchildren, and they have pasture land for sheep that they trade. In addition to the parents' eight children, there are four children, I am told, who have the attributes of Telemachos. His woman, once a lovely young girl of purity and innocence, is now fat and old before her time like her mother. Rumor says that Telemachos has tired of her and while he still is generous in caring for their needs for his own children's sake, he visits this woman seldom. I wonder if she is sad or glad.

Perhaps my son's moods toward us depend more on his general feeling of contentment with others beyond his family rather than his concern for us. I have never understood why he made different rules for me and for Nausikaa at different times. Sometimes he is kind and considerate. Then without warning he changes into a mean and controlling tyrant for many turnings of the moon. I wonder what determines these changes—his character or his pleasures beyond his palace?

My own eyes told me that Medon has meant more to my son than just a hunting friend. Telemachos gave a wife to Medon about ten years ago to father children for the future, but Rumor says that she has been a wife in name only for most of those years. My son and Medon spend much of their time together, I am told, as they did in their youth. Perhaps my son has lost interest in his mountain girl, or the girls at the market. But then these are stories that Rumor tells, and we know we can't believe most of them.

Rumor has been busy on Ithaka lately as she flies to tell me that Telemachos is buying a dancing girl from the East at the marketplace and is bringing her to live here and dance in our palace. She will be close to him so that he will not have to travel far to have her on the nights that he is not with Medon. She is said to be beautiful and has caused great disturbance in the wine house where she dances. So many island men desire her and go to see her dance that there are no sitting places available each night. The men now stand all evening at high tables while they drink strong wine and wait to see her. Men fight to have her, and she is in danger at all times.

As King, Telemachos demanded that the owner sell her to him and was willing to impose his royal power on the owner in order to get her. So Rumor says. Men on the island are angry with my son, and grumbling is heard all through the hills and in the market, I am told. They resent his keeping her for himself, and other leaders on the island want to share her and make her into a public woman for all to share. These are the stories. If they are true, my heart is sore for her.

My son seems not to care about the opinions of others and will face the village leaders at their monthly meeting soon. His sons are embarrassed and asked him not to do this and not to shame their mother. They knew about the other woman in the hills, and other girls at different seasons, but they argue that at least the King took care of the hill woman's whole family. The peasants sold their daughter in order to eat, and their King ruled their home. With that agreement, at least the family prospered. Though the girl had no choice, it was a fair bargain, according to the men on Ithaka.

But taking the dancer home to be his bedmate for everyone to see and talk about is not only humiliating to his wife, but it is madness. We heard that Agamemnon paid a high price when he took the Trojan princess Cassandra home after the Trojan War. Klytemnestra already had reason to hate and murder Agamemnon when he sacrificed their daughter, but bringing another woman to live with them after the war was more than any wife could endure. Certainly Nausikaa is not Klytemnestra, but I worry about how she will feel.

Moreover, my grandsons are not pleased. They worry that they will not get the best wives because of the reputation of their father. If this story is more than false Rumor, my son's lack of restraint will cause enormous misery for many people.

When I was a child, I accepted happiness without thought or question. As I grew toward womanhood, I expected that life should be full of the pleasure of love, caring, and helping those in need. Sikelia did not have a divinity that was angry over human happiness and whose jealousy inflicted terrible torment for that good life. Only after I was on Ithaka did I learn about Nemesis, the goddess who punishes mortals for too much happiness or riches. I realize now that I had the treasures of loving and being loved, the marvels of nature's nymphs, the light of Helios and the music of Apollo that made each day a wonder. I was too easy with laughter that Nemesis heard, and my prayers of gratitude have done little to mollify her.

I wonder now if the goddess sent the hero Odysseus as a weapon to wound me for those pleasures. Perhaps Nemesis, in her divine jealousy and retribution, sent the winds to blow the ships of Odysseus off course and land him on the shore of Sikelia where he saw me and decided my dark fate. Since coming to Ithaka I have tried to remember the errors of my past. I have attempted to be humble and silent when life was good so that Nemesis should not notice the palace of Telemachos. I should have realized that the gods learn about all things, that Hermes flies throughout the world and Rumor carries his stories. Nemesis must have been wild with envy over our brief joy in the family of Nausikaa and now punishes us daily with her sharp barbs of pain.

Nausikaa and I have not mentioned the dancing girl, but I have heard whispers that Telemachos says that he bought her in order to protect her from all the men of the island. The owner of the wine house where the girl lived was willing to sell her each night to the highest bidder. My son insists that he did not buy her for himself but for her own safety. I am plagued with doubt and have difficulty believing that it is my son's heart that impels him to act in this situation.

The gods darken my thoughts about everything.

The dancing girl named Nauriteia is now in the palace and dances each night at dinner. She is exquisite with gold rings and bracelets and jewels around her hair and on the hems of her veils. Telemachos is enraptured, and I hate him. He cares nothing for his wife's suffering and no longer shares their bedchamber. I watch Nausikaa when she comes to dinner, but more and more often Nausikaa and I take our dinner in our own rooms alone or I eat with the weavers in order not to see this exhibition. I understand why Nausikaa's smile no longer reaches her eyes—like the dancing girl whose large brown eyes, once deep and warm, are slowly growing cold as stone. Why do men take the best of life from their women and don't even notice or care?

The Wine God has control of my son again. Desire and drink rule my son, and he owns the dancer.

My Merchant and his sons arrived this morning. It has been too long since my eyes have touched him. His hair is almost white, but he is tall and straight and well muscled, and his teeth are still strong and white. He could tell that life on Ithaka has changed from the few years of the children's growing when the evening banquet was filled with laughter and songs and stories. Now, the poor dancing girl performs, and the men who are my son's guests laugh and bang their cups and yell for her to show more than the veils allow. They do not appreciate the art of dance, and treat her like a common winehouse woman. She is humiliated and looks only at the floor. It is a disgrace.

Nausikaa rises to say that she is not well, and we both go to our rooms. My son is again seduced by Dionysos, as he has always been when he wants to hide from himself the wickedness that he does to others.

I wrote a note to apologize to Cadmus about the changes in our palace so that he will understand my reserve, and I hid the parchment as always in his special robes. He says that he will stay on Ithaka for two suns, so we may speak together. There is always someone around me, so we may not be allowed to speak. Just seeing him is enough to fill my heart.

Nothing in life stays the same. Everything changes, especially the good and cheerful times that are illusory. Life is like the waters of the sea that move and alter constantly.

Yet, as I consider it, the sea itself is as it always was. It is a mystery.

The years roll on and Arête has grown into a beautiful young maiden. Men from Ithaka and afar pay homage to her, and fathers have spoken to Telemachos about an agreement for her dowry. I worry about the kind of place and the type of man who will take her. One day Telemachos told me that he fears for her. He said that he would kill the man who would hurt his daughter. Perhaps he remembers Nausikaa's illness, but I don't think so. He says that he is looking for a prince who lives in a land close enough for him to visit and to see how she is treated. I smile at his new understanding of woman's position in life.

After ignoring Arête for all of her years, he suddenly feels the gladness that squeezes his heart when he looks at his exquisite daughter. He does not realize that the women he hurts are also the daughters of fathers who may suffer because of their child's treatment. His blindness and irrationality baffle me.

Despite the concern my son expresses about a daughter's position, there is no one to shield Nausikaa and Nauriteia the dancer from their pain. Nausikaa has watched two daughters born to the dancer who was once beautiful and desirable but now has lost the lightness of her step and the gladness in her smile. She is privileged like Nausikaa and me, I am told, so she spends her time in a distant corner of the palace in isolation, caring for her two daughters and waiting for Telemachos to give her a baby boy to make him glad.

I think so often about Nauriteia, the dancer. She has given life to two of my grandchildren, two girls whom I long to know. She may be lonely because I have heard that there is no one to befriend her. The servants are beneath her, and she treats them as she thinks they should be treated. Yet she too is owned by the King so cannot be free. She belongs nowhere and with no one. I am very sad for her. I know what loneliness is. But can I be her friend when just her presence brings such pain to Nausikaa? My loyalty to Nausikaa is first, but my heart is sore.

Nausikaa no longer visits the weaving room since King Telemachos came to me and told me to make room for the dancer's loom. She will now be a weaver in the palace. I began to object, but he said with anger that she is now a weaver. There was no argument. I know that she has lost the lightness of her body and the delicate beauty of her face that enticed my son when he first saw her. Her body is heavier, and her face is lined and sad and without the vibrant color that distinguished her. She no longer dances for the men. And she has not given the King the son that will prove his virility. Now she must work in a different way for her food and shelter. Her two daughters accompany her everywhere so that she can protect them from the men roaming the palace. This includes my son, I suppose.

At first the weavers, who have heard stories over the years, did not speak to her or her children until they watched me welcome them and work with her for several days. Nauriteia is not to be blamed for her fate or the treatment she received in our palace. And certainly her children are young and innocent. Gradually, the weavers started to help her, and the spinners started to teach the girls how to spin. They are still too young, but everyone is getting comfortable together.

They seem to like being here. The girls especially love my garden. I am certain that being with us must be better than the indignity of dancing for drunken, slobbering men who have no respect for women—or for the art of dance. And being in the weaving room and garden all day is better than being shut up in a room above the maids' quarters. Nauriteia is not a fine weaver, but her garments can be kept for the servants or slaves, so her work helps all of us.

I explained my situation to Nausikaa. "I am sorry to hurt you."

"I understand, Mother, but I cannot go into the room so long as the dancer is there. I feel shame for both of us, and I cannot look into her face."

We embraced and wept for the fate of women. I understand her position, but the loss of Nausikaa among us grieves me. It is not an easy life for any of us. Only Telemachos seems indifferent to all of this in his continued search to fill the longing in his heart.

Ithaka held a celebration of games, and Telemachos and Nausikaa, as King and Queen, presided over the festivities in the amphitheater. They are handsome, and Ithaka was proud. There were banquets in our palace each evening, and markets were open all day and night where food and drink and everything else desired by mortals were available for the right price. The games went on for four days.

The men of Ithaka spent many months preparing fields for play and terraced benches for seating. My grandsons, grown tall and strong like their father, were very excited and worked hard to make the games a success. The servants scrubbed and cooked, and the men of the palace made many arrows and spears and other implements for all of the games to be played. Many ships from the surrounding islands arrived before the games began, and men set up their sleeping places on the hillsides near the palace.

Everyone was excited and grateful for the blessings that the gods showered on them. Our boys could hardly sleep for anticipation. They had been practicing for different events for many circles of the seasons, and now they were ready for this great challenge.

I asked permission to bring my weavers, who had their first days without work since they were young children. They dressed in new robes with lovely colors and designs, and they bathed and brushed each other's hair. They said that they felt like free women, and they danced around the room. I warned them about Nemesis, and they were subdued. They stood around while my maids arranged my hair and oiled my skin for softness. They said that I am beautiful, but they say those things because they feel affection for me, I am certain. I know that I love them.

My weavers were allowed to sit with me on the new amphitheater benches to watch the festivities for two days. We brought food and water for our noon meal and returned to the palace for the evening meals. We laughed, and they learned to cheer, and they tasted the freedom that most men enjoy as their daily fare. They could hardly sleep with the excitement of those two days. We have shared much in our lifetime together.

The games were filled with wonder and enthusiasm. Telemachos did not compete because he is the King and host. But Medon won second prize in the javelin. That was amazing for a man of such years. Laertes won a laurel wreath for the bow and arrow. It is said that his strong shoulders and arms are like his grandfather who has been lost to us. Alkinoös won the laurel wreath for wrestling. Playing with his brothers and his friends for all the seasons of his growing has also given him great strength like his grandfather.

Ikarios, who cares more for gardens and mosaics and birds and his dog than battle, who dreams of sailing to discover the world, did not participate in the warrior competitions. But Ikarios loves to run and is recognized throughout the island as he runs up and down the mountain paths and across the fields. Nausikaa has long said that he resembles her father and brothers who were tall and slender, but powerful. He won the competition for running long distance, and he stood proudly with his laurel wreath. We were all grateful for the sons of the godly Telemachos and his beautiful Queen.

A young Prince named Aristander, who comes from the kingdom of Olympia near Mt. Lykaion on the mainland, lost himself in the beauty of Arête. He sat at the banquets with his father, King Koritos, and could not remove his eyes from my beloved Arête. Strong and handsome, quiet and well mannered, he offered Arête the laurel wreath when he won the competition for jumping. She accepted the wreath with a reserved smile, but I knew that she was pleased. When the games were over and the last celebration ended, King Koritos and Prince Aristander asked to speak to Telemachos for the hand of his daughter. Telemachos, I am told, thanked the King and his son and said that he must speak to Arête, for on his island the woman's wishes are considered. I am stunned to think that Telemachos could believe these words. I am also happy to know that Aristander was pleased but worried that his fate depended on the emotions of my granddaughter, who is young and inexperienced in the expectations of suitors.

King Telemachos called a meeting of Nausikaa and Arête, who asked that I be present, and told his daughter of the offer. Upon her marriage to Aristander, Arête would be Queen of Olympia since the wife of King Koritos lost her battle at an early age with the spirits of birth when their second son was born.

My son said to Arête, "King Koritos told me that his son has watched you for four days, has made inquiries on Ithaka, and is pleased by your beauty and your modesty. The King and his son believe that the gods shine down on you. You will make a lovely queen, and they feel that you will be happy in their palace. He said that your happiness is important to his son." Arête's face took on the rosy glow of sunrise, and she showed the pleasure of one who is smitten by the arrows of Eros.

"I do not know Prince Aristander," she said with trepidation, "though he is handsome and seems to be kind."

She kept her eyes on the floor as she thought about the situation. I was deeply touched when she turned to me and asked my opinion.

"Perhaps she could take time to know him," I suggested to Telemachos. "He and his father need not return home immediately to Olympia."

Telemachos responded with enthusiasm to my proposal, "I will ask the King and Prince to be our guests for several weeks. At the end of that time if the two young people want the binding ceremony, I will agree to a wedding feast. I shall speak to them tomorrow morning."

Arête was grateful and very excited. Nausikaa had much to discuss with Telemachos, while I went with Arête to her room. We talked into the night.

I try to feel pleasure when I see the two young people walking and talking together in the public courtyard or sitting in the garden of trees where Arête invites me to share tea with them. And my heart glows when I hear Arête's laughter, and I see his smile shining down on her. But then my throat closes with pain and the loneliness that I will feel when she is gone. She has visited with me for almost all the days of her lifetime, and I feel as though together we are one. I know she will choose him. Telemachos tells me that she will not be far away on the land east of Ithaka and that he will visit to be sure she is safe and happy. I try to smile with gratitude, but I doubt that he will keep that pledge. Promises mean nothing to him.

We are weaving wedding robes for my son and Nausikaa, and on my own loom I am weaving Arête's gown for the wedding feast. It must be more beautiful than anything I have ever woven. It will be flowing silk with a silk veil in the soft colors of the sea and sky, and the breeze will make her feel free rather than imprisoned. I try to convince myself that her fate will be different from mine. I work into the night to complete her flowing robes.

The binding ceremony was this evening followed by a great banquet with all of the village leaders and, on my request, their wives. It was a joyous time with food and wine that seemed endless. Seeing the dignity of Telemachos and King Koritos and the limits of their drinking, the other men also restrained themselves and there was no drunken violence. I felt that I was home on Sikelia, and for one evening I was proud of the man my son had become. Yet, I could not stop weeping when at last I was alone.

Today my sweet girl became Queen Arête and after the midday banquet I watched her sail east to Olympia. She begins a new life, and Nausikaa and I weep together. I cannot write more.

In the long days and endless nights I feel only loneliness. But how can I feel alone and friendless when I am surrounded by my weavers, when Nausikaa comes and goes after the dancer and her daughters go to their room, and when work fills the light and darkness of my life? I realize that only the rolling seasons of Arête's growing brought warmth and pleasure of summer days even in the chill of cold storms. When Arête was running around and talking and asking questions or chatting constantly, there were moments of happiness in every day, a sense of being filled by her presence and her love.

Now, only the rare visits of my Merchant's galleys can replace the emptiness with feelings of wellbeing and joy. Then the brief days fly by like the winds. I watch his galleys set sail from the small western port of Ithaka and desolation returns. Do the gods know such loneliness or is this despair kept for mortals? It cannot be mine alone, can it? Surely Nausikaa shares my misery, but we do not speak of it. Our eyes meet and fill with the waters of sorrow.

Eurykleia becomes weak with age—another loss. She has been my Lachesis. I think of her as the Fate of good Fortune because of the story that Eurykleia told me after Father Laertes descended to the Lower World. She could not stop weeping when we lost him to Persephone. I brought her to my bedchamber and made her some tea that would bring her rest. She lay back on the soft mat I had set up next to my bed. She began to speak of her youth and the happiness of being a princess until she was stolen by traders of the dark.

"They planned to sell me at a slave market on the coast of the hot sands in Ægypt. They were thrown off course by the winds of chance and arrived on Ithaka. I heard them speak of it. They believed that I had brought them bad luck so they were willing to sell me cheaply. Or, if an Ithakan refused to buy me, I would be sacrificed to the god of winds before they left Ithaka's shore. King Laertes saw me at the market.

"Much later King Laertes told me that when he saw me tied and standing with other slaves to be sold, I touched his heart. It was my good fortune from Lachesis that Laertes bought me and saved me from a condition of slavery that could have been unbearable.

"In the House of Laertes, I was treated like one of the family. Even the Queen was as kind as she could be, beating me seldom after I began caring for the baby Odysseus. After Ktimene was born Rumor told me that Laertes warned his Queen that if she beat me again or treated me with less than the respect that I deserved as a princess from my homeland, he would find a way to punish his wife. The mother of Odysseus told the King that if he took this slave as his new wife, he would never see me alive again. He promised never to touch me, but it is rumored that he never touched his Queen again either. Thus, they had only one son.

"Once Laertes told me that he considered sending me back to my homeland, but he could not lose the vision of me in his palace. He asked me to forgive him for his weakness. Then he said that he also feared that I might be lost at sea or taken by pirates again. I remember kneeling and kissing his hand for his kindness. From that day I lived a life that was almost full." She smiled her sweet smile that I have come to love.

When she finished her story, Hypnos touched her with his wand. As he flew away, she closed her eyes and enjoyed a deep sleep for the first time in many days.

Now she stays with me and I care for her as she cared so lovingly for my Lord, my son, Father Laertes, and for me in these long years. If she lies down, she cannot rise from her thick pad, so after we help her up in the morning she sits in the soft chair that I used for Nausikaa many years past. She enjoys the sun in the garden and is soothed by the soft breeze of Zephyr. She remains gentle and smiles with gratitude when I feed her and minister to her other needs. My heart is sore when I think of her leaving us.

Eurykleia has left me, and my chest bleeds from the knife of grief. I am comforted only by the hope that she is now united with her beloved Laertes, who surely resides in the Garden of the Blessed in the Lower World.

PART FIVE

1. Dark Clouds Descend

My son has long substituted battle for love and games. It is said that his hunting voyages are really raids on the settlements and kingdoms on the islands north and along the shores east of the sea that surrounds Ithaka. I worry that his reputation will bring disaster on this island, for Retribution follows evil ways.

Everything changes yet some things seem to stay the same. I have never been able to predict how Telemachos will live or act. Sometimes I admire him and sometimes I despise him. I remind myself of the little boy in my arms, and love floods the shame that I often feel for him. My son and grandsons have been hunting in the hills of Ithaka for many rolling seasons. Now that my grandsons are as tall and as strong as their father they are hunting outside the island. I have long realized that it is more than searching for animals. It is pillage. It is murder and destruction of those who are not our enemies and who have never attacked Ithaka. My heart aches when I hear that my son brings home treasures that include slaves.

At the last full moon my son announced that they were going to sea to find wives for my two oldest grandsons. My heart stopped. Pictures of my abduction flew by my eyes, and the river of sobs threatened to overcome me. I excused myself and left the banquet for the comfort of my altar.

Telemachos and his sons have been gone for several new moons. Will they be lost like the great hero Odysseus? Or are they making a similar journey around the shores and islands of the Great Sea? We may never see them again, but I say nothing of my fears to Nausikaa.

My days are filled with weaving until I am too tired to write the heavy thoughts and fearful images that fill my mind. We wait again day and night.

Telemachos and my grandsons returned today. The whole palace met them in the courtyard as they entered the main gate. The weavers stayed on the stairs and cheered with everyone else. Laertes and Alkinoös were beaming as they led their handsome wives to the Great Room. As we sat together feasting in the Great Room, my son told of their adventures and success in bringing home worthy wives.

"We sailed to Corfu where we met that land's great lord with seven daughters. Lord Lexanos welcomed us when he learned that I am the son of Odysseus, the hero of the Trojan War. And he was honored to offer two of his daughters to the grandsons of Odysseus. There was a great celebration in that land as my sons had the pick of the lovely daughters of marriageable age."

My son continued in a self-important tone, "Laertes chose the first daughter Marua who should be overjoyed that she will eventually be Queen of Ithaka. And Alkinoös chose the second daughter Nerua, another beauty as you can see. Let us drink to their long and productive life on Ithaka. May they have many sons." We all raised our cups and our voices in greeting the two girls who smiled and giggled with the pleasure of this attention.

The sisters are very close and happy to be together. I too am delighted for them. I would have gladly come to Ithaka, or anywhere, if my sister had come with me.

Ithaka's wedding celebration for both princes began soon after their arrival. I hope that I was wrong in my observations, but the sisters appeared to be disappointed that Ithaka was not so elegant as their homeland. They looked around with eyes that said we were all beneath them. The weaving may bring them down to our level.

The new wives were allowed to rest for several days after the wedding festivities. Then Telemachos announced that their job in the palace was weaving. Marua burst out laughing, assuming that he was joking. She did not realize at that time that Telemachos does not make jokes. He is deadly serious and thought that she was laughing at him. Insulted, he repeated his order then rose from the table and walked away.

After their weeping subsided, the women were led up to the weaving room, and they were not pleased. I welcomed them at the door. I had two looms ready and prepared for them to start weaving to show us what they could do. They started to look around at what the weavers were doing. They were surprised and gradually awed at the beauty of the robes. They were also shocked at the weavers' clothing. My weavers and I laughed. I explained our Phoenician-style men's clothes and why we wore them to stay cool and to give more freedom to our arms. They seemed to understand, but they were skeptical and resistant. The hot season has descended on the island, so I knew that they would eventually join us in the comfort of our clothing.

The story of the two sisters is an interesting one, I think. In the weaving room they stayed by themselves, and it took some time for them to speak to the other weavers, and only when necessary. When the summer days made the heat and discomfort in our weaving room intolerable, in spite of the air coming through the windows, they asked permission to replace their long robes with the short sleeves and openness of our garments while they worked. Despite this submission to our ways, they seemed separate from us and stayed distanced from the other weavers. They treated me like a servant and did not share in our meals or eat our stews, even when it was cool enough for me to have the fires going on the balcony. Instead, they ate their morning meal before they came to us and left the weaving room before the middle meal in order to eat by themselves or among those worthy of their attention. When Marua was very large with child, they stayed away from the weaving room and attended to each other below.

When they were forced to return to our room, they refused to lower themselves to ask for help or guidance in improving their work, so they never improved. They declined our invitation to join us on our bathing days, even when Nausikaa came to the inlet with us. The weavers frowned at their aroma when they entered the room each morning and were anxious about their bringing vermin among us. I shared my weavers' concerns. I rearranged the room and placed the two sisters alone in a corner nearest the door. This is where they remain.

For many years, Ithakans have spread stories of my herbs and their curative effects—the salves that take away boils, the aloe that cures cuts and burns, and the teas that scare away coughs and headaches and other illnesses. It has been difficult to care for all the people coming to the palace for my assistance. As I have been weaving less when my fingers swell up with pain and I wait for my teas to take effect, Naela and her daughter Penelopeia have become the organizers and teachers in the weaving room. I have been working to instruct others in the secrets of herbs and plants. Nausikeia and Pero and Agape have been of great benefit for their cleverness and curiosity. Of course, we cannot eliminate all the ills of this island, but sometimes if they follow my directions someone recovers. And often my teas make leaving this life gentler. It is a comfort for all of us to be of assistance in these most painful and difficult times.

Ikarios, my youngest and cleverest grandson, has taken a wife. Though Phylia came to the palace with joy, I watch her and feel that she is not happy here. Ikarios met her while he was running alone in the hills. Telemachos had been urging him, or bullying him, to take a wife and give him grandsons. I guess Ikarios thought that this pretty young girl was as good as any. He started to visit her and her family and urged his father the King to ask for her hand without demanding a large bride price. She is the daughter of one of the leaders of the island, and the family was honored. She was flattered and grateful that the King's handsome son wanted her above all other girls on the island. She had no idea what life in the King's palace would be.

They had a grand wedding, like the banquets arranged for the other two sons, and Phylia came to live with us. Almost immediately after the wedding feast Telemachos told me that she would be a weaver, and I was to teach her the art. Then my son and his two warrior sons went pillaging along the shore of the land that leads to Mycenae. Ikarios said that he was newly married and could not go. Instead, he went running, as he often does, through the hills and valleys of Ithaka.

A servant led Phylia to the weaving room where the two wives of my other grandsons were busy at work. Phylia looked around with disdain and said that she expected that the wife of a Prince would not have to work like the slaves of the palace.

The wife of my eldest grandson, who would someday be Queen of the island and who was now far along with her second child, said with a loud, clear voice, "On Ithaka, all important and noble women are weavers. Perhaps you would prefer to stay all day in a small room where you do no weaving and have no value to anyone. We consider it a privilege to learn the art from Lady Penelope."

I was astounded. Marua had always treated me as a lesser creature because she was the daughter of a King on Corfu, a larger island north of Ithaka, and was unaware of my royal birth. Suddenly she was grateful for what she had learned from me? I saw her lower her head and glance with a tiny smile at her sister. I could not speak for anger that Marua thought I was foolish enough to believe her deceitful flattery. I looked at my weavers and saw smiles of pleasure on their faces. They want to believe the best of everyone, especially if someone respects me.

My weavers, who no longer consider themselves as slaves but as free artisans who are confined by circumstances to the room they have come to love, looked at Phylia with frowns. She had not begun her life among us in the most propitious manner.

Phylia must have realized that she was suddenly among enemies because she had insulted all of us. She lowered her head. I took her to an empty loom, gave her the yarn, and told her in a restrained voice to set up the loom. Everyone secretly watched her while she struggled with the new type of loom. Now that she was appropriately subdued by her own misguided pretensions, I went over to help her and to explain the new looms that we had redesigned over the years. She listened quietly and worked throughout the day to set up the yarns correctly. At the noon meal, she sat in a corner by herself because the other women were not yet ready to forgive her haughtiness. She ate the stew from a cup because she did not yet have a bowl of her own and was clearly not accustomed to the flavors and textures. She did not like it. Nor was she pleased when she glanced around at the other women enjoying their special meal. At the end of the day after the work was done, I did not release her to go down to the banquet with the family. Instead, I walked her around to show her the work being done by our weavers. She was silent, but her eyes widened at the beauty of their garments. I knew that her learning was just beginning. I hoped that she would improve more than her two sisters-in-law have done.

Phylia has returned to the weaving room with eyes lowered. Subdued, she set to work immediately. Her weaving is very primitive, as it is throughout the island.

Occasionally, a family sends a child with interest or talent to me to learn the art, and she stays with us for many rolling seasons. When I feel that she has become accomplished enough to return to her family with the ability to weave garments that can be traded by her father for their family's needs, she says goodbye to us. Sometimes the girl does not want to return to her family and wants to live with the weavers instead. In that case, if she is a gifted weaver, we deal with her father by offering him one third of everything that she weaves. Then he can trade her goods at the market. She will provide an income for the family, and her father will not have to feed or clothe her or offer a dowry to get rid of her. I must admit that I send him the robes that are woven more quickly, often with a looser weave, but still lovelier than most garments on the island. The finer cloth and designs we keep for the royal family and for Cadmus.

Nauriteia and her two daughters are now living in the weaving room with us. One day she came to me with tears on her cheeks and begged to remain overnight. I brought her to the garden and we talked quietly together. She said that she cannot protect herself or her daughters if she remains in the room originally given to her by Telemachos.

"He lost interest in me long ago," she said in shame, "but I was still considered his woman. After this time has passed without giving him a son and the men realize that he does not visit me or care about me, they think that I am available to anyone. I have kept them out of my room until last night. Now I know that my daughters, though they are young, will be next. Please help us. Protect us, please. My daughters and I will work hard for you and will be grateful forever."

She was on her knees with her arms around my legs, and she was weeping, "I did not know when I learned the art of dancing in my homeland that all men would think badly of me. Where I grew up, the best dancers were admired and treated with respect for our virtue. I had a special place in the palace that protected me. Then I was abducted from the marketplace where I had always felt safe. When I arrived on Ithaka and was bought by the wine merchant," she sobbed, "I learned another way of life. Then I thanked Fortune that the King bought me and saved me from the sad life with the wine merchant who would willingly sell me nightly to the men of the island. I did not understand that the King would also want me for his bed and would not appreciate the beauty of my art."

Realizing that the King is my son she said quickly, "Forgive me, Lady. You have always been kind to me and to my daughters who love you. I did not mean to offend you. But please, I beg you to help us. We have no other friend on this island." And she covered her face with shame and sobbed as I put my arms around her.

"You have a room full of friends," I said to her, "and we will be glad to have you stay with us. You are welcome." My maidservants then went to her room below and brought up the few things that belong to her.

They now have a space too small for the three of them at the base of her loom, but they seem to be content in their safety and smile more freely.

I must tell Nausikaa that Nauriteia and her daughters are living with us. Perhaps if I explain why she begged me to stay with the weavers and how she has been treated since leaving her homeland, Nausikaa may be willing to visit our rooms. Nausikaa is a generous and kind woman and would not want to see anyone abused. It is not the fault of Nauriteia that she came to this palace, I will say to my lovely Nausikaa. I pray to Athene and Hera for guidance.

Phylia has progressed rather quickly considering the quality of her weaving when she came to us. The weavers also began to help her and suggested ways to sit and move more efficiently. They realized that she was working very hard to please. Marpessa even volunteered to be her loom mate so they could stand and work together. Unfortunately, one day she reversed all of the goodwill that she had gained in the many new moons she had been with us. She sent young Briseia, the daughter of Nauriteia, to get a skein of yellow yarn. We have several shades of each color on the shelves of our storage room, and there is only one window for light in that room. The child did not recognize the subtle shades and brought back the wrong yarn.

Phylia let loose the anger that she had apparently been holding behind her teeth and screamed at the child, "That is not the shade that I sent you for, stupid girl. There is enough foolishness around here without wasting my time and delaying the completion of this robe."

Phylia threw the skein of yarn at the child. A sound like breath went throughout the room—then complete silence. No one moved. Briseia started to cry, and I went to her. The weavers and maids do not treat each other with cruelty. We do not humiliate each other.

I put my arm around the child and took her to the storage room to explain the different shades, which she knew but had not recognized in the dimness of the storage room. I wiped her face, and she picked out the correct yellow and walked slowly back to Phylia. By this time no one would look at Phylia, who clearly knew the mistake she had made. Even Marpessa, the quiet one, showed disgust.

Phylia began to weep and ran out of the room. She did not return that day or the next.

Several days passed before she returned. I am told that she went to Ikarios to complain about the weavers, and about me, and said that she is not treated well. He went to Telemachos who spoke to me. I told him what happened.

"I knew that she was responsible," he said. "She gives Ikarios no peace with her tongue that should be cut off. I will speak to her."

A maidservant told me that Telemachos told Phylia that she could make a choice—she could go back to weaving and apologize for her behavior or she would be sent back to her father with her small bride price. The size of the bride price was degrading enough, but she also knew that being returned to her father was a humiliation to her family that would not be forgiven—or forgotten. No man would ever want her again, so she would be a burden to the family. Her father may well throw her out of the house to survive, or not, on the land, or he could take her to the marketplace where she could be sold as a slave. The alternatives were terrible.

She returned to the weaving room with eyes lowered and whispered that she was sorry for her temper. The weavers stopped and gave her their full attention. She said that life has not been easy for her, and she burst into deep and wrenching sobs. My weavers, who never forget but are always willing to forgive, returned to their tasks to show that she was one of us again.

I took Phylia to the garden where I made mint tea and we talked.

"It was difficult for me also when I first came to Ithaka against my will, but with time I made a place that is comfortable for me," I said. "I hoped that you would begin to enjoy the friendships of the weavers who are gentle and kind women. And I hoped that you would come to trust me to talk whenever pain overwhelms you.

"Weaving is not a competition—it is an art," I said. "The only thing I will not accept," I whispered, "is letting you insult and hurt the people who work together in the weaving room. They do not deserve it."

She nodded and thanked me humbly. I let her sit in the garden and think about what I had said and what she might offer to my weavers. When she joined Marpessa at the loom, she worked diligently without complaint. I noticed also that she whispered something to Briseia who smiled and nodded. At our midday meal, Phylia asked to share the rabbit stew. She is trying to be one of us.

She is still a child, almost as young as I was when I arrived on Ithaka.

So far Phylia is doing better, and her work is improving. I do like her and feel sorry for her disappointments. People think that marrying a king or a prince offers the happiest and most fulfilling life. Instead, I think that the success of one's marriage depends on the nature of the woman and the man, not on his position. Perhaps it is only my situation that leads me to such a conclusion.

Not everyone has done as well as Phylia. After long seasons of patience I have asked Telemachos to allow Marua and Nerua to weave by themselves. I asked that a small room be set up for them to be together in their work. I said that I could not teach them anything more. I have tried, and I have ignored their insults and rudeness. They kept the robes that they wove for their own families until my grandsons complained about the inferior work. Marua and Nerua were humiliated and angry when their robes were kept for the servants and I sent the better work to their families according to their needs. It is amazing how their pride kept them looking down on us even when they never reached the heights of my weavers. One day I finally admitted to myself that I do not like these women and decided to avoid them when possible.

They have closed their eyes to growing, not only as weavers but also as women. As a result of their characters, they are losing much that could give them pleasure in life—and give pleasure to everyone around them.

I have hesitated to confront these weaknesses in my grandsons' wives. They are family, and I feel that I have failed in teaching them about what is important and what is not. Perhaps Corfu failed them, and they will never feel good about anything that they have. They seem to think about nothing, do nothing, and learn nothing. They are both despondent, and my grandsons are miserable. The evening banquets are uncomfortable. There is little to say and little to make us laugh. Even their babies offer little joy. Each one now has two daughters, and my grandsons are bitterly disappointed that they do not have sons.

Nausikaa is sad and feels that her husband chose foolishly when he chose wives for his sons. I think that Telemachos does not know his sons and therefore does not know what would please them. And he certainly did not recognize the characters of the two girls he chose. But then Telemachos knows little about people. He only knows what makes him feel good at each moment and cares little about others. He is so like his father.

The only positive thing about this story is that we now have more room for Nauriteia and her two daughters. They have space for their three mats and sleep more comfortably together. It is a pleasure to have Nauriteia among us, for she is now a fine weaver and everyone has affection for her.

Cadmus has been on the island for two days. Seeing him would be enough to bring life back to my spirit, but there is something else that he brings to me. Throughout the years, on each visit, he has passed to me hidden sheets of parchment on which he has written the history of his life and of my family—how my brother the King has continued the tradition of peace and prosperity in our kingdom and how my second brother has created huge lemon and orange groves that produce food for trade. Each of my brothers has a family of sons and daughters who make their parents proud. I am happy for them. They always treated me with kindness and love.

Cadmus also tells me that my sister resides inland and so he cannot see her. But he hears that she is well and has a family that is grand. I must believe that.

My mother has not done well. One day when she was screaming at a servant, she fell to the floor in a swoon. Unable to speak or move for several new moons, she finally went silently into the Lower World where she is still in a rage, I am sure. Sadly, something about my mother's fate never allowed her to find pleasure in the sunshine of her days. Now the darkness encloses her forever. It is a story of unnecessary misery.

Beyond my family's stories, my Merchant friend also offers me leaves of wisdom. With every sheet of parchment I learn new words, unfamiliar ways of speaking, and opinions or ideas that no one else on this island would ever consider. After every visit I have been left thinking about my life and my fate in new ways.

I am not alone in my admiration for my friend. He and Ikarios have had long discussions about the world that the Merchant knows. Ikarios cannot seem to get enough information about the Merchant's experiences and what other kingdoms and peoples are like, where and how they live, the languages they speak, their manners and beliefs and laws. I was surprised to hear when I approached them at the banquet last night that Cadmus was describing Sikelia and my people. My throat closed with longing, and I held back my tears. I sat quietly and listened. We were early for the feast and so sat together as Cadmus told us of my brothers and their families, of the continued success of their peaceful way of life, and of the wondrous oils and wines that still make that kingdom famous.

"Their weaving takes second place only to the robes of Ithaka," he said, as he glanced at me beneath his eyebrows.

I could feel the heat rise in my face as my grandson smiled proudly at me. I felt that my grandson, who has always been close to me in his interests, looked at me with new eyes. Ikarios asked me how I remembered my homeland, and I contributed to the pleasure of the conversation until others arrived and we became silent.

We all sat at the banquet table long after the food was consumed and talked with Cadmus who told stories of the world.

My son said something that I don't remember and Cadmus answered, "The art of Lady Penelope has brought fame to Ithaka throughout the shores of the Great Sea."

I felt my cheeks flame, but Cadmus continued, "Queen Dido, who built Carthage into a rich and glorious kingdom and who will forever be remembered for her passion for Aeneas and her love of her land, admired Lady Penelope's weaving. I am told that she was wearing a robe woven by my Lady when the Carthaginian Queen met her untimely death. Even Hades must have been awed to greet the beautiful Queen in her glowing robe into his kingdom."

I raised my eyes brimming with sad tears and he went on, "I have gained some measure of fame myself by trading with kings across the shores of the Great Sea the splendid robes woven by the gifted Lady Penelope, Queen Nausikaa, and their weavers."

He paused. The brightness that his praise of our weaving had brought to his eyes suddenly dimmed. Some different thought made him frown.

Then he said quietly but with purpose, "Now the reputation of Ithaka has altered. Its lust for war and raids has spread to the western shores of the Great Sea and to the eastern islands beyond the Peloponnese. From the Pillars of Hercules, to Libya and Sikelia, to Krete and beyond, I have heard stories of bloodshed brought by the Ithakan royalty. The family of Odysseus is quickly losing the glory that once brought honor to this island."

"Is this a criticism or a reprimand I hear from our guest?" my son asked with outrage in his voice and his eyes.

"Neither a criticism nor a reprimand, Lord, but perhaps a warning for friends I have known for all the years of your life. Rumor has spread that settlements all along the shores of the Great Sea are preparing for your next raid. They are getting ready to wage war against you."

Laertes with the quick anger of his father said, "We fear no small settlements of weak and cowardly men."

"Would you know fear for your people if those settlements combined into an army that attacked Ithaka?" Cadmus asked. "It is told by Rumor that such an army is being formed. It may take time, but care must be taken to protect your island."

While Cadmus was speaking, the color drained from the faces of my son and grandsons.

Ikarios stood and said with disgust, "I have told you that you would bring down destruction on Ithaka with your warlike ways."

Laertes bellowed, "Why should we listen to a coward whose fear makes him run to the hills instead of standing with his kinsmen in our raids?"

Ikarios quickly challenged the accusation with his own question, "Why should I stand in blood and see the suffering you bring upon peaceful settlements unprepared for battle? Is that what you call bravery? It is like the heavy sandal that steps on a small hill of ants and takes pleasure in the killing. There is no courage in that." Laertes stood and drew his sword.

In fury Telemachos yelled, "Stop! You would kill your brother over words? Has Eris overtaken our kingdom? Not in the House of Odysseus and Telemachos is there such strife to make us kill our kin."

Nausikaa had sat throughout with silent tears marking her cheeks and her heart.

Before he spoke once more, Ikarios looked at his mother then at Telemachos. Quietly he announced, "I am leaving with Cadmus to sail to the ports of the Great Sea. I will be gone for both cold and hot seasons in order to learn the ways of gods and people. Cadmus has agreed to take me with him and teach me in order to help my King when I return," he said.

When Ikarios declared that he was leaving with Cadmus on the next tide, everyone gasped. His wife screamed. She became so hysterical that two guards carried her to her room. Poor girl. She is left without a child or hope for the future.

Cadmus and Ikarios left today on the dawn's tide. Before they left, they came to my room and told me that they would stop at Sikelia so Ikarios could learn about my family and my homeland. I am full of gratitude and tears.

Phylia sobbed uncontrollably when they left, and I fear for her health if she does not learn the art of accepting her fate. I will spend more time with her and urge several of my weavers to befriend her. Keeping her busy may help. So much depends on how long their journey will last. But for now, I have little expectation of soothing her soon.

Long seasons have passed since Ikarios left his wife in order to sail the seas. One day Phylia stayed with me after the weaving was done. We went to the balcony garden, and I made tea with the evening meal of lamb, roots, bread and cheese, and curd with fruit and honey. We sat quietly for some time, and I waited to hear what she wanted to say to me. When it was almost dark and Helios was ready to sleep, she began to tell me how unhappy she had been since she came to the palace.

"Ikarios never saw me," she said. "He was not unkind, but he hardly spoke to me or touched me when he was here. He did not seem interested in me. He thought only of the world, of plants, of the skies and sea, and of what other people think. He never cared about what I think. Please do not be insulted if I tell you that I would have been happier if I had married a simple poor herdsman who felt affection for me and wanted me."

She stopped for some moments then proceeded with tears filling her large eyes, "Am I so ugly, do I look so bad that he cannot care about me? And now he is gone for long seasons, and he may never return. I may never have a child to make me a woman admired. I may spend my life alone like you, and I would rather throw myself into the pit of Hades than be alone forever." Phylia began to sob.

I sat quietly for some time; then I began to tell her about my life. I was careful to explain that her fate is not mine.

"It is true that my life has been one of waiting, but yours need not be the same. Perhaps Ikarios has the curiosity of his grandfather, and he must travel for a short time to satisfy that longing for knowledge. But it is not his fate to travel the seas forever. Cadmus, the greatest merchant in the world, will not let anything happen to keep him from returning home. Cadmus will bring him back to us with the belief that home and family are the most important gifts in life. After Ikarios sees great kingdoms like Carthage and Sikelia, Ægypt and Phaiakia, Krete and Tyre, and other places poorer and less developed, he will return to improve Ithaka, I am certain. If you are happy to see him and let kindness control your tongue, he will be grateful and pleased to be back. He will tell you his stories and you too will grow from his experiences. Cadmus will teach him how to be gentle and caring to all of us.

"Remember, Ikarios has grown up with men who respect only hard battle. When he was a little child, he was loving and happy and enjoyed my garden and the beauty of nature's gods. Then his father and brothers laughed at what they thought was weakness and forced him to share their hunting and killing. He ran into the hills to be away from them, but their power still confused him about the nature of men. Cadmus will teach him another way of life, a way to show manliness without violence and strength with tenderness.

"It is important that he is away from Ithaka while his father and brothers are plundering the nearby lands," I suggested, hoping that I was correct. "If the gods allow, Ikarios may bring peace to the men of Ithaka and will give you the family and life that you desire. Pray to the gods, and prepare yourself to be worthy of him when he returns."

"Thank you, Lady," she murmured as she took my hand and said that she could sleep now. I spread a pallet and blanket for her. She lay down on the floor of the balcony and whispered to Hypnos to bring lovely dreams instead of nightmares.

I understand her pain and frustration with Ikarios gone on the seas with Cadmus. She is without a child and does not know if he will return. She is lonely and without love. I understand.

Phylia is now sleeping on the floor of my room. I do not know how long she will stay with me, but calm seems to enclose her. In her weaving and friendships she is doing far better than Marua and

Nerua, who refused to interact with anyone beyond each other. I fear that their attitudes, which brought poison into the weaving room, will always keep happiness far away. I am glad that I put them in a room by themselves for their weaving. The problem was not my weavers—it is their own arrogant natures. They believe that Corfu is the only acceptable place to live and that everything about Ithaka, the tiny island in the Ionian Sea, is beneath them. I agree that Ithaka could be much better, but the three wives together could improve it so much. Instead, these two disdain everything and everyone and stay by themselves. Because Nausikaa is Queen, they speak to her, but I have seen Marua and Nerua make faces behind her back and it enrages me. Nausikaa's homeland, like mine, is far more beautiful and elegant and civilized than either Corfu or Ithaka. Yet, these two young girls believe they are superior. Hubris always amazes me, especially when there is no basis for such conceit. Phylia, at least, is learning the ways of kindness and curiosity. She will become a great woman if her husband returns to love her and give her the family that fills her dreams.

Poor Phylia. The loneliness and frustration of waiting are driving her mad, despite her attempts to control herself. I try to think of ways to fill her time until Ikarios returns, but her passions occasionally overcome her. Sometimes when her bad temper takes control of her warm nature, the weavers keep their eyes on their looms and frown. It seems to happen around the same time of each moon's growth, and nothing seems to soothe her except one of my teas. When she screams with the pain of her bleeding, I take her to the garden, put her pallet on the floor, give her my special soothing tea, and she sleeps for the day. When she awakens, she sobs with the misery of another barren month. At least she does not strike out at my weavers, but rather weeps and suffers by herself. I have learned not to wait until she insults someone before giving her the tea.

Her sadness has been made more intense by seeing Marua and Nerua with their children. Yet they also are pained by not giving sons to the palace of Telemachos. They seem to be more concerned about satisfying the King than pleasing their own husbands. And the King only frowns or growls at them. I do not understand this. But Phylia would be happy to have even a daughter, she told me once. She longs for the softness of a baby and is pleased to care for the babies of other women, though the green spirit of Jealousy torments her. Ikarios has been gone with Cadmus for several seasons, and I do not know how much longer Phylia can survive this agony.

One day she even asked me if I thought she could return to her father with her dowry and if he would accept her so that she could remarry. I would have interceded for her with Telemachos and his sons and argued that Ikarios may not return, but I suspect that Phylia may have a different motive. I saw her look at a guest one evening and knew the look that he returned. If my son or any man on Ithaka suspects that she wants another man and would take him to her bed, her disloyalty to her husband will bring sorrow beyond her imagining. She would be stoned and he would be hanged. I told her to think hard on what she wanted and the trouble it would bring down on her and on the man she wants. She seemed shocked and was frightened that I had guessed. She lowered her head in shame and sobbed. I put my arms around her and held her close. I whispered that her secret was safe with me.

"There is a difference between desiring and giving in to desire," I said. "Helen and Paris, filled with lust, caused the destruction of many thousands of men and of a whole kingdom," I reminded her. "And Paris was killed by his appetites. You may not cause another Troy, but you will bring down untold pain and suffering if you allow passion and loneliness to control your actions."

She was silent for some time. Then she told me humbly that she will live in the weaving room from that day until Ikarios returns. I feel relieved by her decision but wonder where I will put yet another pallet. My weaving room may save her life, as it has saved so many women in this palace.

How could I judge her or shower recrimination upon her when I too am pursued by my own secrets and desires?

2. Invasion and Its Aftermath

Since the days of the great games on Ithaka when the sons of Telemachos showed the world their prowess, Telemachos and his two elder sons have been raiding the settlements and kingdoms on islands of the Great Sea and on the mainland east of Ithaka. I have heard that they have sailed up and down the coastline and have, as Cadmus warned, become widely known for their cruelty and greed. Since my two grandsons brought back their brides, they have been going farther and farther away from Ithaka and staying away from home for longer periods, sometimes for many swellings of the moon.

When Rumor whispered these stories to Nausikaa, she confronted Telemachos in my presence.

"Why," she asked, "do you bring such suffering to people? Why do you need to do battle and leave a legacy of hate to Ithaka instead of a name that all people can admire?"

"I will not be questioned by a woman," he roared. Demanding his right to absolute power, he continued, "I am King of Ithaka and son of the godlike Odysseus. My sons and I are protected in order to fight for the honor of the gods."

"And what of other men's sons? Is it always their fate to be slaughtered by you and by my sons? What honor is there in that?" Nausikka asked.

Telemachos said in a low and frightening voice, "It is their fate, stupid woman, and say nothing more of it."

I have been torn with foreboding. Each time new slaves are brought to Ithaka, the atmosphere becomes darker with misery. But Telemachos has ignored everyone. I cannot tell what has happened to him. Must he relive his father's Troy for the remainder of his days in the Upper World? Does he await his father's return to show Odysseus the heroism of a son? It is all a waste.

Terrible affliction has been brought to my family and to Ithaka.

Last week we saw the world's revenge when Telemachos returned without strength to walk and without his second son. Alkinoös left his breath on the shore of a far land, and Telemachos may not survive his terrible wounds. We have been in mourning for Alkinoös since the empty pyre was lit as a tribute to the warrior's spirit, and Nausikaa and Nerua wail in grief and tear their hair, as is their custom. The two little daughters of Alkinoös and Nerua look terrified and hide in my garden and in my arms. They stay in my bed at night and refuse to leave my room. I think that their mother's screams and sobs frighten them more than the darkness brought down on the uncertain palace. I cannot describe the desolation I feel when I look at what the actions of Telemachos have caused to our family. I hardly have the energy or desire to minister to my son or to try to wrench him back from the shore of the Underworld.

Telemachos is on fire with disease brought on by his wounds. He moans day and night and fights over and over the battle that took Alkinoös. He does not know where he is or who we are. His arm was injured so that Laertes and his guards cut off his arm below the elbow and used fire to burn the skin together. By the time they returned to Ithaka, his arm was swollen and purple above the elbow and he was no longer aware of his surroundings. We had to cut above the swelling and stitch the skin together after washing and draining the wound. Then we kept soaking the wound to get all the evil out of it. His skin is still hot, but Nausikaa is with him feeding him drops of water and tea. Servants bathe him every hour, and we pray to the gods of medicine that our teas calm him and cure the fire in his body.

We are doing everything we know, but I feel fear every time I see Medon at my door. He is still my son's closest friend and is helping Laertes direct the small army of warriors who now protect the palace from those on Ithaka who would take advantage of our weakness.

Several days after Telemachos and my grandson returned from battle, Medon explained to me what happened on their journey.

"We invaded Pylos, a kingdom beloved of the gods, and took the young daughter of King Antilochos and twelve women and children as slaves. We also raided the markets and stole much wealth from that kingdom. We were driven away from the shore of that land when warriors from Sparta joined the guards from Pylos. It was in the battle with Spartans that Alkinoös met a swordsman stronger than himself, and King Telemachos lost his powers as a warrior. No longer will he be ready for battle," Medon said with sorrow.

And no longer will he take his men on raids to insure his name as a hero, I wanted to add.

"What happened to the princess? Do you know her age?" I asked my friend.

"I do not know, my Lady. There was such confusion after the King was injured that I do not know if she is among the slaves that we put on our ship. I will try to find her," he said as he arose to leave.

"Bring her to me when you locate her, please. I will make inquiries also. How terrified the princess must be, regardless of her age, if she was abducted from her homeland." I could only think of Agape and prayed to the gods that nothing has been done to hurt the princess.

I did not tell Medon that one child from Pylos was dressed like royalty and so she may be the Princess. Or she could be an attendant to the princess. I do not want my grandson Laertes, the new King, to take revenge on her for his father's fate. I have kept her with me, isolated in my room, since the first day she arrived, but I do not know who she is. Her hysteria at being captured frightened the soldiers, and they would have killed her upon their arrival home, but I told them that I would see to her. Relieved, they gave her over to me and to Nausikaa who also agreed to take her.

We do not know her name. She came to us tied with rope, as I was once tied, in order to keep the child from jumping overboard on the journey to Ithaka. Though she will not speak or eat or even rise from her pallet, I am concerned that she might jump from my garden balcony. For that reason, I tied her hand to the bed with soft yarn and assigned one of the maids to watch her and to keep her safe. She is protected, but nothing calms her except the comfort that sleep brings. As she realizes that our rooms offer her kindness and safety, she may allow calm to soothe her. It will take time, but the sorrow will never leave her.

I sat for some time wondering what Telemachos will be for the rest of his life even if he does survive the fire in his blood. How will he meet his father when Odysseus returns from his journey? Will my son ever again raise his head to meet the eyes of other men? Where is his pride now—this hubris that destroys kingdoms and people?

Medon is saddened by the condition of his friend the King. He sits by the side of my son and grieves. Medon fears that the army of Pylos will invade Ithaka, even as the Greeks brought retribution to the walls of Troy for the abduction of Helen. I heard him talking to Laertes in the Great Room, urging my grandson to gather all the men and boys of Ithaka to prepare to defend the island.

Laertes, sounding like my son, called Medon a coward and said, "The men of Pylos are not such fools as to defy the gods and attack the home of beloved Odysseus." I heard his empty remarks as I sat with my son.

Ignoring this hollow arrogance, Medon begged, "Let me fortify the walls and gates of the palace, my Lord. Then if we are attacked, at least the palace can be defended until the assault is put down," he argued.

I was so proud of my young friend's intelligence and loyalty. Medon remembers the days he was stolen from his family and brought to Ithaka. He has told me so in our pleasant talks in my garden on so many warm evenings. Yet, he has forgiven the House of Odysseus for denying him his family and giving him ours. He calls me his savior, and we have remained friends. Now he shows me that his judgment far outweighs that of my son and grandsons. He has fought for my son, though I know that he never wanted to assail other lands.

"Should a slave dare to tell a King what to do to protect his people?" Laertes roared with rage. "I could run you through with my sword, you fool. Only your deep friendship with my father protects you, but let me hear no more of this from you or I will forget your history on this island. Now leave us and leave the kingdom to the King." Medon bowed and turned away.

Laertes is now King and believes that his new title means that the gods have given him wisdom as well as absolute power. He has the pride and folly of his father but without the stratagems and cleverness of his grandfather. We are doomed.

Nausikaa and I went to Telemachos to ask him why he brought such shame and destruction on our family and what he will do to save us, but he was still in the land of unknowing and could not even hear or see us. I realized that speaking to him of his choices was useless. He is his father's son.

When we believed that Telemachos had been brought back from the gates of the Lower World where Hades reigns, Medon came to the weaving room to visit with me. The look of his eyes held both desolation and exhaustion.

I asked him the reason for his sorrow beyond my son's wounds, and he said, "Oh, my Lady, what we have done!"

Suddenly he burst into tears. I was shocked because this was not the Medon I had known since my son was a baby crawling the floors of the palace. I asked him to follow me, and I took him into my garden. When we sat down and we sipped the mint tea that he likes so well, I asked what he meant.

He began to speak with a break in his voice, "Lady, as you know the kingdom we plundered was Pylos, a land beloved by the gods and by Lord Odysseus." Of course I knew that, but he needed to tell his story once again and I listened.

He continued, "The winds of Aiolos drove us off course. We did not know that we had sailed the distance to Pylos. When Telemachos saw the activities of a thriving port and market, he did not take the time to inquire where we were. We tied up our ships away from the port, and he gave the order of invasion. We did not know that this was Nestor's kingdom, Nestor, the friend of Odysseus and the generous and wise friend Telemachos visited when he went in search of his great father. Many years ago it was Nestor who opened his gates to us as though we were his kin, and now we have invaded his land. Nestor, we have learned from the women we enslaved, has long been walking in the Elysian Field, and his grandson Antilochos is now the King of Pylos.

"It is his daughter we abducted when she and her handmaidens were visiting the markets. Since our women are not allowed such freedom on Ithaka, we had no idea that royalty was walking the streets on Pylos. By plundering that kingdom we defied the laws of loyalty and friendship, and I fear that King Antilochos will come in war for his daughter. The gods smile on such vengeance. The Pylians knew who we are and where our kingdom is when we left their land. Telemachos announced his name and lineage loudly throughout the marketplace. They and their Spartan allies will come for the princess."

"Have you spoken to Laertes again about your fears and how to return the princess before Ithaka is attacked?"

"Yes, my Lady, but he has no memory of Nestor's kindness to Telemachos since Laertes was not even a dream at that time. He says that returning the princess would be a mark of weakness, that he is his father's son and the grandson of the heroic and godlike Odysseus, and that he will not show such frailty. It would shame his father who cannot speak for himself at this time, he says. I have great fears, my Lady. He calls me a woman and sneers at me." He looked down with shame.

"We also have another problem, Lady. We cannot locate the princess. She may have been killed on the shore of Pylos or taken as a slave by one of our seamen who left for his home after we arrived on Ithaka. Or she may be in the marketplace as a public woman, though I have made inquiries and cannot recognize royalty among the girls and women there."

He said quietly, "The gods have no sympathy for mistakes. They will punish Ithaka, I am certain."

"I too am certain," I answered. "Can you start secret preparations for defending Ithaka and hope that a treaty may be made by returning the princess when they arrive here? She may be in the palace among the workers. Nausikaa and I will look for her."

Medon sat silently for some time with thought wrinkling his brow. Then he said, "Perhaps to save the princess, Antilochos may stop an invasion if we return all that we took from their land and repay them for the damages we made. We cannot make up for the deaths of those in the market, but they may accept some reparations. I shall try to talk with Laertes today. He is hard at work with his men repairing the ships and making new weapons, but he may speak to me. If he would listen and think hard on the consequences and if we could locate the princess, we might be saved."

Standing up godlike he said, "Thank you for hearing me, my Lady. The gods hear your prayers. Please ask them for this favor—that Ithaka may survive the errors of our past."

With renewed determination Medon left the garden. I sat watching the lights of Helios dance on the waters in the distance and felt little hope. Where have the gods been for me in the long rolling years of my life? Why would they listen to me now? I walked up to my shrine, knelt down with my forehead touching the cool mosaic floor, and wept through my prayers.

My poor Nausikaa. Despite her courage and strength, she suffers deeply. Her family is in tatters. Arête is lost to us by distance and marriage, and we hear nothing of her that might bring us comfort. Nausikaa's husband, my son, balances on the edge of this upper world and the Kingdom of Hades where her second son resides, and her weak and impotent son Laertes has become King of Ithaka. He is driven by hubris and is therefore useless. We hear nothing of Ikarios.

Nausikaa spends day and night with my son, and his condition of mind and body drags her into shadow with him. Last night I visited their room, and I left feeling that all hope for Ithaka is lost. Today we talked briefly together outside of his room.

"How have I failed?" she asked me. "How have my sons, who were once so beautiful and full of confidence and laughter, become the cruel warriors that they are? Why did they not learn from me the lessons of the better gods?" She put her head down and wept.

I held her hands and answered, "I have known the same doubt about my son as you have about yours. How could Telemachos be so like my Lord Odysseus when his father was away during most of his growing years? And your sons are also the image of their father. Is it in the nature of men to pass on their qualities to their sons? My mother was not like my sister or me. But men copy men in order to know manhood, it seems.

"You have been a tender and loving mother," I reassured her. "You cannot fight the fate given to each one of us, and in the House of Odysseus a man's fate is to be a warrior. Only Ikarios seems to have the character of his namesake, my father, who glorified peace rather than war. We must struggle through the darkness that denies us the answers and become the best that we can be. Perhaps when Ikarios returns, we will see a man different from the other men of Ithaka.

"I would not want you to be anything other than what you are," I said quietly. "We all love you, Nausikaa, and will always be here to help you."

"Thank you, my Mother," she said softly as she dried her eyes and walked into the room that holds the shadow of my son.

Preparations have kept me busy night and day. The House of Odysseus will never be proud again, as it once was, and our lives will forever be filled with regret. We pray to the gods to forgive us for the folly of our kings.

After we spoke in my garden, wise and noble Medon, unknown to my grandson who ignored his pleading, sent several men on two fishing boats to Zakynthos, the island south of Ithaka. The men are to watch for a fleet coming toward us. He ordered the men to set up a series of warning fires to be lit along the coast when the enemy galleys appear. For several swellings of the moon, all was silent in the night.

During this time Medon also met quietly with men across our island to warn them of a possible invasion. He told me of his plans and discussions with the Ithakans. Some of the men who never went on the raiding parties in the past believed that they would be safe. They were naïve enough to assume that they would not be involved in an invasion.

"I warned them that if we are invaded, and I believe that it will happen, all the men and boys, old women and babies would be slaughtered and the young women and girls ravished and stolen to be sold as slaves. That is the way of war," he said sadly.

In his warnings he told them that the army of Pylos had an agreement with Sparta, and the two armies would join together to avenge the loss of the princess. Ithaka would be no more.

The men on the island respect and like Medon, I have heard over the years. Thus, when he told the Ithakans that war was coming, most of them believed him and began to learn how to use their hunting weapons for war. They were also making heavy leather armor, Medon told me.

"I say all this to you in confidence, Lady, because our men will need large supplies of bandages and medicines for the wounded. I beg you to plan all of this quietly but to plan well. We both know that if Laertes learns of these plans made without his permission, the young King will take my life for moving behind his back. He would call it treachery."

Nothing makes sense in a land about to be destroyed by a king without wisdom.

I instructed the weavers to finish the robes on their looms then to weave only plain blankets and smaller cloths. "These are not for trade," I told them, "so weave as much as you can as quickly as possible. Use up the yarn that is not dyed." They were confused but followed my instructions. I began to store bandages, aloe and other salves, and poppy and lotus to ease the pain from the wounds that I anticipated. I sent out my gatherers to get whatever plants and herbs were in season and began to make the potions in quantities larger than ever I have made. I called Pelias, the Chief Potter since Pheidopos joined the shades in the Lower World, and asked for more large jars and amphorae to hold the herbs and potions in readiness. My weavers were baffled when I placed the pithoi and amphorae in my garden and in the storage room with our yarns and robes, but I could not explain to them why I was behaving so strangely. I also stored huge quantities of bandages and potions in the corners of the weaving room and in my shrine until I could hardly stand before the small altar. Medon instructed me to store as much of the palace's gold and bronze treasures as I could in the weaving rooms. I hid plates and cups among robes in the storage room and among the plants of my garden. When we had no more space in the weaving rooms and in my bedchamber, my errand boys and maids even wrapped the gold and silver pieces in oiled leather and buried them among the fruit and nut trees in my tree garden, hoping that the assailants would not find them. We filled the cisterns with as much water as they would hold, and we gathered as much fruit to dry as ripeness permitted. My time was filled each day, and I wove little and wrote nothing during these weeks of preparations.

I also worried about the stores of food that would be necessary to feed those of us in the palace as well as our fighters and the people who came to us for protection. I asked our Chief Cook to smoke as much meat and fish as he could preserve. He promised to use the most trusted servants in the kitchen in order to start drying the fruits and vegetables, as he could, without letting the rest of the palace know why he was doing this. We talked of an attack, and I said I trusted him to do what he could to conserve as much food as possible. We did not know how much time he had to do all of this, but he said he would do what he could. I thanked him with deep gratitude.

King Laertes was seldom seen in the palace and never at the marketplace during this time. He stayed among his men who were repairing the ships in the small western harbor on Ithaca. When he came to the palace briefly, it was to observe the making of weapons by the craftsmen and to give them orders. He did not visit his wife and daughters, I am told, and did not even see his mother or ask about his father's health. It was as though he was in hiding.

I spoke to Medon about our need for food if the island were attacked. In the absence of the King and his leadership, Medon went to the marketplace and asked the merchants to offer their grains, olive oil, wine, and other foods for storage in the palace high above the landing of the army. He even bargained for pithoi of lentils, which the palace rarely consumed but which I liked and used in stews. The merchants refused until Medon promised to return the foodstuffs if they were not used or, in the event of attack, to repay the merchants after the battle to defend the island was ended.

He assured them that they—and their families and slaves—would all be protected in the palace and would be fed during the invasion. Some of the merchants who liked and trusted Medon complied and gave their grain and oil, sacks of dried beans and lentils, and other foods from the East; some of them said they would offer the enemy their stores in return for protection of their stalls; and some said that they did not trust Laertes or Telemachos who had taken whatever they desired in the past and never reimbursed the merchants for their wares—or women. A few of the merchants simply refused to help the King and would not participate in his war, they said. My son's behavior was having dire consequences.

Medon urged all the people of the marketplace to leave the shore and go into the hills as soon as the enemy ships were in sight in order to save their lives and those of their families. He could do nothing more than warn. Our courageous friend did his best. By acting without the King's permission—or knowledge—he put his own life in danger in order to protect the people and our island.

Feeling safe with a palace at the top of Mt. Aetos, or in the galleys that he was repairing on the other side of the island, Laertes ignored everything around him and saw none of these preparations. He remained under the illusion that the gods were on his side. My son stayed in his sleeping quarters recovering from his black wounds and the loss of his hero son.

Finally, the guards stationed on the shore of Ithaka saw the fire on the highest hilltop on the island of Zakynthos to our south. This was the warning that an army was sailing to invade us. Medon had planned well. A messenger came to the palace to tell us that we had fewer than seven dawns before the invasion of twenty or more ships.

When Laertes learned about the attack, he became hysterical and in panic started to blame everyone but himself. He was furious when he learned of the plans of Medon and was about to run Medon through with a sword for sneaking behind his King's back and defying his instructions to do nothing. I could not believe my grandson's irrational response. Nausikaa and I screamed at Laertes and called him a fool. He stopped, in shock that we would dare to speak to the King in this way. We reminded him that he would need every warrior he had to defend the island. We reminded him that Medon's loyalty had protected his father throughout his life. Subdued but still angry, Laertes asked Medon what had been done and what was yet to be done. I felt only contempt for my grandson.

We all went to speak to Telemachos who had little strength to hear our story or to give advice. He was still alive, but he could hardly sit up and his eyes looked empty. He fell asleep as we were describing the situation.

I looked at my grandson and said, "If you are now our King, then act like a leader. Show your people that you are a hero that they can follow. Medon, who cares only for the survival of Ithaka, has been preparing the island for defense and will work for you. He bows to your power and has always been loyal to your father and to you."

I did not say that Laertes should be grateful for the intelligence and cleverness of Medon. That would have inflamed the proud fool standing before me. Medon knelt and kissed the hem of my grandson's robe and asked forgiveness in this time of trial. Mollified by the subjugation of his father's friend, Laertes told Medon in a haughty manner to follow him and they would discuss the preparations.

We heard the horns of rams announcing danger across the island. Medon had extensive plans already in place and shared his plans with my grandson who was overcome with confusion and fear. Apparently, Laertes was courageous only when he and his father could surprise and attack helpless men. Within hours men with their weapons and armor began to meet in the amphitheater for orders. King Laertes announced to the men that Medon was his general and would implement the plans for defense. Everyone was to follow the orders of his general.

Medon then took charge of the organization. The men who were experienced in war through their pillaging were already instructed on where and how to fight. Others who kept arriving in small groups began instructions in war. Battlements were set up behind the marketplace across the island east of Mt. Aetos and the palace. Besides the hours spent each day learning the skills of battle, men were busy building fences and fortifying the palace walls and the bulwarks near the markets.

I learned that the markets would be the first line of defense. Many of the women and children who worked the stalls of the market were allowed to leave by their husbands or masters. Within several days they began arriving at the palace. They brought as much as they could carry in food and bedding, but they needed water and places to sleep as soon as they arrived. We planned to use the palace courtyard as well as the amphitheater to bed and protect the people. Our warriors would sleep in the fields surrounding the palace while the wounded would be cared for in the palace Great Room. So many people streamed through the gates of our palace to be assigned their places. I knew that food would be a problem in the days to come, though all of the storage rooms both underground and above the ground were full.

Nausikaa and I began to organize the people. Everyone was terrified and wanted only to hide, but we put them to work to collect water at Arethousa, the nearby spring, and to set up makeshift tents in the fields outside of the palace gate. Many of the women and girls said they could weave or spin, so I sent them up the stairs to Naela and Nauriteia who put them to work, as they could. I told them that we needed more covers for sleeping mats, and those could be woven by anyone who knew the basic skills of weaving. Naela put more looms—the older ones that were in storage—on the balcony overlooking the Great Room, Nauriteia supervised these weavers, and that kept the women busy. The boys too young to fight were sent to fill wagons with leaves and pine needles to fill the mats. We sent the men too old to fight to bring back more goats and sheep and pigs for the pens that Medon had built near the palace stockade. We had to be prepared to hold out against an army that tried to starve us out. We put some of the animals in the holding pens, and additional sheep with nursing lambs we put in the garden of trees to protect them. I had learned some of these strategies from the singers and merchants who told the stories of Troy, but I had no idea of the quantities that would be necessary.

The grains were almost ready to be cut in the fields, so men, women, and children worked together to cut the grain before the invasion. The stalks were collected and stored for the livestock at the palace. The distant village and mountain people were encouraged to carry their sacks of grain higher into the mountains with as many of their animals as possible. They would have to survive in the caves and woods, they were told. We feared that the fields would be burned by the enemy and all of this year's grain supply would be lost if we did not save it before the war began. The people worked fiercely from the first fingers of dawn to the light of Selene until exhaustion overcame them, and they slept where they fell in the fields.

Nausikaa and I met with the cooks and those in charge of keeping our olive oil and wine and foodstuffs protected. We explained to them and to the servants our situation and assured them that they were safer in the palace than anywhere else on the island. We needed all of them to keep us safe and fed, I told them.

Medon had stored the grains and lentils from the merchants in the dreaded grotto on the side of Mt. Aetos and in a shed that he had built next to the grotto. All the servants joined together to carry those sacks of grains and foods that our cooks now stored near our kitchens and in the old weaving shed. There are caves near the summit of Mt. Aetos, not far from our palace, and Medon stored foodstuffs in the caves as well. Every part of the palace became a storehouse or a place for sleeping families. They also stored more amphorae filled with olive oil and wine in the old weaving shed and elsewhere among the artisans' sheds.

Then I gave instructions to start baking hard bread day and night and to store it safely while they continued to roast and dry the flesh of both animals and available fish from the markets. More hard bread and dried meat would be needed for the army and for the people from the markets, I believed. I also added that anyone found taking food for themselves would be punished severely. All foods would be cooked and served from the kitchen where some of the women from the island began to help to prepare, cook, and serve the food. No one said anything, but I could tell that they were as frightened as I was.

Nausikaa and I went to Telemachos to share what we knew. We had decided that he should be brought up to my bedchamber so that their sleeping room could be used for food storage or later for people as the food was consumed. I would sleep in the weaving room, and the young girl who might be the princess would share my pallet.

Telemachos was sitting up in bed, tears filling the lines in his cheeks as we talked. He listened with eyes closed as though he could not look at us for what he had brought to Ithaka. We did not say that we had warned him of this day. We just assured him that Laertes and Medon were leading the army that would defend Ithaka. We brought him some food, which he did not eat, and some water with wine, which he did not taste. Guards came into his room to carry him up to my bedchamber, which was stocked with bandages and large jars, or pithoi. I wanted to remind him that we need him to lead us and that he requires strength to do so. But that night he was not ready for responsibility.

I believe that we will not survive the coming war. I awoke one morning thinking of the beautiful ring that I had denied myself all the rolling seasons of my aging. There was no longer need for denial. I called Periphetes and showed him the ring in the hardened clay. I asked if he could free the ring without damage to the gold or the glorious green stone. He had a questioning look on his face, but he said that he would try.

If Periphetes can do this, I thought, I shall wear my Merchant's ring every day of my life and even into the cold home of Persephone where it will warm me.

Long moons have passed since I last put brush to parchment. It is time that I write the story of the invasion. Perhaps if I write this sad tale, the nightmares will soften and I may sleep again.

We waited for several journeys of the dawn while our men stood guard at various points on the island's shores. Then the attack was made at the marketplace, as Medon predicted. He had flags flying there to make the enemy think that the markets were busy. Instead, most of the stalls and tents were full of our men ready to do battle. The rest of the tents held the imprudent people who remained to greet the invaders, and they perished on that first day. Many men from both armies went into the Underworld on that day—and in the months that followed.

When the Pylians invaded Ithaka, we were not ready. For those of us who lived for peace, we could never be prepared for the carnage that followed the assault; for those men who loved the excitement of battle, they too were awed and eventually horrified by the extent of destruction on our island.

The wounded from Ithaka, when possible, were carried to the palace where we tended them. The courtyard was already full of women and children and a few old men from the marketplace, and they helped to carry water and food and bandages to the wounded in the Great Room. We lined up the poor bleeding men on the floor and tried to staunch their wounds. Two of the maids were in charge of dispensing the poppy tea, but only on my instructions to certain of the men. We needed everything for those who were in greatest need and for those strong enough to ward off the cold breath of Thanatos. My weavers were frantically weaving more bandages, and the younger ones were busy washing the ones already used.

Medon had stored great quantities of water in the cisterns beneath the palace, so we could bathe the men before washing the cuts, putting salves on them, and stitching up their deepest wounds. I remembered my Father, then later Cadmus, telling me that keeping wounds clean was essential for healing. Cadmus once said that on the lands where bathing was frequent, death from a wound was less common than in the settlements where people seldom bathed their bodies, as on Ithaka.

Though we worked to keep men and their blankets and pallets clean, some of the men we could not hold back from Hades. But with our teas they went more quietly to the god of the Underworld than those who lost their breath on the battlefield filled with screams and brutality.

Pyres were built in the center of a wooded area in order to hide the numbers of dead from the enemy. We had no time to bury the bodies, no time for ritual or mourning. Young boys and old men were put to work keeping the fires ready to embrace the dead and send them on their way to the Lower World. There was no time for preparing the bodies, for wailing, or for the tearing of hair. This was all devastating for our people. We tried to keep the names of the dead but were unable to separate the ashes for their families. It was a frantic time, and we did not have the experience to guide us in the ways of war, survival, and its aftermath.

One day Periphetes brought my ring to me. It is beautiful. I wear it on a chain given to me by my dear Father a long lifetime ago. Both my Father and my Merchant are close to my heart. I will be ready when I go on my final journey.

The battles on the eastern shore of Ithaka began and ended daily, according to the whims of the kings, I suppose. I could not understand the meaning of it all.

One day when Laertes brought some wounded to us, I asked him, "Why can we not return the young princess with an apology and end the war?"

He looked at me as though I had lost my wits and said haughtily, "A hero does not apologize and surrender." Oh, the power and folly of hubris. The war continued.

The people living in the courtyard, the fields, and the amphitheater were frightened, and their fears became anger turned against each other. There were arguments among the women and endless quarrels among the men who came to the palace for food and rest. We had a rule against the people relieving themselves against the walls of the courtyard, and when someone tried to do so those who followed the rules rose up in anger. All of these problems were evident in the field outside the courtyard also. Though Medon assigned village elders to supervise the people living in the fields and on the benches in the amphitheater, there were quarrels constantly about food or space to sleep or some other nonsense. At least I thought the issues were trivial and foolish. But then, I was dealing with the wounded and dying every day.

We knew that the elders were having a terrible time keeping order. Only when Medon could be in the courtyard to keep the people busy or when they were sleeping were they almost quiet. We tried to organize them into groups for particular jobs, and that helped to bring some measure of order to the palace. But not enough. And not for long.

When the cold season arrived, all the problems became worse as we tried to keep the people warm and protected from freezing rain or snow. The weavers were kept busy making heavy blankets with wool of all colors until our beautiful yarns were depleted. I thought how long and hard so many people had worked to produce those splendid yarns, and now those blankets would be placed on the rough ground and given hard use. Then I thought of the people freezing in our open courtyard, in tents, and in makeshift coverings, and the loss of the dyes and yarns no longer seemed important.

Nausikaa and I, like Medon, were exhausted with working day and night, and I did not know how long we could continue to do everything. Medon, especially, was worked to the limit since he fought bravely in battle every day then tried to cope with the issues among the people when he should have been resting. Consequently, we set up a guard of wounded warriors who were not yet ready to return to battle but were able to walk and carry weapons to exert authority. This plan worked very well in helping us and the village elders because the people admired and respected their wounded heroes.

How did the war on Troy last for ten years, I asked myself every day. I knew that we could not endure such daily onslaught for that long.

After many moons our food supply was getting low because some of the grain brought up from the marketplace was infested with insects. The Chief Cook spoke to Nausikaa and to me about this situation. He was shamed and could not meet our eyes.

"We cannot last another growing of the moon without using those foods full of filth," he said.

"Is there any way to get the insects out of the barley and other grains?" I asked.

He thought for some moments then suggested, "We can cook them and as the water boils in the large pots, the crawling things may rise to the surface. I can skim them out perhaps, but some of them will still remain."

"Will the people see and taste the tiny worms?" I asked.

"I don't know, Lady," he whispered in embarrassment. "Perhaps it will not bother many of the people who live poorly. They eat such things in their daily meals."

I thought of Zeila and her children and the pot of food that smelled so revolting. Who knows what was in that pot? But I did not say anything.

Our cook is proud of the meals he has provided to the palace, and now I was asking him to serve what we would give to the swine.

I felt sorry for him, but I asked, "Or can we hide the remaining insects in the grains by chopping up fruits like figs and dates, almonds, and orange and lemon peels and honey and cooking it all together?"

He smiled and said with amusement, "The strategy may work, my Lady. I will see to it. But I will keep our good grains for you and the royal family."

I thanked him for his kindness then shocked him by saying, "You will serve me what you prepare for others. If one suffers, we all must suffer together. Use the good grains to grind for bread flour. You might also stretch the food supplies by making thin stews with small pieces of dried meat and vegetables. You have been generous with your delicious roasted meats, but we cannot do this hereafter if our supplies are getting low. I will give you herbs that I dried from my garden to give flavor to the watered stews. I realize that it is difficult to feed all of these people and the troops without generous supplies, but I rely on you to think on how to do it. I am sure that we will get through this difficulty together, and you will be honored for your work in all of this."

He bowed and said, "Thank you, my Lady." Then because he had much to do, he left quickly to return to the kitchen.

From that day I let Nausikaa deal with the food issues. I did not look forward to meals in the days to come.

One night, after what seemed like forever, Cadmus and Ikarios returned to Ithaka. Under the protection of darkness, they hid the galleys on the western shore of Ithaka near my bathing place. I thought that this inlet was known only to my women, to me, and to the trusted guards that protected us. However, Ikarios too must have known of this place that was not so secret as I had imagined. In the darkness, they climbed the steep path to the palace and were almost killed by the guards at the gates and around the walls. Fortunately, several guards remembered Ikarios and let them into the palace grounds.

I was in the Great Room tending to the sick men, and I heard the commotion when they entered the courtyard. Thinking that the enemy had broken through the gates, I stood at the door ready for a sword through my heart. I preferred to join Persephone in the Dark Realm rather than be captured and enslaved beyond what I have already suffered. When I saw Cadmus and Ikarios, tears filled my eyes, and I could not speak. They both grabbed me and sat me down on the floor outside the door of the Great Room. The Great Room floor was covered with the sick and dying, so close together that we could hardly step between the men, and the stench in that room was unbearable. All furniture had been stored in various rooms throughout the palace, so we sat and ate on the dirt floor of the courtyard wherever we could find a space. They gave me a drink of water. After Ikarios embraced Nausikaa, who was also tending the wounded, I suggested that we go up to the balcony garden so we could talk in quiet. Nausikaa said that she would remain with the sick men.

"They need my attending," she said bravely.

Ikarios and Cadmus were shocked to see the condition of Telemachos when we walked through my bedchamber. He was thin and gaunt and had aged a lifetime. He was sleeping in my bed and did not awaken when they spoke to him.

When we finally sat down in the garden and were drinking weak tea, they asked me what had happened to Ithaka. They had heard rumors of the invasion, they said, but they could hardly believe what they saw below. As briefly as possible, I told them the sad story of a kingdom ready to fall.

"We were correct in our fears," I told them. "After the invasion, the enemy warriors roamed the valleys and hillsides and set fire to anything that could grow in the future. For the length of time that the enemy has occupied our land, no planting has been done. I have not seen it for myself, but I have been told that it is a bitter sight to see the blackened land of Ithaka where once there was green life."

Before I could finish my story, there were frantic shouts and loud banging on the main gate. We went to the stairs to see what was happening. Soldiers brought several wounded men to the Great Room door while shouting something about the King. As we ran down the stairs, I could see that the first of the wounded was Laertes. Before she realized the situation, Nausikaa came forward and said that there was no space to put the new wounded men in that room. Then Nausikaa saw her son and swooned. As the maids attended to Nausikaa, I examined Laertes and knew immediately that he was too close to the doors of Hades to pull him back to us. With the help of Cadmus and Ikarios, we carried Laertes and the seven other wounded men into Nausikaa's room that was now empty of food stores. Some of the men had to sleep sitting against the walls, but Laertes and another warrior were laid on pallets.

All through the night Nausikaa bathed her son, wrapped his horrible wounds as best she could, and gave him poppy tea. I begged her not to use the salve that cured. We kept the medicines for the men with hope, and we both knew that it would be useless for him.

"We will need more than we have for those who will benefit," I said sadly. My heart was torn in shreds.

She stared at me with horror at my cruelty. Then she looked around at all the men in need, and she put her head down and sobbed. I cannot describe that night.

Hearing that Laertes had been wounded, Marua ran into the Great Room and retched at the sight and stench of the wounded. Before she could be taken to her dying husband, guards carried her back to her own room, which she was sharing with Nerua and on rare occasions with their daughters. By morning, the breath escaped the lips of Laertes.

Marua, her sister, and their daughters stayed in their room screaming and ripping their hair and cheeks. Both Marua and Nerua had refused to tend the wounded since the invasion began. Food was brought to their rooms, which they never left. I knew that they would be useless when we first brought them to the Great Room for their help, and they continued to be useless even when Laertes was brought bleeding to us. So we left them alone in a room where they had been hiding in terror from the beginning of the war.

Marua would not go to Laertes even in the hours when he struggled to survive. He never saw his wife, and she never said goodbye to him. Word went out across the palace, and hatred took the place of contempt toward the two sisters.

Nausikaa was the hero on that evening and in the days that followed. Mourning was required for her beloved son, our King, but she knew that the living needed her time and energy. Despite the stories that would be spread by Rumor, she refused to spend the days wailing and tearing her hair until his burial mound was built outside the walls. It was a mound of stones much smaller than what was worthy of a king. I am shamed by my feelings, but it was what he deserved.

Nausikaa stayed with the wounded until the moment when we prepared the body of her son for the burial in a field not far from the palace. I chose the robe to wrap him for his journey to meet Hades because she was too distraught to make such decisions. But at the shortened ceremony, her courage was amazing. Both Cadmus and Ikarios stood by her side while Medon helped Telemachos stand tall in spite of his shame. Ikarios told the people in the palace to be quiet and not to scream and wail so the enemy below would not know that an important hero had fallen. The women wept quietly and tore their hair while the men stared straight and made no sound. It was not a funeral befitting a king, but it was the best we could do in the middle of war.

Rumor spread the word that a greater army was forming to attack Ithaka, which would be known as the second Troy. In the King's name, Medon had sent messengers out to the islands surrounding Ithaka to ask for men as reinforcements for our army. Our men were exhausted and Medon feared that we could not defend the hills around our palace much longer. The reinforcements never arrived.

In the meantime, we continued to care for the wounded, and some of them returned to the fighting. The women and children living in the courtyard of the palace had their work, which they accomplished every day, and everyone was hungry because the portions were smaller and smaller. Sobbing was commonplace, and Fear wrapped everyone in his blanket.

One afternoon Medon and Ikarios came through the gate looking pale with green fear. They asked to speak to Cadmus who had sent one galley home to Tyre with his sons while he himself had remained on our island to offer help for our survival. In the second galley, he had stores of grains, which he shared with our people. But beyond the food that he provided, just his being near was a comfort to me.

The presence of Cadmus was essential to us, for he also had knowledge and medicines to help the sick who were wounded or who were living too close together in the courtyard. We feared that spirits of the Underworld were sweeping through the palace with dark disease. Too many of the warriors and those in the courtyard and now the servants were coughing and suffering with fevers and other ailments. Nausikaa and I also struggled to remain on our feet to help, but I suspected that we might not be able to continue much longer.

A decision had to be made without delay. The exhaustion and despair of our two leaders, Medon and King Ikarios, made a new plan necessary. Cadmus joined us, and I led the three men up to my garden where Telemachos sat in silence. I made them herb tea and served them bread and curds without honey. They could not eat. Then I listened while they talked.

"Our side is losing," Ikarios said, "but we do not think that the enemy has yet realized this state of affairs. A strategy must be shaped to end the war before our island is completely destroyed. The enemy continues to use fire to defeat us, even as they had burned the marketplace and the hillsides earlier in the war. After killing the people who worked the land and refused to leave it even for their own safety, the enemy stole the livestock left behind and razed orchards, grape arbors, and farmland. Most people have gone high into the mountains where they are starving, it is said. Some of these men have returned to help us to fight, but they are not warriors and fall quickly. There is no honor in watching our men slaughtered."

He paused and then resumed speaking softly, "There will be little left for the island's survival, even if the enemy retreats now, unless our small army changes its plans. We have tricked them so far by seeming to have more men than we have and moving the men around, but that cannot last much longer."

Ikarios and Medon looked to Cadmus after they finished their bleak summary of our situation.

The Merchant asked simply, "Why do you not sue for peace by returning the princess and the slaves and the wealth taken from Pylos?"

There was silence.

Medon glanced at me then asked, "Would that not reveal our weakness so that King Antilochos would know that he could annihilate the whole island—and the other surrounding islands in our realm?"

Then Ikarios asked, "Who could be our messenger? How could we do this as a gesture of peace and friendship, rather than defeat?" Cadmus smiled at my grandson with a look of admiration, perhaps for learning his lessons so well in the seasons that they had traveled together over the Great Sea.

Cadmus responded, "I know King Antilochos. We have traded over the many seasons of my sons' growth. He does not know that I am here, nor could he know that Ikarios did not take part in the ravishing of his marketplace. I could go as your emissary because I am a man of peace rather than your military ally, and I could speak for you. If he would speak with me, I could set up that meeting for you as the new King."

Refusing to look at his father, Ikarios asked, "What could I say in defense of our actions against Pylos?"

Cadmus also ignored Telemachos as he answered, "If his daughter Laodike has been cared for and has not been harmed beyond her grief in not being home with her beloved family, then there is a possibility you can resolve this situation quickly. Do you know where she is?"

Medon looked at me and said, "I have spoken to my Lady who believes she might know who and where the princess is. We have been in contact, the Lady and I, and she has been hiding the princess for her own safety."

Cadmus smiled at me then turned to Ikarios, "With the princess to barter, you could tell King Antilochos that you have been sailing with me to see the world and returned to find your kingdom in the middle of an unwanted war. You could say that your father Telemachos is seriously wounded and is unable to attend this meeting, and your two brothers have been sent to the realm of Hades for their poor judgment in attacking his kingdom and taking his daughter. You could say that her quick return physically unharmed is her only desire and yours. Tell the King that you are shamed by the actions of your father and your brothers. Stress that King Telemachos has suffered greatly for his recklessness.

"Reassure him by saying that you are the new King of Ithaka, that you have not been a warrior though you have been trained to fight and will do so if it is necessary to save your island. Say that you have wanted only peace for your kingdom and ask that no more men be slaughtered for the wickedness of one man, though he is your father whom you honor in other ways. Assure him that you recognize the grievous damage that has been done to his people and your own. The battle should end now, and on your honor you will return his beautiful daughter and her attendants and will make compensation for what has been taken from him and his people

"You should say all these things, then you remain silent and await his decision. In the meantime, you must be certain of the princess's identity."

Without hesitation Ikarios said that he would do it. Telemachos sat looking at the stone floor in silence and shame. I remained silent.

Cadmus returned from his meeting with King Antilochos of Pylos. The King's concerns were centered on whether his daughter was safe and how she had been treated.

Over tea, as before, wise Cadmus spoke to us, "Their army is made up of three smaller armies. Sparta supports the two kings who came for the young princess. She is the daughter of King Antilochos of Pylos and the betrothed of King Agarreus of Mezapos at the southern tip of the Peloponnese. Their armies are determined to regain her. Unless you return her unharmed and you sue for peace with their kings immediately, they are readying themselves with reinforcements to destroy your island."

Ikarios asked, "Is it too late to return the child?"

Cadmus responded, "I don't know. It is never too late to return a woman child with her virtue intact. Or has she been spoiled for her husband?"

Ikarios turned to me and asked, "Grandmother, Medon tells me that you have been hiding the princess. You are certain of her identity and can bring her here?"

I said, "My Lord, I have a new and gifted weaver since the start of the war. She may be the daughter of a king. When the captives were taken into the palace, I saw the work in the robe she wore, and I asked her name. She did not answer. But there was something more than the weaving that interested me. Despite her terror and grief, several women seemed to attend her with great deference and respect. I asked the guard for her. He seemed eager to dispose of her.

"When we took her up to my room, the child was hysterical. I gave her a calming potion and for several days she slept or wept. We also took her attendants to sleep among the weavers in order to calm the child. They seemed grateful for our protection. We took her and her attendants down to the inlet where we bathed and oiled her, washed and dried their robes, then brought them back to the weaving room where they have been living with the weavers. She does not speak, so I do not know her name or origin. Nauriteia and her two daughters have been particularly attentive and kind to her, so she has been well cared for. If she is the princess in question, then Ithaka may be saved."

Ikarios said, "Bring her to us now."

I went to the weaving room, took her hand, and led her to the balcony. With fear in her eyes, she entered the garden and knelt in submission to the Lord with the frown.

Ikarios gently asked her name, but fright held her lips closed. Cadmus said quietly that since he knows her father, perhaps he might talk to her. Ikarios waved his hand in agreement. Cadmus raised her from her knees and asker her with a smile to sit.

"You will not be hurt," he said. "Lady Penelope's weavers are safe in this house."

She looked up at me with troubled eyes, but she seemed to relax when I smiled and nodded my head.

"We simply want to know your name and the name of your father. Are you married—or betrothed?"

At first she shook her head, then she nodded at the word "betrothed." I put my hand on her shoulder and tears filled her eyes.

Cadmus said softly and kindly, "Please tell us your name. We want to help you."

She began very quietly, "I am Laodike, daughter of King Antilochos and great-granddaughter of King Nestor of Pylos. I was taken with six other women and several boys when our kingdom was attacked. All others around us were sent to the kingdom of the Underworld." She stopped with a sob.

Cadmus asked, "Have you been hurt by any man since you were taken from your homeland?"

Her face flamed in humiliation at being asked such a question, but she shook her head "no" and raised her chin in pride.

"Let us plan how to end the war," Cadmus said as he turned to Ikarios and Medon.

Nausikaa and I took Laodike up to my shrine where we stood together in prayer to Hera and Athene. Then we sat together and talked for the first time. Despite some differences in language, we learned much about her family and the beautiful land of Pylos.

When Phylia learned that Ikarios was to go behind the enemy lines to speak to the King who has brought such devastation, she begged him not to go.

She sobbed, "I cannot lose you again so soon. I am with child. We need you."

Ikarios held her in his arms as he said softly, "I am proud that a new life will be born out of all this, but you must understand that we may not survive if the war does not stop now. I do this to protect you and, now, my son who will someday be King. If he lives through years of battles, can I leave a land in ruins for him to lead? You have not seen the desolation of this island with this war. Troy defended itself for ten years and then was destroyed and the people murdered or enslaved. Is that what you want for this land and for the family that we hope to have? I must have peace in order to rebuild what has been lost so that he will be proud to be lord of this land. Do you understand?"

Phylia looked into his eyes and said with love and remarkable deference, "Yes, my Lord."

He smiled and kissed her lightly on the lips then turned and said gruffly, "Let us begin immediately to put our plan to work."

I was filled with love and admiration for the man Ikarios had grown to be and with wonder at my beloved Cadmus.

A temporary truce was made when Cadmus and Ikarios met with Antilochos.

Our future depended on Laodike, I was told. She had been staying with the weavers and had remained in our rooms at the top of the palace since she arrived on Ithaka, so her virtue had been preserved. And she had been treated as all are treated in the weaving rooms. Gradually, the kindness of the weavers and our child helpers penetrated the wall of grief, and she began to eat and drink. I noticed that she particularly liked the stews that my servants made according to my instructions, even without the rabbits and other meats, and she enjoyed the curd with cooked fruits from our trees. I gave orders that she should eat what she liked. Each day she spent time on my garden balcony to enjoy the sun and soft breezes. Zeila or someone else was with her at all times. When I could spare some moments for rest, I would go up to the garden and make chamomile tea, and she and I would relish the lovely fragrance. We felt the peace and possibility for the future, even without language, at those precious times. She began to answer my smiles, and I looked forward to her company.

Everyone talked to her and helped her with her weaving. She was curious and pleased to learn new methods and weaves. While she was with us, she wove a lovely robe with the help of my weavers. Naela told me that Laodike was proud of the robe and smiled when one of the children suggested that her garment was worthy of a queen. Finally her lovely face gave the gift of smiles to everyone around her. However, she was a child torn from her family, and her longing for home remained in the sadness of her eyes while she was with us.

One evening while I was tending to the wounded, I received word that she was to be prepared to meet with her father on the next greeting of Dawn. I let her sleep quietly among the weavers, and when Helios began his climb into the skies I woke her.

I whispered, "You are to dress quickly in your best robe, and King Ikarios will come for you soon." When her eyes widened with fear, I reassured her, "Wherever you go, I will be with you. You will be safe." I could tell her no more.

We both bathed quickly and dressed in robes worthy of royalty. With a frightened look, she began to weep and held on to me begging me not to let her go.

"The King of Ithaka is an evil man," she said. "I saw him slay innocent men and guards who protected me. He will slay me."

I held her tightly and assured her, "The new King of Ithaka is a kind man and wants only what is best for you. Dry your eyes. He will not hurt you, and Cadmus will be with you," I said.

"Promise that you will come with me, Lady Penelope? I will not fear if you are with me."

I smiled and gave to her my loveliest silk veil, which I wove long years before, and arranged it over her beautiful black curls. Then we descended the stairs with her maids behind her, and several guards leading us.

Laodike and I were taken quickly through the Great Room and Courtyard. Her attendants were with us. With her head down and her veil over her face, she could not see the horrors of the wounded and the sick. We wanted to spare the child this shock at least. The moans and the stench we could not avoid. My grandson King Ikarios, Cadmus, and Medon met us outside the gates. Ikarios did not want me to accompany them to the base of the mountain, but I insisted.

"The path is too difficult," he said, though he did not add that I am too old and there was danger.

"I promised Laodike that I would be with her," I said, "and such strong men can assist me when the way becomes difficult."

Cadmus smiled, perhaps at my temerity and determination, and assured me that we would be safe. The child let go of my arm and stood tall with dignity. Perhaps she recognized Cadmus as a friend. Several of our soldiers as well as the guards, boys, and women who had been taken at Pylos joined us, and we began the difficult descent to the Pylian camp near the ruined marketplace.

When we arrived at the camp, King Antilochos and King Agarreus were waiting, surrounded by the gifts of compensation. King Agarreus remained in the background, frowning silently. Laodike and her father exchanged smiles, and he asked about her health.

She answered far beyond her years, "Father, I have missed you and my mother, my brothers and sisters, and my people, and I was deeply saddened when I was taken from my homeland. But my captors have been kind. Lady Penelope's weavers are protected in this house. I stayed in safety with them, and they taught me many things. I have come to love my Lady and her famed weavers and am grateful that she shared her food and teas and knowledge with me. With their help, I wove this robe that I am wearing. I am certain that Mother would be proud to wear it, and this beautiful veil is a gift from Queen Penelope who created it. Please end the war, Father, and let us go home."

"Were you told to give this speech?" he asked.

"No, Father, I speak with honesty and honor, as I have been taught by you and Mother. The King who took me away from my homeland was cruel, but the present King is a good man, I am told, and I have been treated very well."

My grandson apologized to the princess for her suffering in being separated from her home and thanked her for her gracious words. Then he told her that she could go to her father. She ran into her father's arms, and they both wept.

We all sat together in the King's tent and feasted. I was grateful to rest. Laodike said that this tea was good but not so good as Lady Penelope's teas. We all laughed. While we ate, we discussed how we could help their wounded before they started back to Pylos. When we were ready to leave, Ikarios made a promise of brotherhood and friendship that will never be broken. King Antilochos thanked Cadmus for his role in his present happiness and assured Ikarios of the future friendship between our kingdoms.

With that simple bond, the terrible war with its suffering, death, and devastation was ended.

As I turned to go, the King thanked me also as Laodike ran to hug me and kissed my cheek. We shared the tears in our eyes.

"I will miss you, my child," I said.

With her sob echoing in my ears, I left and did not turn back. Too often I have said goodbye.

The way up the mountain was long and arduous.

Dear Friend, I must express my memories of our leave-taking so that you will know my heart. After I slept a sleep so deep that I might never have returned from the realm of Hypnos, Nausikaa wakened me and said that you were leaving Ithaka immediately. I knew that I would never see you again in the Land of Light, and I felt that all that I am would be in shreds. Any moments of contentment would forever be lost to me. Waiting for your visits has helped me to survive.

I bathed and put on my most beautiful robe to be prepared to greet you, but when I walked down to the Great Room, I could not speak. I was grateful when you asked if I could walk beyond the gate of the courtyard so that we might speak privately. I watched you say goodbye to Nausikaa, Ikarios and his Queen, and to Medon, and they all had the waters of sorrow and admiration in their eyes. I turned and led you through the gate and longed to follow you wherever you would take me. I wanted only to remain with you for the years that are left to us, but I knew that was impossible. You would return to your wife of good fortune and your glorious sons. It had to be.

We stood touching eyes, and I saw you look once again at the ring on my chain. I touched it to my lips, and you took my hand. The words you spoke then will always be with me.

"My lovely Penelope, thank you for your friendship. You have enriched my life beyond what imagination or Fortune could design. As you might have guessed, this is my last journey over the Great Sea. It is time for me to rest and enjoy the home and gardens that I have built for my last years. But as I do so, I shall look out to sea where the sun descends and where you are. Always my mind and heart are where you are. I wish only that we might someday meet again under the light of Helios before the Lower World claims us for all time."

He stopped for a moment. Then he continued, "There will always be a favored place for you in Tyre, if the gods grant us such a gift. Goodbye, friend of my heart."

You kissed my hand with warm lips, turned, and with your mariners behind you, walked down the path to the port. On my hand there was a tear left by the water of your deep brown eyes. I was so breathless with suffering and the longing to hold you to me that I could not speak. I could hear my sob as I watched you go.

Slowly I walked back into the Courtyard, my head held high, and I knew that my family understood for the first time the cord that bound us.

As I walked past them, I said only, "I am tired. I shall rest."

I walked up to my garden and remained there in long days and nights of silence until my throat could open for the words to speak, to write, to tell the story of Ithaka's Great War.

Cadmus, I am told, left our port after the Pylians sailed. They probably met on the seas as their ships sailed east to Pylos and

Tyre. My thoughts and my heart go with him as I consider long into the night what he has meant to me.

Beyond love, my Merchant has given me a language of learning that has sustained me. This treasure has kept my mind and spirit alive during the endless seasons of being chained to the rock of Ithaka. Always eager to know everything, I have shared with him the words that allowed me to understand and experience a world that I could have never known otherwise. He has made it possible for me to name the thoughts and feelings that have explained my time on earth and the life of those around me. Without Cadmus, I would have lived in a wordless dungeon of darkness like most of the people on Ithaka, perhaps like most women everywhere. I know now that, regardless of the limitations imposed on me by the Fates, my dear friend has given me treasure that even the richest kings would envy. How can I ever repay him for offering me the best of what life can be?

3. A New Beginning

It will take many rolling seasons to return Ithaka and the palace to their former life. The wounded are recovering and taking their places in settlements throughout the island. The green shoots are coming up through the scorched land, and we expect the earth to begin producing within the year. The flocks of sheep and goats have diminished in size and must be restored for our weaving and our food supplies.

When the war ended, many people were angry with Telemachos and our family for bringing down on them such death and destruction. Ikarios and Medon work long and hard to settle their grievances. Despite their resentment about Telemachos, the village leaders chose Ikarios as the leader of Ithaka and surrounding islands. They know that he had no part in the ruin of Ithaka, that he in fact brought peace again to our island, and that he has restored a measure of hope and well-being to our land. And Medon continues to be greatly admired and respected as a hero.

Our palace needed much work and still requires further cleaning and repair. So many people lived here. The gardens need planting, and the weavers are hard at work reusing yarns for robes and gowns that must be replaced. Periphetes and his men are repairing the mosaics that were broken with hard use, and he is planning a mosaic floor for the huge courtyard.

We are grateful that the islands around us responded to the pleas of Ikarios and have sent us generous supplies of seeds, grains, and animals to help renew the food and livestock on our island. Perhaps they know that our family gave away all of our stores of food and other goods to the people who came to our doors for protection. Olive trees and grape arbors, orange and lemon groves, and gardens are being replanted all over the island, and Ikarios has people working to help each other grow strong together. The marketplace is being rebuilt, and the large eastern port may be useful once again in the seasons to come.

Phylia and Ikarios are happy with their son Tydeus, and she is with child again. They look forward to having a large family. Phylia is beaming with good health and the kindness of her husband, and I am pleased.

Marua and Nerua and their daughters have been returned to their homeland with most of their bride price, which was difficult to raise at this time of need and suffering on our island. But we all felt that they offered us nothing, and we could give them nothing that they wanted. I never told anyone that I found Nerua with a guard in the Garden of Trees the night before the invasion. They were terrified, but I told them that if she returned to her homeland nothing would be said that would lead to her stoning. She asked to go home the next morning and Marua agreed to go also. Sadly they had to wait until the end of the war, but now they are gone and are free of all ties to Ithaka, as we are to them.

I pray that the gods will not penalize me for allowing her to go away without punishment for her violation of our codes. It is difficult to know what the right path should be—penalty or forgiveness for defying the gods and our laws.

I will be so busy in rebuilding the stores of woven goods for trading that I will not have the energy to write for long turnings of the moon. I am content that I could complete this story of Ithaka's war and the return to order once again.

I am struggling to weave even the simple robes now. A thin veil is covering my eyes and taking the sharp edges from my world. And only my herb teas soften the pain in my hands. It has been a problem for some time, but Nausikaa and my weavers have hidden this from Lord Telemachos. When he learns that I am no longer in charge of the weavers and I no longer produce the most exquisite robes, he will take my room from me. He has wanted it since his sons were married, but he has longed for it since he spent his days in my room and the garden during his recovery. I heard that Telemachos plans to keep the sleeping room and garden for himself and Nausikaa and will make three spacious rooms out of the weaving room. My son will give one new room to Ikarios and keep the others for his grandchildren's nursery. They will be large and comfortable with air for breathing. I don't know where I will go.

As the light is taken gradually from my eyes, I will need the scent of my garden and of the sea even more. I will need my shrine where I can continue with great effort to write my whispers in the dark. What will life be when all this is lost to me, when I can no longer feel and smell my plants, when I can no longer see the glorious rays of rose and apricot and bronze as the sun moves down to welcome sleep, when I lose the blue and purple wines of the shining waters that touch my homeland across the Great Sea? When sight and touch are gone, what will life be? I try to hide these feelings from Nausikaa who has enough of her own trials to contend with.

All Hope has flown from the House of Odysseus. We learned today that my Lord Odysseus will never return home to wife and son. A seer who sees the future and the past, like Teirisias, arrived on Ithaka and revealed the fate given to Odysseus in the Lower World—that from this second long journey overland he will never return alive to Ithaka. Why did my Lord never tell us this in long years past? Why did the seer delay so long in bringing us this news? Why did they keep me waiting to waste my life in emptiness? I think of returning to my homeland, but who would be there to remember me after so many turnings of the cold seasons? And what of the dream of Tyre? Who would care for me there when I cannot care for myself? Perhaps there is no land under the watch of Zeus that would have a better place for me than rocky Ithaka. It pains me to write this.

My son is overcome with grief at the loss of his father. I believe he imagined that when the old king returned from his travels, Telemachos would earn forgiveness from his father. Instead, like me, my son has waited for a lifetime. In despair, he spends much of each day in the garden and speaks to no one except Nausikaa. I wonder if his fate has not been worse than mine.

Since his illness and the loss of his father until they meet in the Lower World, my son spends every day sitting in my garden and looking out to sea. Often he even sleeps in his chair all night and does not want to be taken to his room below. Perhaps it is time for me to ask to be moved. Perhaps he needs the garden more than I do.

Today when I walked into my garden to inquire if Telemachos needed anything, my son was sobbing, his face awash with tears. I thought he was in pain, and I asked what I could do for him. For some time he could not speak.

As his tears subsided, he said quietly, "I have no peace. My Father is with me in night dreams and day dreams. Always throughout my life, my hero Father came to me in the night and called me to follow him. 'Come, share my adventures,' he would say. 'Show me your courage. Show me how you slay strangers in foreign lands, how you fill our coffers with the treasure taken from others. Show me how you lead your men and your sons to follow my example. Become a hero in my wake.' My noble Father would chide me and groom me to be a hero known throughout the world like him. The same dream came to me over the years, and I struggled to model myself like the hero I longed to be.

"He has been with me always, mocking me, urging me, making me feel like a hero or a failure. I almost lost my beloved Ithaka."

He stopped and held back tears. Then he continued, "I lost my brave sons trying to please the shade of my Father. I beg Hypnos not to let me sleep. But now my Father comes to me in the shining light of my days. Even this beautiful garden, which gives me small comfort, cannot stave off his shade. He will be satisfied only when I join him, and we can walk together through the Field of Asphodel blustering with the other heroes of the Great War. Only then will I feel calm and know the happiness of having my Father once again. It is the longing of my life."

I had never known the depth of my son's suffering at the loss of his father. He never spoke of it. I thought he was cruel because he took pleasure in the pain of others. I never realized that he was trying to be strong like his father but did not know what a good man's strength really was. And when my Lord returned from his journey to Troy and boasted of his adventures, he increased his son's desire to be what he thought a hero is: a hard, cruel adventurer feared by all. If only he had a model of strength with kindness throughout his growing years, he might have been a different man. Then his days might have been filled with value and serenity. He would not have been driven by a dream that turned into the nightmare of his life.

What could I have done differently? Have I been denying my role in what my son became? Or was his father's fate the chain that bound my son and me to tears and longing for what we could never have? How can we fight the fate given to us, and would we be punished even more by the gods if we tried? Can the answers to these questions come in our lifetime or must we await the Nether World to learn our weaknesses when it is too late to change them?

Sometimes I think that human life is a horror, a horror that can never be altered no matter how we try. Lady Athene, please give me the wisdom to understand, rather than deny, my fate and the courage to accept what is immutable.

I have thought long and deeply about the sad fate of my son. His life was designed on the fate of his father, the renowned hero of the Trojan War and the enduring hero of the long journey home to Ithaka. Refusing to confront who he was and what he might have been, my son wasted his own special gifts that he and everyone around him might have enjoyed. Instead, he longed to emulate, to be, his warrior father Odysseus, who was unique and without peer. As the poets now tell us, he was the man of many turns: resourceful, long-suffering, intelligent beyond all men, clever, wily, deceitful, strong in battle and devious in plans, brave, curious, persuasive with his golden tongue, respected, admired, feared, a leader among men, and beloved among the gods. Even the noblest kings of the Greek and Trojan forces could not match him. But his son, who grew up without his father as a model to teach and encourage and love him, longed to be this greatest of men and so would forever fail. My son was given a fate at odds with all that he might have been had he been raised by a gentle man like my own father or Cadmus. And thus, he struggles and suffers even into the moment when Thanatos will guide him into the home of Hades.

Reminding myself that at last the pain of his life will be over and that he will finally and forever be with his beloved father somewhat eases my heart.

On this year's visit for trade, Cadmus remained at home, as I knew he would. Although he is in fair health, his son says, he is no longer strong enough to sail the seas. Poseidon takes pleasure in sending storms to torment him. For what reason I do not know. There is no justice in wounding a good man like Cadmus.

Today it was Polybos, Cadmus's second son, who visited me. Like his older brother, Polybos brings me stories of his father and the world, so we had a long and pleasant discussion over the midday meal in my garden. I told him that if he should visit me on his return journey home from his travels on the Great Sea, I would send the chest that is a gift to his glorious father. It is filled with the papyrus and leather sheets covered with my silent marks.

"Lady," he said, "I assure you that my father is eager to read the work of your life."

He went on softly, "My father told me that after he reads your story, he will bury your trunk in safe ground outside the city of Tyre, far from the sea, so that in the years to come someone may find it and also know the story of the Ithakan Queen's courage." I am not certain that this comforts me. But if Cadmus and the gods approve, so be it.

Polybos then said, "My mother has moved into the next world, and my father remains in the large, rambling home that he built for his old age.

"My father is not born of nobility, but he is a wealthy man," he said. "The house and gardens are grand and have all the comforts and splendor that even a queen would admire. We own a small fleet of merchant galleys for his three sons and grandsons, including my two sons," he said with a proud smile. "His servants keep him company, and his large family has separate houses on the grounds so he is visited daily, as is his due. And his gardens keep him busy and agile. He is not alone, my Lady, but he is lonely for the sight of you, which, he told me once, has sustained him through all the hardships of sea and land. He wishes that you might visit Tyre when you know about your Lord's fate. My father does not believe that your Lord will ever return, if you will forgive me for my candid speech." He lowered his eyes in discomfort.

When I said that Odysseus would never return, on the word of a great seer who visited me recently, his son expressed his sorrow for my loss and for the endless years that I have waited. I was touched by his kindly manner. We sat in silence for some time as gentle Polybos, so like his father, sipped his tea.

Then in a serious manner he looked into my eyes and made this offer, "I could take you to Tyre and to my father when I stop on Ithaka to pick up the chest on my journey home. I cannot turn back to Tyre now, or my men and their families will suffer in poverty for the loss of their shares.

"We will make the galley comfortable for you, my Lady, and you will enjoy the beauty of the sea. Please consider this offer as a serious one because my noble father would want me to say this to you. We have great men of medicine, not like the Medicine Man on this island, I am told. We could care for you. There is a man renowned for medicine of the eyes. He helped my father greatly. I cannot promise a cure for anything, but it is more than this island offers to you. If you are not happy in my father's house, I promise you that we will return you to Ithaka and your family when you tell us it is time to leave us. We want your happiness and the contentment of our father, who has only your well-being in his heart." As he rose to leave, he said, "Please consider this offer, my Lady. We will speak again when I return."

Then he took his leave by kneeling and kissing the hem of my gown. I pray to the gods to protect him and his beloved father.

When Helios moved his chariot toward the west, I watched the shadows of the two galleys sail out of the port below. I was filled with turbulence. I felt both joy and fear, but mostly trepidation. I may sail away from Ithaka to the land of Cadmus where I have always wanted to be. Is it too late for such happiness? Am I too old and frail to take this long journey? If Cadmus becomes ill and leaves this life for the Garden of the Blessed below, I would be alone, without family to care for me, without Nausikaa to see to my needs. But would it be worth challenging Fortune for the joy of even a few turnings of the moon, for a week, or even one day with my dear friend? His son urged me to consider this new future. I will think on it—and dream, and wait.

Today I arose from my bed and decided that I must begin to walk, to move, to get back the lightness in my step. Yesterday Polybos offered me a new life—if I dare to take the challenge. Perhaps I should prepare for it. I bathed and dressed and asked my maidservant to take me down to the courtyard where I could walk. The sun felt good. I walked for a short time then climbed the stairs and decided to extend the time each day while I wait for Polybos to return.

Telemachos has never fully recovered. His war wounds took more than his arm from him. His legs are too weak for support, and he requires help in climbing stairs and walking. He continues to spend every day in my garden where the Sun God and the soft breezes give him comfort. He sits in the chair once occupied by Father Laertes and Eurykleia and thanks me for my teas and the stews that are still made daily. He is so fragile that even his voice is almost too weak to hear. I think that it is time for me to give up my room and garden so that he can enjoy his last days before darkness. I have been considering where I will go, and it pains me to think of losing all this that I love. He is my son, after all.

Today I told Nausikaa and Telemachos that it is time for me to move to a room below. This bedchamber should be theirs, and the adjoining rooms should belong to Ikarios and his family. Nausikaa knelt and kissed the hem of my robe as she thanked me. She has known of my son's needs but did not want to send me away from my garden, the only home I have had on Ithaka. The tears ran down the gaunt cheeks of my son as he looked out to sea. He knows that the journeys of the Sun God left to him are few. In his first kindness to me in long seasons, he said that I can leave the wall hangings of my homeland, and he will see to it that they are protected. But Nausikaa, always the thoughtful and loving Nausikaa, said quietly that perhaps they could put two of my hangings in my new room, and the two woven pictures of her homeland could be put up in their new room beside the ones I leave.

I looked at her with tears of gratitude. Our homelands, which we both love and remember, will be mingled beyond my lifetime—unless I take them all with me to the home of Cadmus. I have said nothing to anyone about my Merchant's offer.

It took two days to find and prepare a room suitable for me. It has always been a room assigned to guests of the palace. Nausikaa and Phylia chose the room next to the gate that leads to the enclosed Garden of Trees that I had planted soon after I arrived on Ithaka. The trees are now large and offer shade in the hot season and protection from winds and rain in the cold season. Servants moved my loom and yarns as though I could still weave each day, and they moved my personal things, including the chest with my writing. When I left my bedchamber and my garden balcony, I knew that I would never visit them again.

When I said goodbye to my weavers, they wept and hugged me. The pain is like fire in my chest. They lose their home too. What will become of them?

After I was moved to a room below, the weavers were also removed from my rooms and put in a large shed near the kitchen and the craftsmen. It was the space that they occupied when I first arrived on Ithaka. I went to visit them once. Only once. I longed to see my weavers again and to talk to these women whom I have loved for so many years.

They were surprised to see me, but they seemed pleased. They showed me their robes, but there was no pride or joy in it. Their room was shadowed with only the light from wall torches and the two doors that were kept open for a bit of air and light. No mosaics brightened the walls of stone. The floor was packed earth. The room was as it used to be. Suddenly Naela, who was in charge of the weavers despite her age, said quietly how much she missed our weaving room at the top of the palace where we lived and worked together for so many years. Without urging, each woman said what she missed.

"I miss the light and fresh air."

"I miss the garden and the scent of the flowers and herbs."

"I miss the smell of the sea."

"I miss the colors of the sea and the sky."

"I miss the teas you made every day."

"I miss the stews that you made."

"I miss the smells of the cooking."

"I miss not being hungry."

"I miss the lyre and Karua's songs."

I stopped them to ask where the lyre was. "The guards stole it, my Lady. They said that women were not worthy to touch the sacred lyre. 'That is man's gift from the gods,' the men said."

I frowned and said that I would look into it. I saw several women smile.

Maruna and others continued, "I miss the herbs that take away head and belly pain."

"I miss the bathing and being clean."

"I miss the journeys for the flowers and roots."

"I miss the dancing."

I was amazed that there was so much of our life together that they treasured and now missed. I suddenly realized how much alike we are.

They went on, "I miss being safe."

"I miss the stories every night."

"I miss the children."

"I miss Arête and Nausikaa."

"I miss the visits by the godly Merchant. You were always radiant when he visited."

"I miss the panels of your childhood home."

"I miss the mosaics."

"I miss your kindness and the safety," said Nauriteia with tears in her eyes. The dancing girl who found home among my weavers.

All of the weavers became silent as we remembered and wept.

Then Agape, who had been without speech for so many rolling years, said quietly, "I miss all of that but mostly I miss you, my Lady. Helios has taken the light from our life, and the gods have turned their backs on us."

I felt the tears wash the dust from my cheeks as I said, "I miss all of you and our life together. It was not the life we all might have chosen, but you made my days richer than they would have been without you, my dear friends. The gods may not allow me to visit you again, but I want you to know always that you and our memories fill my waking and sleeping."

Each of my weavers—even the new, young ones who have no long history with me—came to me, knelt down, and hugged my knees. I kissed the cheek of each one before she rose and returned tearfully to her loom. Then I arose and, with my maidservant to assist me, put the darkness and stench of the sheds within my heart as the weeping of my weavers followed me.

After I recovered from my visit to the weavers, I called for Ikarios and asked him to have the walls and ceiling whitened and the floor of the weaving shed transformed by the mosaics of Periphetes and his workmen.

"They are slaves," he reminded me, "and they work in a tradesmen's shed."

I told him that the yarn and fabrics had to be kept clean to be worthy of trade. I reminded him that the women are now living in the dust and dirt of potters and ironworkers and others who make the articles that are essential for the efficient management of the house.

"But the weavers bring wealth to the palace," I said. "For all the years of my life on Ithaka, trade with this kingdom has depended on the weaving. As I once told Laertes and Mentor, I say again that, like Periphetes, these women are artisans, not ordinary slaves that haul and clean. The room must be bright or the women will lose their eyes to the darkness. They need decent food because it takes many rolling years to become a great weaver, so they cannot be easily discarded.

"No one should be easily discarded," I added softly.

"The weavers must be protected from the men who use and beat them each night," I insisted firmly. "And guards stole the lyre that Cadmus gave to them. They deserve a new lyre. Cadmus would be grieved to know what has been happening to the weavers he admired so well. And while it will not lessen the pain from the brutal men, the music may reach the gods and help these gifted women forget the sadness of their days—even for a few moments each evening."

With his head down, Ikarios thought for some time. Then he hugged me, kissed my cheek, and said that he would see to it.

Apparently Ikarios is building a new room about the size of the upstairs weaving rooms, and Periphetes and his men will prepare it with a mosaic floor and clean white walls. The women now live and work together for their safety. The women are now fed proper foods for their health and they are protected, I am told, by guards who have been chosen for this honor. I am proud of my grandson the King and grateful to Cadmus for all that he taught Ikarios in their few seasons on the Great Sea. Ikarios learned to read and write and plans to teach his children to do so also. I see much of Cadmus in the character and affections of my grandson and wish that my son in his youth had taken the opportunity to know and to learn from this noble merchant.

Periphetes came to my room today. He told me that he had whitened the ceiling and walls of the new weaving shed. He said that he was making large tiles for the floor and would alternate light blue and white to brighten the room and keep it clean.

"They are not mosaic designs," he said, "but the tiles will create a room to please." He added, "Ikarios has become more generous with their food, and they are guarded each night. Medon has been assigned to find a fine lyre for the women." We thanked each other, and he kissed my hand.

He murmured, "My Lady, the weavers are grateful for what you have done. And I remember every day that I owe my life to you." Then he left my room. He did not tell me that the other craftsmen were angry from jealousy, but I wonder.

Periphetes has aged greatly, as we all have, but his assistants give him strength, and his mind is still filled with the beauty and wonder of his art. What a gift he has been to our palace and to my life!

The garden near my room is beautiful with fruit on all the trees that I planted, oranges, figs, dates, apricots, pears, pomegranates, and almonds. The garden is enclosed by a high wall, and under the branches the garden is cool and comfortable in the hot season. It is private and quiet with paths for me to walk among the trees, and I walk or sit there for much of the day in the shade. I have a small altar where I pray and offer libations to the gods that protect me. I could be living in a worse place, and I am grateful.

My maid brought Pheres to me today. I asked if he would bring fruit to the weavers whenever my trees are laden with the gods' gifts. He promised to do this throughout the bearing seasons. My weavers will be happy.

All day and night, I hear the cries of sheep and goats and dogs reminding me of life, and I enjoy Nausikaa's daily visits. I think that she needs to get away from the dark moods of Telemachos, and I am glad to sit under the trees with her and sip tea, which she orders. I had asked her if she would have a lyre given to Karua, the weaver whose songs are more beautiful than the sounds of the birds. She told me today that Karua has her lyre, and all the weavers wept with joy when she began to play.

While Naela is in charge of the weavers, Nausikaa is now in charge of collecting the plants for dyes and the medicinal herbs and flowers for illness, salves for wounds, and teas for pain. Her assistants in collecting and making the medicines are Penelopeia, Naela's daughter, and Zeila and Nausikeia, the daughters of the peasant woman who went too young into the home of Hades. They have been given a small section of the kitchen to make their brews, as the seasons require, but they say that it was more convenient when we had the fires near the doors of the balcony garden. Then they could go on with their weaving while the plants were cooking. Now they must remain in the kitchen while the potions are being made. Occasionally they come to ask my advice about someone's problem and what to give the person or about the recipe for making something, so I am able to see them and talk with them. I enjoy that and still feel needed.

Telemachos has moved to the Underworld where Hades opened the gates to welcome him. It was a gentle passing from this world to the next. When Nausikaa tried to awaken him this morning, the dark cold had enclosed him and all breath had been released. All of his guilt and suffering are now left behind in the light, and he will be comforted by the shades of his father and other heroes in the Field of Asphodel.

I sit in my room and write by the light of a lamp, and I think about my son's life. I know that he is with his father at last, and I should be happy that he is at peace. Why cannot my weeping stop?

Why does the sobbing wrap me in sadness that will not end?

The days of mourning go on. The funeral was large, and men from all parts of Ithaka and the surrounding islands came to pay respect. I suspect that the admiration is for Ikarios and not for my own son. But the burial mound was enormous, almost as large as that of Father Laertes, and the feasts were sumptuous. Nausikaa and I are grateful that Ikarios and his Queen showed his father the tribute required for a king. They brought me to the field so that I could witness that honor was paid to my son and his family. When I entered the field, the crowd stood up and cheered, and I was humbled that they still remember me. If Telemachos accomplished little that was admirable, at least he gave me Nausikaa and gave life to Arête and to my grandson, whom I deeply admire and love.

It has occurred to me that there should be a large burial mound in honor of Odysseus, and it should be built near the ones for Father Laertes and Telemachos. The three generations of the House of Laertes should be honored and remembered. I will mention it to my grandson tomorrow. I know that this will please him.

The moon grows large and small, over and over, and I wait.

Periphetes and his wife Phylo occasionally visit me in the garden in the evening after the banquet. They tell me stories of the palace and of the dear friends who enriched me in long years past. She says little about the weavers. Perhaps she wants to avoid subjects that she knows will hurt me because I miss them. This saddens me, but I am glad to be alone with these friends and to know that they remember and honor me.

A new servant attends me. She is kind. I am taking longer walks each day, sometimes even into the fields beyond the palace walls, but mostly I wait and fear that it may be too late for a sea journey in my lifetime if Polybos does not come soon.

Nausikaa and I talked long today about the changes made by Ikarios in the palace. It is now a place where I would have enjoyed living in years past.

"First," she said, "to protect the women from the lust of the guards and other men in the palace, Ikarios has married the servants according to their wishes. Some of the younger weavers now have husbands and are large with child. Ikarios built barracks with separate rooms for each couple outside of the walls of the palace. The married couples go to their rooms after their evening meals and their work is done each day.

I immediately asked, "How can the women be protected from beatings? Or are they protected?"

I could not bear to think of my weavers being hurt by husbands who have the right to do so on Ithaka.

Nausikaa smiled and said, "When Ikarios offered brides to his men, he said that the rules of marriage will be changed in his palace. No man is to touch his wife or children with his hands unless he touches them with love. No man is to slap or push or hit or punch or kick his wife or children. No stick or weapon may be used against a wife or child. To violate this law will result in losing his family and being exiled from Ithaka for life. Any man who works in or near the palace must abide by these rules or be banished and lose his place on the island."

I laughed with delight and asked, "How did the men accept this?"

Nausikaa also laughed and said, "At first they were dumbfounded and began to argue. 'It is man's right to control his wife and children.' 'How can we control them without using our hands or feet?' 'They will think that we are weak and lose respect for us.' And they went on and on.

"Ikarios allowed them to speak, and then he asked several questions designed to allay their fears, 'Am I weak? Do you respect me? Do my wife and children honor and respect me? I have never hit my wife or children, and they love me more for it. Women admire gentleness, rather than cruelty, and they will treat you with greater affection and deference if you treat them kindly. I learned this from the wisest and kindest man in the world.'

"As the men grumbled, King Ikarios continued, 'How would you like to be beaten whenever I, as King with the authority and power to do so, decided to beat you? How would you feel if your wife had the strength to beat you with pots or tree branches if she got angry? Would you feel good about her if she beat you because an old law allowed her to do so? If you do not want to abide by these rules, do not marry. But I tell you that the women in this palace will no longer be available to you to satisfy your lust on any of them. You will leave the women in this palace alone. If you marry, you will not dishonor your wives by taking other women. It is a new and kinder day, and you will be heroes for your strength and willingness to change this world from harshness to kindness. And your families will admire you for it.'"

"What happened?" I asked.

"Most of the men, except the old ones, agreed to the new laws and have taken wives," Nausikaa said. "And the women are elated to have their own man and children. Except for two men who were banished for beating their wives, so far the new rules are succeeding, and laughter has replaced gloom among the slaves and servants."

"Were all the weavers forced to take husbands?" I asked as we held each other's eyes.

She understood my meaning and answered, "No. Several weavers chose to stay with their friends whose love they could not bear to lose. They keep their rooms in the maids' quarters." I smiled with gratitude and relief.

I wonder about the design of my life had my husband been with me and showed compassion and tenderness, as Ikarios has decreed. What an amazing man my grandson is. No wonder Phylia smiles when she and her beautiful children visit me. Recently, Ikarios came to ask if I would like to attend the celebration for his eldest son's fifth birth remembrance. I was so happy that he asked. I wanted to attend all the activities, but I stayed only for the banquet. I get tired. Even writing is difficult, though it still fills the barren spaces of my life.

I sit in my room, too cold in winter and too hot in summer, since they moved me from my weavers and my garden at the top of the palace. The weavers send messages through Medon or Phylo to tell me that they miss me and think of me every day. I smile. They are not allowed to roam freely during the workday and are busy with their new families at night, so they cannot visit me. I remember how we danced and giggled quietly and slept in the weaving rooms in order to be safe.

I did not know then that that time was good.

Today I told Nausikaa that the sons of Cadmus are to take my beautiful chest and everything in it home to their father the next time they stop at the port of Ithaka.

"I promised Cadmus that he would have the chest that he originally gave to me as a gift long years ago," I explained. She agreed to see to it.

Then I continued, "I may go with them to visit my friend in our late years. They say that the large, rambling house and extensive gardens are beautiful and that there are separate homes nearby that accommodate his whole family, as our palace does. I will not be alone, they tell me, and I will have medicines far beyond Ithaka's standards when I need them. Of course I shall miss you and your wonderful family and my dear friends on Ithaka, but this will be my last chance to see the world that I have never known and to see my dear friend once again. If it is my fate that time is still before me, I shall make my decision when they arrive to trade."

Nausikaa looked at the ground, and I saw a tear roll down her cheek.

She said softly, "Yes, my Mother. I shall tell Phylia." Then she left me with the fear and anticipation of a new future.

And so I wait.

Sometimes Nausikaa or Phylia comes to me and tells me the gossip of the palace. They come into the room to see that it is cleaned, that my clothes are changed, and that my bed has fresh and softly woven blankets. The first servant was sent out of the palace for her neglect, but she was young and cared little for me. Now my new servant does what has to be done. I am comfortable, but I still miss my balcony garden and the sight of the sea.

Nausikaa has been very ill for longer than she would tell us. For some time I have watched her skin lose the color of sunshine and noticed how slowly she walked when she came to see me. I asked if she were well, and she insisted that she was. When she did not come to my room for several days, I went up to visit her. She looked terrible and asked me if I would stay to share her sleeping room at the top of the palace. Now I stay in my former room and care for her, with the help of her maids who also love her. Each day she occupies the chair that Telemachos enjoyed on the balcony. She says that she can breathe easier when she sits in the garden, and she seems to be more at peace when I am here to sleep on the floor next to her each night. The servants made up a pallet for me, and I can make her the teas that keep the pain away. Each day I make broth that sustains her, and each day I bathe her twice to let her know by a gentle touch that she is loved and still among the living. I try not to see the large lump in her breast and the lump lower down.

Just moving my beloved Nausikaa from her bed to the chair in the garden requires two maids. She is so weak. Yet, she is still the sweet and gentle woman she has always been as she thanks me for my attentions and my presence. I am devastated with sorrow and the fear of losing her. I cannot bear it.

Such emptiness. After many years of brief but glad visits, my dearest friend Cadmus no longer comes to Ithaka. Perhaps the gods had feared that the moments of joy with him would have turned my head away from the life that was designed for me. The gods need not have feared, for we cannot change our fate. Helen and Paris and the fires of Troy taught us that lesson long years ago. His beautiful son Polybos will take my writings away on his next visit to our island. I await him with fear that it may be too late, but I have feelings of conflict also. If he comes while Nausikaa is fighting the battle against Thanatos, how could I leave her? She has been my friend, daughter, and sister since she came to this palace. We have been chained together all the years. How could I let her face the darkness without me to ease her suffering? Yet, if Polybos leaves without me, what would Ithaka be for me when Hades takes my lovely Nausikaa into his dark kingdom?

Why do the gods fill mortal life with so much suffering?

Nausikaa has left us. Nothing can fill the loss of Nausikaa. The palace is desolate.

I cannot write more…

I think of the long sleepless nights I have spent in writing my story in order to keep the shapes of Chaos from my mind.

I have come to believe that Athene knew my fate and gave me three gifts in return for all that has been taken from me—my magic loom, the knowledge to make these shapes that speak to me and perhaps to others who know how to read them, and my dear friend who opened the doors of my mind and spirit. These gifts alone have kept my heart from turning to stone.

In this life of endless loneliness and waiting, light fades from my world. Would a sea voyage revitalize me and bring Hope back to my spirit?

My life in sun and wind and silence will soon be over. I remain in the sleeping room where the bed connects earth and sky, but weaving is long past. My eyes are weak and, like twisted roots of the aged olive trees or the ginger that makes the tea to comfort me, my fingers are gnarled and have little control over the designs. Even the brush is sometimes difficult to hold, but I still take pleasure in writing. Only my herb teas that I make on the balcony offer relief. I can see little in the light of two small oil lamps to write the silent songs of the night. So now, to the consternation of my maidservants, I write during the day on the balcony. I fear that my friend may not be able to read these scratches, but Cadmus will preserve them despite their condition.

Cadmus. He is with me night and day. I wonder how the Fates brought that beautiful man to me so long ago.

Sometimes I reside in a small space between the Underworld and this world where sand and sea and sky mingle. Suddenly I am taken by an unknown god to an unknown place that cannot be real. Yet, I go willingly to be young again and to relive my youth. It is more than dreaming or remembering. I am there, talking to my father or sister, to Cadmus or Arête or Nausikaa. Yesterday, or maybe weeks ago—time is no longer clear—I called Eurykleia who was with me once again. If I can believe Phylia, I had a long conversation with Eurykleia until my maid shook me, and I lost my dear friend to the shades that surround her.

Later, Phylia came to my room to ask me if I am well. I knew that my maid sent for her because my mind was wandering again on that landscape that comforts me but no one else. Then I feel frightened that I cannot even control what I think and what I say. For most of my life I had control over nothing but my own mind, my weaving, and my writing. And now even that is gone. I could accept this new condition if everyone else did, but they are upset and feel that Chaos has overtaken me. I feel both fear and shame that they may see what I have always hidden from those who would judge me. I fear that they may tie me down so that I cannot wander, even in the land behind my eyes.

I must finish my story before I am locked in that middle world forever.

This morning I saw the shapes of the galleys owned by my Merchant's sons. My maid confirmed that they are the Cadmus ships. They were in the distance, like dots, sailing toward the port below my garden. They have come in time for me to make my decision. I must finish my story so the chest filled with my writing can be locked for the journey.

Epilogue

I sit in my garden, sipping chamomile tea with lemon and honey. I consider how I want to express the ending of my story, the purpose of my time in the world of sunshine. Perhaps I can say it this way.

We are each alone in this life, but memories of gentler moments and papyrus pictures that I draw have helped me pretend that isolation is not my fate. Mine is a life of imaginings. I dream that the songs I sing go out across the seas and my friend smiles. I dream that my pictures could somehow touch the hearts of my father and sister. I dream that they have been happier in this life than I have been. My mother remains a mystery to me. I dream that this chest designed with leaves and flowers and scrolls will reach all women, and they will feel less lonely in their solitary rooms and hostile hovels. I dream that Odysseus and my son loved me but were also trapped by what they learned and by what was expected of them. I dream that women in the future will not depend on the rules made by others but will be free to create rules for themselves. I have difficulty imagining what such freedom would be. I dream that the gods will someday care about the pain that life brings to mortals and will make our days soothing and safe. I dream that I will see my beautiful and loving Arête again, and she will be standing with her beloved mother on the shore. She will be smiling with the silver sand at her feet, the breeze in her hair, and the sea in her happy eyes.

Finally, I dream that the gods will be kind and that the sands of my memories will be washed out to sea where they will touch the shore of Tyre and the heart of my friend. I pray that my gentle Cadmus will read this, and we will meet once again to touch hands and smile into each other's eyes. Among those I have loved, I hold a special place for my Merchant in the garden of my heart.

Perhaps after all, this silent song to love is, like waiting, the meaning of my fate.

Postscript

This novel is a fiction based on the fiction that we know as Homer's *Odyssey*, its characters, myths, legends, and setting. Freely drawing from Homer's epic and its major characters and from more recent historical and archaeological discoveries, this volume is my invention and my dream of what Penelope, in that time, would have been.

Glossary

Achaians—A general term for Greeks, including Ithakans
Aegean Sea—Body of water between Greece and Troy
Ægypt—Egypt
Aeneas—Trojan hero; Dido's lover; founded Roman Empire
Agamemnon—King of Mycenae; leader of Greek forces
Agape—Child violated by guard; saved by Penelope; a weaver
Agarreus—King of Mezapos; betrothed of Laodike of Pylos
Aiolos—King of the winds
Aithiopia—Ethiopia, rich kingdom south of Ægypt
Alcippe—Birthing woman on Ithaka
Alessos—Chief Builder and stonemason on Ithaka
Alkinoös—King of the Phaiakians and father of Nausikaa
Alkinoös—Second son of Nausikaa and Telemachos
Amphinomos—Penelope's suitor
Amyklaios—Penelope's great-grandfather
Antilochos—King of Pylos; grandson of Nestor
Antinoös—Despised leader of the suitors
Aphrodite—Goddess of love, passion, and beauty
Apollo—God of music, prophecy, and medicine
Arachne—Girl turned into a spider for challenging Athene's weaving
Ares—God of war
Arête—Queen of Phaiakians; mother of Nausikaa
Arête—Penelope's granddaughter
Arethousa—Spring on Ithaka
Argives—Like the Achaians, the Greeks
Argos—Old dog that recognized Odysseus on his return
Aristander—Son of King Koritos of Olympia
Ascanius—Son of Aeneas
Artemis—Goddess of childbirth, children, and the hunt
Atē—Malevolent deity of error and irresponsibility
Athene—Goddess of wisdom and the art of weaving
Atreus—Father of Agamemnon and Menelaos
Autonoë—Maid to Penelope

Briseia—Daughter of Telemachos and Nauriteia the dancer
Cadmus—Phoenician merchant, teacher, and beloved friend
Carthage—Kingdom ruled by Queen Dido in northern Africa
Cassandra—Trojan princess; captured by King Agamemnon of Greeks
Chaos—Disorder; believed to have power of a deity
Corfu—Island north of Ithaka
Cyclops—One-eyed monster and enemy of Odysseus
Danaans—Greeks (see Achaians and Argives)
Demodikos—The King's bard on the island of Sikelia
Dido—Queen of Carthage and lover of Aeneas
Dikē—Goddess of justice
Diomedes—Greek warrior in the Trojan War
Dionysos—God of wine
Doria—An older weaver; dies of old age and work
Eileithyia—Goddess of childbirth
Elysian Field—Realm of happiness in the Underworld
Eris—Deity that causes strife
Eros—God of erotic love; son of Aphrodite
Eumaios—Swineherd and loyal friend to Odysseus
Euminoös—Penelope's young brother; killed by Odysseus
Euphemos—Prince who wed Ktimene
Eupithes—Father of Antinoös, leader of the suitors
Eurykleia—Nurse to Odysseus and Telemachos
Eurymedousa—Nausikaa's nurse from Scheria
Eurynome—Penelope's nurse on Sikelia
Eurynomeia—Head housekeeper of the palace on Ithaka
Fates—Clotho/thread of life; Lachesis/chance; Atropos/fate
Field of Asphodel—Area of Underworld without suffering
Furies—Infernal deities; torment violators of family ties
Great Sea—Mediterranean Sea
Hades—God of the Underworld
Helen—Most beautiful woman; "caused" Trojan War
Helios—God of the Sun
Hera—Queen of the gods; wife of Zeus
Hermes—Greek God; son and messenger of Zeus

Hippodameia—Maid to Penelope
Hippotho—Birthing woman for Nausikaa
Hypnos—God of sleep
Iason—Jason; husband of Medeia whom he abandoned
Ikarios—King of Sikelia; father of Penelope
Ikarios—Third son of Nausikaa and Telemachos
Ilithyia—Goddess of childbirth on Sikelia
Ilium or Ilios—Another name for Troy
Iocasta or Jocasta—Mother and wife of Oedipus of Thebes
Ionian Sea—Body of water between Italy and Greece
Iphigeneia—Daughter of Agamemnon; sacrificed to Artemis
Iphthime—Penelope's sister
Ithaka—Island home of Odysseus (and Penelope)
Iulus—Son of Cadmus
Kalypso—Immortal; kept Odysseus prisoner for eight years
Karua—Weaver and gifted player of the lyre
Karumna—Weaver
Kefalonia—Island west of Ithaka; includes kingdom of Sami
Kirke—Immortal who turns men into animals
Klytemnestra—Wife of Agamemnon, whom she murdered
Koritos—King of Olympia
Krete—Island in the Mediterranean Sea southeast of Greece
Ktimene—Sister to Odysseus; friend to Penelope
Laertes—Father of Odysseus
Laertes—First-born son of Nausikaa and Telemachos
Lakedaimon—Portion of Greece, which includes Sparta
Land of Burning Sand—Africa
Laodike—Daughter of King Antilochos; abducted from Pylos
Lefkos—Island north of Ithaka
Lethia—Weaver disloyal to Penelope and Odysseus; hanged
Lethos—Eldest son of Cadmus
Lexanos—King of Corfu
Litae—Daughters of Zeus; mitigate problems caused by Atē
Lutto—Weaver who brought Chaos and hostility to weavers
Lykaia Lakedaimoneia—Beloved goddess on Sikelia

Machaon—Penelope's grandfather
Marpessa—Weaver
Marua—Wife of Penelope's grandson Laertes
Maruna—Weaver
Medeia—Wife of Jason; killed their sons in revenge
Medon—Saved by Penelope; friend to Telemachos
Melanthios—Goatherd killed for disloyalty to Odysseus
Melantho—Maid disloyal to Penelope; hanged
Menelaos—King of Sparta; husband of Helen
Menoitios—Emissary to Odysseus on Sikelia
Mentor—Ithakan elder and friend to Penelope
Mezapos—Land of King Agarreus
Minos—King of Krete
Morpheus—God of dreams; son of Hypnos (Sleep)
Mt. Aetos—Site of the palace on Ithaka
Mt. Etna—Volcanic mountain on Sikelia/Sicily
Mt. Lykaion—Mountain in Lakedaimon
Mt. Olympos—Home of the gods and goddesses
Muses—Goddesses of music and poetic inspiration
Mycenae—Kingdom ruled by Agamemnon
Naela—Assistant to Penelope as weaver and herbalist
Nauriteia—Dancing girl bought by Telemachos; a weaver
Nausikaa—Wife of Telemachos
Nausikeia—Weaver; daughter of peasant woman Zeila
Nemesis—Deity of anger, jealousy, and retribution
Nereids—Virgin Deities of the sea (fifty in number)
Nerua—Wife of Penelope's grandson Alkinoös
Nerunome—Birthing woman for Penelope
Nestor—Late King of Pylos and friend of Odysseus
Nymphs—Beautiful Deities of rivers, forests, and mountains
Odysseus—King of Ithaka; hero of Trojan War
Olympia—Kingdom in the Peloponnese
Ormenos—Palace guard who violated Agape
Paiëon—God of medicine
Palamedes—Greek warrior

Pandares—Eldest brother of Penelope
Paris—Trojan prince who took Helen to Troy
Pelias—Chief Potter in the palace of Odysseus
Peloponnese—Mainland of southern Greece
Penelope—Queen of Ithaka; wife of Odysseus
Penelopeia—Weaver and herbalist; daughter of Naela
Periphetes—Artist of mosaics on Ithaka
Pero—Weaver; sister of Zeila and Nausikeia
Persephone—Goddess of the Underworld
Phaiakians—Peaceful, kind people; brought Odysseus home
Phedressa—Weaver; friend and beloved of Agape
Pheidopos—Chief Potter when Penelope arrived on Ithaka
Phemios—Bard/singer in the palace of Odysseus
Pheres—Adopted son of Polykas, the farmer; Zeila's son
Phoenicia—Land on coast of Mediterranean Sea (Lebanon)
Phylia—Wife of Ikarios, Penelope's youngest grandson
Phylo—Weaver; wife of Periphetes
Pillars of Hercules—Western Mediterranean Sea (Gibraltar)
Polybos—Son of Cadmus
Polykas—Chief Farmer for the palace on Ithaka
Poseidon—God of the sea
Pramneian wine—Wine used as medicine
Pylos—Kingdom in southern Greece once ruled by Nestor
Sami—Kingdom on the island of Kefalonia
Scheria—Homeland of the Phaiakians and of Nausikaa
Selene—Goddess of the moon
Sida—Weaver; suffers from varicose veins
Sikelia—Homeland of Penelope; also called Great Island
Sikelos—People of Sikelia (Sicily)
Sisyphos—Figure tortured in the Underworld
Sparta—City in Lakedaimon, ruled by Menelaos
Sychaeus—Husband of Dido; killed by her brother in Tyre
Teiresias—Seer in the Underworld; foretold Odysseus' fate
Telegonos—Rumored son of Odysseus and Kirke
Telemachos—Son of Odysseus and Penelope

Thanatos—Personification of Death in Greek mythology
Thon—Boy helper to Penelope and to Zeila's young sons
Thora—Weaver disloyal to Penelope and Odysseus; hanged
Trojans—People of Troy; defeated by the Greeks
Troy—Kingdom in what is now northern Turkey
Tydeus—First-born son of Ikarios and Phylia
Tyndareus—Childhood friend and betrothed of Penelope
Tyre—Island and town in Phoenicia; home of Cadmus
Underworld—Lower World of Hades; Land of the Dead
Zakynthos—Island south of Ithaka
Zetheus—Prince from the neighboring island of Kefalonia
Zeila—Peasant woman; died of cancer
Zeila—Weaver; eldest daughter of Zeila
Zephyr—The West Wind
Zeus—God of thunder and lightning; most powerful god

Acknowledgements

My deepest appreciation to Robin Stratton and Big Table Publishing for producing my work and for being the publisher every author dreams of meeting; to Michael C. Keith for his friendship and his determination to see *Penelope's Song* in print; to Robbin Cuddy for her artistic talent; and to Marlene Tholl, an amazing editor.

I can never express my gratitude enough to the wonderful writers and friends who read my manuscript at various stages of the writing process: Marlene Tholl, Grace Farrell, David Orsini, Ann Suter, Stephanie Rivera, Susan Aylward, Sally Burke, and Michael C. Keith. Their writing talent, knowledge, and generosity have been treasures to me. To Je Banach and our workshop group at the first Yale Writers Conference in 2012, thank you all for your encouragement, editorial suggestions, and enthusiasm for Penelope. It all came at the perfect time. To Gregory McNab, my appreciation for your endless belief in me, your patience, and your devotion; to my children, Kenton, Robbin, Elizabeth, and Susan; my grandchildren, Eamon, Miles, Neve, Reece, Kieran, and Meghan; my sister Lorraine; and to Eamon, Carl, Anne, Nicholas, and Marlene, thank you all for being in my life and for teaching me the depth of family love. And to Giancarlo Maiorino, Grace Farrell, AnnMarie Janicki, Sally Burke, Susan Aylward, Sarah Holmes, Eunjoo Woo, the late James Healy, the McNab family, and other friends and former students who have enriched my life every day, there can never be a gift that I could give you for all you have done to keep my life balanced and full of pleasure and good humor.

Without Homer's *Odyssey*, its translators and editors, this novel could not exist. And without the classical scholars who researched and wrote about that world, I could not have written this book. My special gratitude to Elizabeth Wayland Barber for her brilliant books on women's weaving; to Oleg Polunin and Anthony Huxley for their wonderful book on *Flowers of the Mediterranean*; and to Grace Farrell and Jan Doyle, founders of the Carolina Fiber and Fiction Center in

Richmond, RI, for their instructions on weaving. Finally, I thank the Brown University English Department, especially Professor David Harry Hirsch and Professor Keith Waldrop, and Classics Professor Michael Putnam for their encouragement and for supporting my interest in the relation between ancient Greek and Latin literatures and American writers. That fascination is evident in my publications and throughout my years on the faculty at the University of Rhode Island where I decided long ago to write Penelope's story.

About the Author

Lois A. Cuddy has a Ph.D. in English from Brown University and is Professor Emerita of English, Women's Studies, and Comparative Literature at the University of Rhode Island. A member of Phi Beta Kappa, she is the recipient of a Woodrow Wilson Fellowship and the Teaching Excellence Award at her university. She published *T. S. Eliot and the Poetics of Evolution*, co-authored two other scholarly books, and wrote articles on both classical and modern authors. Long fascinated by the Homeric tradition (including variations and subversions of the classics), she felt it was time to turn to fiction in order to tell the story of Penelope and her world. She now resides in Richmond, RI, with Greg and their Maine Coon cats, Darwin and Wallace.

Made in the USA
Middletown, DE
17 June 2015